KILL HER TWICE

KILL HER TWICE

STACEY LEE

putnam

G. P. PUTNAM'S SONS

G. P. PUTNAM'S SONS
An imprint of Penguin Random House LLC, New York

First published in the United States of America by G. P. Putnam's Sons,
an imprint of Penguin Random House LLC, 2024

Visit us online at PenguinRandomHouse.com.

Library of Congress Cataloging-in-Publication Data is available.

ISBN 9780593532041
1st Printing
Printed in the United States of America
LSCH

Design by Maya Tatsukawa
Text set in Dante MT Pro

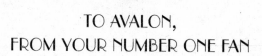

TO AVALON,
FROM YOUR NUMBER ONE FAN

1
GEMMA

IN 1932, LOS ANGELES WAS A CITY OF REINVENTION. IT was a place where mountains could be moved and rivers reshaped, where even stars could fall from the sky and walk around on Earth. The blood of an Angeleno coursed through the veins like gasoline, primed for the explosion that would drive progress.

"Stop looking like we're about to rob a bank." I tied my straw hat tighter.

My older sister, May, with her long arms gripping the steering wheel of our father's flower delivery truck, did not look poised for progress. In fact, she looked like she was waiting for the truck to drive her.

Around us, customers hunted bustling City Market for deals on the last of summer's bounty—corn, stone fruit, zucchini—though it was already October. "Pretend you're the lead in one of those Hollywood flickers. We're stylish women in the latest robin's-egg-blue Cadillac about to go for a drive."

The Mule, what we called our old Ford Runabout pickup, was definitely not robin's-egg blue. More like turtle-egg brown.

May frowned at me, a tiny Y crease forming between her tea-steeped eyes. Even when she was annoyed, she had the kind of beauty that drew eyes and tripped feet. "Are you wearing lipstick?"

I pressed my lips together. "As a matter of fact, yes. Lulu Wong's Noir Red." The silver-screen starlet and our hometown celebrity had the dark-red shade made vegetarian for her. "Here, you wear some too. Put it on quick." I plucked the tube from my clutch.

"They'll think we're hussies!" Her serious eyes blinked double time.

"They already think that." If I'd had enough money, I would've gotten the kohl pencil for drawing on Lulu Wong's tiger-charming beauty mark, a mole round and perfect enough to stop a tiger in its tracks. "Oh, forget it. Work the gears. Let's get this bucking mule on the road." I swept my hands toward the exit of City Market, where Ba had carved a niche selling flowers among all the produce vendors. But few bought blooms during a depression. Save for a few big orders placed during the Summer Olympics, it felt as if flowers came to our stall to die. We'd only sold a third of our inventory this morning, mostly the cheaper lilies. But this time, we weren't going to simply donate them around town like we always did. Ba wouldn't approve, but he was sixty miles away and might not return for many months.

"You and your big-thinking head," she muttered, using a Chinese expression for someone with grand ideas. "I have a bad feeling this will get us married off for good." With grudging movements of her hands on the gears, May eased us forward.

I snorted, though my leg began to jitter with annoyance. With fewer eligible maidens in Chinatown than bachelors, Ba had always told us that his three fierce clouds—Mei Wun, or "beautiful cloud," for May; Gam Wun, or "fresh cloud," for me; and Pan Wun, or "wishful cloud," for our youngest sister, Peony—would blow favorable winds to our family. But with the city's plans to bulldoze the heart of our community for a train station, May and I worried the winds would scatter us to new households sooner than we were ready to go.

"They won't like us selling at Westlake Park," May groused, crawling us along. The Mule bucked, tossing us like rice in the wok and clattering the buckets in our truck bed. One of the City Market sweepers shook his broom at us. May gave him an apologetic wave. She had always been the nicer one. Reaching San Pedro Street, she gunned us out of the lot, her face growing dark again. "Remember how Guitar Man tried to visit the park?"

"Of course I remember," I grumbled. Our friendly Chinatown bum, who always carried a guitar case, had been so distressed at being ordered to leave the park, he'd gotten on the wrong streetcar and ended up near Pasadena. The city preferred the Chinese keep to Chinatown, except when we were selling here at City Market, located two miles south. Los Angeles relied on our produce. Of course, if they swept us out of Chinatown, their dinner plates would suffer, but by the time they figured that out, it would be too late for us. "Guitar Man spits a lot and scares people. We are not going to scare people. We are a delightful vision. Aren't you always telling me people judge with their eyes first?"

May shifted gears and the Mule bucked again. "I was talking about show business."

A truck rumbled by, sweeping dust through the Mule's doorless entries.

"Well, this is a kind of show. Our feminine wiles will go a long way." I eyed her pale-green dress, wishing it was more à la mode, which was French for "fashionable." May sewed our dresses from castoffs like old curtains and tablecloths. Though her creations were clever—she had split a doily to make the collar on my own dress—they always had a washed look to them.

Her tongue clicked in annoyance. *"Feminine wiles?* Sorry, Gemma, I left mine at home next to my girdle."

"And along with your sense of adventure," I said breezily.

"Along with my *sense*, you mean. How much did that lipstick cost?"

I made kissy lips at her, and she groaned. If we were going to sell our flowers to the beau monde, which was French for "the upper crust," we had to look as presentable as possible. Lipstick was a minor investment for a bigger payoff.

Traffic wasn't heavy on a Saturday afternoon. The white tower of the new city hall saluted us several blocks northeast, toward Chinatown. Buildings passed in streaks of concrete and brick, each day bringing more EVERYTHING MUST GO! signs and longer soup kitchen lines. I imagined all the business we'd find in Westlake Park: couples strolling the lake, families walking their dogs. Westlake residents could still afford luxuries, unlike those in most neighborhoods, who could barely buy the necessities.

"I bet we could make twenty dollars today," I said. That would more than cover our flower costs for the month.

"How do you figure we'll do that, short of clubbing people over the head and taking their wallets?" Her nose started to twitch, as it always did when something bothered her.

"It's very simple, May. We quadruple our prices."

Her posture slouched as the wind blew out of her. "That's it. I'm turning around. It's clear your noodles have gone mushy."

"Keep your hair on. Westlake people are used to paying certain prices for things. If we didn't quadruple the prices, they might worry over the quality."

"I see. So we're doing them a favor."

"Absolutely." A little risk-taking was what was needed to keep our heads above water a little longer. Despite my airy demeanor, my stomach clenched like the grinding of the clutch. We wouldn't have had to take such risks if we weren't being kicked out of our houses in the middle of an economy that had belly flopped. It was bad enough that Ba had gotten sick. Now it was up to us to save ourselves.

She cut her gaze to me. "I suppose you also have a cage to sell to a lion."

The wealthier neighborhoods of Westlake folded around us, with its elegant mansions moderne, fussy Victorians, and Spanish haciendas, fronted by spacious lawns. The stately brick buildings of a fancy girls' school stretched half a block, where girls played basketball on a court so pristine it would make Peony weep.

Soon, the tropical oasis of Westlake Park spread before us with its glamorous palm trees and meandering footpaths. An assortment of canoes and paddleboats floated on an artificial lake. Pumping the brakes, May eased us up the driveway leading to the boathouse, which oversaw the park. Diners gathered under the shade umbrellas of a picturesque café glanced in our direction.

I prayed that the Mule wouldn't buck. "Make a left."

May rolled by the crowds, then turned into the driving lane that encircled the lake. Azalea bushes screened lovers' alcoves. Weeping willows swayed gently in the breeze.

Before reaching the band concourse anchoring the other end of the lake, I pointed to a palm tree. "Park under there."

If someone wanted to lodge a complaint about us at the boathouse, they'd have a good quarter mile to walk.

Pedestrians cast us curious gazes, their eyes skimming the words painted on the side of the truck: CHOW'S FLOWERS. We flipped over crates to build an attractive display on the truck bed, topped by a showstopping potted orchid with its cascade of miniature purple slippers. Though I doubted the plant—our most expensive item—would sell, orchids gave off good energy. I scribbled prices on a chalkboard, then slashed those prices as if we were having a sale. The orchid I marked at seven dollars slashed to five dollars. Last, I gathered broken petals and blooms into a basket and looped it on my arm.

"Afternoon, folks," I chirped, rolling a bright-pink bloom between my fingers. "Get your flowers for your lady loves. Won't you come look? We've got roses, freesia, daisies, zinnias, and mixed bouquets in astonishing and dizzy-fying combinations."

May raised an eyebrow at me. People began to drift closer.

"Oh, Harold, these are just like the ones we got married with." A woman with a violet hat pointed at a bouquet of white roses, which I had tied with baby's breath.

"The white ones are the most fragrant." I beamed a smile at them that Ba referred to as one of my eye-catching "Gemma facets."

"We'll take them," said the violet hat's husband, not even blinking at the price.

"Wonderful. You can pay my sister, and I'll wrap these for you." We usually used newspaper, but today I had brought the waxed tissue paper that we reserved for the extra-fancy bouquets. I threw May a wink, which she did not return. More customers approached. More flowers changed hands.

I couldn't help noticing a handsome couple leaning against a stone divider several paces away. The woman tilted her Max Factor face toward the man as she twisted the heel of her white pump with its little bow in the dirt. Her powdered nose was fleshy, the kind of "money nose" that the Chinese believed attracted wealth. Plus, only someone with money would wear white pumps to a park. The young man carried himself with the cultured air of a violin and seemed to be listening to her with only half an ear, his brown eyes studying us with his haughty eyebrows tweaked. A fedora created shadows over his smooth face.

Max Factor left her boyfriend's side and sifted through the bouquets, touching everything as if it already belonged to her. Her young man watched her with the half-annoyed look of someone waiting for a late train to arrive. With a squeal, Max Factor held up a bouquet of bloodred roses, which cost a dollar. He nodded, his smile not reaching his eyes. As May took it for wrapping, the young man lifted himself off the wall and swaggered his pin-striped suit to where I was standing. "Dollar, huh?" he said in a low voice.

"That's right, and worth every penny. You can see how happy they make her."

We both looked at Max Factor, who had buried her fleshy nose in the bouquet.

He snorted. "I could buy a whole chuck roast for that."

"You could. But I doubt it would look as nice on her dresser."

"Freddie, pay the lady," Max Factor called, waving.

He pulled out his wallet, and his long index finger riffled all his bills, more than our entire savings. "You people have a good racket going."

The Gemma facet grew an edge. "I don't know what you mean, sir."

"You can get these at City Market for a quarter." His gaze corralled mine, and my stomach clenched at being called out. "I think you just came here to fleece us."

"Freddie, what's taking so long?" Max Factor's Cupid's-bow lips pouted. "My mother's waiting for us, remember?"

May narrowed her eyes at me. "Gemma?"

My gut warred with the loftier part of my brain that cared about things like image and pride. "Good news, May," I said loudly. I didn't take my eyes from the man, even though he stood a good head and shoulders above me. "This nice gentleman would like to buy our showstopper. Could you fetch it? It's for the lady's mother."

Freddie's straight nose flared. He glanced at the price—five dollars—and his eyebrows became hooks.

"Oh, Freddie!" Max Factor gushed. "Mother will love it. You are so dear."

I swore Freddie's bills screamed as he ripped them from his wallet.

The air swept out of my lungs, and I tried to project serenity. "Orchids prefer indirect light, and they're sensitive to hot tempers. But if you give them lots of love, they will reward you with many years of good fortune." I stepped aside in case he was tempted to pick me up and plant me in the nearest pot.

May brought the orchid to him, cutting me a glance that said she knew I had done something bad, something that might affect our family honor. May's expressions were always specific.

Freddie and Max Factor strolled away down the footpath, passing a pair of policemen coming from the other direction. The pair made a beeline for us, kicking my pulse up a notch. Had the bad deed caught up with us so fast?

"Say, what do we have here?" said the shorter one, a high-energy Chihuahua sort with a twitchy mustache.

"Good afternoon, Officers." I flashed them one of the Gemma facets.

"You got a permit?" barked the Chihuahua.

Conversation died around us.

"Absolutely." The word fell smoothly from my forked tongue.

I'd figured we would need a permit but had hoped no one would actually check. May sidled up. Two bright spots of color had appeared on her porcelain cheeks. Despite her discomfort, she was as fair to behold as a waterfall pouring off a slender cliff, even without lipstick. The men couldn't help staring at her. I beamed a smile in her direction. "Sister, give it to them."

She withered me with a look. With all the ice she was generating, we could use her to store meat. "Why, sister, I thought *you* brought it."

"Me? Oh, dear. I'm afraid my sister would forget her pretty head if it were not already screwed on."

She fixed her lips into a tight smile. "If this pretty head didn't have to do the lion's share of the work, I suppose I might've remembered that permit."

"*Lion's share.*" I guffawed. "More like lying-about share."

"Officer." May bent a frown at the larger officer. He was more a Rottweiler type with his dark scruff and muscular build. "Isn't there a law against abusing one's sister?"

The Rottweiler shifted from foot to foot, glanced uneasily at the Chihuahua.

The Chihuahua sneered. "Look here. You're not supposed to be—"

I swished my skirts becomingly. "Officers, we don't wish to pull you into our unseemly family squabbles. If you don't mind overlooking my sister's embarrassing and, frankly, not surprising oversight"—with a *hmph*, May stuck up her nose—"we promise to remember our permit for next time. Please, a rose for your troubles." I handed each a golden bloom from my basket, along with a palmed dollar, enough for a pack of bootlegged beer.

A little sugar in the teapot was how business got done here in Los Angeles. Someone once tried to convene a grand jury to try to root out the corruption, until someone sweetened the jurors' tea as well.

Both pocketed their dollars. "Don't let me catch you without your permit again," said the Chihuahua, twirling the rose against his squarish nose.

At last, the pair wandered back to the footpath. New pedestrians replaced the ones who'd shied away, and business picked up again.

"You were born for the screen," I dropped into May's ear. "Lulu Wong better watch herself."

"It wasn't all acting," she grumbled, hooding her eyes and lifting her chin. Her look said I would have to pay for this bad deed in the next life. Or maybe even this one.

2
MAY

OUR MA STOOD AT THE WINDOW, RUBBING HER SWOLLEN belly as she considered the darkening sky. I'd always loved studying people's faces, and hers was my favorite. But tonight, her face had a folded look about it, like a handkerchief carried too long in the pocket. "Fourteen dollars today," she said in Cantonese, the language we spoke at home. "We can stay in business for another month. But November and December are dead months. How will we get through?"

Few blooms grew in the cold months, and Ba usually supplemented our income with odd jobs, like repairing leaking roofs or roughnecking in the oil fields. But no one would hire a couple girls for that, especially these days, when folks would work a full day just for a bowl of soup.

"I can look for sewing work." It was the one skill I had, even though my hand cramped thinking about the additional work.

Ma's face folded tighter. "You can barely keep up with ours."

Gemma, sitting across from me at our round table, glanced up from her bowl of fried rice. She had wiped off her lipstick and subdued her chin-length hair with a pin. Yet hers was a face that was rarely quiet, even when she was saying nothing. "Don't worry, Ma," she said. "We'll manage. I have some ideas."

I gritted my teeth, having had my fill of Gemma's ideas for

the day. Beside me, Peony began to fidget. Even though she was already twelve, she still had the energy of a cricket and wasn't trusted yet to make the tea. She was small-boned like Ma, her face always open, with eyes the color of the golden lotus paste used for special desserts.

"I do have some good news," said Ma, still looking out the window toward the Los Angeles Plaza, the old city center, as if listening for the watery tinkling of the circular fountain.

"Yes, Ma?" I asked.

"The Moys have asked about you. Their oldest son, Wallace, just graduated from the UCLA"—she pronounced the English initials in a Chinese meter—"and is ready for a wife."

Gemma's eyes turned mirthful. She wiggled the fingers of one hand as if mimicking a scuttling beetle and mouthed "Bug Boy." When we were kids, the knock-kneed Wallace was always chasing us around with creepy-crawlies—grasshoppers, spiders, earthworms. I could not imagine a more dismal husband. I swallowed wrong, provoking a spasm of coughs. Peony slapped me on the back, and I dodged out of her way. Despite her petite frame, Peony's limbs packed a heavy wallop.

"Girls," Ma chastised, not missing anything. The window screeched when she opened it, and a breeze shot through the room.

After composing myself, I asked, "Er, what did Wallace study?"

Ma began making a circuit through the living room half of our large room, using her foot to push a bucket of leftover yellow paint closer to the wall. "Nature. He's an"—she switched to English—"ex-something."

Gemma, who'd been hiding her mirth in her teacup, set it down with a loud ha! "Ex-terminator, possibly?"

I shot her a dirty look. A black mushroom in my bowl suddenly looked like a squashed cockroach.

"Why do you have to go to college to learn how to kill bugs?" asked Peony. Now we were all speaking in English. Only Ma preferred speaking in Cantonese, even though she'd been born in San Francisco. But once we got going in English, it was hard to turn the horses around.

"Not exterminator. Starts with *e*." Ma abruptly stopped in front of our chintz sofa, clutching her stomach. Breathing through whatever pained her, she stared thoughtfully up at Ba's crisp paintings of bamboo reeds, intermingled with the pictures of happy babies we'd torn from magazines so that the new baby would be good-natured. A train rumbled from nearby Alameda Street, and Ma returned to the window. We'd grown up hearing it, but recently I'd found myself noticing the sound more often. Maybe Ma had too. "The train station may be coming soon. Plans must be made."

Before Ba was sent to the sanatorium, Ma never paid much attention to matters outside the home, like politics or lawsuits. But like all of us, she was doing her best to fill in the spaces his absence had left, including making decisions for the family. Gemma and I had dropped out of school and taken over the daily work of the business, even though we hadn't known how to sell flowers. The cobbler assured us that when cataracts took his vision, his other senses amplified, enabling him to carry on with his work, but we had barely broken even these past six months.

My arms squeezed tightly against my sides, like one of those women who lay in boxes for magicians to saw in half. I resented that train station for pushing us in directions we were not ready to go. Though I was nineteen, of suitable marrying age, who would take care of this family if I were to leave? Gemma and her big-thinking head couldn't be bothered with the little things that needed doing, like painting the truck so people didn't think we ran a shoddy business.

Gemma examined a cube of tofu between her chopsticks. "Maybe those railroad tycoons will win this time and we can all stay."

The three major railroads had mounted a last effort against the city's order to build a union station on Chinatown, an order backed by the Supreme Court itself. The matter had made strange bedfellows of the Chinese and the railroad magnates. They didn't want to empty their pockets to pay for a terminus uniting all three networks, and we didn't want to lose our homes, our community. The thought of being forced to leave made my head clang with questions. Where would we go? How would we manage to set up house before Ma gave birth? Where would Peony go to school? Unlike the railroad magnates, we didn't get a say. Any day now, the city would pass its final judgment.

Ma grunted. "As long as officials can be bought, we will never be secure. Otis Fox has a dragon's hoard of money."

Gemma made the kind of face reserved for bad smells. Millionaire Otis Fox of Fox Cosmetics had spearheaded the "Take Back L.A." committee leading the charge for the building of Union Station. He considered Chinatown a nest of vipers that needed stamping out. And if his son, Philippe, won a city council seat next month, he wouldn't even need that dragon's hoard to get his way.

Ma's eyes floated to me, stirring at my rice. "Your ba thinks it will be a good match."

Gemma stopped eating. Peony picked at a callus on her palm. I glanced at our father's chair, remembering how family dinner was his favorite part of the day. Many fathers frowned upon children speaking at the table, but not him, and we all missed him, especially Ma. When he'd begun coughing up mouthfuls of blood, the doctors at the French Hospital had recommended total rest at a health resort located in the desert of San Bernardino to dry out his tuberculosis-ridden lungs. As he was a spry man not yet forty, used to hauling heavy loads as a bricklayer before starting our flower business, they estimated he'd be out in three months. In a cruel nod to the day he'd left—April Fools' Day—he'd been at the sanatorium already twice that. How much longer would it be? And what did it say about the state of his condition that he had approved of a suitor from afar?

"Why is it a good match?" asked Peony, casting me sympathetic glances. She knew I wasn't ready to be married.

"The Moys live in Pa-sa-de-na"—Ma pronounced each syllable as if laying down a winning hand—"on their own ranch." They owned a successful canning company by the Los Angeles River, and though most Chinese couldn't be citizens and therefore couldn't own land, money was like water. The stronger the stream, the more easily it wound its way around even the staunchest rocks.

Peony blinked at the nonanswer.

Ma lowered herself onto the sofa, her face flushed, panting lightly as she studied the teakwood ancestral altar we kept stocked with flowers and incense. Gray hairs were ambushing the black ones on her head. She deserved an easier life. If we all married well, she could have that eventually.

"So when's the piggy going to market?" asked Gemma, mirth returning to her face. I kicked her under the table.

"They will be coming for dinner Friday. Your father insisted you should meet first and 'get to know each other,' the American way." Ma lifted her feet onto a low table, grimacing. "In my day, all we needed was a matchmaker to ensure both families were reputable, and a fortune teller to read the stars. There was no need for all this Hollywood drama." She wiggled deeper into the couch. "But good wives will defer to their husbands." She raised an expectant eyebrow.

I rolled a loose thread between my fingers. I was the oldest, and duty called. The Moys were respected, even if their son was odd as the number one. I should count myself lucky that it wouldn't be a blind match. That might have worked for our parents, but this was a new age. "I will meet him, Ma."

Maybe I had been born to the stage, because the dents that seemed to be a permanent part of Ma's expression these days smoothed at last. A missing bottom tooth gave her soft smile character. "You can wear my marigold dress, but you'll need to take in the waist."

AFTER DINNER, I TOOK MA'S DRESS AND MY NOTIONS BASKET TO the abandoned apartment three doors down that I used as a sewing room. With the threat of Union Station looming for the past few years, the three other families who used to live on our floor had moved to mixed neighborhoods like East Adams as the landlord had failed to make necessary improvements. Why fix the roof of a condemned house? Ba didn't want us to move— whether because of stubbornness or optimism, I wasn't sure. When he left for the sanatorium, Ma elected that we should stay put so we could welcome him back to a familiar home.

"Evening, Stuffy," I greeted the dress form that Peony and her basketball crew had found in the old Mercantile lot. "You ever feel like you're stuck in one place with no mind of your own?"

I fingered the tiny iridescent feather I'd recently pinned to the headless torso. "Sorry, of course you do."

Pushing aside the calico curtains I'd constructed from old bedsheets, I cracked the window that looked south toward Apablasa Street. Bing Crosby crooned from the boardinghouse of bachelors next door. Music was one reason I loved coming to this room. The other was to people watch, though most were already tucked away in their nooks.

I pulled a chair to the window and began ripping out a seam in Ma's marigold dress. In either direction a motley collection of old brick and yellow stucco buildings—and even a few wood structures—soaked up the last of the dusk. Still visible were the red pails Ba had installed on each doorstep. We filled the "cheer buckets" with our unsold flowers—Ba's idea for sprucing up our embattled strip of the world.

Bing's last note died out, and the sultry hit "Midnight Murderess," made famous by Lulu Wong's hit movie of the same name, began its rocking melody. My gaze floated to the iridescent feather, which had inexplicably shown up in our mailbox last week, along with a card that read, "Your turn for luck. Lulu."

Lulu had been two years ahead of me in school, but a school play had brought us together when I was nearly twelve, and she, fourteen. I played a fence, and she, a willow tree, which meant we did a lot of standing. After the play was over, she invited me to the two-room apartment where she lived with her ma and her younger sister. "Since I know you can make wood interesting, would you like to recite some plays with me?"

Two years later, we learned of an upcoming role for a Chinese girl in a movie. The "Oriental" look had grown popular in the movie industry. Agents in big Cadillacs even trolled our streets for extras.

"Let's audition," she begged me, the signature tiger-charming mole on her cheek as bright as an evening star. "What do we have to lose?"

I looked at her in surprise. Though I'd loved the thrill of transforming into someone else on the makeshift stage of the Wongs' small flat, the idea of doing so publicly put squirrely feelings in my stomach. Lots of folks considered girls in show business to be loose in morals, even hussies. Perhaps she didn't care. She'd survived scandal before, after her no-account father took his delivery truck and lit out for Nevada when Lulu was twelve and her younger sister just learning her ABCs. But I could never bring shame to my family.

Before her audition, I gave her a tiny iridescent feather, which I'd found by the river, for luck.

Lulu's rise to fame had been described as "meteoric." By the time she was eighteen, she'd moved her ma and younger sister out of Chinatown, and now they all lived together in Beverly Hills with the other movie stars.

Maybe if I'd been so bold, we'd have more than rice and vege-tables in our bowls and I wouldn't have to worry about marrying Bug Boy.

"It must be very dull being a millionaire," I told Stuffy.

Stuffy had no head, but I couldn't help thinking she was laughing at me.

3
GEMMA

I STEPPED OUT OF OUR SHABBY STUCCO AND INHALED the Chinatown air, which smelled of fried dough, old cigarettes, incense, garbage, and, mind-bustingly, the ocean, seventeen miles away. Ba said I had the nose of a bloodhound like him, useful in the flower trade. I sniffed again. There was something else. A thick layer of clouds seemed to pin down the sun, casting everything in gray. Maybe gray had a smell too.

Or maybe it was simply the scent of irritation lifting off May, who was managing to inspect me from head to toe without tripping, a frown marring her delicate face.

"For heaven's sake, at least let some day go by before getting fretty," I griped.

"Tie it like this." May showed me the knot on her blue neckerchief, a twin to mine.

As if that weren't matchy enough, she had made us both jumpsuits of medium-blue oxford cloth, styled with rolled-up sleeves and cuffed pants and our short straw hats. She thought these new uniforms gave us a more professional look, and since I was working out how to pitch her my new idea, I didn't complain.

At the Esteemed Friend planter, a three-foot-high strip filled with gardenias, we rubbed our hands across the brick Ba had inscribed with our Chinese names. Touching the brick was our way of honoring our family. If a family is harmonious, all will be well.

We trekked toward the abandoned horse lot where May had made us paint the Mule last night. Apablasa Street hadn't yet woken up. But soon, the tofu seller would hang his FRESH TODAY! sign, the cobbler's hammer would start knocking, and the herbalist would pull out his wooden tub of longevity turtles, warning, "Watch your fingers!"

The weeds had grown long in the abandoned horse lot and looked like spirits rising from the grave. My ears perked up. At the far end of the lot, past hitching posts still swinging with rope, a strange buzzing seemed to be coming from the stables. Maybe it was the ghosts of vegetable sellers past. The area used to pulse with horses and people on their way to City Market.

I stamped my cold feet and coughed at my skittishness, hating the slipperiness of being afraid. One fear led to another, and soon you were skidding down a mountain. Life gave us plenty of opportunities to be afraid, and an equal number of chances to punch those fears in the nose.

An orange blur streaked by. I yelped, scaring a scream out of May.

The herbalist's tabby peered back at me, all head and little body. The man shaved the animal to keep down the fleas but allowed her to retain the hair on her head, "for dignity," though I thought it made her look like an overgrown dandelion. With a scowl in my direction, May pulled out her driving gloves.

The Mule still stunk of her new coat of emperor yellow. As May warmed the engine, her gaze rested on the basketball net Peony had nailed to the closest hitching post. "Poor Peony hasn't seen her basketball mates in a while."

None of us had time for leisure since Ba's illness. "You should worry about your new mate, Bug Boy." I'd been ribbing her ever since Ma brought him up. "At least you'll have someone to kill the cockroaches . . . unless Wallace would rather chase you with them."

May didn't take the bait. "Maybe he won't be as bad as we remember."

"That is a very poor standard for a husband."

Casting me a sour look, she chugged us toward the farms on Valley Road. The uneven pavement jostled my bones, still sore from yesterday's painting.

I groaned. "Please, May, drive as fast as possible so I can really feel those bumps."

"Anytime you'd like to drive, I'm happy to trade places."

I slid down into the bench seat. She knew I would rather paint a dozen trucks by myself than work all those gears and pedals. Ba had taught May but had fallen sick before teaching me. Had it not been for a quarter "tip" to the evaluator, I would've failed the road test. But maybe I would learn just so I didn't have to hear May lord it over me.

The San Gabriel Mountains north of us were beginning to turn from purple to yellow, like someone had punched them. We motored by the county hospital and soon after arrived at the farm of one of our suppliers. Straight rows of blooms surrounded the adobe house in both directions, peppered with colorful geraniums, which were said to keep beetles off the other flowers.

Angel Barajas, a young farmer with a broad nose and a wide smile, moved piles of flowers from a wheelbarrow to our buckets. May and I slipped on work gloves and pitched in.

I plucked up a yellow mum, eyeballing the rows of its older brethren dying on the stalk. "Crisantemos?"

Angel's smile pulled wider. "Sí, señorita."

"You ever sell dead flowers?"

May grabbed two bunches of daisies, one under each arm. "Where are you going with this?" she asked me in Cantonese.

I polished up a smile. "Chinese people love drinking chrysanthemum tea."

"We're not in the tea business, sister," May sang through her clenched teeth, back to English. She was predisposed to not liking my ideas, especially ones involving new business ventures.

"But we could be," I sang back.

"Actually, we will have many dead flowers soon, and you're welcome to them. We're switching to all vegetables in the spring. I was just writing a letter to your papa."

"We'll be sorry to lose you," said May, surveying the man's neat fields.

Angel aired his hat. "Me as well. The problem with flowers is you can't eat them if no one buys."

"Of course." May gave him an encouraging smile, though I knew she was worried. Half of our suppliers had gone out of business in the last year alone. But we'd manage, somehow.

After securing the last of the flowers, we returned to our seats, and May gunned off before I had even grabbed the seat handles. Back to the abandoned horse lot we rumbled. We'd prep the stems there before taking them to City Market. Its closeness to home meant easy use of the facilities should we need them before heading out for the day's work.

My sister drove with her gaze tightly focused on the road, as if someone was pulling us along by a string connected to her nose. I knew she was worried about replacing Angel, but I also suspected I was getting dished a serving of silent pudding for my tea idea. At least I had ideas and didn't spend all my time fretting. I started whistling "Pop Goes the Weasel," the song with no end.

When she didn't respond, I did my other whistles—two-note, parrot, train, come-hither, I did them all.

"Stop that racket." The Mule bucked as if agreeing with May. "I wish you would take our situation more seriously. We just lost a grower, I have to marry Bug Boy, and you want to jump a train with an unknown destination. Dead chrysanthemums, indeed."

"Don't be a martyr for us. If you remember, I advised against Bug Boy. Wait until something better comes along. A rodent man, at least."

May took a swipe at me, but I dodged out of the way.

"If you want to block the marriage hand, you have to think bigger." I undid the knot in my kerchief and wiped the sweat off my brow. "Selling chrysanthemum tea might help get us through the winter."

"Who's going to buy it?" May blew the hair off her face. "The same poor Chinese who are already watering their porridge? Plus, we'd be stealing away Dai-Sang's business." She was so fired up, one bump in the road could rocket her into space. Pulling into the horse lot, she killed the engine. "You're always bossing me around without thinking through the consequences," she huffed, then stomped toward the cargo bed.

I met her on the other side. "You know what your problem is, May? You lack vision. White people drink tea too."

She guffawed. "Would you buy tea made by someone you think carries disease?"

"Did you not learn anything from Westlake Park?"

"Yes. That if you ever ask me to go there again, I'm running in the opposite direction." She began untying a bundle of old newspapers that we used to wrap bouquets.

"We sold all our flowers because we were as pretty as a picture, and you know it. Chinatown has an image problem. But I don't see that anything can be done about it, as long as the press insists on giving people like Otis Fox their attention, and never us."

I picked up the top newspaper, where a picture of the weasel holding up his fist accompanied the headline "Fox, on Behalf of Take Back L.A., Says 'Chinatown Must Go!'"

I read aloud:

> In a passionate speech to members of the city council, Fox claimed, "The Chinese are, by nature, drunken and slovenly, even their women. As a species, these messy goblins reek of mysterious odors and prefer their dark, labyrinthine alleyways so as to make their crimes and many hideous perversions harder to discover."

"Well, how do you like that?" I asked.

"What?"

"*Hideous perversions.*" I showed her the paper, pointing at the words. "He must have seen the herbalist's tabby."

May shook her head and smiled. But a fly buzzed near her face, and she took off her hat and swatted at it. Another swooped in, then sped toward the stables, where even more flies were buzzing. My gut whispered a warning. Peeling red paint and a wide, doorless entry gave the stables the look of a rotting carcass.

"They're coming from there," I said. The gray had lifted, but the place was still raising the hairs on my arms.

With a frown, May rehatted her head. "Let's finish this and get moving." Grabbing her clippers, she began trimming excess leaves into an empty bucket.

Children came here to play. If something foul had moved in, we should find out. "Something's wrong. I'm going to investigate."

"An animal probably crawled in there to die. Don't go in. We have work to do! Wait!"

I crossed the dirt lot toward the stables, weeds grabbing at my ankles. The wood building was long enough to house ten stalls on each side. We'd discovered a cat with kittens living in one of the stalls a few years ago, but Ma wouldn't let us keep them, saying she had enough mouths to feed. Occasionally, vagrants would find their way into the building. But besides the flies, the place seemed spookily quiet.

I could feel May come up behind me. Dirt and gravel crunched underfoot as we crossed the threshold.

"I can't believe you're dragging me in here just to see a dead animal," she muttered.

"I hope that's all it is." The reek of manure along with traces of sawdust and rotting wood made me sneeze four times in a row. *Four* in Cantonese sounded too much like the word for "death" and was very unlucky. There was something else too. That gray smell again.

May tugged at my sleeve. "Maybe we should just go."

The flies were zipping around the stall farthest from the door to the left. I switched my gardening shears to a more defensive grip, just in case.

As I drew closer, I couldn't help noticing footprints on the floor, which was covered by a fine layer of dirt. The prints were as large as Ba's. A chill snaked up my arms, and I hugged myself.

"Oh, for heaven's sake, let's just get this over with." May, who had been trailing me, pulled me to the end stall. "See, it's just—"

A scream exploded from her lips.

4
MAY

A WOMAN LAY SPRAWLED IN ONE CORNER OF THE STALL, her legs ending with oxford pumps. Pencil-thin black stripes ran the length of her cream suit. I forced my eyes to follow the lines, dreading who I would see. A tendril of hair down her left cheek pointed at a unique birthmark. A tiger-charming mole.

All the bones in my spine seemed to shake loose. It was . . . Lulu. I shrieked, a hair-raising noise I'd never made before, but I couldn't stop it.

Gemma grabbed me. "Shh, May, be calm."

"Oh, ancestors," I babbled, tears coming. "She's—she's—"

"Yes, dead," Gemma said in a tight voice as we clutched at each other.

I couldn't look away, caught by Lulu's eyes, wide open in shock. They suggested she had not died naturally. I whipped around, as if the killer might still be here, watching us. But there was no one, only a dry and empty nothingness. Even my shrill screams had been sucked away.

On-screen, Lulu had always appeared sophisticated. Mature. But now, save for her faded lipstick, her delicate face with its high cheekbones was bare and almost childlike, framed by her short, waved hairstyle. Her mouth was pursed, as if blowing a kiss.

My knees nearly gave out at the oddness of her expression,

and a sour taste coated my mouth. *No, no, no. Not you, my old friend. Oh, Lulu, what are you doing here?*

A memory of her playing dead on the pine stage of our schoolhouse superimposed itself over the vision in front of me. She'd relaxed all her muscles, even her tongue, so that she really did look tragically corpselike, save for a youthful bloom over her cheeks.

She'd popped up from the floor so suddenly that I'd jumped back, nearly falling. "Okay, now you play dead."

This time, there was no acting. She wouldn't be getting up ever again.

A fly landed on her upper lip, and a shudder ran through me. Gemma caught me before I fell, pulling me back to the stable door. "Come on, we've got to call for help. Mr. Yam has the closest phone."

I stumbled to the exit on legs as unfeeling as two sticks of white radish. The morning sun hurt my eyes, the earlier haze having burned away. "How long do you think she's been there?" I gasped, feeling my stomach bucking.

Gemma shook her head. "I don't know. But when I think back, I remember the buzzing from earlier. I didn't know it was the flies then. I wasn't even sure it was a real sound."

My flat Mary Janes sounded too heavy on the pavement. The iridescent feather floated into my mind, sent only a week ago. *Your turn for luck,* she had written. I hadn't yet replied. Guilt flooded me. If I had gotten in touch with her, would things have been different? Who had brought her so low?

A rising panic was closing my throat, and I forced myself to breathe. "Poor Lulu. How could this happen? Her poor mother."

"And Bettina," Gemma muttered, referring to Lulu's little sister, one of Peony's classmates. She hadn't "fit in" well at her local school, so she'd returned to our school in Chinatown. "Steady, sis. I know you were friends, but we can't fall apart yet." She handed me a hankie, and I dabbed my wet eyes, for once glad for her take-charge manner. With a glance back at the stables, she pulled me along over gravel that crunched like bones. "Should we call the police?"

"Of course we should call the police."

"Like *they* ever help," Gemma griped.

I grimaced, remembering how the police were supposed to investigate the vandalism of several Chinese businesses last year but dropped the case when the businesses couldn't cough up enough funds to keep them interested. "Even if they don't like us, they'll have to do something. She's famous. If we don't report it, they might think we had something to do with it."

Gemma scowled. "It's just, this is going to rain hell down on us. I just know it."

"What do you mean?"

"Chinatown already has one foot in the grave. The Foxes of the world are going to use this to push us all the way in."

All the gloomy possibilities began to take shape in front of me. People already believed Chinatown to be mysterious and sinister. Proponents of Union Station certainly played up that angle. Whatever last efforts were being pitched by the railroads—not to preserve our homes, but to save their pocketbooks—would be ripped away.

I focused on putting one foot in front of the other as we hurried to One Dragon Grocery, a hundred paces from the horse lot. The store's faded bricks all seemed to be leaning to one side. Had they always been that way? Even the flowers we'd put in Mr. Yam's cheer bucket all appeared to be crooked in one direction. For a moment, I almost believed Lulu's murder had caused the ground here to shift. But even if the earth was sound, a howling wind had blown through Chinatown, wreaking damage that would be felt for a long time. Maybe forever.

The scent of red flower liniment drifted from the entrance, where a knee-high statue of a stone dragon stood guard. Mr. Yam, the grocer, was always up early. Inside, his spindly form arranged sacks of rice, a lick of black hair all that remained on his even scalp.

"Mr. Yam!" panted Gemma. "It's an emergency. We need your phone."

He unbent himself, his joints popping and creaking. His eyes were the gray of old spoons. "Come in, come in." He gestured to the telephone on his counter.

Gemma picked the receiver off its candlestick base and dialed. "Operator, please connect me to the Central Police Department." She fingered a basket full of haw flake candies; the small red cylinder packages looked like tiny firecrackers. "Hello? . . . Yes, someone has died. We think she was murdered." Her voice trembled and she cleared her throat. Mr. Yam fumbled the pot of tea he was pouring, spilling it onto the counter. "Yes, *murdered*." Gemma glared at the plank floors. "Please come quick. We're at Apablasa Street by the horse lot . . . My name? It's Gemma Chow."

Mr. Yam pushed two cups toward us, then clutched his arms around him.

We nodded our thanks, though my hands shook so badly, I dared not lift mine.

"Was it anyone we knew?" Mr. Yam licked his thin lips.

"Lulu Wong," I whispered.

"Oh. It couldn't be." His breath fell out of him, and he looked on the verge of collapsing.

If I hadn't seen her with my own eyes, I wouldn't believe it either. She had been so full of life, of promise. No one ever expected she would go into show business, the soft-spoken girl whose dresses always fit too large on her boyish frame. But I knew.

"What was Lulu Wong doing here?" Mr. Yam leaned back against the pile of rice sacks, his thin face heavy with dismay.

"Maybe visiting someone?" Gemma blew distractedly at her tea.

I frowned, rubbing my clammy palms against my pants. Lulu ran with a different crowd nowadays. I had been the closest to her, and even I hadn't kept in touch. "Maybe she came to shop for her mother?"

Mr. Yam frowned. "If so, she would've stopped here. Wong Tai put in an order for more red flower liniment and hasn't picked it up yet."

A police siren wailed from the direction of Alameda to the west, sounding annoyed, as if the hand cranking it were doing so reluctantly.

"Excuse me, girls, I must wake up Mrs. Yam." The grocer stepped around a wooden barricade that marked a crumbling spot on the ceiling, then disappeared up the stairs to his living quarters. Mr. Yam and his wife were like the sun and the moon, one early to rise, the other, late.

Gemma and I set off back toward the horse lot, me dragging my feet again, but not due to numbness. I didn't want to see Lulu like that again, dehumanized. A victim. It was bad enough that someone had killed her. I pinched my neck, thoughts of her suffering threatening to shatter me. A second death would come in the form of scandal, her twisted body held up for viewing like some circus sideshow, her fame recast as a cautionary tale. They would kill her twice.

People had begun to appear on balconies or from the doors of the lodging houses lining the street. A black cruiser with a boxy top pulled up. Its window rolled down, and the crackling noise of a police dispatcher filtered through. A man peered at us from the stingy shade of his porkpie hat. His face had the unenthusiastic droop of one not easily amused. He draped an elbow over the window, his peanut-shaped nose flaring. "You the one who called?"

"Yes," said Gemma. "Officer . . ."

"*Detective* Mallady."

"Detective Mallady. I'm Gemma Chow, and this is my sister May."

I nodded at the man. Beyond him, a young officer in uniform sat at the wheel, his gaze darting around him.

"The victim is Lulu Wong," Gemma stated simply in her no-nonsense business voice. Thank goodness for her levelheadedness. My own head felt as jumbled as a tangle of blooms. "We found her right up here in the stables."

The young officer parked behind the Mule. As Detective Mallady exited the car, his seat cushion groaned, and the door uttered the kind of unpleasant noise not made in polite company. Even his car didn't want to be here. He nodded to our truck. "That yours?"

The Mule looked cheerfully out of place in the drab setting. "Yes," said Gemma.

Mallady pulled his trousers higher over his thick middle. His broad shoulders caused his rust-colored suit to bunch, though better posture and a good ironing could help. "Chow's Flowers. What are you doing here at this time of day? Shouldn't you be out selling those?"

"We always stop here before City Market to prep the flowers," Gemma said easily.

Mallady frowned at me. I showed him the clippers I had stored in my pocket. The door slammed, and his partner emerged from the car, a wide-eyed man in his early twenties. He assessed us with the nervousness of a pigeon on the lookout for cats, his shiny new badge throwing around glints of sunlight. "So who's Lulu Wong?"

Gemma rolled her eyes. "She's a movie star."

The young officer scratched at his cheeks, which had the bumpy red look of a recent shave.

Mallady snorted. "Come on, Officer Kidd. Let's see what we've got. You two, stay here."

Kidd withdrew a baton from his belt and followed Mallady across the dirt yard.

"Let's go," said Gemma, setting off after them.

I planted my feet. "They said to stay here."

"But we're the ones who found her. And I don't trust them to do a good job. Mallady looks like he'd rather be anywhere else, and that Officer Kidd looks newly minted."

I didn't move, as if I could stop this horror from continuing by standing still. "Who would want to kill her?" I finally voiced. "Who would do such a thing?" Lulu might've had her share of on-screen enemies—she was always cast as the villain—but off camera, she had been caring and warm. Sometimes, instead of reciting plays, we'd read the dailies posted on the news wall on Alameda to the elderly and the illiterate.

"I'm just as upset as you. But we owe it to Lulu to keep an eye on matters. We need to make sure justice is served, don't you see? She might've been a somebody when she was alive, but now, who knows?" Gemma gazed up at me, her face as earnest as a daisy.

Worry trapped my breath in my chest. Lulu's wealth and

fame would give the investigation a push. But for how long and how far? In the end, she was just a dead Chinese woman, without even a father to speak for her. Would she matter enough? I said a prayer and nodded. Lulu was gone, and I could not afford to stay in this moment. She needed us. Plus, though Gemma might be bolder, she was also more foolish, and it was my duty to keep folly's hand off her.

The scent of incense drifted by from one of the bachelor buildings, and my mind floated back to when I had seen Lulu six months ago at the White Horse joss house. After she'd nabbed her first role at age sixteen, I hadn't seen her much, and then not at all when she'd moved to Beverly Hills. I'd just refilled the gold bowls in the main temple with fresh camellia—something Ba made us do every week. In the adjacent ancestral hall, a figure in a dark jacket and a silk headscarf bowed at the altar. Leaving her to her privacy, I exited to the courtyard, which featured a fountain centered by a horse.

"May?" The woman had followed me. She pushed back her scarf.

"Lulu? How are you?" I set down my bucket, reaching out to embrace her, then pulling back. Now that she was a big star, perhaps it was inappropriate.

To my surprise, she pulled me close, placing a kiss on my cheek. "I'm well." Her smooth brow with its straight hairline furrowed. "You are a hard person to reach." Her voice, huskier than most girls', seemed to have ripened into a fine rice wine, sweet and rich with honey notes.

I murmured an apology, remembering a call I hadn't returned and a letter I'd written but never mailed. Somehow, I'd convinced myself that her new life didn't leave room for her old one.

"I think about you often, May. I miss our times together. Ma asks why you never come around."

My expression fell, hating that I'd disappointed a woman who'd always welcomed me. "I am sorry," I mumbled. "Time just got away from me. Hollywood must be exciting." I bit my tongue, realizing how foolish that sounded. "I mean, all the people you must be meeting."

"I didn't love it at first." She wended her scarf around her arm. "I was being treated like a circus pony, trotted out, petted, and fawned over. But I got tired of other people holding the reins. So I took them back. Act like you have power, and you just might get it."

"Okay," I replied, though I wasn't sure what she was talking about.

"I'll call you next week. We'll get French dips." She pretended to clamp a cigar at the side of her mouth and waggled her eyebrows.

I laughed. "Of course." We had dreamed of ordering French dip sandwiches at a diner near Chinatown, though I couldn't imagine the gossip that would be provoked by the sight of us eating together, the famous Lulu with the ordinary May. People might think she felt sorry for me or, worse, that I was trying to elevate my own status.

Those thoughts seemed so petty now.

I forced my limbs to follow Gemma toward the stables. Creeping inside, we stopped behind the first stall. At the last stall, Kidd was writing in a notebook.

Mallady stood beside him, his hands on his hips. "Definitely rigor mortis." His voice echoed off the walls. "Look at her neck, fingers, limbs. That puts the time of death in the last six to twelve hours. If it was a murder, whoever did it would be long gone." He swatted a meaty hand at the flies, then bent down. "There's a cut on the side of her head."

The word *murder* slithered around my head like a water eel among the lotuses.

"You think that's what did her in?" Kidd's pencil paused.

"Who knows," Mallady grumbled. "I don't see any other marks. Could be poison."

"Like Dixie Doors."

Gemma glanced at me, her eyes large. Dixie Doors was a local beauty pageant winner from Glendale who the police had found murdered in a local park last year. The police never did catch the killer.

"Dixie Doors was strychnine," said Mallady. "This doesn't look like strychnine. Ah well, let the medical examiner figure it out."

Kidd was back to scratching his cheeks. "But what's a dame like that doing here? I wouldn't bring my horse to this dump if I owned one."

"Maybe meeting a lover, a tryst like."

Gemma's eyes flicked to the ceiling, and she shook her head. When I'd known her, Lulu had been a dutiful and virtuous daughter. I couldn't imagine her skulking around in old stables meeting lovers.

"Yeah, look at her lips." Kidd's voice had gone high, and he started shaking out his legs as if he were preparing to make a run for it. "It's like she was waiting for a kiss."

Gemma clicked her tongue in annoyance. Mallady glanced over at us, his aluminum-colored eyes crimping. "I thought I told you to wait outside."

"We just want to help solve her murder." Gemma strode right up to the last stall, with me at her heels. The sight of Lulu's frozen face with her kissing lips sucked the air from me. The cut Mallady had mentioned was visible, a spot of dried blood above her left ear that I wouldn't have noticed without his having pushed her hair aside. Something red—blood?—smudged her right sleeve near the wrist of her cream pantsuit. Had she attempted to wipe the blood from the cut with her right sleeve? She was right-handed, but that was a long way to stretch. Surely she would've just used her left sleeve. My gaze fretted about on her silk pantsuit with its stylish wide trousers. Who had she been coming to see?

Mallady crossed his arms, reminding me of a grumpy sandstone pillar. "If it is murder. She could've just wandered in here drunk, fell over, and hit her head."

Gemma snorted loudly. "If you knew her, you would know that Lulu wandering in here drunk is as likely as her flying in with wings. She was Buddhist and didn't drink."

"I'm a Catholic, but that doesn't stop me from sinning," said Mallady.

"Besides, we were here painting our truck last night until sundown," Gemma added with impatience. "We didn't see a soul."

"Write that down," ordered Mallady, and Kidd scribbled in his notebook. "She a friend of yours?" Mallady's mouth twitched to one side.

"Yes, we knew her," I answered.

"Yeah? How?"

"Lulu was two years above me in school," I said, willing my voice not to quaver. Kidd's pencil scratched the silence. "She left school to be an actress. She is well known for her role in *Midnight Murderess*."

Kidd looked up from his notebook. "I saw *Midnight Murderess*. That was her? She was evil, the way she painted her face and scared all those men to death." He shuddered, glanced back at

Lulu, and shuddered again. "Girl like her must have had a string of boyfriends."

Gemma scoffed. "Movies are not real life."

The detective steered his grouchy face to me. "You know anyone who had it out for her?"

"No," I replied stiffly. It felt wrong to be talking about her while she was stretched out in the corner, attended to only by flies. "We were all happy for her success."

Mallady pulled off his hat, whose indentation had marked his face with a second frown. "I suppose it could've been a robbery. Love and greed are the biggest troublemakers in my business. She had money, didn't she? I don't see a purse anywhere."

"Even if it was a robbery, it was still a murder, and I hope you won't rest until you find the killer." Gemma's jaw clenched, and her arms spooled tight around her. "He should be hanged and quartered."

Mallady raised an eyebrow, and for the first time, his face took on a glint of interest. "We'll find the *truth*, don't worry."

The word *truth* batted around in front of us like a moth.

Gemma's mouth buckled, as if trying to cage all the doubts piling up behind it.

"May? Gemma?" Mr. Yam poked his head into the stables along with the Filipino cigar maker and the herbalist.

I lifted a hand in greeting. "We're here, Mr. Yam."

"Good Lord, the townspeople have arrived," Mallady muttered. He raised his voice. "Folks, this is a crime scene. Girls, let's go. Kidd, call an ambulance. Then rope off this area. There goes my morning."

"Yes, sir." Kidd hurried after his boss, who was already halfway to the exit. I got the impression that the junior officer was only too happy to move on to more mundane matters.

Gemma began to follow them, but Lulu's anguished face beckoned to me. Swallowing my revulsion, I drew closer, lowering myself. Through the small hole made by her lips, I could see that some of her dark red lipstick had rubbed off onto her front teeth. "I wish you could tell us what happened," I whispered.

"Let's go, May." Gemma held out a hand. I was about to take it. But then a ray of sunlight from the broken roof crept over Lulu's head, and something glinted beneath her black waves. My finger trembled as I pushed aside her hair. She was wearing gold earrings.

"Look." I showed Gemma. "If the motive was greed, wouldn't they have taken these?"

Gemma's eyes went as big as moons, and she bent closer. "They're cranes. See the long legs?"

I slowly nodded. In Chinese culture, the birds represented longevity. But they also signified long-lasting love and fidelity. Cranes stayed with one partner for life. "So who did Lulu love?"

5
GEMMA

AN AMBULANCE CARTED LULU AWAY TO THE *TSK, TSK* OF
cameras. While reporters for the *Observer First, L.A. Daily,* and
Chinatown News collected stories, I did my best to assure our
shocked neighbors, despite my own sawed-off nerves. Their conversations pelted me from all directions.

"Bad luck will follow," said someone.

"Who could've done such a thing?"

"Chinese haters. They are coming for us all."

"Hush. Disaster follows from careless talk."

That last bit was spoken by our stately herbalist Dai-Sang,
one of Chinatown's respected leaders, whose tall face always
harbored a deep thought.

May floated around like she was a Goodyear Blimp, only air
holding her up. The shock had been especially great for her, as
she had known Lulu the best. I remembered one wretched winter when our whole family except May had come down with
influenza. With us all half-delirious, May snuck out to sell some
of Ba's inventory in her handbasket. Lulu, then fifteen, offered to
help. The two took the streetcar to the newly opened Grauman's
Chinese Theatre, where they sold the blooms to tourists.

Both mothers had been as mad as boiled owls when they'd
found out.

For the thousandth time since Ba had been gone, I wished he was here. People always came to him when they had trouble because he always knew what to say and do. Once, I'd broken May's new scissors trying to cut off a stick of sugarcane. She was mad enough to stab me with them. After making me apologize, Ba showed us both how to repair the scissors with a new pivot screw. What would he do in this situation?

Well, one thing he would *not* do was break into hysterical fits.

After helping Mr. Yam organize a "comfort committee" to check in on Lulu's mother, including collections for a gift basket, May and I finally processed our flowers. I shook my limbs loose. I'd been holding myself as tight as a trussed duck, as if I could keep all the bad energy, like gasoline fumes, from seeping in.

"Let's donate these to the hospital." May tied twine around the last bunch of daisies. "By the time we get to City Market, it'll be close to noon. And this day has wrung me out." She *was* looking as green as a cabbage leaf around the edges.

I held my tongue, not ready to surrender our flowers. Though noon was closing time at the market, whoever had murdered poor Lulu would not take our wages too. Not if I could help it. And selling flowers was better than brooding at home over the cruelty of the world.

"Fine," I said amiably. "I'll deliver them. You go home and keep an eye on Ma." I wiped off my tools and tucked them into an old potholder, trying not to look suspicious. If May knew I was planning to sell again at Westlake Park, she might feel compelled to tell Ma, who didn't need another thing to worry about. Ignorance served all.

May leveled her gaze at me. "But you don't drive. I'll come with you."

"I don't drive because I'd rather *you* do it. Anyway, I do have my license." I jutted my chin. Hadn't I resolved to learn just a few hours ago?

Before she could disagree, I quickly maneuvered into the driver's seat. Home was only a short walk away, but May slid into the passenger's side and cast me a thorny gaze, judging me in the way only she could do. "First, let's see if you can make it the two blocks to home."

I switched on the key and pressed the starter. The Mule made sounds like she was trying to cough up a hairball.

May pressed a finger to her temple. "You forgot the choke. Start again."

"Right." I turned off the starter, this time remembering to release the choke valve and jiggle the timing lever before trying again. I lifted the throttle, and with a *vroom*, the Mule bucked, snapping back both our necks.

Two dents like rabbit ears appeared between May's eyebrows. "This is a bad idea. The point is to bring the flowers to the hospital, not wind up in the hospital."

"Stop worrying. I'll never get better at driving if I don't just do it, and I don't need you looking over my shoulder. In fact, I was planning on cruising around afterward, to practice my left turns. I'll be home before dinner."

"You're up to something."

"Am not." How did she always know?

May sagged against the seat. "Whatever you say. I'm too tired to argue. Wiggle. You're wasting gas."

I parked in front of our dingy building, then followed May up the stairs to our apartment. "Just need some peanuts," I told her frowning face.

Inside, Ma had started scrubbing the floor, even though we had done it this weekend. Chores were her way of working off anxious energy. May pulled out one of the kitchen chairs. "Ma, come sit. I'll finish that."

Ma relinquished her brush to May. "It could've been one of you. What if it had been?"

"It wasn't," said May.

I ducked into the room I shared with my sisters and grabbed my tube of lipstick. Returning to the living room, I headed for the door.

"Gemma?" May's voice was stern.

Somehow, she had seen through my jumpsuit pocket to the lipstick hidden inside. I lifted my chin. "Yes?"

"I thought you wanted peanuts." Her eyes patted me down for clues.

I coughed. "Yes, I did." Fetching a handful from the sack on the counter, I hurried back outside, trying not to step on my own tail again.

Soon, I was back on the road. I nudged the Mule to a jogging pace, which was fast enough for me. A horn honked from behind. "Move faster, you road hog!" the driver yelled.

I threw out a hand and gestured for him to pass. "Go around, flower hater!" He couldn't hear me, but it felt good to yell back.

I bumped the curb on a right turn, and the dark archway of the Second Street Tunnel came into focus. The Mule sputtered and kicked up a fuss, as if trying to dissuade me from the path I was set on. Ignoring her, I drew in a deep breath and held it, letting Bunker Hill swallow me.

When May and I were kids, we'd heard that if you held your breath in a tunnel and made a wish, the wish would come true. We tried it out, wishing for the poundcake being raffled off for the school benefit, and won. We'd been holding our breath in tunnels ever since.

As the Second Street Tunnel chugged by, I crammed in as many wishes as I could: for Lulu's killer to be caught, for Ba to come home soon, for Union Station to be stopped, for juicy roast duck. A small man, Ba had always had a big appetite when it came to roast duck, and he'd passed it down to me.

The car in front of me slowed unexpectedly, and my lungs clamored for oxygen. But I refused to let all those wishes go, even though May would say I had wished for "more than my allotment" and they wouldn't count anyway. According to her, we could only make one wish per tunnel pass. We'd always played by different rules.

At last, sunlight poured over me, and I sucked in great gobs of air all the way to the park.

The ornery Mule kicked again, maybe to protest our destination.

"Life is a gamble, you nag. Maybe we'll get lucky again."

Pulling into the driveway by the boathouse, I slowed to a crawl, hoping to creep by the café diners and afternoon strollers as noiselessly as possible. It occurred to me I should've wished for a hassle-free afternoon. If I ran into those two coppers from the last visit, they might not be so forgiving this time. Echo Park lay a couple miles north and drew rich people, just like Westlake. Sure, it was sometimes closed due to its popularity as a movie backdrop, but why not check? No need to take unnecessary risks even when gambling.

I was just passing the spot where we'd set up previously when the Mule backfired, causing nearby pedestrians to startle and recoil. A terrier yipped frantically at me. Then, with an ear-splitting bang as if someone had fired the fatal bullet to end her suffering, the Mule let out a whine and died.

"No," I wailed. Wrenching the wheel, which now felt frozen,

to the side, I used the truck's last bit of momentum to pull it off the road, braking when I felt the wheels hit the curb. The Mule came to rest in a spot next to a large garbage can. There was no cool palm tree to rest under, not even a fig leaf of shade. "Come on, girl. I didn't mean to call you a nag." I reset all the gears, then tried to start again from scratch.

Nothing.

On the bright side, at least I wasn't blocking the road. But now I'd be the one having to walk a quarter mile to the boathouse to find a telephone. That didn't seem quite fair, even though it probably was. I imagined May's face when she learned what I had done. Worse, our mother's face, already puffy with water retention. Well, if I had to suffer their looks of dismal disappointment, I wouldn't do it empty-handed.

Applying Noir Red, I set up shop and wrote out prices on our chalkboard. The Monday crowd was thinner than Saturday's, and not as free with their money. Or maybe I was driving them away with my distracted salesmanship, twitching like a pigeon every time I thought I saw the permit police.

After three hours, I'd only made two dollars. It was better than nothing, though not enough to ward off the trouble headed my way if May found out I'd lied to her again. But I was getting tired of standing in the sun. Plus, the heat seemed to be lifting the scent of duck droppings off the pavement and serving them to my nose. There were downsides to having a good sniffer.

I packed up. Time to find a telephone booth. I fished the key out and tried the engine one last time, as if I could surprise the Mule into action. Nothing happened. Sighing heavily, I dropped the key into my purse, though I wondered why I bothered. As far as I was concerned, if anyone could revive this dead horse, they deserved her.

I hiked down the footpath, carrying a basket of the choicest flowers, just in case I encountered customers along the way. Fortune favored the prepared, after all.

My feet had begun to swell, and the narrow toes of my black boots were pinching. The lapping of the water as boaters paddled by—ordinarily a soothing sound—today stirred the contents of my stomach, and my head felt too hot and heavy. I took off my hat and fanned myself. Lulu's grim face appeared in my head. She had been twenty-one. I hoped the newspapers would be kind.

"Fancy seeing you here again." A man's voice lifted my head from his polished shoes to his face, finely crafted like a violin. My feet slowed, recognizing the young man named Freddie who'd bought the showstopper. A sleek fedora that looked as if it'd been made of steel sheeting topped his head at a jaunty angle. Dark eyes that never needed to glance away rolled over me.

"Fancy that." I moved around him, but he sidestepped in front of me, bringing his chin to my eye level. I would never go out with a man with a pointed chin, which indicated someone who must always have his way. In fact, thanks to our ba, who often treated us as the sons he never had, I could not think of a single thing I needed a man for. Well, except having babies, and I wasn't a baby-raising sort.

The chin jerked behind me toward the Mule. "Business must be slow if you've got to peddle your wares by foot. 'Course, that makes it harder to sell those obscenely expensive purple monstrosities."

I managed a tight smile. "I'm so glad your mother-in-law liked her orchid. If you don't mind—"

He tugged at his gold cravat, a perfect contrast with his crisp gray suit. It was a pity May was not here to admire it. She'd iron her hat if she could.

"My girlfriend's mother, you mean. Well, yes, she loved it. But I doubt it'll make it to the other side of this week with her black thumb. She even kills dried herbs."

Guilt pinched me in the side. *Shake it off. The showstopper is just a plant, and no longer your concern.* "Tell her to keep it in the shade and mist it frequently. It's tropical."

"The humane thing would have been to leave it in the tropics instead of siccing desert dwellers on it."

"If you're trying to get a refund, I'm sorry, but all sales are final. Now, if you don't mind, I need to find a telephone booth. And your girlfriend must be looking for you."

"She's not here today. Who are you needing to call?"

"I don't see how that's any of your business."

"Suit yourself." He tipped his hat to me, then stepped aside.

Rolling back my shoulders, I marched on. The boathouse with its colorful umbrella shades lay another fifty paces away.

"By the way, there's no telephone booth at the boathouse."

I stopped and looked back at him smugly watching me. "Where's the nearest one, then?"

He shrugged. "I haven't the foggiest."

I grimaced, my basket creaking under my arm. This was a fine pickle. Well, I would just have to head toward the main boulevards and see if I could find a booth. Or maybe this fellow was playing a trick on me and there actually *was* a telephone at the boathouse.

"Seems to me, if you needed to use a telephone, you would've driven your jalopy to the boathouse, and since you didn't, perhaps you are having some transportation issues. Am I right?" He threw me an unsettling, triumphant grin, like a demon who had tricked me out of my soul.

Was I hallucinating? My knees trembled. I must have a touch

of heatstroke. "That's quite a deduction, Sherlock. How hard it must be for your neck to support such a big head. Goodbye." I had more important things to attend to than arguing with this dandy. I set off again toward the boathouse, just to look like I was going somewhere. But, damnable pinching shoes, my foot missed its step, and I felt myself stumble. I caught myself, but the world seemed to be spinning.

A hand caught me by the elbow. "Easy, miss." The man relieved me of the basket. The smugness had left his face.

"I am fine." I shook off his hand and tried not to sway. "It's just . . . the heat."

"It's not even eighty degrees. When's the last time you drank anything?"

I snorted, though my mouth was parched. "Why? Are you a doctor, in addition to a detective?"

"Correct. Dr. Frederick Winter. I think you are dehydrated."

I squinted at him, but it was hard to focus.

His face drew closer, searching mine like a beggar looking for change. "Come on, Miss—er, what is your name?"

"Just Gemma."

"Gemma. Let's get you something to drink. How about you wait on that bench, and I will fetch a refreshment."

"I am not in the habit of trusting men who have accused me of fleecing them."

He frowned. "I can assure you that, as a doctor, I have taken an oath to do no harm, so you have nothing to fear from me unless you're planning to force me to buy your flowers again."

He helped me to a bench in the shade of a magnolia and set my basket beside me. Then he made his way to the boathouse, somehow covering the distance in less than a minute without looking like he was in a hurry.

With my bottom planted, the world stopped shifting about so much. Maybe it *was* dehydration. I hadn't drunk anything since this morning's tea.

A couple of women walking a poodle cast me snooty looks. Even their poodle bared its teeth at me. I never liked dogs, after a policeman's Doberman pinscher tried to take a bite out of my leg after my sixth birthday.

As the women swept by, one whispered loud enough for me to hear, "Who does she think *she* is?"

I lowered my eyes, shame breathing fire on my neck, and the women passed.

This was what fruit mold felt like. Fruit mold couldn't help where it planted itself. It was just trying to live its life, like everyone else. I loosened my boots. The breeze through my thin socks felt as heavenly as summer rain, and magically, the throbbing in my head lessened.

So Freddie was a *doctor*. I hadn't figured the blue blood for a working man, let alone a healer. No wonder he helped me. It would look bad for his reputation if he didn't.

In short order, the man returned with two glasses of lemonade and slid onto the bench beside me.

"Thank you." I drank thirstily, the icy goodness pouring through me. I hardly noticed when he took my wrist and felt for my pulse. I snatched my hand away.

He took my empty glass and passed me the second one. "This is for you too." He pulled a paper bag from his pocket. "Shortbread?"

"Is this usually part of your service?"

"Only for the patients who need sweetening." Before I could think of a snappy response, he asked, "Have you been dehydrated before?"

I scoffed. "You make it sound like I did it on purpose. I happen to be a fan of water."

"Your sister's not here today. Where is she?"

"She wasn't feeling good. Why does it matter?"

"Is she ill?"

"Not exactly." I fed myself a cookie, reluctant to tell him about Lulu's death. We didn't need his sympathy, even though I seemed to have no problem enjoying his charity. But he *was* a stranger. And strange men who came in his particular shade did not have a good history when it came to women in mine. Then again, he did just go out of his way to help me. And he was a doctor; perhaps he would have some insight into how Lulu had died. I washed my mouthful down with more lemonade and focused on a mallard putting around in the water. "We witnessed something horrible this morning." As briefly as possible, I told him.

The smooth planes of his face turned grim. "Poor Lulu Wong. She didn't deserve that." He gripped his knees and stared hard at the lake.

"You knew her?"

"We ran in similar circles, yes." He blew out a breath. "Well, that explains it."

"What?"

"You're still in a bit of a shock. Your skin's clammy, your pulse is elevated, and you're dizzy enough to fall over, all made worse by not drinking. Good news is, you're on your way to recovery."

A truck rumbled up the driveway with ABE'S AUTO SERVICES painted on the side. Freddie hailed the driver and went to speak with him, then pointed to the Mule, a few hundred paces away. The driver motored toward the Mule, and Freddie returned to me.

"Who was that?"

"I took the liberty of calling one of my patients. He owns an auto shop. He can fix anything, even old jalopies. Feeling okay to walk?" Setting the glasses in my basket, he picked it up, then offered his arm. I ignored it. I did not like the idea of taking any more assistance from him than I needed. "I thought you said there wasn't a telephone at the boathouse."

"No public telephone. They let me use their private line."

My cheeks pinked. He knew they wouldn't have let someone like me use the private line. "Thank you. What is his rate?" I only had five dollars. Usually, we'd get car fanatic Moses in Chinatown to help us with repairs for the reduced rate of Ma's famous scallion pancakes.

"Forget it. He owes me."

"But then I will owe you."

"I can't take money from a damsel in distress. It's against my principles."

"I bet you see plenty of damsels in distress in your work as a physician. How do you stay in business?"

"As long as I can avoid the flower sellers, I do okay."

"Well, it's against my principles to owe a debt." Especially to someone like him. One moment, he was vexing me as if for sport, and the next, hovering like a nurse maid.

"I'm afraid, then, we are at an impasse." He walked as stiff as a telephone pole beside me.

"Say, could I interest you in a truckload of flowers? You only gave your girlfriend a dozen last time, when a true gent would've gotten her a dozen dozens."

A smile tugged at his mouth, and he shook his head as if hoping to dislodge it. "If it makes you feel better, I will take them to my clinic across the street."

"It does."

We reached the Mule, where Abe, a neatly combed young man with his name stitched on his army-green jumpsuit, had already started working under the hood. He nodded at me. "Miss. Looks like you have a bad fuel pump. Take me a second to replace it."

"Thank you, sir."

Freddie gestured to the driver's seat, and I slid in. He took his off his jacket, taking the time to fold it neatly over his arm before wandering to the engine, where Abe was tinkering.

Lulu's face appeared in my head again, flies landing on her skin, the bizarre mask that would be her last.

"Gemma? Are you alright?" Freddie was peering in from the passenger side. My knuckles had gone white from gripping the steering wheel.

I released the wood. "Yes. Er, as a doctor, you must have seen many, er, dead people."

All his hard angles seemed to soften. He scooted into the passenger seat and leaned back, causing his hat to tip up. "Yes, I have. I even interned with the coroner's office for a few months."

"She had a small cut on her head above the ear, but not much blood. Is it possible to die from an injury like that?"

He blew out a breath. "Sure, if the blow occurred at the right angle and velocity. Bleeding inside the brain can cause pressure that can be fatal." His eyes were the walnut brown of a good writing desk. "The medical examiner should be able to figure that out. He'll do a thorough examination, including toxicology reports."

"You mean, to find out if she was poisoned."

He nodded.

"Detective Mallady said it probably wasn't strychnine." From Dixie Doors's death, we'd all learned that strychnine was an excruciating way to die, and the thought that Lulu might have similarly suffered had been worrying me. "How would he know that?"

"Strychnine shuts off motor control. The resulting spasms can contort the body in an unnatural way, perhaps freeze the face in a grimace or a clenched jaw. Eventually the muscles tire so that they can no longer draw breath, and—" His eyes traveled to my face. "Well, let's just say, the detective is probably right. I'd recommend letting the wheels of justice turn. The truth will come out."

A river of anger coursed through me. Sure, the wheels of justice turned for some, but others they just ran right over. Lulu Wong was wealthy, but she had also been Chinese. Which part mattered in the end?

6
GEMMA

THE NEXT MORNING, WE BYPASSED THE HORSE LOT ON our way to City Market. Lulu's body had been taken to the morgue and the stables roped off, but an uneasy feeling squatted in my bones, like an alley cat who refuses to shoo off the porch. Lulu might be at rest, but she wasn't at peace. Until her killer was found, that drat cat wasn't going anywhere.

I scanned the front page of the *Observer First*—the city's main newspaper—while May worked the gears. Happily, she hadn't noticed our new and improved steed, and I wasn't going to tell her. Between the upcoming annual Hollywood ball—the Pannychis—and the Yankees winning the World Series at Wrigley Field, Lulu's photo appeared, her smile bright, her eyes focused somewhere off the page. I read aloud:

Rising Starlet Discovered
Dead in Chinatown

The body of Chinese actress Lulu Wong was dis-
covered in Chinatown's Old Apablasa Stables early
Monday morning. Police Chief Hank Wagoner called
the find both "disturbing" and "unusual" but declined

*to comment further on this open investigation. The
actress was twenty-one.*

*Lulu Wong starred in six pictures in her short
career, including her most well-known role as a
villainous mistress of the night in Midnight Murderess. An investigation is underway and an inquest
has been called. No suspects have yet been identified.*

*Located in the east section of Chinatown, the old
stables are within the boundaries scheduled for clearing in favor of the new Union Station.*

*For Otis Fox of Fox Cosmetics, also head of the
Take Back L.A. committee, the news did not come as a
shock. "How many more people have to die before we
finally drain out the brackish pond of Chinatown?"
Mr. Fox said. "This time, they ate one of their own,
but next time, it could be you or yours."*

"That blowhard makes it seem as if Chinatown is somehow
responsible," I growled. "There's even a picture of him." Otis
Fox's piercing eyes stared out at me. Black whiskers drew a thin
loop around his mouth.

May's face was bunched into a scowl. "We don't know if the
attack even took place in Chinatown. They won't even call it a
homicide."

"I'd say it took place outside the stable. There was only one
set of footprints, and they weren't hers."

She nodded. "Plus, it seems like an out-of-the-way place to go
and murder someone. It's more a place to hide someone after
you've"—she grimaced—"done the deed."

"What *was* she doing on this side of town?" I murmured
before continuing to read aloud.

"She was a rising star, and we will all miss her," said director Emil Serège of Capsize Pictures, where Miss Wong was filming her latest movie, A Far East Affair.

"She was my dearest friend," added Hettie Bright, who starred alongside Lulu Wong in her last motion picture, Fast Fortune. *"I can't imagine any devil wanting to hurt such a pure soul," Miss Bright said.*

Miss Wong is survived by her mother, Mrs. Rose Wong, of Beverly Hills, and her younger sister, Bettina.

"That's it?" May made a tight turn into City Market, where sellers had already begun unfolding their tables and setting out their produce. "They didn't mention any of our stories."

I shook my head. Not a single Chinese person was quoted, even though we'd all shared our best memories of Lulu with the reporter from the *Observer*. Even that weasel Otis Fox got his word in, using Lulu's death to advance his own agenda. I certainly hoped the police were doing their job better than the reporters were.

I flipped through the paper, but there were no further mentions of Lulu, though an ad urging readers to elect Otis Fox's son, Philippe, for city council, sure flicked a finger in my eye. The slogan "Fox for Progress!" overlaid a picture of an oncoming train. As they say, a tiger father has a tiger son. If he was elected in November, Chinatown was as good as gone.

May backed into our stall in one straight shot, then killed the engine. "Something odd is going on."

"You could say that again."

"I didn't mean Lulu." She patted the dashboard. "The Mule didn't buck once our entire ride."

I coughed as Freddie Winter's smooth face appeared in my head. I'd managed to keep the entire episode at Westlake Park a secret from her, stashing the two dollars I'd made in an old gardening glove. Accounting for it on our ledger would raise her suspicions. "Er, well, maybe it's worked out the kinks all on its own. You know, like how you have to wear a pair of shoes a few times before they stop squeaking?"

She raised one of her slender eyebrows. "The Mule's almost thirteen years old. More likely, she's on her last leg and can't buck anymore. Which means she could die soon, maybe even leave us stranded somewhere. I think we should get her looked at." She tucked a loose strand behind her ear and arranged her hat over her head.

"I say we don't fix what's not broke."

She let out a prim snort. "That's a lazy way to live."

I sighed, deciding to let it go. She'd woken up in a foul mood after a night of tossing in our bed. The discovery of a new fuel pump in our engine was hopefully one mystery that wouldn't need solving in view of the larger mysteries at hand.

We set about trimming our flowers, squinting as incoming trucks blew dust around us. Our stall neighbor and chief competitor, Mr. Magnusson, an ex-boxer we sometimes called Make-Me-a-Deal, had already set up his table and was yelling out his catchphrase to passersby.

"Do you think the Yams would allow us to join them?" I asked. The grocer and his wife had arranged to visit Lulu's grieving mother tomorrow night.

May threw me a wary look from beneath her straw hat. "I would like to visit, but I doubt Wong Tai would be pleased to have gawkers."

"We're not gawkers. We're the ones who found her daughter; plus, you're her old friend. It would make sense for us to be there in case she has questions."

A pained expression marred May's perfect skin as she watched me briskly clip carnation stems at an angle. "And to ask her questions, you mean."

"Fox will use this to push for Union Station. We can't let that happen."

She pruned her own stems with prim snips, and green confetti dropped into our waste bucket. "It's only been a day. We should give the police a chance to do their job."

"The police have never made Chinatown a priority. You think Lulu being famous will change that?" My voice went high. Even Make-Me-a-Deal stopped yelling, grabbing the straps of the only pair of overalls he owned as he peered at us. I lowered my voice. "The city's going to make their decision on that train station any day. If the police don't find her murderer soon, people will believe Chinatown murdered her. Then there goes the neighborhood." A pigeon swooped into our stall, and I threw my arm at it, chasing it away. "You know, May? I think we were meant to find her. Somehow, Lulu led us to her because she knew she could count on us to solve the crime."

She let go of her breath in one huff. "We're just two girls. We don't know the first thing about investigating. Not to mention, who would ever believe us?"

I narrowed my eyes at her. May grieved for Lulu maybe more than all of us, but she was as annoyingly dutiful as she was beautiful. "Sounds to me what you're *really* saying is, don't fix what's not broke, except in this case, it *is* broke. Pretty lazy way to live."

She attacked a bunch of daisies with renewed vigor. "You think I don't care? Lulu was . . ." She clamped down on her lip, as if stopping words from coming out.

"What?" I prompted.

Her shears paused, but she shook her head. "You can't just

go sniffing around every time a breeze floats by. We've already lost a day's wages, and look." She threw her hands toward Make-Me-a-Deal, who was showing a man in a crisp suit his roses. "Make-Me-a-Deal just nabbed Mr. North."

I scowled. Mr. North worked for the Beverly Hills Hotel, where he arranged events like conferences and opening-night parties that required lots of expensive flowers. Ever since Ba had gone to the sanatorium in San Bernardino, Mr. North had seemed reluctant to give us business, as if he didn't trust us without Ba.

The gent nodded at me. His black hair grew in a thick tussock, like mondo grass, upon his egg-shaped head. A lavender cravat bloomed at his neck. I reached for our showiest candy cane roses, but May slapped my hand. "You know we can't do that."

Ba and Make-Me-a-Deal had agreed not to beggar a customer whom the other had already engaged. "Do what?" I asked, innocently waving around a few flowers so Mr. North could see what he was missing.

May crossed her arms tightly in front of me. "We have a family to take care of." Her superior tone always made my ears ring. "I wasn't a good friend to her, and I must live with that. But we can't afford to make enemies. Ba is counting on us."

"Exactly. And looking out for Lulu Wong means looking out for Chinatown, where our family might not be living for much longer if they build the station."

Her gaze drifted back to Make-Me-a-Deal, smiling broadly as he took Mr. North's order.

Feeling her soften, I added, "All I'm suggesting is that we ask Mr. Yam if we can join them. If he says no, then fine. But if he says yes, we'll make sure to bring Wong Tai our finest roses. What do you say?"

7
MAY

BA HAD ALWAYS SAID THERE WERE TWO TYPES OF people in this world. One made things happen, like Gemma, who could spin the world faster if she dug her foot in hard enough. The other let things happen. As Gemma and I rode in the back of the Yams' 1924 Ford Model T dressed in our most somber clothes— calf-length gray dresses with double stitching and pressed collars, together with oxford shoes—I decided that tonight I was a third type, the kind that wondered what just happened.

Even though both the Yams and Ma had agreed that our visit would be appropriate, the thought of reinserting myself into the Wongs' life had me wanting to turtle my head.

As promised, Lulu had called the week after I'd run into her at the White Horse joss house six months ago. I planned to meet her at a diner famous for French dip just a few blocks away, and was shocked when she pulled up to our building in a fancy red Cadillac. Embarrassed by all the onlookers, I ducked in, urging her to make a quick getaway.

She peeled off, causing more heads to turn.

With a hearty laugh at me shrinking into her white leather seat, she patted at her stylish silk headscarf. "You've forgotten how to embrace an entrance. Our French dips can wait. First, we're going for a ride." Soon, we were speeding up Roosevelt

Highway, hemmed in by the aquamarine Pacific Ocean on our left and a wall of white sandstone on our right. "How are your sisters?"

"Peony's still busy with her basketball and her mystery novels. They can't write them fast enough for her. Gemma's top of her class," I said with a measure of pride. "Ba's pleased, but Ma's worried no one will want her because she's too smart."

"Is your ma worried about you?"

"I don't seem to have that problem."

She laughed, but then her smile mellowed. "Nineteen's too young to settle down."

Agreeing seemed like a complaint, so I didn't answer, though I could feel her watching me through her cat-eye sunglasses. Ma had been Gemma's age—eighteen—when she married Ba, who was twenty.

After catching each other up on more family members, she slumped a little in her seat. "I know things aren't looking good for Chinatown, and I'm sorry about that."

"It's hardly your fault."

"No. But some people think I could do more."

I smoothed the pleats of my plain linen skirt, seething at the wrongness of it all. They were taking away our homes, yet we were made to feel guilty for it. "To leave a place is not to abandon it."

"No." She pulled the car onto a turnout that overlooked the ocean. Killing the engine, we stared out at the moving, shushing landscape, me musing over how different my life would be if I had auditioned with her. Maybe she was thinking how different her life would be had she not auditioned. She doffed her sunglasses and placed a warm hand on my arm. Her eyes sparkled. Without the smoky makeup she always wore on the screen, she looked like a schoolgirl with a secret to tell. "How would you like to be an extra on my next film? The pay's good, and it's mostly just standing around."

"I—I don't know what to say."

"Yet your *face* is saying a lot. You want to do it, but you're thinking those 'good daughter' thoughts. We are all given roles to play in this life, and yours is more than a wife and mother. It's time to step onto a larger stage. A stage where you can decide where you want to stand."

I winced, feeling like she had pressed her thumb into a fresh bruise. "But I do want children one day."

"And you can have that. Having a career doesn't mean giving up on love." She winked, making me wonder if she had personal experience in that regard. "Think of the opportunities. I'd introduce you to people, people with influence. We need more girls like us in the industry. I know you're good, May. You're a natural. Don't tell me you don't love it."

I bit my lip, imagining how nice it would feel to cruise through life in a red Cadillac, to breathe in the ocean whenever I wanted. But with no father around, Lulu had never needed to worry about shaming the family name. Her mother had always supported her acting. Maybe I was just making excuses. My tongue felt suddenly tied. "What is this movie about?"

"I can't tell you yet. But I've finally been given the opportunity to do something groundbreaking."

"What?"

"I get to play the heroine."

I grabbed her fingers and squealed. "That's fantastic." Lulu always played the villain. It'd never occurred to me that she might play anything else. Would having a Chinese girl as a heroine shift perceptions of us? Might some come to believe we weren't so bad? Lulu could move people to tears. If anyone could do it, *she* could. I had felt like crying myself in that moment.

She faced the ocean again, her profile as resolute as carved jade. "See, sometimes you can't just open the front door to air the house. Sometimes you have to come from the side, through a window. Sure, it's work to lift it, even a crack. But once you get your fingers under it, the lifting gets easier. And when the sweet breeze fills the spaces, change will follow." Those last words came out with adamance, and I caught a glimpse of the girl who'd always been quick to help, but polished into something sharper. Her grip on my arm had tightened, and she released it. "You can let me know next week, but I hope you say yes."

That was the last time I spoke with Lulu. Ba had been given his diagnosis the following week, and I never called her back. Yet she had still sent that iridescent feather for luck. She had still held out hope for me to join her in Hollywood, returning the tiny plume so I would have the same luck as her.

I wiped away a tear and tried to refocus on the conversation. Gemma was updating the Yams on Ba's progress, the last of the daylight casting her face in gold. "Phone calls are not encouraged because they are too taxing on the lungs."

Mrs. Yam peered back at us from the front seat. "But you write him regularly?" She had the sort of doubting voice that expected a no even for questions that must surely be answered with a yes. She pushed her knitted cap off her ear. She always wore a cap to keep her qi from escaping from her head.

"Yes, Auntie," said Gemma. "His last letter said he was playing a lot of cards, but they can't play pinochle because it gets the patients too riled up. Also, he was dying for a malted milkshake."

Mr. Yam chortled. "Everyone likes ice cream since Prohibition. We should start selling it in the store. They have it on sticks now too."

Mrs. Yam groaned. "Don't be a noodle. We don't have a freezer." She returned her attention to us. "Is your father receiving the newspapers?"

"Yes," I answered. Ba would find out about Lulu through the papers. Our letters wouldn't travel as fast. He would worry about us, with a killer loose in the city. It was bad enough being separated from us and forced to rest when he had always been a person of strong yang energy, like Gemma. I took more after our ma, with her quieter yin nature.

"Sales of candy and cigarettes have gone up in the past few days," Mrs. Yam said darkly.

Mr. Yam sighed in exasperation. "Don't worry the girls."

I rubbed at a stain on the leather seat. Candy and cigarettes were popular offerings on family altars. People were appealing to their ancestors for protection against bad luck. Ma had even started making mooncakes for our altar, a time-consuming endeavor that would show great sacrifice. Though Ba raised us Lutheran, we always honored our ancestors, which meant showing them respect in good times and bad.

Mrs. Yam read directions from a slip of paper. To my knowledge, no one from Chinatown had visited the Wongs before. When Lulu moved, it was as if she had passed the velvet rope into a place we didn't belong. But had someone resented her success?

We passed a corner full of unemployed men holding signs, including one that read I CAN DRYWALL GOOD, then an empty-looking drive-in restaurant advertising oyster sandwiches for twenty cents. Eventually, the neighborhood changed from commercial buildings into structures with better bones. A Victorian hotel wearing a stole of bougainvillea neighbored a studio in the style moderne with starburst windows and geometric designs. Larger residential lots streamed by. Some wore their mansions up front for all the world to marvel at. Others hid their villas deep among the foliage.

We entered a tree-lined neighborhood of elegant homes with streets named after constellations. The Wongs lived on Andromeda Lane, a quiet street with not a shred of litter, whose sidewalks did not contain a single bump, like they'd been ironed flat. My breath stalled as I took in the picture-perfect setting. How had it gone so wrong?

Mr. Yam cut the engine in front of a red stucco dwelling. Compared to the mansions we had passed, Lulu's place was a cottage. Ivy crawling up the side gave the place a homey look. The windows were clean, and the plants lining the walkway, pruned.

"Looks nice," said Mr. Yam, his positive energy like sweet to his wife's sour. "Shall we?"

We unloaded our gifts from the community—vegetable buns and containers of sesame noodles, five-spice tofu, pickled turnips, and dried red dates to flavor soups and promote general health. There were also our candy cane roses and the vial of red flower liniment Wong Tai had ordered.

Mr. Yam smiled at me as we carried the goods to the front door, his stringy arms strapped around a crate. "You are good girls."

I reflected his smile. He was an easy man to like, with hard-working hands and an amiable face that didn't expect anything in return. I hoped I would find a partner with such attributes one day, as they would make for an easier life.

Mrs. Yam rapped three times with the brass knocker, then stood back.

It was said that Lulu employed servants, but Wong Tai herself answered the door.

She was as tiny as I remembered her, at just under five feet, with the posture of a chair. Her fine-boned face looked drawn, and two puffs had appeared under her eyes. Good living hadn't filled out the lines trouble had carved in her face, which was now shadowed in exhaustion. I had the urge to steady her, as if she was made of cardboard and might fold at any moment. Behind her, Lulu's sister, Bettina, appraised us shyly from under the folds of a robe that dragged on the floor. Her face, still round with baby fat, was hidden by thick black glasses.

"Ah, Teddy, Lu-Chin." Wong Tai embraced both Mr. and Mrs. Yam.

"Black hair should bury white," Mrs. Yam greeted Wong Tai with the Chinese condolence, patting the woman's back with small thumps. The two stood the same height, but Mrs. Yam was a chimney of a woman, whereas Wong Tai, clad in a simple outfit of loose pants and an overlarge sweater the color of seaweed, was more a stovepipe.

Mr. Yam bowed his head. "Your daughter was the pride of Chinatown. This outrage must be answered." Shadows hid the anger on his face, but we could feel it in his tone.

Wong Tai took a step back, pulling her seaweed sweater tighter around her. "What do you mean? Lulu is still the pride of Chinatown."

Mr. Yam's eyes slid to Mrs. Yam. "Well, of course. We will never forget her."

Wong Tai's quick eyes drank in Gemma, then me. I felt myself shrinking. But her face contained no blame, only mild surprise. "Chow daughters, it has been a while," she greeted us in Cantonese, the warm base notes of her voice reminding me of Lulu.

"Auntie, we are sorry for your loss," I murmured.

Gemma added the Cantonese expression "May your grief be restrained."

"What is all this talk of grief? Come in, come in." Wong Tai was strangely composed after such a tragedy, though she'd always been the quiet sort. But grief has many faces. When Ma's best friend passed, she refused to talk about it for months. I wondered if Wong Tai was having the same reaction.

"Hello, Bettina." I bent to embrace the girl, sadness enveloping me. This was as close to Lulu as I would ever get now. She felt warm and a little moist under the chenille, which smelled of some expensive tuberose fragrance. It must have been Lulu's robe.

Gemma tugged one of Bettina's wispy braids and handed her a thick packet. "Peony says hi. Your classmates wrote you letters."

Bettina sniffed and nodded. The girl was usually as bubbly as a spring, though, of course, not now. "May I go to my room?" she asked her mother.

"Yes." She fondly stroked her daughter's braids. "You can help me make your sister's favorite almond tofu later."

Bettina retreated down a hallway, hugging her packet to her.

We followed Wong Tai through a tasteful living room that didn't look quite lived in, with its pastel curtains pressed into sharp pleats, and scalloped chairs whose seats still looked tight and springy. How had the woman gotten along in Hollywood with her halting English and reserved manner? And with one daughter left to raise, would she remain here? After three years of refined living, surely she would not move back to our neighbor-hood, with its uncertain future and shabby feel.

Unlike the living room, the kitchen felt cozy, with warm yel-low cabinetry and dabbed with the perfume of homemade meals and fragrant pears. A faded teapot sat on the counter, and Wong Tai's worn apron hung neatly on a hook.

Gemma arranged the flowers in a vase while I placed the food in the latest-model Frigidaire. The sight of jars of Chinese condiments was reassuring, a nod that being Chinese had still mattered to the Wongs. There was chili, plum, and soy sauce, but not oyster sauce, since Lulu had a shellfish allergy. I closed the door, then eyed the kettle on the stove. It would be rude to make tea for Wong Tai in her own house, but she looked like she could use some. Mrs. Yam glanced at me, taking in the crisis I was having, and announced, "Please allow May to make tea for you."

Wong Tai distractedly patted her hair. "Of course. I am sorry—how is your father?"

"Very well, thank you," I answered, not wishing to burden her with more.

"And your ma?"

That question felt more loaded. Ma and Wong Tai had been cordial, but their relationship cooled after Ma fetched me early one afternoon from the Wongs' small Chinatown apartment. She found Lulu and me wearing our slips, Lulu in full stage makeup, a red ribbon tied around her arm, and me in tears from her stirring performance. Lulu and I both snapped to attention, hiding our faces, as if we'd been caught doing something shameful. Ma had never heard of Cleopatra. "Let's go, May," Ma had stated, her face a mask. We didn't even stay for the special high-mountain tea Wong Tai had brewed. Hollywood had come knocking on Lulu's door soon after.

Wong Tai's gaze gently pressed me.

"Our ma is fine." I shined a too-bright smile. "She has sent some sesame paste." I showed her a jar of Ma's homemade sauce, which required much labor to grind.

Wong Tai clucked her tongue. "She didn't need to do that, and you didn't need to come all this way, though I am glad you did. I only wish Lulu was here as well."

Speaking words of comfort, Mrs. Yam pulled out a chair for

Wong Tai at the round table. "You have not slept. Teddy can stop by Dai-Sang's tomorrow for lily buds."

"I can do it myself."

Mr. Yam glanced up from where he had been inspecting a sagging drawer. "It's not far. Chinatown has not forgotten you." He pressed in the words kindly. "We want to help however we can. I can try to fix this drawer if you want."

"I think the police broke it when they searched the house." Wong Tai winced. "But don't trouble yourself; I will hire someone."

Mr. Yam scratched his head, maybe wondering why anyone would pay good money to fix something when someone had offered to do it for free.

Gemma opened a canister of rosebud tea, a soothing brew that the Yams had brought for rattled nerves. She sniffed the dried blooms. Rosebud tea cost twice as much as chrysanthemum. Before Gemma got any ideas about buying dead roses, I pulled the canister away from her. She made a sour face, then brought teacups to the table.

Mrs. Yam spoke in low tones to Wong Tai. "How was the inquest?"

Wong Tai moved her hands like dove's wings, fluttering about. "That Detective Mallady asked me so many questions— whether Lulu takes cocaine, whether she is in debt, how many boyfriends she's had." She snorted. "She's never had a boyfriend. I wish she would bring a nice young man home."

If Lulu had a boyfriend, why hadn't she told her mother? Perhaps the boyfriend hadn't been a "nice young man." *Having a career doesn't mean giving up on love,* she'd said. She wouldn't have tossed out something like that without knowing it to be true.

Seating herself, Gemma quietly unstacked the teacups.

"Auntie, do you have any idea who could've done this?" I held my breath. Gemma inserted her questions like she was passing out daisies. It was hard not to accept them. I could never be so forthright, even though I longed to know the answer as well.

"Done what? Why does everyone keep talking as if she is gone? Lulu is just away." The woman had the jittery energy of someone who gets a second wind after a night of no rest. "She'll be back soon."

Gemma watched me steep the tea, her troubled expression matching my own. Wong Tai was clearly confused. "When was the last time you spoke with her?" asked Gemma.

"Sunday afternoon." Wong Tai's dove-wing hands landed, and Mrs. Yam covered them with her own. "Bettina and I were spending the weekend with my cousin in Anaheim. Lulu called to tell us not to wait up for her when we got home because she'd be out late rehearsing. She was meeting her coworkers from *A Far East Affair* at seven that evening."

That was Lulu's latest movie, the one she had called groundbreaking, as she was playing the heroine.

"Which coworkers?" Gemma asked.

"Hettie Bright and Carey Stone. Hettie said Lulu never showed up."

Gemma snuck a look at me, her eyes round. Lulu was small potatoes compared to Hettie Bright, the doe-eyed ginger who always played the ingenue. Hettie had called Lulu her best friend in the news article. Had the feeling been mutual? As for Carey Stone, we'd all squealed when we heard Lulu's next on-screen love interest was the dreamy golden boy who the press had labeled "America's heartthrob."

I poured the tea, and the scent of rosebuds daubed the heavy air. Mrs. Yam released Wong Tai's hands and distributed the cups.

"What time was this phone call?" asked Gemma.

"Four o'clock." Wong Tai leaned over her teacup and inhaled. "You see, she left our phone call briefly to answer the door, and I happened to glance at the clock."

Gemma and Mrs. Yam leaned in. I sank into a chair, my thoughts whirling like clothes in the spinner. Whoever had visited Lulu while she was on the phone with Wong Tai might have been the killer. "Did she mention who was visiting her?"

"No." Wong Tai's face shuttered tight for a moment. "We didn't realize she hadn't come home until we were leaving for school the next morning."

"Did any of the neighbors see?" asked Gemma.

"No. But . . . Bettina found mandarin oranges in the living room. I know I didn't buy them, and if Lulu had bought them, why put them in the living room?" She glanced toward an empty fruit bowl on the counter. "The visitor must have brought her the oranges."

The Chinese brought oranges when visiting, though of course, it could've been anyone.

"Mandarin oranges are not in season," mused Mr. Yam.

"Do you still have these oranges?" asked Gemma.

"The police took them to check for poison. How ridiculous. *Poison.*"

The word left an oily film in the air, and Dixie Doors, the pageant queen whose poisoning case had never been solved, stepped into my head. For months, people could talk of nothing else. Then the case reached a dead end, and gradually, people moved on.

A metallic groaning sounded from a door that had to lead to the garage. "Oh, that must be Cole. The police found Lulu's Cadillac in the old Mercantile lot. Cole went to fetch it."

Gemma and I eyed each other. Visitors who wanted to keep a low profile often parked in the Mercantile lot, a junkyard full of discarded things like old sinks and bottles. While I didn't know who Cole was, the Mercantile lot was located squarely in Chinatown.

"Could she have been going to Fragrant Bamboo?" Gemma asked. "Maybe she and her costars were just getting a bite to eat."

I nodded, having thought of the same thing. Fragrant Bamboo was only a short walk from the Mercantile lot. It was the only place the three could have gone with privacy, with its back entrance for people who didn't want to be seen. It was rumored that many a deal had been inked on the white cocktail napkins of C. Y. "Cash" Louie's windowless hideaway, like the signing of Jean Harlow to *Hell's Angels*.

"The police interviewed Cash. He said Lulu didn't come in that night."

"But why would she have left her car there?" Mr. Yam asked.

A door opened and closed. The sound of men's shoes clopped heavily on the tiles, and then a man in a baggy suit with a gold watch filled the doorway. Now, this was a man who walked into a teahouse with heavy boots, a man who would require no subtlety to portray on a stage. His head swung from side to side, taking us in with tight eyes that indicated someone who always tried to beat the amber light at an intersection. "Hello?"

Wong Tai introduced us, switching to English. "May I introduce Mr. Cole Stritch? He is Lulu's manager. Have you found Lulu yet?"

Gemma angled her eyebrows my direction. Wong Tai was clearly having trouble accepting Lulu's death.

"Mrs. Wong, Lulu is gone, and we must get her affairs in order," Mr. Stritch announced in a gravelly voice that bounced around the room.

Though we used American titles for the Yams, it sounded strange to hear Wong Tai addressed as *Mrs.* instead of with the formal Chinese honorific *Tai*, which was similar to *Madam*. The man dropped his trilby hat on the table, and Gemma looked at it as if it were a horse biscuit. Ma did not abide hats on tables. Mrs. Yam didn't look too pleased to see it either.

"Sunday, I shall take the car, like we discussed."

Standing, I busied myself fixing the roses to fall evenly in the vase. Gemma never arranged them symmetrically.

"So soon?" asked Mrs. Yam.

Wong Tai's face soured. "Cadillac gave that car to Lulu, but I think it's too fast, and too red, like Hettie Bright's hair. Even the doctor warned her about it."

It seemed a strange thing to warn a patient about. Then again, motor vehicles were the second-leading cause of death last year, according to the newspaper.

"Still, Lulu might need the car." Wong Tai's posture bent a little, her head bowing like a lily feeling a breeze.

"Now, Mrs. Wong, you've had a terrible blow. Please trust me on the car."

Mrs. Yam poked up an eyebrow. "Letting go takes time." She did not favor Mr. Stritch with eye contact.

"We can help sell it when Wong Tai is ready," said Mr. Yam, pretending to inspect a spatula. It was impolite to contradict a guest, but there were other ways to express disapproval.

"Ownership has already been transferred," Mr. Stritch snapped.

"So who bought it?" asked Gemma. "I certainly hope not one of those nuts looking for a shot of fame."

The man gripped the back of the chair I had occupied with his yellow-stained fingers, as if he had a mind to snap the thing in two. "That is none of your business, and I would appreciate you dropping the matter."

A familiar flash of lightning crossed Gemma's expression. I put a hand on her shoulder before she sprang from her chair.

I got tired of other people holding the reins, Lulu had told me. Was Mr. Stritch one of those people? He certainly seemed an easy man to set off.

Mrs. Yam sucked in her breath, and Mr. Yam stopped fiddling with the drawer. He cleared his throat. "Perhaps Wong Tai has had a long day and would like to rest."

"Actually, I am a bit tired, if you don't mind." Wong Tai gave us all an apologetic smile and nodded at Mr. Stritch. "Cole, come by Sunday at five for the car."

"Sunday at five, then." Giving us a hard look that pushed creases between his eyebrows, Mr. Stritch set his hat back onto his head, then saw himself out.

Mr. Yam gave Wong Tai a short bow. "If you need anything, please do not hesitate to call."

Wong Tai saw us to the door. Before we left, she hugged Gemma and me close. "Lulu always admired you girls. You must come back when she is home."

I had dreaded facing the blame of a mother whose daughter I had failed. But seeing the woman's falsely hopeful eyes was a hundred times worse. I cradled Wong Tai's ice-cold fingers. "Auntie, I wish we had been better friends to Lulu."

Her face crumpled, giving us a horrified glimpse of a mother who had tragically lost her daughter. She pressed her hands to her face. When she released them, she was composed again, but there were tears in her eyes.

Lulu had been the pride of Chinatown. And now she was its deepest sorrow.

8
GEMMA

AFTER MAY AND I BRIEFED PEONY AND MA ON OUR VISIT
with Wong Tai, I hiked to the bathroom down the hall from
our apartment and scrubbed my face. That lug nut Cole Stritch,
with his yellow teeth and rotten-fruit cigarette odor, sure put a
kink in my nose. He was a jobajoo—a freight train—who didn't
care about running over anyone or anything in its path. It didn't
make him a murderer, but I had my suspicions.

In the tight space, I wiggled into my pajamas, wondering why
I bothered to close the door. Ever since the families on this level
had vacated for the mixed neighborhoods, we'd had the exclusive
use of the facilities, which May had spruced up with cherry-print
curtains. Then I returned to our apartment, where the smell of
the misshapen mooncakes that Ma was teaching Peony to make
hung in the air.

I headed straight for our bedroom. Peony, sitting on her single bed by the window, didn't even look up from her book, *The
Murder at the Vicarage* by Agatha Christie. "Must be a real page-
turner," I said.

Peony hunched tighter over the book. At the center of the
room, May folded back the quilt on the big bed she shared with
me and smoothed the wrinkles out of it. She couldn't stand to get

into a rumpled bed. Glancing up at Peony, May slid her big eyes to me and shrugged—a look that said, *She's mad.*

"So, Peony, how would the detective in your novel investigate who murdered Lulu?" I asked, hanging my dress. "Where would he start?"

Peony scowled. "It's a 'she'—Miss Marple—and I don't know."

"What's wrong, Peony?" May asked.

Peony shook her head, her scowl deepening.

"Shaping the mooncakes is the hardest part," I said, even though I knew that wasn't the reason for her mood. Sometimes you could trick the truth out of someone by feeding them a false theory. It was human nature to want to correct each other.

Peony slapped the book shut and tossed it in a basket under her bed. Her annoyance was making her bedsprings squeak. She got the single bed because she kicked when she slept and her motor ran too hot. "Why don't you ever take me along? I miss out on everything."

There it was.

May divided her hair into three portions for braiding. "We could hardly fit you into the Yams' car. Plus, you need to stay here and watch over Ma. You're our watch girl. She could go into labor early, and who would fetch help?"

With a grumble, Peony withdrew a basketball from under her bed and started tossing it up, spinning it with a flick of her wrist. Before Ba got ill, she'd spend long hours playing basketball after school with her friends, but she only played on the occasional weekend now.

"We tell you everything, don't we?" I asked. "Plus, you're our inside connection to Bettina. Remember, we're clouds. We do our best work together, covering each other." I flounced into the bigger bed, causing May to wobble and mess up her braid.

May coughed in annoyance and pushed my leg with her foot. "You have the grace of a barrel of lard."

"Oh, ouch, you hurt my feelings. Plus, you need to trim your toenails, unless you're planning to catch a husband by clawing him like a fish from the river."

Flipping onto her back, Peony cradled the ball to her and stared at the ceiling with its glazed bowl light. Her faded coverlet hung off her bed. It would end up on the floor by morning. "Miss Marple would ask, who gains with Lulu dead?"

I pulled my quilt up to my neck. "Obviously it's not her ma, her little sister, or her father." We had heard he died a few years back.

"It's not always about the money," said Peony. "Who are the people in her life? Start with the mandarins. Where would you get them out of season? Maybe you can find who visited her."

"Alright, Miss Marple," I began. "First stop in our investigation is to talk to Mr. Takashi tomorrow." He owned a citrus stand in City Market. "We should also talk to Hettie Bright and Carey Stone." Of course, Lulu's famous costars might not talk to a couple of nobodies like us.

Peony gasped. "If you talk to them, then you *have* to take me."

"Hold on, now," said May with a huff. "Who said we're *investigating* this case? That's what the police are trained to do."

"I don't know why you put so much stock in the police. It's been three days, and no one's been arrested yet. And with Wong Tai in no shape to push them, someone has to take charge."

May tied off her braid, then coolly appraised me, trying to burn sense into her head with my eyes. "This is a big case. After Dixie Doors, the police will want to prove they can actually do something."

Peony rolled her ball under her bed. "Do you think the cases are connected?"

"We don't even know how Lulu died yet." May whacked her pillow into shape.

"Lulu and Dixie were both found in places they weren't supposed to be," I said as the possibilities set my gears to spinning. "Both young and single women."

May watched me with her sensible brown eyes, eyes that resisted both flattery and nonsense, as if heaven had known she was destined to receive a lot of both. Eyes that always knew when her sister had boarded the train to what-if city.

"Peony," I called, "turn off the light."

AT CITY MARKET THE NEXT MORNING, MAY HELMED OUR BOOTH while I marched down the aisle to the fruit section. After seeing no news in the paper about Lulu's murder, my nose detected the mothball stench of inaction. The trail was already getting cold.

Mr. Takashi, a widower whose white cowboy hat provided a cool contrast with his brown skin, nodded at me from behind a table laden with crates of fruit.

"Hello, Mr. Takashi. Do you sell mandarin oranges?"

His short brown hands sorted through a pile of apples, tossing them in one crate or another. "When they're in season. You won't find them before November."

"I know someone who just received some as a gift."

He stroked his white triangle beard. "You can fruit them early, though it's a lot of trouble to baby them. Probably a hobby gardener with nothing better to do. I could ask around, but it would help to know the type."

"Type? Er, I'm not sure."

"What did they look like?"

"I didn't actually see them." Even though it was barely nine o'clock, my shoes had already started to pinch.

"I can think of at least eight varieties." He tapped his temple.

"I'll get back to you on that."

I returned to our stall, where business was slow. May was reading the *Observer* behind cheerful bunches of carnations. With a sigh, she rolled up the paper. "Maybe there are no articles because the police don't want to hamper the investigation."

I snorted. "When Dixie Doors was murdered, the papers didn't spare the ink." For weeks they delved into every corner of the beauty queen's life, like how growing up as a miner's daughter led to her kitchen beauty products using mica. They even included her recipe for Shimmer Cream. "That settles it. We should definitely pay Detective Mallady a visit."

"Why?" Her nose crinkled.

An autumn breeze blustered through the market, throwing leaves at us.

"We need information, and the papers aren't giving us anything. We need to see what *kind* of mandarins they confiscated, and whether they have a lead on the earrings. Plus, I want them to know someone's waiting for answers. Wong Tai won't do it, and there's something off about that Cole Stritch. It's his tight nostrils. People like that are always hiding something. I mean, did you see them? Bet you couldn't push a melon seed up—"

"Why would he kill the goose that lays the golden egg?" She tapped her newspaper roll against her palm.

"I don't know, but we should find out."

"In case you had forgotten, there's a murderer on the loose." May's glare was intense enough to bend the carnations. "One who has killed a Chinese woman. Before I am married and buried, I *will* take care of this family. I promised Ba."

"All the more reason to find the killer before he strikes again.

We're just poking our heads in, helping them get the job done as fast as possible. You don't have to do anything but sit pretty."

THE CENTRAL POLICE STATION WAS ON THE WAY HOME TO Chinatown and just around the corner from city hall. A stone façade with an archway in the dead center formed the bottom half of the building. The front entrance seemed to ward visitors away, with its stingy windowpanes and dark wood. A second story in a lighter stone featured yet more arches, one on either end.

"This building is too symmetrical for me," I said. "Look where they put the flag. Right in the boring middle."

May followed my gaze to the roof, where the flag was planted. "You and your middle-child issues."

"Symmetry curses the middle to mediocrity. Ever a point of reference. Never the point."

"It's a flag. If you're not going in, I'm leaving."

I almost felt sorry for May and her ruler-straight ways. No wonder she excelled at sewing, which required neat and ordered stitches for things to work out.

I filled my lungs with air, nervous energy snaking through me. The newspaper wrapping the bouquet I was holding crackled, and I relaxed my grip. We'd never been inside the police station. Most people I knew did their best to avoid this place if they could help it, just as the police avoided us. If a problem required solving, we figured it out ourselves. Like with last year's vandalism of Chinese businesses—after the police dropped the case, the Benevolent Society set up neighborhood patrols. Eventually, the vandalism stopped.

But with Lulu's murder, there would be no figuring it out ourselves. If we wanted answers, we needed to ask.

I marched up to the stay-out doors. May's feet punched the stairs behind me, as if the ground had erupted in flames and it was her job to stamp them all out. Poor May. I had burdened her all these years. Without her practical hand to keep me grounded, who knows where I'd be? Timbuktu, or maybe jail. I shivered at the thought.

Inside, metal ceiling lamps bounced a glare off black and white tiles that spanned the floor in an eye-dizzying diagonal. Two women occupied a black oak desk, one at a typewriter, the other speaking into a telephone headset. File cabinets took up most of the wall behind them.

The woman at the typewriter blinked at me through winged glasses. "May I help you?"

"We'd like to see Detective Mallady."

"Concerning?"

I gave her our names. "We'd like to ask—" The woman warily pulled back her head. "That is, we'd like to *offer* some information about the Lulu Wong case."

May stiffened, probably bracing for the lie I would be telling. With a nod, the receptionist lifted a phone receiver to her ear and relayed our message.

"What information might that be?" May dropped into my ear.

"Keep your hair on."

Five minutes later, we were being shown into an office where Officer Kidd, the rookie from the stables, sat in one of the chairs opposite Mallady, taking notes. The room stunk of pickles and stale tobacco. I invoked a silent apology to my carnations, which, though hardy, would probably not survive the night here.

Mallady's familiar misshapen face seemed focused around an unlit cigar—not the nickel White Owls, but a hand-rolled one. On his filing cabinet sat a box of expensive Prosperity cigars, printed with its smiling Chinese woman with rosy cheeks, whose tight dress fit like a second skin. Pretty as a picture always sells. "Kidd, let's finish this later." With a sigh, he closed a file on his desk.

The young officer grimaced at the sight of us. Maybe we reminded him of the murdered Chinese woman. He hastened to the door, somehow managing to knock over the container of cigars. Mallady let out a string of choice words that seemed to box May's ears.

"Oh, sorry." Kidd's shoes squeaked as he bent and began cleaning up the mess.

I presented the flowers to Mallady. "These are for you."

Mallady eyed the bouquet as if it might contain explosives, but I set it on his desk anyway. The visit was not off to a grand start.

May sat so primly on the edge of a chair that someone could probably remove it and she wouldn't notice. Occupying the entire leathery length of mine, I gripped the armrests, then flashed one of the Gemma facets. "So what did the coroner say?" Might as well plunge in the net while the ocean was calm. Something might come out.

Mallady's face pinched tighter around the cigar. I bet even if I stuck a foot on his chin, I couldn't yank that stogie out with two hands. After a moment, he removed it from his mouth. "He hasn't issued a statement yet."

"Well, do you have any suspects?"

Mallady's gray eyes became prongs. "Do you think I would tell you if I had?"

"Of course not," said May, sitting poised as a potted lily beside me, "and we are glad you take your job so seriously."

Mallady nodded. "Now, what information have you brought me?"

Come on, girl, think . . . Maybe I could trick the truth out of him, like with Peony. "'The killer left the *silver* earrings'"—I watched his face carefully for a reaction to my misstatement, but saw none—"'which means theft wasn't a motive. It was personal.'"

"Have you come to give me information or harass me with your unfounded theories?" He plugged the cigar back in his mouth. Baiting the truth wasn't as easy with him as it was with Peony.

May made a polite throat-clearing sound. "Don't mind my sister. We just want to help. Why, the citizens of Chinatown are counting on you. You'd be a real hero if you solved the case."

He sat up straighter and tugged at the sleeves of his jacket. It was almost surgical how May and I worked, me cutting, her sewing back up.

"Especially after Dixie Doors." Sometimes I couldn't stop a good poke in the eye. Sure, we were annoying him, but he was annoying me. We represented a community in grief. We paid taxes too. He owed us *something*, even just a helpful attitude.

May slowly turned a Medusa-like gaze upon me.

"I'm a busy man." Mallady's cigar wagged like a finger. "If you cheeky chits don't spit out what you've come to say, I might start to think you've really come to interfere with my investigation."

My heels dropped with an irritated clap, and I had to control an urge to get up and start boxing him. *Cheeky chits*, indeed. May had turned to stone herself. The only noise came from Kidd, who was still cleaning up the cigars, their wrappers making crinkly sounds. Sensing us all watching him, the man hastily reshelved everything, tipped his visor, then left.

I managed a smile. Boxing Mallady would accomplish nothing, especially since I didn't know how to box. Perhaps I would learn. For now, brains must be my weapon. "Of course, Detective. It's this. That mandarin oranges aren't in season."

"And?"

"And if you can let us look at the fruit you confiscated, we can help you find the source."

"They've been sent to the lab, as I'm sure you know."

"Could you describe the fruit? Wrinkly? Smooth? Approximate diameter? Belly button?" The more balls you throw at someone, the more likely they will throw one back.

His grimace sank deeper, like a horseshoe that had fallen into the mud. "No, I will not describe the fruit." He stood, his chair scratching the floor tiles. "Is that all? I would warn you not to waste my time again. Good. Day."

AFTER A HASTY DEPARTURE, MAY GUNNED THE MULE THE LAST half mile to Chinatown. I slunk down into my seat, releasing a whistle like a teapot just come to a boil. "Well, that was like climbing a sinking ladder. At least we know the mandarins are being tested. Maybe Wong Tai or Bettina can describe the oranges."

"We might've climbed a rung. While you were clapping your trap, I snuck a look at his desk calendar."

I sat up. A bigger truck passed, throwing dust in our faces, but I hardly noticed. "Don't stop there."

"Now, why would a detective be going to the Pannychis?" She glanced at my confused expression. Hosted by the *Observer*, the annual gathering of L.A. dignitaries and Hollywood elite did not usually include lowly police detectives. "His calendar said, 'Pannychis with O.F.'"

"Who's O.F.?"

Her eyes glinted. "Someone with an interest in this case."

I considered for a moment, then slapped my knee. "You mean Otis Fox?"

She nodded.

Fox Cosmetics supplied the movie studios, so it wasn't

surprising that Otis Fox would be in attendance. But why would he invite Mallady to the ball of the year? More importantly, what was he expecting in return? "When is that party?"

"Tomorrow night at the Beverly Hills Hotel, as always." Her eyes narrowed. "No. Forget I mentioned it." She waved a gloved hand at me as if to clear the air of my bad ideas. "If it is Fox, maybe he and Mallady are just friends."

"And I'm a chicken foot. Mallady could hardly afford to run in such huffery-puffery circles. Think, May. Chinatown is Fox's number one priority. And now Mallady has a Chinatown problem on his hands—Lulu—that Fox has already angled to his advantage. He's got the money to pay off Mallady to sit on his hands. Chinatown looks bad, and that railroad measure passes. Only someone missing his head could fail to see the connection."

She took a pothole too fast, tossing us up like dice. We came to a jerky stop on Alameda. While we lived east of Alameda on the side of the Los Angeles River, roughly half of the fifteen blocks that made up Chinatown were located in the "Old Mexico" district to the west.

Gathering our unsold bunches, we picked our way down the uneven pavement toward the stately Garnier Building, Chinatown's unofficial city hall. Many hours of my life had been spent agonizing over Chinese primers on the second floor of that building, where they kept the schools and temples. It was thought that institutions that exerted authority should be on the highest level, closer to the heavens. But I thought they just wanted to prevent us from escaping, like how they kept the city jail on the top floor of the Hall of Justice.

"Afternoon, Mr. King," I greeted the owner of King's Emporium, one of several businesses on the first floor. He was swabbing his windows, making the pom-poms on his hat swing, and there was a faint sulfuric odor in the air mingled with the sweet notes of incense. Sandalwood had been especially pronounced these past few days as ancestral altars were dusted off and restocked. The specter of Lulu Wong's murder would hang over Chinatown for many weeks to come, assuming we had that long.

Mr. King's face lost its scowl when he saw us with a bright bunch of chrysanthemums. "Thank you, girls. Chrysanthemums are the kings of flowers."

"Already closing up?"

The dusting of freckles on his tan face twitched. "Wicked boys threw eggs." He looked behind us at the street, now holding only a neutral stream of cars. "Second time since the tragedy."

A bitter taste washed over my tongue, and I gave May a dark look. "The joke's on them, giving up good eggs like that."

"They got Mr. Yep's too," he said, nodding to the bookseller's shop next door. "Got eggs all over his new book display. He went home with a stomachache."

"We are sorry, Uncle," said May. "We hope tomorrow will be better."

We left flowers in Mr. Yep's bucket, then cut a wide berth around the wok seller, Mr. Ng, or as we called him behind his back, No Good. He never took flowers from us because he considered our family of three girls unlucky. Through a screen of metal spatulas, ladles, and cleavers, his mistrustful eyes zeroed in on us, and his mouth clenched. Instead of squinting back at him, I kept my gaze forward, only because he might've had eggs thrown at him too.

"You see, they're coming for us," I said to May.

"Who, exactly? Eggs always start to fly whenever they say something bad about Chinatown."

"It's the mob effect, like the Massacre of '71." I spat on the street. May threw me a disapproving look but held her tongue.

After a police officer had been wounded in a feud between two rival Chinese associations, a horde of angry Angelenos lynched eighteen of the "foreign Chinese devils," most of whom weren't even involved in the quarrel. It poured acid on me every time I thought of how no one ever paid for the deaths. We were supposed to lick our wounds and move on, just like now.

"Lulu Wong would've been an attendee at the Pannychis," I stated, my idea now fully ripened. "They'll all be talking about her. Plus, Hettie Bright and Carey Stone might be there. We'll pretend we're delivering flowers. No one will notice us as long as we look like we belong. Mr. North knows us."

"He'll also know he didn't hire us."

"We'll make something up. We just need to get a bead on what's going on between Mallady and Fox."

We filled three more buckets with zinnias, which should last the week. Zinnias were as tough as tortoises. May was as tough as tortoises too, marching back to our truck. "If O.F. *is* Fox, don't you think he'll notice two Chinese girls crashing the party? He's got a special nose for our kind."

"He hires *our kind* to fetch and carry. As long as we know our place, he won't look twice at us."

"No. Way. Besides, the Moys are coming for dinner tomorrow." The Mule dipped as we both climbed in at the same time.

"They're coming at five. That's plenty of time to entertain Bug Boy *and* prevent the miscarriage of justice." Actually, it would be tight, but May didn't want Wallace anyway.

"The answer's no. We are not gumshoes." Starting the truck, she buttoned her lip and refused to look at me.

I watched two men argue over a taxi and decided to let it go. She'd change her mind. It was only Thursday afternoon, after all.

9
MAY

THIS TIME, I WAS NOT GIVING IN TO GEMMA. TALKING TO Detective Mallady at the station was one thing. Spying on him at the ball of the year was an entirely different matter. True, the professionals did not seem to be pursuing the investigation with the rigor I thought was due, but Gemma's attic was drafty if she thought we could waltz into the most elite party of the year and snoop around. We'd stick out like two flies on a cobweb. Not to mention, the place would be crawling with security and picture snappers. So not only could we be arrested, we could be photographed while being hauled away. Instead of taking care of this family, I would bring shame and disgrace.

I rounded the corner, a cold sweat breaking over me. Plus, I still had to iron the marigold dress, patch the quilts before the weather started turning cold, sharpen the scissors . . .

"May, look." Gemma's attention was focused across the street, where out-of-work men sat cracking melon seeds near the herbalist's wooden tub of floating turtles.

"So? They're always there."

"No, not them. Isn't that Wong Tai's Buick?"

A gray Buick sedan waited discreetly in the shade of a sycamore. It certainly looked like Wong Tai's car. "Maybe she's here for groceries."

We crossed the street. The men were bricklayers, except for one. No Good, the wok seller, in his black jacket and pants, took up the whole bench, his limbs sprawled like a spider. A bricklayer called out a greeting. "Look, it is the Chow sons!"

My smile erased, but Gemma guffawed, proving their point about us being unladylike. Noticing my expression, she elbowed me. "Oh, come on, May, don't waste energy on being mad. They are just stuffy old men who can't handle the idea of girls doing a man's work because it means they could be out of a job."

Our herbalist, Dai-Sang, gave us a distracted nod. He seemed to be in an animated discussion with our neighborhood bum, a man with the shape of a jug. His name was Gee Fa, but we called him Guitar Man because he always carried a guitar, or at least the case, though Ba said he'd once been a gardener before his mind had grown weak.

The man had set down the guitar case and was cupping something near his face—maybe a cigarette. He showed us as we approached. "Little Leaf."

A small turtle with yellow spots did indeed look like a sun-dappled hydrangea leaf.

"Where will you keep it?" asked Dai-Sang, wiping his elegant fingers on his apron. "You can't just carry it around with you. It needs a good pond to live in."

Guitar Man lifted his brown face and intoned, "Nature will provide for both Little Leaf and me. Wherever I go, I find food and a place to lay my head." The words were like a poem. He always spoke in simple, musical phrases, which were a delight to my ear, even though his black-and-white hair looked like it had been trimmed with gardening shears.

No Good sneered, but the bricklayers laughed. They wouldn't have if Ba were here. Guitar Man enjoyed smelling our flowers, and Ba let him help us make bouquets on special occasions.

"If nature doesn't provide, I bet Little Leaf will taste good in a soup," said one of the men.

Dai-Sang grunted, his sharp features twitching. "Just don't stay in those stables. You know there's a killer on the loose, right?"

Guitar Man seemed to shrink, cradling the turtle to him. He was a big man, a hand taller than Ba, who was five foot seven, but a perpetual hunch cut Guitar Man down by a few inches and made his belly pooch. I hoped he was getting enough to eat. After he shared the scallion pancake Ma had made him with a squirrel, Ma refused to give him any more, but if Ba met him on the street, he always gave him the packet of peanuts he kept in his pocket.

"Lulu's car passed me on Macy Street that night," Guitar Man told us now.

Gemma swiveled her face to me. Macy Street was just north of us and led directly to the horse lot. "What time, Uncle?" she asked.

"A couple hours after sunset. My nose follows the smell of the jasmine bushes, which smell best in the evening."

"Was Lulu driving her car?" Gemma pressed.

The bricklayers all began talking at once.

"He also saw Herbert Hoover at the Chinese New Year Parade," said one.

"And the Wright brothers gave him a ride in their airplane," said another.

No Good watched, his eyes moving by fractions, like a rifle seeking a target. Ba always said even the meanest person had a good side, you just had to find the right angle. But if Mr. Ng had a good side, he was the type who didn't want you to go looking for it, his dour expression like a curtain of knives warding people away.

Ignoring them, Guitar Man solemnly shook his head. He had the half-distracted gaze of a man who saw dragon-lions in shadows, which he fixed upon a mark on the pavement. "Lulu wasn't driving, or she would've stopped for me. She gave me a hundred dollars for Christmas."

One of the bricklayers grabbed Guitar Man's hand and pumped it. "I always wanted to shake the hand of a millionaire!"

"We should get home." I pulled Gemma toward our apartment, but she shrugged me off.

"Uncle, what did the driver look like?" she asked.

"A white demon."

More laughter punched the air. Guitar Man's face curdled and he spat. He stretched up to his full height, and with one hand clutching his pet, he picked up his case and started swinging it. The bricklayers shrank back and scattered. Guitar Man had a good arm; he even pitched for the neighborhood games now and then. No Good rose from the bench and backed away. Dai-Sang clucked his tongue and returned to his shop.

"Serves them right," said Gemma. "If you rile a turtle, don't be surprised if you lose a finger."

We passed our hands along the family brick, then ducked through the rotting door of our building. At least the tiled stairs and the floors were sound. As we made our way down the hall, our front door opened, and Peony stuck out her head. "Shh. Ma's napping."

Gemma cast her a look of confusion. Ma often napped in the late afternoon, but why the need for extra caution? She could sleep through a marching band, which she had proven during last year's Lunar Parade.

Another head emerged beside Peony's, the wispy threads of her light-brown braids a contrast to Peony's thick ropes.

"Bettina," exclaimed Gemma. "Is your mother here?"

"She's making an offering at the joss house." Bettina wrung her hands. "She thinks the ancestors have been playing tricks on us, hiding Lulu, because our offerings have been too meager."

Peony pulled Bettina inside. "Quickly. We don't have much time," she said in a hushed voice. "Her ma will be back soon."

I closed the door behind me and untied my hat. "Why all the secrecy?"

"Bettina needs us," Peony said, as if that should explain everything. Without even washing up, Gemma and I joined the girls at our kitchen table, which was already set with two half-drunk teacups. Peony refreshed Bettina's cup, pouring too fast and splashing tea onto the table. I grabbed the tea towel, noticing a hole in the fabric as I wiped up the moisture. I'd reuse it for the diapers I still had to make for the new baby.

"Go on, Bettina," said Peony. "Show them what you showed me."

The girl dug a crumpled envelope from her plaid jacket, which she had hung on her chair. Pulling out a paper, she unfurled it on the table. Gemma and I scooted closer, both of us reading. The note was written in loose Chinese characters, as if the hand writing it didn't care for rules.

虎啸山崩, 我會銘記你的言行.

Tiger roars; mountain tumbles. I will remember your words and deeds.

"I found this in her things. I *know* that my sister was m-murdered." The trauma must have put a stutter in Bettina's speech, as I didn't remember her having one before. "But Ma doesn't believe me."

"Who could've sent this?" Gemma flipped the note over, but the other side was blank.

"I d-don't know."

"Maybe the tiger refers to Lulu," I said. People sometimes called Lulu a tiger, symbol of great yang, or male energy. "But what about the mountain?"

Gemma's eyes narrowed. *"I will remember your words and deeds.* Is that a threat?"

"If she held on to the letter, perhaps not. Did you show this to your ma?" I asked.

Bettina nodded. "She doesn't know where it's from and said to burn it. Mr. Stritch said it was p-probably just fan mail. He said all movie stars get fan mail, good and bad."

"Do you believe that?"

The girl's round shoulders had migrated to her ears, and she collapsed them. "Ma trusts him." Her eyes had begun to fill, and she rubbed them under her steamed-up glasses.

Peony offered her handkerchief.

If Mr. Stritch was somehow involved with Lulu's death, and Wong Tai trusted him, then Bettina would have to watch what she said.

"But do you trust him?" Gemma asked.

"I don't know." Bettina wiped her glasses with Peony's handkerchief.

Peony placed a hand on Bettina's arm. "It's okay, we won't tell your ma."

"I heard Lulu arguing with him once. He said, 'You're asking for a war that's gonna take both of us down.'"

"What kind of war?" I asked.

"Lulu told me I shouldn't worry about it." Bettina's voice had become even smaller.

"When did this happen?" Gemma probed.

"The day after Lulu's birthday on March 14. I remember because Lulu offered him a slice of her birthday cake."

That predated my last conversation with Lulu, who had visited the week before Ba had left us on April Fools' Day. *A Far East Affair* was going to be groundbreaking, she had said. "Lulu was playing the heroine for the first time. Maybe the war had to do with that?"

"If so, it could've been anyone who didn't want her to be the heroine." Gemma tugged her kerchief free from her neck and patted her face. "Did Lulu ever mention anyone threatening or scaring her?"

Bettina wiped her palms on her dress. "She came home upset a few months ago. S-s-someone kept stealing her script. She thought it was another actress."

Gemma locked eyes with me. A jealous actress could certainly be motivated to kill. "She didn't mention any names?" Gemma asked, snapping out her kerchief with one quick motion.

"No. Only that it made her look irresp-sp-sp—"

Peony pitched in. "Irresponsible."

Bettina nodded again.

"Do you have any idea who the visitor on Sunday could've been?" Gemma probed, and when Bettina shook her head, she asked, "Your ma mentioned you found mandarin oranges. Could you describe them?"

Bettina made a fist. "They were this big, but flat, with shiny sk-sk-skin."

"Tight skin or loose?" I asked.

"Loose. Plus"—Bettina looked from Gemma to me, then down at her fist again—"they were very sweet."

I gasped. "You ate one."

Her eyes filled again. "I don't think they were p-poisonous."

"Well, that's a relief," said Gemma.

"Don't cry, Bettina." Peony patted her on the back. "We'll help you catch whodunit."

"That's right, Bettina," said Gemma, though her gaze was once again fixed on me. "Girls from Chinatown have to help each other out."

I glared at her, though my glare lacked fire. Maybe it was seeing the once-cheerful Bettina reduced to a stuttering child. Or maybe it was because I hadn't been there for Lulu. I'd assumed that as the world rolled out the red carpet for her, she no longer needed me. But hadn't she reached out, so many times, even tried to pull me onto the stage with her? Ba had gotten sick, but had a feeling of unworthiness stayed my hand as well?

Circumstances might have changed for Lulu, but *she* hadn't changed. And now I'd never know if she'd been happy, or if I could've somehow disrupted the evil headed her way. My temples throbbed, and some cruel fist squeezed my heart. Here, at last, I could help her. But at what cost to our family?

Finding the right path was as easy as following a twisty bindweed to the root.

For now, I was going to that huffery-puffery ball.

FRIDAY FLEW IN, SOONER THAN I WANTED IT. IN THE BATHROOM mirror, I smoothed my hairline, which tweaked to one side, and powdered my nose. Ma's marigold dress fell in elegant folds around me, the bust and waist taken in. My stomach seemed to have risen to my rib cage, though I don't know why seeing Bug Boy, *Wallace Moy*, should have me feeling so giddy. It was more likely tonight's scheme at the Pannychis was to blame.

When I returned to our apartment, the acrid smell of

something burnt filled my nostrils. Gemma and Ma were huddled over an almond cake with a blackened top. Peony stood by the open window, sweeping a fan to blow out the telltale scent. She wore the same grumpy look she'd been wearing since we told her she couldn't come with us to the ball.

"I'm sorry, Ma. I thought I had set the timer." Gemma twisted the pleats of her russet tea dress, which I'd spent an hour pressing flat. *I* should've made the cake and made her press her own pleats.

"They will think we don't know how to cook." Ma fanned the cake with her potholders. She wouldn't throw it out—we never wasted anything—but would probably cut off the black parts later and serve the cake as breakfast.

"I shall take the blame," Gemma said dramatically.

Ma sighed. "Fetch a towel and wrap it before it stinks up the whole neighborhood. May, go buy something at Happy Moon. Hurry. It's nearly five o'clock!"

Donning a sweater, I grabbed my purse and hurried to the bakery two blocks over.

Careful not to get my heel stuck in the train tracks, I crossed busy Alameda toward the Plaza in the Old Mexico district, hurrying by the flophouse on the corner. Ravens splashed about in the fountain at the center of a round courtyard.

The line between Chinatown and the Mexican district had never been as sharp as people liked to think. We attended school with Mexicans, and a few lived on our street. They saw our herbalists, and we bought from their weavers.

A familiar figure with his rounded shoulders sat on the edge of the fountain. It was Guitar Man, his guitar case set by his feet. Remembering the incident with the bricklayers, I considered checking in on him. But as I drew closer, he appeared to be in earnest conversation with a woman about my size, her face hidden by a wide-brimmed cloche with a spotted guinea feather. Her dark hair suggested she was probably Chinese or Mexican, given the area. I doubted she was one of the cats from the flophouse. Guitar Man was shy around women. Plus, where would he get the money?

Mind your own business. Time's a-wasting.

Happy Moon Bakery was located at the mouth of Olvera Street, where tourists came to browse stalls selling bright blankets, hats, and shoes. The vendors had already begun to close their umbrellas and store their merchandise.

Before entering, I ran my hand through the traffic-red geraniums we had left in Mr. Moon's cheer bucket. Still hardy. He loved geraniums, which kept the flies away. Inside the shop, most of the cakes were gone. Mr. Moon, wearing a skullcap and a striped apron, was ringing up a sale for another customer. Holding back my hair, which Gemma had raked smooth and glossy with our broken comb, I peered into a glass case with an assortment of leftover pastries—a single butterfly cookie with its sticky, glossy top, and custard tarts whose centers had broken. There were also almond cookies pressed in the center with their namesake nut—a dozen for a quarter—and one of Mr. Moon's trademark strawberry cream cakes, which, at forty cents, was steep, but might give a better impression than almond cookies.

"Hello, May, how's the family?" asked Mr. Moon. The baker had a melancholic face, not at all like a happy moon, though he was kind.

"They are well, but I'm afraid Ba is bored. He wants to be back among the flowers."

"I'm sure he misses his favorite flowers, you and your sisters. So what can I get you?"

"I'm still deciding."

"Take your time."

From behind me, a man spoke briskly. "I'll take the strawberry cake, plus all the almond cookies."

"Excuse me." Straightening, I glared at the man, a young fellow who looked only a few years older than me. He wore a slim gray suit with a marine-blue tie. A fedora cast a shadow over his eyes, and his cheeks had the smooth look of one who didn't need to shave often. "I was going to get that cake," I informed him, hooding my eyes.

"I distinctly heard that you were still deciding."

"Well, I have decided. And since I noticed it first, that gives me a prior claim to it."

"*Noticing it*. Is that all it takes to claim something?" He smiled, a smile that went crooked on one side, like it couldn't be bothered to make the full effort. I got the distinct impression he was making fun of me.

"In this case, yes." I shunned him. "Mr. Moon, please wrap that cake for me."

"Sorry, he called it first." A dimple broke out on the baker's usually placid face.

I watched in disbelief as Mr. Moon handed the young man a pink pastry box, blood rising to my cheeks. How could Mr. Moon refuse me? He'd known me all my life, whereas I don't remember seeing this fellow around Chinatown, even if he was Chinese. This rudeness could not stand, though I could hardly get mad at Mr. Moon, who was like an uncle.

"I wish you the joy of eating such ill-gotten fruit," I told the young man, lifting my nose. "Good day, Mr. Moon."

"Oh, I will enjoy it," the young man tossed back. He lifted off his hat. "Hello, May."

10
MAY

"WALLACE MOY?" MY HANDS FLEW TO MY BURNING cheeks. "How did you know I was here?"

The young man replaced his hat. "Your mother. I ran to catch up with you."

"Well, I hardly recognize you. You—" What? Slimmed up? Shot taller? Not to mention got handsomer. My jaw had fallen to an unattractive elevation. "You've grown."

"Eight years will do that to you." He paid Mr. Moon. We said our goodbyes, and Wallace opened the door for me. "Last time I saw you, you and your sister Gemma were playing the Cast Your Lot game."

My cheeks grew warm. The game involved writing out the alphabet on the sidewalk, casting a stone, and finding the initials of your future husband. "Feels a little like we're still playing it," I said, regretting it instantly.

He laughed. "I'm glad you said that. It feels a little silly to me too. All this fuss just to get settled down. Sort of takes the fun out of things."

Somehow, the words flicked a finger at my nose, even though I hadn't been keen on meeting him. As if dating me would be the opposite of fun. "I'm not ready to settle down either." A couple of ravens cawed from the thick branches of an oak tree, sounding like a chorus of laughter. At least the air had cooled, soothing my hot skin.

"Ah. Don't tell me your parents are putting the squeeze on you, like mine."

"Well, maybe a little pinch."

He nodded, suddenly solemn. "I was sorry to hear about your father's illness. I hope he'll be on the mend soon."

"Thank you."

He shifted the cake to one arm and offered me the other. Together, we crossed Alameda. Instead of searching the ground for bugs like I remembered him, he moved with the light, confident strides of someone who knew where he was going. My breathing no longer came easy. If this were a play, he would definitely be Prince Charming.

He caught me staring and grinned. "What's wrong?"

"The last time I saw you, you were telling me my sweetheart cake had cactus bugs on it. Put me off sweetheart cakes for a long time."

He chuckled and held up his hand in surrender. My grasp on his arm fell away. "Okay, I was a twit. But I wasn't lying. The red dye used to stamp the cake is made from the cactus bug shell. Also in haw candy and hair dye."

"Yes, yes, I know cactus bugs are perfectly harmless now." My voice sounded too loud, more like a donkey braying. Since when had I felt self-conscious around Bug Boy?

"Actually, my boss is allergic to them. He ate red cake and his ears swelled to the size of pears. It's the chitin in the exoskeleton that induces cytokine production—" He cut himself off with a sheepish chuckle. "Sorry, I'm probably boring you. You know, May, if you were serious about not being ready to settle down, maybe we could help each other out." His dark eyes flicked to me. Those eyes were still full of mischief, but the kind that invited you to join in.

"Oh?"

He refocused on a bit of newspaper stuck to the sidewalk. His two-tone saddle shoes were worn thin, looking almost out of place with the sleek suit, like a grandfather clock in a modern skyscraper. "See, my parents have been expecting me to get married after I graduated." He shook his head. "We had an argument. Anyway, they said as long as I was 'trying,' they'd back off. So . . ."

I stiffened, feeling a flame race up my spine. "So you want me to pretend to date you."

"Only for a couple weeks, just so they know I tried. But only if that would help buy you some space too." He gripped the back of his neck, obviously uncomfortable.

I did want the space, and it should have been easy to agree. But somehow, it didn't feel easy at all. More like stepping into a minefield. I forced a smile. "I think that's a fine idea."

He held out his hand. "Friends?"

"Friends." We shook. I hadn't bothered with gloves, and the touch of his hand sent a charge through me. Hiding my blushing cheeks, I set off again toward our apartment with him in tow. "Since we're being honest, I wondered if you could manage to leave by six tonight? My sister and I have, er, plans." Gemma had an elaborate lie arranged, but this was simpler.

He let out a half laugh. "As long as I get to sample the cake."

A glossy cream-colored Chrysler with matching rims was parked in front of our building.

"Is that yours?" I asked.

He patted the hood. "For our pretend-dates."

When we returned to the apartment, our table had been

extended with the square card table we used for mahjong and spread with a red tablecloth. Each place featured a celadon bowl and a pair of chopsticks set elegantly on notched ceramic rests. Ma was showing the Moys Ba's collection of bamboo reed watercolors while, in the kitchen, Peony and Gemma were placing food in serving bowls.

"Oh, good, May's here," Gemma sang. At the sight of Wallace, she clapped her hands together. "Wallace, did college do this to you? If so, all the boys should go."

Wallace laughed. "It's good to see you too, Gemma. Peony." He nodded to our youngest sister, who was bringing a soup tureen to the table. She nodded back, still grumpy and thoroughly unimpressed with our visitors. Ma hung Wallace's hat on a wall hook.

Mrs. Moy took my hands in her small, bony ones and angled her long face at me. Long faces always gave the impression of sternness. "May, you have bloomed into the fairest rose."

The woman carried herself with the air of a diplomat's wife, and it was hard to tell if her comment was sincere. Her husband, a stern man whose reddish skin almost glowed against his jet-black hair, grunted in assent.

"You are too kind, Auntie, Uncle," I demurred, not just out of politeness. Praising a person's looks always felt unearned, as we had no hand in the set of our eyes or evenness of our foreheads.

"Did you knit that sweater yourself?" Mrs. Moy turned over my hands, studying the scalloped hems along my wrists.

"Yes." A prick of heat warmed my collar. Mrs. Moy's dress looked store-bought and probably designer—a crisp sheath like a hosta leaf. We must have looked so shabby with our homemade dresses.

"May is very handy," Ma added. She had replaced her usual mandarin-collared jacket and pants with a pleated dress that accommodated her stomach. "Sews clothes, tablecloths, curtains, many things."

Mr. Moy eyed our tablecloth, which was actually something we got at a church sale. Wallace, who had been chatting with my sisters, glanced at me and smiled.

"Come on, everyone, eat while it's hot." Gemma unlidded the pots, circling briskly about like an eggbeater in a bowl. We were on a schedule, after all.

We arranged ourselves around the tables, and Gemma ladled the soup.

Ma, whose stomach prevented her from scooting into the table, spread a linen napkin on her bump. "I heard Wallace graduated with honors."

Mr. Moy waved dismissively. "He did okay," he said in the self-deprecating way the Chinese used to deflect praise to their children. "Of course, I would like it if he joined the family business, but kids have minds of their own." He rubbed his chopsticks with a napkin, as if he didn't trust them to be clean, then adjusted his bowl like a steering wheel until he settled into the right lane. He certainly was a man with quirks, and I wondered if Wallace had inherited them.

Wallace had neatly placed a water chestnut into his mouth and was chewing thoughtfully, as if assessing its sweetness. I did admire a thoughtful eater, which indicated someone who appreciated details. Truth and beauty, the noble pursuits, lay in the details.

Ma, also watching Wallace but less sneakily than me, gently nudged, "Tell us about your work, Wallace." The barest grin crested Gemma's face, and she nudged me with her foot.

Wallace politely wiped his mouth. "I research the medical importance of bee toxins."

Peony stopped chewing. "You mean being stung can be good for you?"

"Not exactly. But in fractional doses, bee toxins can help afflictions like arthritis."

Peony resumed eating, still not looking convinced.

Wallace lightly tapped his chopsticks in his bowl, evening their length. "Did you know, Peony, the queen bee is quite an impressive lady? She can lay over a thousand eggs a day."

Peony guffawed. Ma made a face at Peony's open mouth.

"Well, the queen is certainly robust," I said.

Ma cleared her throat. "The Chow lineage has had many healthy children through the generations."

I coughed, swallowing wrong. Gemma snorted loudly. "Yes, May is very robust."

Ma glared at Gemma. Peony blurted, "I don't want a thousand nieces and nephews."

Everyone laughed, even Mr. Moy, who let out a loud "Ha!" The man might be odd, but I was glad to see he had a sense of humor.

For the rest of the meal, Wallace entertained us with stories of bees, with Ma interjecting every now and then with some attribute of mine—good listener, fleshy earlobes, even temperament—as if he were choosing a horse. I was tempted to throw myself out the open window and hoped all my wifely attributes included the ability to fly.

Gemma plated the desserts, while Peony attempted to pour the heavy teapot. Sucking in her breath through the space between her teeth, Ma brushed Peony away and dispensed the oolong herself, neatly tipping up the teapot at the end to catch drips. Gemma, whose leg had begun shaking, glanced at the clock for the dozenth time—5:58. Mr. Moy cut his cake into three excruciatingly even pieces. We needed to be on our way soon. The ball started at seven, and we didn't want to miss any interaction between O.F. and Detective Mallady.

Gemma flashed me a grimace. The tablecloth on her side of the table began jittering. Wallace glanced at his wristwatch. He cleared his throat. "The dinner was a heavenly offering," he said in Cantonese, an expression that meant the food was so good, even the gods would eat it. "But we should be on our way."

Ma frowned. "But you are not finished with dessert." She glanced at Wallace's half-eaten almond cookie.

"I actually need to stop by the lab tonight. Ma, Ba, Mrs. Chow, I'm sorry. I should've spoken earlier." Wallace finished the cookie and washed it down with tea, then stood.

Mrs. Moy's diplomat's face hinted at displeasure, but she dabbed at her mouth and rose as well. Mr. Moy ate the last portion of his cake. Casting me a worried look, Ma showed them to the door. Gemma retrieved hats and jackets with more eagerness than seemed appropriate.

After they left, Ma put her hands to her cheeks. "Well, he was certainly in a hurry."

Peony, who had returned to her dessert, giggled. "He must be busy as a bee."

Ma crossed to the window and pushed aside the curtain. "This is why meeting first is a bad idea," she muttered. "Better to just marry and make it work."

Gemma, who had already started clearing dishes, ticked her eyes to the ceiling. "Yes, Ma." She was only saying that because to disagree might delay us further. "May, after we finish here, what do you say I help you patch up that old quilt in your sewing room?"

"You? Sew?" I answered, playing along.

She beamed a practiced smile. "Well, I have to work on that wifely attribute at some point."

"I am glad to hear it," said Ma. "Well, this night will be good for something."

CLEANING UP TOOK LESS THAN TEN MINUTES WITH GEMMA, Peony, and me trying to go as fast as possible without looking suspicious. Then I carried the quilt to the sewing room down the hall while Gemma ported a chair, and Peony, my sewing basket.

Once there, I drew the calico curtains, and Gemma and I quickly changed into our woolen gray work dresses, which we'd stashed there earlier.

Peony helped me with my buttons, her fingers still damp from dishwashing. "I wish I could come to that ball," she grumbled.

Gemma worked her stockings over her feet. "I promise you, Cinderella, we're not going to meet a prince."

Peony began to bounce. "Okay, but if you see Clark Gable, could you ask for an autograph?"

I brushed a cookie crumb from her chin. The first time we'd ever seen Clark Gable on-screen was just before Ba went away. "I'm sorry, Pea, but assuming we can get in, we can't draw attention to ourselves. But you are doing an important job, giving us cover."

"That's right," said Gemma. "Like an alibi."

I pulled on my own stockings, my hands suddenly cold. An alibi meant we were going to commit a crime. Was this how the cycle of corruption started? One well-intentioned deed that, like a misplaced foot, led down a slippery slope.

Stuffy the dress form seemed to eye me from her place near the window, the iridescent feather pinned at the top catching my eye. *Your turn for luck.*

We were going to need a lot of it tonight.

11
GEMMA

MAY PILOTED US TOWARD SUNSET, WHERE, TEN MILES
ahead, the party of the year was just getting started at L.A.'s finest inn, the Beverly Hills Hotel. The sun had sunk, and the sky
wore a skirt of garish purple taffeta. That was Los Angeles for
you. Even a depression wouldn't keep her from dressing up.

I tightened my scarf, a zing of nerves shooting through me.
A doorless truck was not the ideal chariot in which to arrive at
the ball, but we didn't have a better option. "Let's talk about the
elephant in the truck. Bug Boy has become a big boy." I waggled
my eyebrows at May, but she refused to look at me.

"Death by pun-shot is how you will kill me one day." Her
cheek muscles twitched. "For your information, Wallace is not
interested in marriage."

I snorted. "Seems he knows a lot about pollinating flowers."

"We will pretend-date to keep all parties satisfied." Her arms
were as straight as railroad tracks, her hands clamped to the
wheel. Even the curls pouring from her shop cap looked like
coils, ready to spring and hit someone in the eye.

I guffawed. "You're putting me on."

She lifted her nose. She was serious.

"Whose idea was that?"

"It was mutual."

Pretend-dating certainly seemed a bold solution to the connubial conundrum, especially for my dutiful, beautiful sister. It gave me new admiration for her. "My, my. Might as well enjoy the sun on your face a little before going to seed. An excuse to go out will come in handy. In fact, I think we should follow that jobajoo Cole Stritch's tracks Sunday night. See who he sold Lulu's car to."

May rolled her head to one side. "You don't think he'd notice this jalopy on his tail?"

"He wouldn't notice Wallace's touring Chrysler."

"I don't think Wallace would appreciate us using him like that."

"Au contraire. I think Wallace would like to be used by you. That's how pretend-dating works. We'll call him tomorrow."

May kicked the Mule faster, passing cars motoring leisurely along, the evening traffic having already thinned. She started shaking her head, as if in an argument with herself. "I really hate this plan."

"You also hate Coca-Cola, beach swimming, basically anything fun."

"This is hardly fun."

Despite my ribbing her, my own worries snagged at me. If Mallady *was* on the take, how would we prove it? Not to mention, who would care? If all the palms were being greased, we would never grasp the hand that could give Lulu justice. "We're just gathering clues from which we will form theories. Remember the horned cucumbers?"

When we were girls, Ba had taken May and me to walk along the Los Angeles River, where we came upon a low plant sprawling in every direction. Using a stick, Ba pushed aside some of the leaves, which were coated with a sticky fur of fine needles.

Orbs of yellow fruit, prickled with thick spines, grew underneath. "Must be tasty, if you have to work that hard for it." Ba
was always full of wisdom like that.

Using sticks, we managed to knock free some of the fruits.
Inside was a sweet-sour jelly you could spread on toast, better
than anything I'd tasted. Like with those horned cucumbers, we
just had to work our way around the needles and hope we'd find
something worth our troubles.

"What about the horned cucumbers?" May said through her
teeth.

"Patience bears fruit."

Soon, the Beverly Hills Hotel crowned a shallow incline,
white lights making the structure appear to float. From far away,
white stucco walls and a red roof gave the hotel the look of a
mission. But there was nothing monastic about it up close. Palm
trees, not just the skinny-trunked common variety but also some
shaped like fans and pineapples, studded a paved driveway on
which was parked a line of cars. A crowd had already gathered
under a roofed driveway.

At the bottom of the incline lay a small lot with delivery vehicles and a service entrance, guarded by two men in suede jackets
and plaid flat caps. Their biceps were so big, their arms didn't
hang straight. "Park there," I said.

The brakes squeaked. May slid in between two delivery
trucks with the ease of notching a button. She'd make a good
chauffeur if women were allowed to do such things. Leaving
our jackets tucked under the seat, we pulled our baskets from
the flatbed. We'd filled them with corsages made from leftover
blooms.

May pressed a knuckle to her lip, and I knew she was counting the hotel's stories—an unlucky four.

But getting her this far had taken all my salt, and I wasn't giving up now. "We'll be careful," I assured her. "Bettina's counting on us, and this is the only lead we have right now."

Her cap sank like a frown. "Fine. We'll go in. But first sign of trouble, we skedaddle. Am I clear?"

"As boiled water." It was important for her to feel like she was in control of the situation, especially when in reality, we didn't know what could happen, and we didn't have a plan if things went awry. If the cage came down on us, I'd have to do what I'd always done—defuse the situation with May's pretty face and use my wit to cut our way out.

After watching the burly guards toss a man out the service doors, we hoofed up the driveway toward the main entrance. There'd be guards up there too, but we might have a better shot at slipping through the crowd unnoticed. We passed handsome roadsters and cabriolets, the noise of people mixing with the brassy sounds of an orchestra. Ivy climbed the archways spanning the hotel's main floor, the leaves reminding me of dollar bills. We crested the top of the hill, where valets in black jackets glided about, debarking clientele from their glossy chariots as efficiently as waiters clearing plates.

I blew out a low whistle. "This crowd's butter and eggs," I said, meaning "high quality." I adjusted my cap. "Remember, walk with purpose. It's easier for people to simply allow you to carry on than to stop you."

"What if their job is to stop you?" She peered toward the main entry, where more burly men with plaid flat caps were busy holding back a press of photographers.

"We hardly look threatening," I said with annoyance, though my limbs suddenly felt heavy. Setting an example, I marched toward the crowd.

A trio of tuxedoed men, none of whom was Clark Gable, stepped aside as I barreled past, stirring up the smoke of their cigars. May hurried to catch up with me.

We reached a red carpet delivering ladies in sleek dresses and their escorts into the hotel. Camera bulbs flashed like a swarm of fireflies, and the photographers surged closer, keeping the burly guards busy.

"That's her!" someone shouted.

As everyone turned to look at the newcomer, I grabbed May's arm and hustled her up the red path, my ears attuned to protests. But hearing none, we made it inside. The lobby opened up before us in relaxed grandeur. May gasped softly beside me. Chandeliers cast dazzling lights upon carpets with dizzying patterns. Armchairs that could fit both May and me, with room for Peony too, sprawled like tufted islands in case you needed a vacation on your way to the main event.

May's gaze trailed to a sleek brunette accepting a drink from her silver-haired escort. "That's what's-her-name."

"Yeah, and that's what's-his-name. Come on." We kept moving to where the lobby angled into the party room, judging by the noise. I pulled May behind a post. "Keep your eyes sharp for Mallady. If he's here, he'll probably be wearing one of those penguin suits. Maybe we should split up—less visible that way. If anyone asks what you're doing—"

"Hello there," said an indignant man in a gold smoking jacket with a black collar, his arms around an ice bucket. "What are you doing?"

I retreated a step. "We're delivering the corsages. What does it look like?" The man's jaw began a slow descent. Before words emerged, I added, "Best let us get on with it. The boss won't like it if the guests' favors wilt."

"What boss? I'm the hospitality manager around here." The ice in his bucket clattered like the warning rattle of a snake, and the nostrils of his reddish nose flared.

"Mr. North, obviously. He's the event planner, isn't he?"

"Well, yes."

"We're the floral assistants. He paid for this service. It'd be a shame to waste good flowers like this. Show him the Sultan's Delight, May."

Her cap had begun to slip over her forehead, as if she was willing it to eat her up. Snapping to attention, May pulled out one of the candy cane roses and twirled it between her fingers. "Shipped in from Santa Barbara this morning," she said, more congenial than me. "Costs a whole dollar a head."

The man peered closer at the bloom, frowning. Maybe he was the sort who couldn't tell a carnation from a cauliflower.

A woman in a black uniform approached. "Mr. Le Strait, Hettie Bright just arrived."

May stopped twirling her flower and quickly put it to her nose, maybe hiding her surprise. I flashed her a triumphant smile. Hettie Bright *was* here. I didn't know how we could corner her to talk with us—or Carey Stone if he showed up too. But if opportunity knocked, we'd be ready to answer the door.

"If you'll just let us do our jobs, we'll be out of your hair in a ticktock," I said testily, taking advantage of the interruption. "You won't even notice us." I began to edge away, with May following along.

Le Strait, who might be better named Le Snob, glanced toward the entrance, then in the direction of the party room. He groaned. "Oh, very well." He pushed his ice bucket at the woman in uniform and hurried toward the entrance.

Horned cucumbers. Just another prickly leaf on the way to

the fruit. I watched him leave, but as I moved off in the other direction, I nearly collided with a woman in a leopard-print silk. "Oh! I'm sorry, madam."

Her escort, a man with a full beard, grabbed her before she slipped. "Steady there, love."

Regaining her balance, the woman touched her arranged curls. Her face bore the boozy sheen of a maraschino cherry. "Those are lovely flowers, aren't they, Georgie?"

"Would you like a Double Happiness corsage?" I held out a wrapped pair of roses.

She took it, a smile enveloping her face. "Pay her, Georgie."

May stepped in closer. "Oh, no, they're compli—"

I shouldered her back. "They *complement* your fine dress."

The man, Georgie, handed me a whole dollar, and I slipped it in my pocket with a smile. This gig was already bearing fruit. "Thank you. Please enjoy your evening."

May's smile was so tight, we could hang our shop caps on either end. "Wonderful," she groused as we set off again. "When they book us, they can add extortion to the charges."

My retort dissolved on my tongue as the party room materialized before us.

"It's like Ali Baba's den," breathed May, staring up at the dripping light fixtures that I suppose did remind one of cave icicles.

I was more focused on the loot stashed at the center of the room—a gleaming ham, coins of cheese, glittering fruit and caviar. I started calculating how I could work my way through all the silks, furs, and feathers and stuff some of the bounty into my mouth without anyone noticing.

May tugged my sleeve. "Look!" She lifted her chin to a dining alcove on the right, where a thin man stood talking to a woman. The Foxes. We moved closer, concealing ourselves behind one of the arches. Otis Fox cut a striking figure, with his swarthy looks and a thin loop of facial hair around his mouth and chin, as if drawn by a black crayon. Piercing brown, almost black eyes seemed made for tracking, his gaze swooping from subject to subject.

Fox's wife was rarely pictured with him in those newspaper articles he loved getting his mug in, but as she stood a few inches higher than him, aided by a puff of shockingly white-blond hair, the two made an odd and therefore memorable couple. A Midwesterner, Mrs. Fox's limbs were sturdy in the way people who grew up homesteading tended to be, and there was a hearty quality to their movement even with the simple act of plucking grapes. By contrast, her makeup was polished and avant-garde, softening a squarish jaw and making her eyes pop with gold and claret shadow. Of course, the wife of the owner of a cosmetics company would be a makeup pacesetter.

A young man approached, and Mrs. Fox embraced him warmly, with a kiss on the cheek. I recognized the Foxes' son, city council candidate Philippe, whose face I'd seen on campaign posters around the city. He was sturdy like his mother, but with the same dark-brown hair with a widow's peak and sharp features as his father. His facile, crowd-loving smile put a stone in my gut. If he won a seat, another, more dangerous breed of Fox would be born: someone who could not only pay bribes against Chinatown's interests but also take them.

Mallady wasn't anywhere in sight.

"You stay here and keep an eye on the Foxes," I told May, glancing to the other side of the room, where more arches led to a garden patio. "I'm going outside. Maybe Mallady's out there."

"Well, don't dawdle. We're like a couple of cockroaches in the kitchen right before they turn on the lights."

"Stop worrying. People are more interested in who's looking at them than looking at you."

"Don't take unnecessary risks," she said, hammering in each syllable.

While she stationed herself behind a ficus plant, I casually made my way past the revelers, trying not to look at the food. Past the arches, a hanging garden of Babylon dripped from the patio roof.

I paused by an arch post, getting my bearings. More tables—dinner rounds, as well as smaller but higher cocktail tables—formed a semicircle around a dance floor. At the front, a brass orchestra was blowing out a swingy number. I tried to focus on the men, but the dimmer lighting and the sameness of their outfits was making my eyes cross.

I would need to keep an eye out not just for Mallady, but also Mr. North. Along with funeral homes, the party-planning business was remarkably robust even in tough economic times, and Mr. North was the biggest planner of them all. We needed the small bits he threw us. The former might be easier to spot, being out of his element, while Mr. North presented more of a challenge. He was a man of discretion and more used to shining the limelight than standing in it.

Someone tapped my shoulder, and I yelped, catching sight of a head of black hair. But this was not Mr. North. This man had bedroom eyes and an iconic set of thick eyebrows. The earth ground to a halt, and I grabbed the wall for support. "Mr.—er, Mr. Gable."

His lips folded into a smile. "Could I trouble you for one of your flowers?"

"Flowers?" Suddenly, I was breathless, staring into those heavy-lidded peepers.

"Yes." He nodded to my basket, which was drooping from my limp grasp.

"Oh, of course." I handed him one of the gold-dipped roses and tried to stop grinning like a fool. He tucked a five-dollar bill in my palm, then placed the rose to his sensuous mouth and bowed.

Clark Gable just bowed to Gemma Chow from Chinatown.

He disappeared back into the main room. A fit of giggles bubbled up. My stars, that was certainly one delicious horned cucumber.

Pull yourself together, you ninnyhammer. You have a job to do. Here's your chance to pull the stop on the train, and you can't muck it up getting moony-eyed. I forced my feet to stroll, despite the fantasies developing in my head. What if he'd kissed my hand instead of the rose?

"Gemma?" said a familiar disdainful voice.

The earth pumped the brakes a second time. I'd been made. But instead of Mr. North or Mallady, a young man with the cultured air of a violin tweaked his haughty eyebrows in my direction. Dr. Frederick Winter.

12
MAY

THE PARTY ROOM HAD BEGUN TO FILL, MEANING MORE eyes to avoid. If we got out of this unscathed, I would have to atone in some way, maybe weed the gardens at Our Redeemer, or even polish the incense burners at the joss house.

I passed out flowers and tried to act like I belonged in this scene. When playacting, the hardest part of dissolving into a role for me was the letting go of May Chow, who cared what people thought of her. This was easier done when I could play off a scene partner, like Gemma. But here, I was doing a solo act. *Keep your chin tucked, lashes lowered, tongue pressed to the roof of the mouth to keep from grimacing. Relax the posture, or it will suggest superiority.*

People exchanged pleasantries with the Foxes but didn't linger. I couldn't help remembering the fortune teller's wife, who always pinched our cheeks when we thanked her for donating the foil-wrapped candies at the Chinese New Year Parade. We only stayed as long as we could bear the clawlike grip on our cheeks.

Mrs. Fox, letting a pair of women admire her necklace, cast her brightly shadowed eyes in my direction, and our gazes met for the briefest moment. I shrank back into the main party room, nearly bumping into a group of ladies whose floor-length dresses made them look like Grecian goddesses.

Had she seen me? It didn't matter. She'd seen her share of Chinese servants.

"Oh, look, there's Hettie," cried one of the goddesses, and all turned to look.

A young woman whose ginger curls stood out against a mink fur strode into the room on the arm of an older gent who could be her father. Her face looked pale but luminous. A slash of lipstick in Lulu's Noir Red shade set off her green eyes. She slipped off her coat, and the older gent whisked it away to the other side of the room.

"She must be wearing the new Fox Stardust Powder with the mica crystals," whispered one of the goddesses. "Her face looks ethereal."

"I wish I could get my hands on some. It's flying off the shelves."

"Except gingers really shouldn't wear black. It's so harsh against her skin."

It occurred to me that Hettie might be wearing a black gown—a deceptively simple hourglass design—in honor of Lulu. Few non-Chinese people knew the Chinese color of mourning was white.

Guests flocked to Hettie, and a photographer's bulb went off. I should talk to her. But this was hardly the time or the place. Besides, she wouldn't speak to a nobody like me. And if she did, people were bound to notice, people like Fox or Mr. North, if he was around.

Even as I tried to talk myself out of it, I could feel my feet moving toward her. This chance wasn't going to come again. And if she was wearing black in mourning, surely she had Lulu on her mind anyway.

A group had surrounded Hettie, and I stood back,

second-guessing myself all over again. I should wait until Gemma got back. Gemma could insert herself into a conversation as easily as a key in a lock. No, I would just keep my watch on the Foxes like I was supposed to, and—

Hettie looked up at me, and her eyes, green and slightly bloodshot, widened in curiosity. I gripped my basket. Passing someone her drink, she glided to me, and gazes followed. I resisted the urge to scurry into a dark corner and summoned some poise.

"Miss Bright." I presented her with a flower.

"Thank you." She put the bloom to her nose. "Do I know you?"

"No. I'm May Chow. Lulu was a childhood friend."

"Lulu." The flower fell away from her nose. "I still can't believe it."

I nodded. "Actually—" My throat suddenly dried up. *Speak up, you goose, before the moment passes.* "Actually, my sister and I are trying to get some answers about her death. I wondered if I could ask you a few questions." Her thin eyebrows rounded, and I was afraid I had overstepped.

"Excuse me," said a voice behind Hettie. It was Le Strait, standing as stiff as a wind-up soldier. "Why are you still here? I'm so sorry, Miss Bright. We will have this girl removed."

I shrank back. "I—I—"

Hettie flipped back her curls with some annoyance. "Can't you see we're in the middle of a conversation? In fact, we need somewhere to speak privately, if you could please arrange it."

"Er, right now? You're scheduled to give the opening toast in fifteen minutes."

Hettie's eyes narrowed. "Which means we shouldn't delay."

The whole room seemed to be watching us, and I felt my

entire act coming apart. At least the Foxes' view of me from the dining alcove was obstructed.

"You may use my office. Right this way." But instead of exiting the main room the way we came in, Le Strait crossed into the dining alcove. Holding my face away from the Foxes' table, Hettie and I crossed the room to a door painted the same cream color as the wall. Gemma would worry if she returned to find me missing, but I couldn't exactly leave her a message.

The door led to a brightly lit office. A mishmash of supplies—bottles of wine, cardboard party hats—weighed down an executive desk.

"I hope this will do." Le Strait bowed his head deferentially. He cast me a grim expression, then closed the door behind him.

Hettie sagged against the desk. Black satin pooled around her like a shimmery shadow, featuring dramatic flourishes, like a lace décolletage and handsewn crystals. "Lulu was a dear friend. Are they close to finding her killer?" Her eyes blinked slowly, like butterflies before their wings have dried. A little bit of mascara had clumped on one side of her lashes, as if the hand that had applied it had been distracted. Seeing the details helped you understand the larger picture. But was this face the fragile visage of a friend in pain, or the practiced mask of a killer? Tragic beauty wasn't so hard to pull off with proper motivation.

"The police don't tell us much, I'm afraid. Her mother mentioned you and Carey Stone were supposed to rehearse with Lulu the day she died."

"Yes. We planned to go to Carey's place, but we decided to switch to mine. His place has been a bit of a mob scene lately."

"What do you mean?"

She twisted one of the expensive crystals on her dress, not seeming to care that she might pull it off. "The press has been relentless. They catch a whiff of a story, and they'll keep sniffing around until the next thing comes along. Carey's been avoiding public events like this because of it. At first, we thought Lulu had gotten the places mixed up and would be along. But when she didn't show up, and didn't answer her phone, we figured she might've just been napping." Hettie set her corsage on the desk and began tying her curls into a knot on her head. "She'd been tired lately."

"Was she sick?"

"No." Her mouth twisted to the side. "I mean, she had a bout with the salami, but haven't we all? There's always a deli platter on set."

It seemed odd that Lulu would eat the salami, given that she was a vegetarian. I wondered if Lulu had kept this fact to herself.

"I should've gone to her house," Hettie went on. "She only lived ten minutes away. I feel terrible about that. It's just, she'd been working so hard lately, and I really thought she had fallen asleep."

That sounded like the Lulu I remembered. We'd stayed up until midnight rehearsing a scene more than once. "How well do you know her friends?"

"Honestly, she was kind of a loner. At parties, she was as bold and fun as a brass band. But I always got the feeling she was putting on an act. That she didn't care to be with people."

A memory snuck in, of Lulu and me deciding which snack to purchase from the corner store.

"You can't talk when you eat Milk Duds," I had said of the sticky chocolate caramels.

"Good point. I like talking with you, May. Let's get the Goobers."

I felt Hettie's eyes nudge me.

"Was Lulu . . . happy?" I asked. Guilt pushed at me, and I held my breath for the answer I wasn't ready to hear.

Hettie finished with her hair knot and pulled out a few strands to fall on either side of her face. The Stardust Powder was aptly named, shimmering like the Milky Way on a clear night. "I thought so. She never gossiped or complained to me, and I was her best friend."

The words hit me like little darts. *I* had been Lulu's best friend. Maybe if I had been looking out for her, like a friend should, she would still be with us. "Did she have a boyfriend?" Lulu might not have told her mother about a boyfriend, but what about a confidante?

"Not that I knew of." She shook her head, tiny sequins on her gown spinning the light. "Though I remember seeing her file a nail on one of those green Clifford's Steakhouse matchbooks once."

My eyebrows raised. The wealthy restaurateur Clifford Joust was known for his slogan: *If you want her to say yes, take her to Clifford's.* But surely a boyfriend, if he did exist, would have known she was a vegetarian and wouldn't have taken her to a steakhouse. So why had she gone?

A voice from inside the main room began to make itself heard, tamping down the noise of the crowd. Hettie glanced at the door. Le Strait had mentioned they were expecting her for the opening toast.

"What about any enemies?" I hurried on. "Anyone who might've had it out for her? Coworkers? We heard someone had stolen her scripts."

Hettie's eyes snapped to mine again. "I guess there's always going to be jealousy."

"Has anyone ever stolen your scripts?"

"Me? No. But I've gotten my share of spiteful looks." Her eyes flashed.

"Lulu was playing a heroine for the first time. Surely that ruffled some feathers."

She pressed her pink shell fingertips to her temples. "If it did, I didn't know about it. We all supported Lulu."

"Even Cole Stritch, her manager?"

"I would think so. Cole Stritch has a good reputation. He even represents Juanita, Lulu's replacement."

"Juanita?"

"She goes by the single name. She's a real up-and-comer from New York."

That seemed convenient for Mr. Stritch. Had he eliminated his golden goose in favor of one with the potential to lay even bigger eggs? Why not just have two golden geese? Perhaps this had something to do with the "war" that he thought would take both of them down. Maybe Mr. Stritch had feared for his reputation and decided to replace her with someone less controversial. "Were there any others who might've had cause to hurt her?"

Her chin tilted to one side. "There was a strange incident last month. I remember Lulu talking to a group of Chinese girls hired as background. I don't know what they were saying, but the girls were in tears. Lulu seemed upset when she left them too."

Had one of the Chinese extras sent her the mystery note? "Had they been arguing?"

"I couldn't say."

"Do you remember their names?"

A flush crept over her face. "I'm sorry, I rarely get to know the, er, backgrounders."

"Of course."

"Anyway, after Lulu died, they all quit. Emil has to reaudition."

I felt my jaw tighten, though it wasn't entirely surprising. The Chinese could be superstitious, especially when it came to tragic deaths. People who died violently could come back as hungry ghosts, inflicting their misery on all.

Someone knocked. The door opened and Le Strait poked in his head. "Ahem, Miss Bright, your adoring public is waiting on you."

"I'm sorry I can't be of more help." Hettie's thin eyebrows squeezed, putting dents in her forehead. "But if you have more questions, feel free to call." Reaching for a pen and paper, she jotted down her number and passed it to me.

"Thank you," I said, trying to hide my astonishment that a famous person had just given me the means to contact her. "And if you think of anything else, we're in the phone book. Chow's Flowers in Chinatown."

She plucked up her corsage and tucked it into her hair. "I'll remember that."

I waited a few minutes before venturing out after Hettie, wanting to avoid the spotlight that would shine on her once she rejoined the party.

Returning to the alcove, I cased about for the Foxes. A group of guests at their table obscured them from view. It seemed they were still receiving homage. I crept toward the main room, where Hettie in her black gown stood out like a raven in a cage of exotic birds. Beside her, a man in his fifties was holding a champagne glass. With his blond hair shot with silver, and a solid jawline under cheeks that had begun to jowl, perhaps he was an actor as well. Or maybe he was a wealthy businessman, like Otis Fox.

He grabbed a standing microphone, his movements smooth

despite the telltale glow of alcohol on his cheeks. "New York has their Yankees," he began in a hale voice, pausing for a dramatic moment as the room fell silent. "We have our movie stars." His thin lips peeled into a gummy smile. "I just got back from watching those Yankees beat the stuffing out of the Cubs, and let me tell you, it wasn't half as exciting as what's going on in this room." He let go of the microphone and lifted his hand. "On the silver screen, we can be gods, creating new worlds for people to step in and out of. We can bestow emotions, new beliefs. We can hold people in the palm of our hands, if even for a few minutes." He slowly returned his hand to his side.

The words hung in the air, as sparkly and mesmerizing as the crystals on the chandelier. It was true—people revered Holly-wood, with its limitless space to be anyone, do anything. Had someone taken that belief a step too far? Had one of the "gods" considered himself invincible?

The man giving the toast continued, "My beloved wife, Edith, God rest her soul, used to joke, 'I have cheated on you many times, my dear, at the movies.'" He pointed into the crowd. "Pretty sure she was talking about you, Clark Gable."

People laughed, looking toward a face that had stopped millions of hearts. Dark hair rippled with insouciant curls. A suggestive gaze hooked like a cat's tail. I had to pinch myself.

"Just doing my job, Maurie," Mr. Gable's buttery-smooth voice lobbed back, to more laughter.

"You old charmers." Hettie lifted her glass to Maurie. "To you, Maurie Newman, for keeping the lights on with your mar-velous reporting. Behind that serif typography lies the bold heart of a man with a noble vision—to make Los Angeles the city of the past, present, and future!" Her clear voice projected without even needing the microphone, and applause poured out.

"Flattery will buy you everything, my dear, maybe even that castle you're always going on about. Only instead of Hearst Castle, she'll call it Hettie's Castle," he told the onlookers. "And to you all here, and the rest of Hollywood"—the man held up his flute—"cheers for giving us a good reason to turn the lights *off* with your movies."

"Hear, hear!" cried the crowd.

The guests blocking my view of the Foxes' table parted, and my breath hitched. The Foxes were gone, and their places tidied, with fresh plates and tucked-in chairs. It was as if they had never been there.

I glanced around the room but didn't see a single trace of the wiry man, his statuesque wife, or their politician son. I had lost them. Swallowing my frustration, I moved along the walls and in the shadows, searching. Another man standing near the arches to the patio caught my attention. He bore the stately posture of a diplomat, his oiled hair sprouting in glossy spikes, and a lavender handkerchief tucked into his jacket pocket. It was Mr. North, the event coordinator. And he was looking right at me.

13
GEMMA

FREDDIE WINTER WAS GAPING. HIS USUALLY SHARP EYES wavered between me and the festivities around us, as if not sure if he was seeing things. A bee burst out of the petunias in one of the hanging planters, hovered over my basket, then buzzed off. I was tempted to buzz off myself. Would Freddie give me away?

The young doctor grabbed at his chin, putting a crease in his tailored sleeve. "You and your flowers certainly get around."

Though the night was chilly, a burst of heat rolled over me. A toast had started up from within the main room, but I scarcely paid attention. "The same could be said of you and your airs."

"Speaking of airs, don't tell me you drove here in your jalopy?" His puzzled expression found its way back to ironic.

"Well, the Jaguar was in the shop. You know those English cars are so fussy. I didn't know physicians came to these types of events. Who will they invite next? Grease monkeys? Meat packers?"

"I've heard meat packers are quite respectable. A real cut above the rest." I groaned, and he sailed on, "Personal physicians to Hollywood stars are always invited. When the champagne starts flying, someone's bound to fall off a roof."

A hundred feet away near the band, my gaze caught on a large man getting to his feet. It was Mallady. The other diners at

his table were paired up, but not him. He hoisted the waistband
of his ill-fitting tuxedo pants, glancing around the area with the
unease of a cat on a canoe. He was looking for someone—and I
bet my basket it was Otis Fox. I shrank farther into the shadows.

The toast ended, and the band struck up the carefree hit
"Singin' in the Rain." Several diners abandoned their dinners in
favor of the dance floor. Freddie wiggled his fingers in front of me.

"I'm sorry, were you saying something?" I asked.

"I said, how are you feeling? Any more dizzy episodes?"

"No." Mallady must have spotted the person he was looking
for, because he suddenly grew still, looking toward a group of
people drifting in from the main room. He grabbed his drink
from the table and glugged it down. Then he hiked up his
pants again and crossed the dance floor, his face set in grim
determination.

The target of his efforts appeared. But it wasn't Otis Fox.
Instead, a middling gent swung into view, a chap who bore the
haughty swagger of someone used to being head rooster. A too-
big smile underscored a long nose, close-set eyes, and thinning
once-blond hair. He pumped hands emphatically with whoever
crossed his path.

Freddie was watching me with a curious expression.

"Who is that man?" I asked.

"Maurie Newman, owner of the *Observer First*. They call him
'Mr. News.' I believe he just gave the toast."

I wasn't familiar with the odd name, but since it was the
Observer who hosted this party, no wonder the man was so
self-important. Mr. News certainly wasn't O.F. Unless . . .

I snapped my fingers. "*Observer First*."

Freddie raised one of his cultured eyebrows. "Yes."

Catching sight of Mallady, Newman stopped in his tracks,

waiting for Mallady to approach, his pumping hand at the ready. Newman gestured toward an empty cocktail table centered by a silver basin of strawberries and grapes. One of the servers placed flutes of champagne in front of them. What I wouldn't give to be a fly on their fruit bowl.

Of course, their meeting could have nothing to do with Lulu Wong. Then again, it could have everything to do with her. Mallady had given the impression that Lulu's case was consuming all his time. Surely, he wasn't the kind of man who would spend his leisure hours cavorting with people who made him uncomfortable, unless it had something to do with work.

A woman laughed from a few feet away, where she and her partner were swaying side to side. Her partner held her so close, it was hard to see the woman's face.

". . . I'm usually so charming, women hang on my every word." I caught the end of Freddie's statement.

"Dance with me?" I blurted out. Mallady would recognize me for sure, especially after I fogged up his office yesterday, but dancing could get me close enough to the pair, where I might get a half shot at hearing what was being discussed. Of course, I didn't know how to dance with anyone but a coatrack, but I was sure I could fake it. Freddie was taller than me by a head, and it was dark out here. As long as we stuck to the shadows . . .

"Pardon me?" Freddie was back to gaping, though his face had darkened a shade. You would've thought I'd asked him to strip naked and do the tango.

I suddenly remembered Max Factor. "That is, er, as long as your girlfriend doesn't mind." I glanced around, wishing I had thought of her earlier.

Freddie coughed. "Actually, we are no longer together."

"Oh, dear. I am sorry."

"Well, you would be the only one. I learned she had been all over town with her former beau and realized I didn't care so much."

Mallady and Newman seemed to be finished with the pleasantries and were leaning closer to each other. The time was now, or never. "Alright, then, let's go." I set my basket by the post and pulled him by the arm to the dance floor.

"But I'm not sure this is appropriate," he protested as I put his hand on my back and grabbed the other. I wish I had worn gloves, which would've absorbed some of the sweat pouring from my palms.

The nearest dancers turned toward us, and I drew Freddie closer, looking into the cleft of his freshly shaven chin, as if I had lost change in there. "You must hold me closer. I shouldn't be seen dancing."

"Er, it's customary for the man to lead."

"Well, lead me that way." I ticked my head toward Mallady and Newman. "I need to know what they're talking about." I stepped on his foot, and he grunted, somehow catching me before I pulled him off-balance. "Sorry."

"We are not a pair of yoked oxen," he said through his teeth. "Kindly let me steer the wagon, which will be better for both of us. Why exactly am I doing this?"

I tried to be light on my feet, letting him guide me through a frustratingly circuitous pattern. *"Peut-être, peut-être, is American for you-betcha,"* a blond in a low-cut gown sang.

"I imagine, Freddie, that life must be rather tedious for someone in your profession. All the diseases you must see: typhoid, bubonic plague, varicose veins—"

"Typhoid has largely been eliminated, and varicose veins are hardly—"

"I am merely adding some color to your dull and dreary life."

Freddie's mouth twitched. "You are adding something, I will give you that." At last, he managed to maneuver us to within two paces of the men, close enough to hear their muffled voices. I peeked over Freddie's shoulder, straining to hear. When he attempted to steer me away, I resisted, even though I knew we couldn't just stand there. On a carousel, it was the horse that didn't move that drew eyes.

The song stopped, and a slower, swaying melody took its place. I recognized the flirty strains of "I Wanna Be Loved by You," a song people couldn't get enough of. Here was a chance to linger under the pretense of slow dancing. As partners pressed closer to each other, I was suddenly too aware of the twelve inches separating the doctor and me, an airspace thick with possibility. Freddie's eyes didn't seem to know where to go, skimming over my face before skipping away. Things couldn't get much more awkward between the good doctor and me, but I couldn't pass up this opportunity.

I pushed my face right up to Freddie's chest, feeling it hitch. He smelled like soap. Probably all doctors smelled that way. But there was something else, a hint of musk that made my heart race. "Er, could you kindly turn me around?"

With a sigh, he neatly turned me about in two steps, his graceful footwork and the firm hold of his arm inexplicably putting butterflies in my stomach. Somehow, looking up at him had become twice as awkward. At least he had put my back to the men, whose conversation shaped itself into words.

"New cars, of course," said Newman, with a voice that exuded authority. "Maybe even two-way radios. Imagine if the men could talk to the dispatcher. Save time and, therefore, lives. Worth it, wouldn't you say? So much good can come of this."

Freddie watched my face crease as the memory of Mallady's police cruiser with its staticky radio crackled into my mind. Was it possible to have a radio that allowed you to transmit your voice, like a telephone? But what did that have to do with anything?

"I could lose my job over this," Mallady whispered hotly. "We're talking about a girl's life."

I found myself leaning back so far that Freddie was forced to dip me like they do in the tango. The heat of his chest over mine and the closeness of his face to my thrown-back head made the blood swoosh around my body. May would definitely not approve of this . . . *situation*, but what she didn't know wouldn't hurt her.

"You won't. In fact, I was thinking a promotion might be in order." Newman's voice was soft and slippery. "The girl's already dead. Let sleeping dogs lie."

My shoe slipped, and Freddie barely caught me before I fell. A woman beside me gasped, and her partner pulled her away from us, as if stumbling might be catching.

Recovering my balance, I made tracks across the dance floor, with Freddie following close behind. Had Mallady seen me? My back had been turned, and it had happened so fast.

Hurrying toward the dining room, I caught sight of a trim and well-dressed figure inside the main room, standing as proud as a ringmaster over his circus. Mr. North.

I quickly turned around, nearly colliding with Freddie.

"Gemma, what is going on?" he demanded, concern wringing his features. His bow tie had gone crooked, and his combed hair now tweaked to one side.

Dancers had closed up the space between us and Mallady, but the detective could still be looking for me. "Dr. Winter, you have been the noblest geranium," I spoke quickly.

"Geran—"

"They get rid of beetles, leafhoppers, and—well, the list is long. I have one last bug for you to drive away, and then you never have to see me again."

He choked out a laugh. "And if I don't, how often will I see you?"

"I'll try to keep it to a minimum either way. There's an event planner I need you to talk to."

14
MAY

ACROSS THE ROOM, MR. NORTH TOOK A STEP IN MY direction, as if trying to get a better look at me. I shrank back, my muscles primed for flight. But then an elegant young man with good posture approached Mr. North, gesturing toward the patio from where he had just come. With a nod, the event planner followed the man out.

Had Mr. North seen me? I certainly hoped our misdeeds would not follow us back to Chinatown.

Before I could decide on a course of action, I recognized Gemma's quick-moving figure slipping into the main room from the patio. I emerged from the shadows and edged toward her. Spotting me, she ticked her head toward the lobby, and soon we were making our way back to the hotel entrance.

"I lost the Foxes," I told her as soon as I caught my breath. "I think they left."

She glanced over her shoulder, but there was no sign of Mr. North or Le Strait or anyone else who could have us arrested. I couldn't help noticing two pink spots on Gemma's cheeks, either from the cold or the night's escapades. "Never mind them. I think we got what we came for."

I sidestepped a woman gesturing with her wineglass from one of the stuffed chairs. "It's a good thing you came when you did. If some Hollywood type hadn't pulled Mr. North away just before you came in, you would've tripped over him. What are you smiling about?"

"I'm not smiling," Gemma protested, saddling her lips. "Let's wiggle. We'll talk in the car."

Soon enough, I was steering the Mule back toward Chinatown, cold air pummeling us from both sides. I made Gemma talk first, nearly swerving out of my lane when she told me about Clark Gable. But I quickly sobered when she got to the part about Mallady.

"What's clear is that Maurie Newman—Mr. News—wanted Mallady to stop his investigation in exchange for some police perks."

"Are you sure they were talking about Lulu?"

"Is there another girl in Hollywood who was just murdered?"

"But the *Observer First* is supposed to be neutral. 'Observe and report.'"

Gemma waved me off. "They certainly didn't 'observe and report' what *we* told them about Lulu Wong. They're always saying ridiculous stuff about Chinatown. Like how we sacrifice babies and eat bats."

I nodded. Mr. News had money and connections. His corruption could be far more damaging than Otis Fox's. Fox was the monster who attacked from the front. Newman attacked from the back, casting his influence in unseen ways. "But what's his motive?"

"Business interests. Better transportation into L.A. means more wealth flows into the city, more to float his boat."

Behind that serif typography lies the bold heart of a man with a noble vision—to make Los Angeles the city of the past, present, and future, Hettie Bright had said in her toast. "That'll be tricky to prove. Plus, he said he was watching the World Series in Chicago on Sunday night, which means he has an alibi." A dull ache gnawed at my skull. If the police department was crooked, and so was the newspaper, what chance did Lulu have for justice? I stared too hard, and a car coming from the other direction nearly blinded me with its too-bright lights. "Well, we don't know if Mallady agreed. Plus, why kill Lulu, then pay the police to cover it up? Wouldn't you want to make sure the police were in your pocket before committing the crime? I think it's more likely that someone killed Lulu, and Mr. News saw an opportunity."

"Maybe. But let's not count him out." She rubbed her hands briskly together. "So what did you find out?"

I recalled my conversation with Hettie, starting with the matchbook from Clifford's Steakhouse. "Maybe she went there with a friend."

"You don't go to Clifford's with 'just friends.' We'll ask Bettina about it. What else?"

I told her about Cole Stritch representing Lulu's replacement, Juanita—

"Lucky him. What did I *tell* you about his tight nostrils?"

—and about the Chinese extras.

"They quit?" A sly mouse tail of a smile slipped across her face.

"What are you up to?" I asked, not liking where this was going.

"The Chinese extras quit. They'll be looking for new extras. This is our chance."

"Forget it," I said, grimacing as the wind grabbed my words and threw them away. "What would our parents say?" I was supposed to be taking care of the family, not bringing them scandal. Mingling with members of the silver screen was one thing. Stepping onto the screen itself was completely different.

"This is our chance to see what her day-to-day was like," Gemma pleaded. "Who was Lulu Wong when she wasn't with her family, and more importantly, who had it out for her? We're good at playacting. Need I remind you how many flowers we sold at Westlake Park?"

"Need I remind you how we nearly got ourselves thrown in the pokey?" An image of us being led to the Hall of Justice in handcuffs trooped into my head.

"Opportunity knocks and you're complaining about the noise. Besides, we won't even have to playact. All the extras do is stand there or fan themselves or whatever. Easy stuff. It'll give us access to the behind-the-scenes. We could learn who those Chinese extras were—they must have a record of them—and we'd have access to the leading man, Carey Stone. I didn't see him at the party, did you?"

"No. Hettie said he's been avoiding these events because the press has been hounding him."

"See? It's perfect."

"We don't know the first thing about show business. We won't make it past the audition." I immediately regretted my words, which gave Gemma wiggle room for her machinations.

"With your pretty face and my effervescent personality, I am certain we will get those spots. And we might even make some money doing it."

I felt the familiar tug of her pulling me into a scheme that had RUN written all over it. If there was a war going on, we'd be going right to the front lines. Maybe that's why the extras had quit. If someone was going after Chinese actresses, they didn't want to be the next target. Gemma might not have cared, but I did.

"No." If that wasn't clear enough, I said it a second time. "No!

Do you not care about family honor? Not to mention, we have a business to run, one that's barely keeping afloat." I hammered every syllable. "We can't put our family on the sacrificial altar."

This time, she didn't disagree.

LATER THAT NIGHT, WHILE MY SISTERS SNORED ON EITHER SIDE of me, I couldn't stop thinking about how people hadn't known the real Lulu. She had never been an open book, but I wouldn't have described her as a loner.

One hot afternoon, when the air had felt as wet and dense as if we were wading through warm rice porridge, Lulu remarked, "I'm sweating like a spent racehorse. How do you feel about rehearsing in our drawers?" She'd never been self-conscious about her body, unlike me.

I shrugged. "Acting *is* like peeling off the layers."

She wrestled off her damp dress. Her slip rode up to her stomach, and she pulled it down with a sheepish grin. "We don't have to peel back *all* the layers."

Perhaps not allowing people under the final layer was an act of self-preservation. Had she been lonely? The thought hung on me like a brass weight. I thought she'd been living a dream. But how dreamy could it have been, if it had ended in such a nightmare?

I shifted around, jouncing the mattress. Gemma's breathing didn't even hitch; she was probably dreaming of Clark Gable. I envied her ability to sleep so soundly while my thoughts bounced around like beans in a rolling barrel. I turned my back to her and squeezed my eyes shut, knowing that even in sleep, I wasn't going to get much rest.

THE NEXT DAY, AFTER MEDIOCRE SALES AT CITY MARKET, I lifted the receiver of the wooden wall-mounted telephone in the hallway outside our apartment. As with the bathroom facilities, we were the only ones who used the device. I provided the operator with the Moys' phone number, then perched on a worn stool, riffling through the telephone directory on a side table while I waited. I hoped Wallace answered.

Mrs. Moy's formal voice announced, "Good afternoon. This is the Moy residence. Who is this?"

I clutched wrinkles into my blouse. "Hello, Mrs. Moy. It's May Chow." My voice sounded too high. "How are you?"

"I'm well. And yourself?"

"I'm fine too. I wondered if I might speak with Wallace?"

"Certainly. But, May, it is customary for the man to call first."

I wilted like bluebells on a hot day. "Of course."

"May?" Wallace's clear baritone sounded through the receiver.

"I'm sorry to bother you. But I wondered, could we meet up sometime soon?" I didn't provide a reason in case his mother was listening.

"Ah, so you decided to accept my invitation after all," he said, covering for me without skipping a beat. "How does tomorrow sound?" I swore I could hear him smiling.

After we worked out the details, I returned to our apartment, where Gemma and Peony were readying to do some shopping at One Dragon. I usually did that chore, but Gemma had insisted she go today. Out on the balcony, Ma was whacking a seat cushion with a rug beater.

"Well?" Gemma shook out a shopping bag and cut a glance toward Ma.

Peony squatted atop a stool, buckling her shoes. "Do you have a *date*?" She waggled her thin eyebrows at me, her nose looking extra tweaky.

I sighed. "He's picking me up tomorrow at four."

"Wear the blue dress with the dots." Gemma struck a feminine pose, framing her face with her hands. "And the lipstick."

"We're spying. It's not a real date."

Gemma winked at Peony. "They're going to 'investi-date.'"

The pair left, and I brought our wooden washtub to the balcony, where I filled it with warm water from our kettle. Ma sat heavily on a chair and stuck in her feet. "That feels good," she murmured.

"Wallace and I are going out tomorrow for a drive, if that's okay?"

Her honey-colored irises flickered with surprise. "Yes, okay." She slowly stirred the water with a foot. "Strange. He was in such a hurry to go back to work after our dinner. Still, it is good for one's husband to be industrious. Women should only be pillow generals. How else will the family survive?"

I bit back a response. Wives traditionally advised their husbands only in the private sphere, but that didn't mean we couldn't survive if called to lead.

Ma pulled back the brim of her hat and studied me. "You don't agree."

"We have managed, Ma."

"It is not how it should be. People feel sorry for us. Some say your father fell ill because I have not given him sons."

"Who says that?"

"It does not matter."

"No Good?" The wok seller with his hunched, closed-off posture skulked into my mind.

She clicked her tongue in disapproval. "*Mr. Ng* said the only thing worse than three girls is four girls."

I hissed under my breath. Unlucky four. As the only seller of cooking tools in Chinatown, No Good's words had reach. The man hadn't been so vocal with his disapproval when Ba was here, but clearly his inhibitions were loosening. "Well, Mr. Ng is wrong. We make a good team."

"Maybe this one will be a son." Ma rubbed her belly. "And all will be well."

I bit back my response. Her eyes were closing. Perhaps the baby would be a boy and quiet those doomsayers. If not, hopefully, Ba would be back by then, and—

The faint ringing of the phone caught my ear. Quietly, I slipped out to the hallway, wondering if Wallace was calling to cancel our date.

"Is this my number one cloud?" a familiar hoarse voice asked.

A mixture of relief and concern flooded me. "Ba. You're one day early." He usually called on Sunday evenings.

"Before you worry, I am fine. I am early because they want to try a new treatment tomorrow that might make me drowsy." There was a halting quality to his speech, as if each sentence required an injection of gas to get going. I imagined his wiry form resting in his hospital bed, his head propped against the pillow I'd embroidered with clouds for him.

"What treatment?" I settled onto the stool.

"Pneu-something. Pneu-shoes for the boogie blues?" he joked, always able to pull a smile from me. "Pneumo-peri-toneum," he said finally, every syllable requiring thought. "I sent you a letter to explain it. They have successfully used the treatment on other patients." His assurance had the ring of false cheer.

I rolled the hem of my apron, knowing he kept things from us, the way we kept things from him. Too much excitement could be deadly for someone whose lungs were as delicate as paper bags. "Ma's soaking her feet on the balcony."

"That means she should be asleep by now. Don't wake her. The Mule still cranky?"

"No. I'm not sure why, but she hasn't bucked all week."

"Good, good. What about the other mule, still cranky?"

He didn't have to specify who the other mule was. Ba had mediated more than his share of Gemma's and my arguments over the years, as he did not brook disagreements between us. The son of a concubine, Ba had grown up in a bickering household. When he was sixteen, he left home with a pair of stolen boots and his favorite calligraphy brush and journeyed to America using a birth certificate he'd bought off the black market.

"As ever," I lamented, longing to tell him about our investigation and all the bunco Gemma had cornered me into. Sinking lower onto my stool, I stared at the discolored floor tiles.

"Tell Gemma to watch out for twenty-one down on the crossword puzzle."

"Okay." Gemma and Ba would always do the Sunday crossword together as soon as it hit the stands on Saturday. That was their special thing, just as going for drives was mine and Ba's.

"Any news of the Lulu Wong investigation? I received your letters and read what little news they print on the matter." His tone went rough with disapproval, and I imagined his gentle eyes narrowing. "I cannot help but worry for my family."

"We are fine, Ba, though of course Wong Tai is still in shock. The Yams have been looking in on her."

He grunted. "I have written to Toy Tai, remember her?"

"Yes?" The widow Toy Tai was well known for having three fat sons, meaning she had fed them well.

"She offered to sublet us a room in her house in East Adams."

Move? All the breath left me. We couldn't abandon ship now. That would be like giving up.

"Two of her sons have moved out. They have started families of their own." He cleared his throat, and the reminder that I should be doing the same filled the space between our two ears. "It will be good to have her around when Ma's time comes."

"But Ma's time is soon." Only four weeks away. "Perhaps we should wait until things are more settled."

"It is a burden to live with uncertainty. The railroad decision could vacate us any day. And now, with a murderer loose—" A coughing fit started up.

I stared at a scratch on my arm, a hazard of working with roses. So many forces had conspired to yank us off the stage of Chinatown, but Ba had always resisted. Not only was it home, it was close to the fields where we bought and the markets where we sold. On weekends, Ba loved walking to the river and listening to the trains. He said nowhere else in the world did machines and nature have such interesting conversations.

The cough abated. "Of course, your ma may refuse to move because she thinks that is what *I* want. We all had dreams for the neighborhood. But matters have changed. I have signed the Three Coins proposal. Dai-Sang submitted it to city hall yesterday."

"But you told Ma that Three Coins would buy disaster." Several prominent Chinese businessmen had drawn up the plan for a new Chinese neighborhood. Three coins strung on a red string represented heaven, earth, and mankind, and was thought to attract wealth. But Ba hadn't wanted anything to do with the new plan.

"Yes. I worried that us agreeing to leave Chinatown peacefully did not guarantee the city would honor the agreement, and we would be left with nothing. But with Lulu's death, China-town's image is at its lowest. We must be like bamboo, which knows when to bend so as not to break. We will be left with nothing if we don't bend. For now, May, you must convince your ma to move."

I sucked in my breath, already hearing Ma protest. She would never side against Ba except when it was in his interest. He hadn't wanted to go to the sanatorium, saying our business needed him, but she had insisted.

"Toy Tai expects an answer by Friday," Ba continued. "I must be able to count on you, just in case."

"In case what?" I licked my lips, which had gone dry, as if I had sucked on bitter skullcap. "Does this have to do with the new medicine?"

"Of course not," he said quickly, though I didn't believe him. I pressed my ear to the receiver, as if to hear unspoken words, but all I heard was the rasping of his breath. "We don't know when the wind will shift, only that it will."

In my favorite game, mahjong, each of the four players represented a direction of the wind, with the dealer always being East. But as hands were won or lost, the deal shifted, reminding us that fate was fickle. We had to hold on tight so the things we loved didn't fly away. "Ba, I'm not ready for the wind to shift." My nose had started to run. His leaving had devastated all of us. I could not bear a permanent exit. I dared not even think of it.

"What do I always tell my three fierce clouds?"

"Separately, we can block the wind," I began.

"And together, you can determine its flow." His voice crackled with meaning, but at the moment, I felt helpless to change anything, much less something as important as destiny.

15
GEMMA

A HOT BREEZE SWEPT AROUND PEONY AND ME AS SOON as we exited our building, and I nearly lost my shopping list. I stowed it in the pocket of my blue oxford jumpsuit, which certainly beat skirts in windy weather, and tied my straw hat tighter. Many, not just the Chinese, believed the warm Santa Ana winds that blew down from the San Gabriel Mountains every autumn portended calamity. Once, a whole block burned down after the winds whipped a stove fire into an uncontrollable frenzy.

Peony clutched her own skirts to her, her mouth pursed like a dried goji berry. "While we're at One Dragon, I want to call Hettie Bright," I casually dropped. "Maybe she can get us an audition as Chinese extras."

Peony's eyes grew as big as sunflowers. "Why can't we call her from our phone?"

"Because I don't want May to know yet. Hettie may not be able to get us an audition, and you know how fretty May gets about everything." I held my breath, hating to put Peony in the middle. But what choice did I have? It was the perfect ruse for investigating Lulu's death. They wouldn't wait to fill those roles. The time to act was now.

Peony stuck her braid in her mouth, and her eyes sharpened.

"Only if you let me be part of the investigation. You always leave me behind."

"Didn't you call Bettina this morning? You got some very important information for us." Bettina didn't remember Lulu ever going to Clifford's Steakhouse, which meant I would need to do some additional fieldwork.

"I mean a *real* part, not just when it's convenient."

I sighed. She had a point. May and I dropping out of high school to take over the business left Peony as the main house-keeper, especially now with Ma as big as a house herself. Between school and chores, number three cloud didn't get out much, and with her restless energy, she needed airing most of all. "I'll think about it."

As we approached One Dragon, I caught sight of a truck and a gray Ford Model T, the kind used by city workers, parked by the horse lot. A worker in dungarees was gesturing at the lot while another man listened, crushing a clipboard to his tweed suit. These men certainly weren't detectives. We hadn't seen anyone investigating since the murder.

Peony grabbed my arm. "What are they doing here?"

"Let's find out."

Seeing us draw near, the worker stopped talking. Sweat drib-bled from his forehead to his beard. The man in the tweed suit appraised us, a dark mustache and matching eyebrows pulled up in disapproval.

"Good day, gentlemen," I said. "Are you here to investigate the murder?" May would be tugging my sleeve for my bold intrusion, but Peony stood as straight as a pipe cleaner beside me, her arms crossed and chin up.

"Look at that, she speaks English. We're more in the

mow-down business than the murder business," said the tweed suit, eliciting a chuckle from the worker.

Anger balled in my throat. "*Mow down*? Who gave you permission? This is private property."

"This property is going to be condemned soon, making it more my business than yours."

"But it hasn't been condemned yet," said Peony.

"And we haven't started demolition yet, sweetheart." The tweed suit's patronizing smile struck me like another hot breeze.

The worker swiped an arm across his forehead. "As I was saying, we got more than enough men hungry for the work. They're ready to start as soon as you give the word."

The tweed suit nodded, then wiggled his fingers at us. "Don't you have school or something?"

"It's Saturday," Peony said saucily as I hauled her away.

The dragon statue guarding the entrance to One Dragon eyed us warily as we blazed by into the grocery. Mr. Yam, tapping a pencil at a blank paper, greeted us with the kind of smile that made you glad you stopped by. May said you could tell a lot about a person by how their face aged. Mr. Yam's hinted at a boyhood spent racing frogs and setting off firecrackers past his bedtime, whereas his wife, who was extolling the virtues of bitter melon to a customer, had a scowl that saw rain coming even on a cloudless day.

"Chow daughters, is the devil wind pestering you?" he asked.

"More like those goons outside, looking at the horse lot with their fangs out."

"Ah. Yes, I saw."

"They can't start tearing things down yet, can they?"

He shook his head sadly and took my shopping list from me.

"Many are calling the lot a public nuisance. Lulu's death has stirred the waters."

I shuddered. The eggings were bad enough, but soon they'd be moving us off—first one piece at a time, then all at once. They didn't care about us losing our homes and businesses, or how hard it would be to find new ones. Many of our population were getting older and didn't have the energy or the resources to rebuild, like Mr. Yam, whose joints creaked when he moved. A whole world of sights, smells, and sounds would vanish, and who would miss us? No one. They'd just be glad to see us go.

"Let's see, half a dozen candles, a sack each of cornstarch and millet, dried mushroom, red date, baking soda, two cakes of soap, and a new comb," Mr. Yam read off my list.

I released my shopping bag from my tight grip and set it on the counter. The comb was a splurge at twenty cents, but May's thick hair could use it. "And a tin of beeswax," I added, glancing at Peony's chapped lips. Another fifteen cents.

"Will you need to put this on a tab?" Mr. Yam asked gently.

"No, I have the money." We'd put our tips from the Panny-chis on the ledger, but I had the two extra dollars from Westlake Park that I'd stashed in the potholder. Before he pressed me further, I asked, "Could we make a phone call? Our phone has a bad connection."

"Sorry to hear this." Mr. Yam shook his head, probably chalking our faulty line up to the crumbling state of Chinatown. "Maybe I can take a look at it so you can talk with your ba."

"Oh, don't trouble yourself. It's just . . . temperamental." Hastily, I passed Peony my coin purse, then brought the phone to the far end of the counter, where a busted wooden drawer that didn't match the Yams' built-in counters had been set. The hole in the Yams' ceiling seemed to be growing every day and was now the size of a winter melon. That was a problem of the real variety, and no one would be coming to fix it, ever.

Shaking loose my neck, I gave the operator the number I had stolen from May's purse. Moments later, she was connecting me to Hettie Bright's residence.

The phone rang seven times, and I worried the operator would disconnect us. I ran a finger along the misplaced drawer, whose yellow paint was smeared with something brown, like sauce. Finally, a woman with a familiar smoky voice answered. "Hello?"

"Hello, er, Miss Bright?"

"Er, yes. Who is this?"

I tried not to be too starstruck that the voice in my ear was the one I'd heard in many a movie palace. "It's Gemma Chow. I believe you met my sister May Chow last night."

"Oh, yes. May said you two were looking into Lulu's death."

She projected her words, and I was sure everyone could hear through the receiver. I glanced behind me. While Mr. Yam gathered purchases from the shelves, Mrs. Yam weighed bitter melons on the counter scale.

I lowered my voice, hoping I didn't sound like some fanatical heavy breather. "Yes. I'm sorry for my bold request, but I wondered if you could get us an audition for *A Far East Affair* as extras."

"An . . . audition?"

A nervous laugh escaped me. "Yes." Of course, now she thinks we're social-climbing pariahs. "Joining the cast might help us see what life was like for Lulu in the weeks before she"—I lowered my voice to a whisper—"died."

"Hm." Her voice turned thoughtful. "Actually, they rehired those extras."

"Oh." The word thudded like a wet newspaper.

"We only just started principal shooting, and Emil wants to finish by December. But . . ." Hettie began making a series of musical sounds that people sometimes made when they were thinking.

Suddenly the room seemed too quiet. Mrs. Yam was staring at me from the droopy folds of her knitted cap, her customer having left. Peony cleared her throat loudly. "How is your arthritis, Mrs. Yam?"

At the mention of her ailment, Mrs. Yam returned her attention to Peony. *Good thinking, sister.* Mrs. Yam never shied away from talking about her affliction.

"Emil did mention he needed someone to read lines," said Hettie. "They usually hire people through the agency, but I bet I could get Emil to audition you. I'm annoyed at him for pushing us so hard even after what happened with Lulu." She sighed. "Come at three o'clock Monday to Capsize Pictures. Don't go to Casting, but head direct to Building Four. Ask for Jack."

Bubbles of excitement fizzed through me. *Be calm, not fanatical.* "Thank you. We really appreciate it."

After hanging up, I turned around, and now both Mr. and Mrs. Yam were focused on me. Peony gave me a helpless shrug.

"Were you talking about Lulu?" asked Mrs. Yam, who considered our business her business. At times, it was a comfort, but other times, it rubbed me like static electricity.

"She's been on all of our minds," I said vaguely.

Mrs. Yam grabbed a broom and began sweeping at the grit that had collected around the wooden barricade, including a nut-sized chunk of plaster. "Shame about the autopsy report."

Peony gasped. "Autopsy report?"

The broom stopped. "We visited Wong Tai last night. Mr. Yam

wanted to fix her drawer." She nodded to the odd piece on the counter.

I glanced at the broken drawer, remembering how Mr. Yam had offered to repair it for Lulu's grieving mother. My breath had stopped flowing, and I forced myself to draw in air. "So what did the report say?"

"Lulu died of a heart attack, but of course, Wong Tai still doesn't believe it's Lulu."

"Heart attack," I mumbled, disbelieving. Heart attacks were what happened to old people and didn't seem to offer any clues as to how or where she was killed, or who killed her. It was a dead end to a crooked alley. "What did the report say about the head injury? The blood on her sleeve?"

Mr. Yam wound string around our six tapered candles. "I'm not sure. She burned it." His lips smacked, as if trying to rid themselves of a bitter flavor. "The coroner's office keeps the record, but only family can request it." Mr. Yam pulled a crinkled paper from under the counter and slipped on a pair of glasses. "I'm starting a petition for a second opinion on the heart attack. The people want answers."

Peony stretched closer to the paper. "Will that change things?"

"Maybe not, but we will have our say."

The brown smear on the drawer came into focus, located right on the corner. Was it blood? I recoiled, my arms breaking out in gooseflesh. That sharp point could break skin if someone fell against it. "Mr. Yam," I said, trying to keep my voice even, "I wouldn't fix Wong Tai's drawer just yet."

16
GEMMA

THE WIND WAS STILL WHIPPING US SIDEWAYS BY THE TIME
we set off for home. "If that brown smear is Lulu's blood, then
she might've been killed in the kitchen. Too bad we don't know
anyone at the coroner's office who could get us a peek at that
report."

Peony dabbed beeswax on her frown. "Family members can
request a copy."

"But Wong Tai burned hers. What makes you think we can
get her to request— Why are you smiling like that?"

"Bettina's a family member."

"She's a child."

"They might not know that. You could be Bettina. The papers
said 'younger sister.'"

I nearly tripped into a pothole. "You just struck me with lightning, little sister. But let's not tell May yet either. She's going to
pop when she hears about the audition. One thing at a time."

"Only if you take me with you to the coroner's office."

I began to protest, but an annoyed sigh poured from Peony's
body.

"It's not fair. I know the most about investigating, and you
haven't taken me anywhere yet."

My thoughts sailed around in many directions. If Lulu *had*

been injured in her kitchen, could she still have driven herself to the horse lot? Or had someone driven her there? Guitar Man claimed to have seen her Cadillac being driven by a white demon a couple hours after sunset, though he was unreliable. And why was her car found in the Mercantile lot? We still had a lot of ground to cover.

"Alright, Peony. I can't take you to the coroner's office because the paper said one sister, not two, and it would just look suspicious. But how would you like to investigate the old Mercantile lot with me?" The derelict property was littered with miscellaneous junk, and it would be a long shot to find any clues, but we might as well be thorough.

"I guess," she grumbled, though she started to bounce.

After dropping off our purchases at home, we loaded into the Mule. Soon enough, we were slowly rolling by Cash Louie's famous eatery, Fragrant Bamboo, with its fan palms whipping around like they were doing the hoochie-coochie dance. It was too early for the dramatic fire lanterns on either side of its entrance to be lit, but two workers in caps were hard at work scrubbing its brick walls of . . . graffiti?

"*We hate you dev—*" Peony read. The back half of the sentence had already been rubbed out.

"Deviled eggs," I quickly filled in. "*We hate you deviled eggs!*" I said with mock vehemence and a hillbilly accent. "When did Cash start serving those?"

Peony had twisted around in her seat, still watching the workers. "They broke the roof too."

Somehow, the decorative tiles on the pagoda roof had cracked off. I dropped my attempt to make light of the situation. Peony was no longer a child. Pretending would only frustrate her. It was like the time Dai-Sang's wife, who always gave us haw candy, died, and the herbalist told us she had gone on a trip. We waited for years for her to return, until we realized the trip was permanent.

Fixing a roof was costlier than cleaning up an egging. Cash Louie had told the police that Lulu Wong hadn't come into the restaurant the night she was murdered, but that didn't mean he wouldn't be made to pay. Fragrant Bamboo was the most visible gem in Chinatown. Defacing it was bad for all the businesses here.

We turned into an uneven alley, where I managed to kill the engine just outside the Mercantile lot. High fences on both sides of the entrance blocked the area from view of its neighbors across the alley.

Sliding out of the Mule, we crept cautiously into the lot, which today was empty of motor vehicles. It had once been the receiving area for an old general store, which had long ago burned down. No one had wanted to rebuild because the owner's wife and child had died in the fire, and it was said that their hungry spirits still haunted the charred remains.

Peony clutched my hand, her wide eyes both apprehensive and curious. Minus the junk, the lot could fit at least five vehicles. The paving stones had been artfully arranged, a hint of its more dignified past.

A broken shutter clapped erratically in the wind. Even without the wind, this place wound all my joints tighter. Little kids came here on dares, and the bigger ones to smoke cigarettes. No one ever stayed for long, lest a hungry ghost follow them home.

Was this where Lulu had met her end? If so, what a dismal last peek at the world—an empty gasoline tank, a broken toilet, and other discarded and forgotten things. On the day when I take my last bow, please let it not be to a toilet.

After nothing jumped out at us, Peony let go of my hand and nosed around the junk piles, while I studied the paving stones for anything that would shed light on Lulu's murder. Skid marks slashed the ground in no particular order, and I couldn't tell which might've belonged to Lulu's Cadillac. There were no tell-tale footprints or blood spatter.

Glancing around, a glint from the property across the alley slashed my eyes. A pockmarked concrete wall shielded the view of a stucco building. On the upper level, a face appeared to be watching us through a dirt-streaked window. I squinted, trying to make out the features.

"What are you looking at?" Peony came up beside me, rubbing her fingers on her skirt.

When I stretched my gaze to the window again, the face had vanished. "I think I saw a girl up there." With a full view of the Mercantile lot, she might have noticed someone leaving a Cadillac as red as Hettie Bright's hair. "Let's ask if anyone saw something."

Peony and I hiked down the alley to the front of the dingy stucco building. Three units featured storefronts, with living quarters above, though they all appeared to be closed this late.

The unit with the window facing the Mercantile lot featured a rusty sign for LOW LADDERS, written in Chinese and English. *Low* referred to the surname of the proprietor, but it probably confused people who didn't read Chinese. No one wanted a low ladder. Another sign said, WE DO NOT SELL PAINT. DON'T ASK.

"Well, that just makes me want to ask." I grinned at Peony, whose whole face had pinched into a frown. The front of her cotton dress was dirty, and her braid had come undone.

I knocked. Another gust swiped at us, and Peony grabbed her skirts. Inside the shop, a man with a square face pushed back a curtain and scowled. "We are closed!" he grunted in Cantonese through the window glass. "Go home."

"We're sorry to bother you, sir," I called loudly. "I'm Gemma, and this is my sister Peony, daughters of Chow Wing."

His face remained tucked in a scowl, his gray eyes not quite focusing on either Peony or myself. The curtain yanked shut.

Peony's sharp shoulders lifted. "He's not very nice."

I raised my fist and knocked again. "Please, we just have a few questions!" I counted to five and knocked again.

The door popped open, and the scent of wood shavings and cooking oil drifted to my nose. "Winds blow trouble to my doorstep," barked the square face. His thick arms gestured dismissively. "Go away, before I get my broom."

Before he could fetch the broom, by which I supposed he meant to sweep us away, I said, "Mr. Low, you must have heard that Lulu Wong, the film star, was murdered last week."

The man's face did not change. "Don't know her. But if she was a film star, she was asking for trouble to blow her way too. Proper girls stay at home and do what they are told."

Peony crossed her arms, her gaze creeping to a horse made from red paper dangling from the ceiling above him.

"Be that as it may, Lulu's car was found last Wednesday in the Mercantile lot, a red Cadillac. We noticed your window has a view of the lot and wondered if you had seen it."

"What are you, detectives?"

"I can see how you might make that mistake," I muttered, glancing pointedly at Peony's schoolgirlish dress. "However, we are simply concerned citizens, hoping to find answers—"

"You won't find them here. Now, do I have to get my broom, or will you leave?"

"We'll take the latter. Get it? Ladder?"

He shut the door with a crack.

"Someone needs a cheer bucket," I muttered, setting off toward the lot again. Peony hurried after me. "Don't ever marry a ladder maker, Peony. Too many ups and downs." She hardly seemed to hear, instead looking distractedly behind her. Tough crowd today. "Bah, don't mind that old crab. Say, why are you smiling like that?"

"Because lightning has struck twice today. We made those paper horses in class. I know who you saw in the window."

17
MAY

WALLACE AND I MOTORED DOWN SUNSET IN HIS TOURING Chrysler, the bright orange sky nearly blinding. A leather jacket over a cotton knit shirt and tan trousers looked casually elegant, like he'd made an effort without trying hard. The same could be said of his driving, his right hand atop the wheel, his left arm resting on his open window. Sure, we were playacting at a romantic date. But if we weren't following a potential murder suspect, I might actually enjoy this particular stage just a little.

Wallace caught me looking at him, and I averted my eyes.

"I like the comb," he said of the mother-of-pearl heirloom Ma had carefully worked into my curls.

"Thank you," I said, wondering if it was a pretend-compliment. I had known the boy Wallace to be an annoying prankster, but who was the man? Still a rascal or genuine?

He donned a pair of sunglasses. "So why is this Mr. Stritch a suspect?"

"Bettina overheard him tell Lulu she was asking for a war that would bring both of them down. We think the war was over her wanting to be a heroine instead of a villain. Maybe Mr. Stritch killed Lulu to protect his reputation. Not to mention, he conveniently represented the actress who replaced her, which meant he got paid twice for filling the same role."

Wallace whistled. "They say it's the crocodile you don't see that you need to worry about. But how does knowing who bought Lulu's car help?"

"It's a rare car, and now one with sensational value. We want to see who Mr. Stritch is scheming with, and how much heavier his wallet is getting."

He slowed to avoid a branch in the middle of the road, checking his mirror and going around it. I did admire good driving. "Lulu and I were in the same class, you know, until we moved to Pasadena."

"Were you friends?"

"She'd sometimes play ball with our gang in the horse lot. Guitar Man taught her a killer swing."

I smiled, remembering how all the kids used to love it when Guitar Man pitched. Lulu had always moved with a graceful physicality. Once, she took a dramatic tumble off the bed, pretending to be an ape. I swore she had injured herself, but she popped up, tickling her chin with her fingers, just like an ape would do. A girl like that wouldn't have gone down easily. She would've put up a struggle. But her body had looked relatively unmolested. Either she had known her attacker, or he had caught her off guard.

"After we moved, I didn't see her again until *Midnight Murderess* came out. I remember thinking, how did this baseball bat of a girl fill that entire screen?"

The landscape became a blur of green and brown. When Gemma and I saw the movie, every time Lulu came on, the audience became a bed of coils, ready to spring if she said "Boo!" But we'd been bursting with pride. For Chinatown girls, Lulu Wong had shown us a way out. She didn't need a man to give her status or make her way. The irony that she had been killed just when she was on the precipice of becoming something more, maybe even America's sweetheart, put a fresh ache in my heart. "Hollywood's best villain was Chinatown's favorite heroine," I murmured.

"Indeed. So what will your family do when they build Union Station?"

I sat up primly. "*If* they build Union Station." Toy Tai's offer to sublet her East Adams home inserted itself in my mind.

"That's shaking your fist at a storm." He glanced at me now sitting tightly beside him, squeezing wrinkles into my freshly ironed blue dotted dress. "Oh, I seem to have offended you."

"Of course not." I tried to affect a casualness I did not feel. "We are not really dating. You need not hold back your true feeling."

"Okay. Well, what is your true feeling?"

"That those of us who actually live in Chinatown don't have the luxury of giving up hope so easily." I tossed back my curls, feeling my comb slip free. I caught it before it fell but didn't bother to work it back into place. What was the point? There was no one who needed impressing here. I slipped it into my purse and tied my hair back into a simple knot, fixed into place with a couple of pins.

"I think that's being foolish. 'A man who does not plan long ahead will find trouble right at his door.' Confucius said that."

"He also said, 'The strength of a nation derives from the integrity of the home.'"

A laugh spilled out of him. "I like our pretend-dating. It's refreshing to be with a girl who doesn't worry about . . . perception."

"Has that been a problem for you in the past?" Perhaps he was still a rascal.

"Sure. I once took a girl out for a hamburger. She ate two bites, then said she was full."

"Would you have looked at her differently if she had eaten the whole thing?"

"I would've been grateful if I didn't have to eat hers too. I had bad heartburn after that."

He looked so queasy that I had to smile, even though I was still sore about the "shaking my fist at a storm" comment. But as I stared down at a clock on the dash, I realized what bothered me most wasn't his remark, but that he could be right. Ma had said it herself. *The train station may be coming soon. Plans must be made.* We hadn't intended to abandon ship before the storm was over, but it was folly to ignore a lifeboat drifting by.

We drew up to Lulu's neighborhood, with its trim myrtle trees and bespoke houses, neatly arranged like stylish clothes in a wardrobe. "Turn there. That's her house." I pointed to the brick-red stucco cottage. "Park on the other side so no one sees us."

Wallace parked in the shade of an aspen tree a few houses down and cracked the window. "Nice neighborhood. If I had known we were doing a stakeout, I would've brought newspapers."

"The garage is opening." Cole Stritch was ahead of schedule. "Quick, duck!" It would take too long to crank down the seats, so I collapsed myself the only way I could go—to the middle, with Wallace folding himself on top of me.

"I doubt this is how the professional gumshoes do it," he gasped.

A giggle snorted out, and I began to sweat with the effort of holding myself together. His face was planted in my backside, and I could feel his damp laughter blowing in and out. How could I ever face him after this?

A knock came on the window. With a gasp, I sat up, pushing Wallace up too. A woman wearing a yellow dress was glaring at me, her sagging bottom eyelids rimmed pink. Yapping started up from the sidewalk, and I noticed a scrappy bundle of brown fur pulling at the woman's leash.

"This is a respectable neighborhood," she said through the glass. "You fornicators better leave before I call the police."

I could feel myself flush, probably a deep shade of purple. "We weren't— I mean—"

The garage door had rolled completely open, giving us a view of the back of Lulu's red Cadillac. I didn't see Wong Tai or Mr. Stritch, but surely any minute he would pop out and see us.

"Say, you're the girl we saw at Lulu Wong's house that day she was killed."

"M-me?" I stammered. "No—"

Wallace reached over and rolled down my passenger window. "You saw someone visit her that day?"

"Yes. Her, carrying her basket." The woman pointed at me. "Same black hair tied in a knot like that. Thin like you—you're about five and a half feet, right?"

"Yes, but—"

Wallace coughed out a derisive laugh. "It wasn't her."

"What did she have in the basket?" I asked.

The woman lifted a haughty chin. "I don't need to answer your questions."

"Maybe she doesn't remember," said Wallace, somehow taking a page from Gemma's method of interrogation. It felt nice to team up, like sharing a deep secret.

"I certainly do." The woman's nose twitched like a mouse. "Oranges. Enoch didn't like her either." Her mutt barked. "Ripped the hem off her dress."

"What a charmer," Wallace remarked.

"That black dress was only fit for a funeral, in my opinion. To wear such a thing in this neighborhood too!"

"Did you call the police?" I asked.

"Why should I involve myself with police matters?"

I didn't point out how she had threatened to call the police on us. "What time was this?"

"I *always* walk Enoch at four." A frenzy of yapping followed.

Lulu's Cadillac—a convertible four-seater with the top rolled down—had begun to back out of the garage. I put a hand to my forehead, trying to hide my face. Cole Stritch was in the driver's seat, his thick head fitted with his trilby hat. He eased out of the driveway, and I prayed he wouldn't look our direction.

He muscled the Cadillac off.

Wallace started up the engine. "Nice chatting, ma'am," he said before pulling away from the curb. The woman's mouth drew apart, but I didn't spend any more eye currency on her. "That was helpful. We should fornicate more often." He pumped an eyebrow at me.

"Very funny. Drive. He's getting away."

Five hundred feet ahead of us, the Cadillac slipped around the corner. Wallace caught up, discreetly tailing the Cadillac up Highland and into the rugged hillsides of Cahuenga Pass.

If the neighbor had seen a Chinese girl, had it been one of the extras? Bettina said someone had been harassing her at the studio. If this visitor had killed Lulu, had she then driven Lulu to the horse stables?

"Our man has a heavy foot," said Wallace. "But that's a sweet ride."

"Cadillac V-16. Wong Tai said Cadillac gave it to Lulu."

"Nothing's free. I bet their sales went up after she started driving it around."

The Cadillac sliced in and out of traffic, going at least fifty miles an hour, despite the incline. Straggly eucalyptus trees dotted the hills, eyeing the telephone poles as if fearing that might be their fate too. That was progress, wasn't it? It didn't matter that the trees had lives. If the city wanted them to clear out, they had to go.

Cole Stritch held up a cigarette and let the wind blow away the ash.

"The only thing up here's the Hollywood Bowl," said Wallace. The famed outdoor amphitheater must be having a concert tonight with all the traffic.

Soon, a sign that said HOLLYWOOD BOWL PARKING, 25 CENTS came into view. To my surprise, the Cadillac followed the other cars into the lot.

Wallace pulled to the side of the road. Leaning one arm on the wheel, he raised his sunglasses, revealing eyes drawn in cynicism. "Either his buyer is a fan of the symphony, or your Mr. Stritch just helped himself to Lulu's car."

18

GEMMA

WHILE WALLACE GALLIVANTED MY PRIM SISTER ABOUT town, I drove to Clifford's Steakhouse for a date with the bold Lady Curious—myself. The brick building was crawling with ivy and offered no glimpse into its mysterious interiors. I'd always wanted to take a peek-see into the romantic den, imagining a dimly lit grotto where half-robed lovers fed each other oysters.

A warm gust fought me as I opened the heavy oak door. To my dismay, the eatery was less bordello and more business. White tablecloths topped cozy tables, on which servers were setting silverware and arranging salt and pepper shakers. Since it was barely four thirty, the lights were turned high, and no candles had yet been lit. A piano sat at the foot of a grand staircase with a plush carpet runner. Atop the piano lay a glass bowl filled with green matchbooks.

"May I help you?" asked a man in a tuxedo from behind a mahogany podium. With his crew cut hairstyle and an erect stance, he could've been military before his turn as maître d'. His fin of an Adam's apple levered as he inspected my plain figure. I had chosen to wear my gray dress, a color that could never be accused of cheekiness or high jinks, though the wool was making me sweat.

"Hello," I said in a demure voice. "I am Bettina Wong, sister of the late Lulu Wong."

The posture shifted, as if he'd gone into parade rest. "I see. I am sorry for your loss."

I dipped my head gratefully. "Thank you. You see, my mother and I were trying to get a clearer picture of her life, and as she is no longer here to ask, I wondered if I might trouble you for some information."

"What kind of information?"

"We found one of your restaurant's matchbooks in her purse. Do you remember her dining here?"

"No, and I would remember the Midnight Murderess. I saw the movie twice." He cleared his throat as if he'd revealed too much. "Mr. Joust would know for certain, but he is presently in an important meeting." He glanced behind him and up the plush staircase.

An open floor design gave a view of a dozen tables set far apart for privacy. All were empty save one, at which two men conversed. I jerked back as I recognized Philippe Fox with his dark locks and glib smile. Next to him, a thin man with a trim white beard and neat appearance listened to Philippe speak with slow nods of his head. Neither were eating. That must be Clifford Joust, one of the richest men in Los Angeles. And if Mr. Joust was in an important meeting with political candidate Philippe Fox, the spawn of Chinatown enemy number one, I knew which side of the tracks Mr. Joust was standing on, and it wasn't the side of Chinatown.

"I could have him call you, if you'll leave your card," the maître d' was saying.

As if feeling my anger, Mr. Joust glanced down the staircase, and spotting me, his eyes pushed into me like thumbtacks.

Nearly swallowing my tongue, I stepped to one side, putting the maître d' between us. Mr. Joust didn't know me, and I certainly didn't want him to remember me. Men with both power and money were a dangerous species, the kind of men who got away with murder.

"That's alright," I told the maître d'. "You've been most helpful. Thank you."

With my heart knocking about in my chest, I hurried back to the Mule. Lulu wouldn't have patronized a place that catered to Chinese haters. Executing a clumsy U-turn that nearly took out a telephone pole, I beat a hasty retreat.

SNUG IN OUR BEDS, I RECOUNTED FOR MY SISTERS MY VISIT TO Clifford's. On the small bed, Peony was tossing up her basketball again. Next to me, May rubbed beeswax into her cuticles. "So how'd Lulu get the matchbook?" May asked.

"Maybe someone gave it to her," I said.

"But she didn't smoke."

"I don't know, May, maybe she liked setting things on fire."

She lidded the tin and appraised me with her big eyes. "If I'd realized I'd gotten into bed with a snapping turtle, I would have brought a stick."

I don't know why I was feeling so testy. Maybe it was because my efforts today had borne no fruit for our investigation, save to remind us of the inevitability of Chinatown's downfall. Had I been too skittish? Should I have stayed and confronted Mr. Joust and Philippe Fox? They couldn't have hurt me in full view of the waitstaff, could they?

Then again, the servers worked for Mr. Joust, so if he'd told them to dump the mouthy broad in the river, they probably would've done it.

Maybe it was simply our snail's progress getting the best of me. Ba often joked I would make a terrible fisherman because I had no patience, but I'd be a great dogcatcher. "I just wish we could hurry things up."

May tugged her pillow straight with quick pulls. "At least we learned about the Chinese girl who visited Lulu."

"That's not great news either. Finding out a Chinese girl did it would be like Miss Marple finding out the murderer was her daughter—"

"Miss Marple didn't have children," Peony chimed, spinning her ball on her finger.

"It would be like stomping us out with our own boots. All the Chinese haters would gloat, oh, how they would. They'd build Union Station so fast, they'd probably catch a few of us under the tracks as we were fleeing. Maybe they'd even make us build it, like we built the Transcontinental—"

"Even if Lulu didn't go to Clifford's, she still could've had a secret love." May fit her head onto her pillow and ignored my ranting. "I think we should forget about the green matchbook for now and concentrate on the earrings."

"Bettina said she's bringing the earring box tomorrow." Peony, also ignoring me, wiped her hands on a damp cloth, then drew the curtain.

I sighed. Nothing like sisterly rain to douse the flames of the pity party.

My own head hit the pillow. Tomorrow, I would be fearless to make up for today. We had an audition to nail and mandarins to squeeze. *Tomorrow, you just wait.*

19
MAY

THE SANTA ANA WINDS STALKED US INTO THE NEXT DAY,
playing tricks on us, like blowing our flowers into other stalls.
Even the beggars who roamed City Market for the rotted produce had taken shelter elsewhere. An especially large gust blew
our copy of the *Observer First* skyward. I groaned. There had
been no report on Lulu's "heart attack" anyway.

A neighboring vendor's barrel blew over, dispersing corn silk
all over our display. I got to work pincering fibers from the flowers, as if restoring order to my surroundings would fix the mess
in my head. Ma had written a long letter to Ba last night after I'd
come home from my pretend-date, and I hated getting her hopes
up over Wallace, even if it was for a good cause. And without
more information about Lulu's murder, we were trying to catch
papers in the wind.

Gemma returned from talking to Mr. Takashi, holding her
hat to her head. She had rolled up the sleeves of her navy blouse,
not caring about the sun browning her arms. "He guesses it was a
satsuma mandarin. He'll ask around." She batted me away from
the gladiolas. "I'll clean them. You must be tired. I know you
didn't sleep well last night. You kicked me in the shins, twice."

I stretched back my fingers. When Gemma had shaken me
awake this morning, my eyes had been filled with tears.

"By the way," Gemma chattered on, "I think you were right about getting the Mule's engine checked. I made an appointment with Moses this afternoon."

"Good." She was being awfully helpful this morning, doing the lion's share of the trimming and taking over tedious tasks like dethorning the roses, when I knew she'd rather be moving her mouth than her arms. "What have you done this time?"

She rolled the corn silk into a ball and chucked it into our waste bin. The veil of innocence she'd been wearing all morning blew free. "Fine. Hettie Bright got us an audition to be line-readers, today at three."

So she had gone behind my back. Even after I had told her no. Twice. "So you don't care about family honor. Or our livelihood. Or our *being alive*." I swore the closest flowers wilted a little.

"I know you don't approve." Gemma stepped out of pinching distance and began packing up our unsold flowers. "But a peek at Lulu's work environment might give us information, access to people who need questioning. Like those Chinese extras. And there's safety in numbers."

I took a deep breath. I managed to sound calm, even aloof. "Perfect. You run off to Hollywood. I have a business to run." We still had to find a grower to replace Angel, and what if they charged us more? Worse, what if our remaining growers started closing shop as well? Plus, I had to get started on those diapers for the baby and soap the window frames. I shook my head, as if to shake off the worry woodpecker jabbing at it. "Good luck."

Make-Me-a-Deal glanced over, his scarred ex-boxer's face crimping.

"The business can wait, especially if we—"

"Don't you dare say 'Westlake Park.' "

"You admired that idea, and one day you'll admit it. At least come with me. You don't have to audition. Who knows what morsels the wind will blow to our doorstep?" She snatched a loose page of newspaper out of the air, then wadded it up. "We just have to be prepared to catch them if something good flies by."

I didn't point out that the same wind that gives can also take away. Instead, I maintained a stony silence as we hauled our goods back to Chinatown, both to punish Gemma, and also because Toy Tai's offer to sublet weighed heavily on me. I wish Ba hadn't put me in this situation. It was too big for me, like a truck that was too big to steer.

We made quick work of refilling the cheer buckets in the Garnier Building, though all the cheer had drained out of my bucket. At least business had picked up at Mr. King's Emporium.

Gemma sharply inhaled, her eyes affixed to a sign that read: CLOSE-OUT SALE. People exited the store, their arms full of goods like colorful baskets and little tambourines.

I groaned softly. The wind had taken again, hollowing a soft place inside me. The news would fall hard on Ba. Like One Dragon, Mr. King's Emporium was one of the last petals still clinging to the bloom that was Chinatown. How many petals can a flower lose before it stops being a flower? Before everything withers away and only the memory remains?

No Good's wok shop was also closed, though he had hung a BE BACK SOON sign on his door.

I drove us home, slowing at the sight of a black police cruiser parked in the middle of the street, just outside Dai-Sang's store. Detective Mallady stood at the front of the cruiser, sparring with our neighbors, who yelled back both in Cantonese and English. Ba always said trouble travels in packs like coyotes. What new problem had begun to bark?

"Ridiculous!" railed one bricklayer in Cantonese. "He is as dense as a water chestnut, but he would not hurt Lulu Wong!"

As I tried to make sense of what was going on, Gemma pointed at the cruiser. "Look!"

Guitar Man was sitting in the back seat.

20
GEMMA

MAY PARKED THE MULE AT A CROOKED ANGLE ACROSS from where Detective Mallady and Officer Kidd were arresting Gee Fa for murder. With righteous indignation coursing through my veins, I jumped out of the truck before May could straighten it. To my surprise, she left it crooked, then hurried after me to where the men had gathered, including the herbalist and Mr. Yam.

Dai-Sang shoveled his long hands toward the detective. "This is an outrage! He has done nothing wrong."

"The city just wants to sweep us out of Chinatown as fast as possible," growled a bricklayer, looking toward the horse lot, which was still intact, despite the recent visit by city officials.

Mr. Yam twisted his cap. His brown arms under his neatly rolled sleeves were spotted with age. "You cannot just take him. We have rights too."

I marched up to Detective Mallady, close enough to yank his wide tie. "What evidence do you have?"

The man pushed his porkpie hat up on his forehead, his lips pursing. "Not you again."

"You should be questioning people with real motives and not abducting innocent citizens," I said, jabbing a finger at Detective Mallady's peanut nose. "Gee Fa couldn't hurt a fly."

Officer Kidd stood outside the open back door of the cruiser, engaging in a tug-of-war with Gee Fa over the guitar case. Gee Fa's arms used to be strong when he'd played baseball with the schoolkids, but he hadn't done that in years.

"No take," Gee Fa protested in his broken English. "Lulu was friend. My friend."

Mallady sneered. "Not that I owe anyone an explanation, but an anonymous tipster says Gee Fa saw Lulu's car the night of her murder. We're just going to ask him questions."

Dai-Sang's face grew long, and he cast Mr. Yam a dark look. I knew what they were thinking. Gee Fa would readily admit to seeing Lulu's car that night. What else would he "admit"? It would be easy to hang a murder on him. Once they had a suspect, they'd have no reason to investigate further, and the real killer would get away scot-free.

Gee Fa gave the guitar case a final desperate yank, but losing his grip, he fell backward into the seat. Before he could get up again, Officer Kidd quickly closed the door.

I glared at him. "That is not yours. You can't just take it."

The colorless strip of his mouth buckled, as if finding me distasteful. Avoiding my gaze, he popped open the trunk. "We're stowing it for safety. Police procedure, ma'am."

"Detective, Gee Fa is not fit to be questioned," May said, the reasonable tone she usually used as my foil sounding more anxious than normal. "He barely knows what day it is."

Gee Fa poked his head out the window. "It is Monday, Chow's daughter."

Detective Mallady barked out a laugh. "Sounds fit enough to me."

"You should at least let us come and help translate," I said. "He doesn't know all the words! How do you expect him to answer your questions without knowing all the words?" My sentences spilled over each other, hot with indignation.

"If we have problems, we'll call you." The detective gave me a greasy smile, then heaved his bulk into the passenger seat. With a crank of the siren, they stole Guitar Man away.

After a stunned silence, everyone left behind began talking at once.

"Who will speak for him?"

"He has no family. No lawyer."

"The police want to blame Lulu's murder on one of us! They cannot be trusted."

While Mr. Yam and Dai-Sang tried to come up with names of lawyers or at least names of people who might know lawyers, a man appeared at the edge of the crowd. It was No Good, his long black mustache frowning down to his chin. A protruding belly under slate trousers and a matching mandarin jacket gave him the look of a blade, slicing toward us.

One of the bricklayers spat on the sidewalk. "It is this wind. It has blown bad luck on Chinatown."

No Good appraised May and tsked. "Bad luck, indeed," he oozed, glancing at me stamping my feet behind her. "Chow girls, how is your mother?"

I lifted my chin, itching for a fight. "She is very well, Mr. Ng."

Some of the men stared at us with uncertainty, but Mr. Yam shook his head. "These are good girls. Go back to your shop, old man."

No Good curled his mustache around his finger. "Let us hope the child she carries is a boy. Four girls would doom Chinatown for sure."

Something coiling inside me sprang loose. Balling my fists, I barreled toward the man, ready to inflict damage. *I don't know about Chinatown, but this girl is going to doom you.* His beady eyes widened.

Just before I punched the wok seller in the nose, May grabbed me, swinging me around. "It's time to be getting home, sister," she said between her clenched teeth.

I struggled against her, but her surprisingly strong arms held me tight. "Maybe it is all those cleavers you hang in the window, cutting Chinatown's luck to shreds," I spat at the man.

No Good's body went rigid, but he only smacked his lips. "Without their father, the girls have developed too much yang energy. It was the same way with Lulu Wong, and now we will all pay for it."

21
MAY

MY NECK CRACKED AS I GAZED UP AT THE ARCHWAY OF Capsize Pictures, which rose high enough to let a train through. The word *Capsize* spanned the arch, a sunburst cresting off the top. Gemma stared up with me, no trace of anger left from her dustup with No Good. She released her anger in fits and spurts. I was more the slow-burn type, though my indignation could burn just as hot.

Gee Fa's abduction had been the final indignity. Solving Lulu's murder might never absolve me from neglecting my friend, nor save Chinatown. But it wasn't just Chinatown at stake anymore. It was Gee Fa, a man who had no use for politics or train stations, who would rather smell a flower than worry about his next meal. The possibility that the lowest among us might take the fall for the murder of Lulu Wong, she who had risen the highest, was a double crime that I could not let stand. Family honor would have to take a back seat during what I hoped would be a short ride through Hollywoodland.

We passed through a set of wrought-iron gates, and I was surprised to see a courtyard full of men and women of all ages gathered around a door marked CASTING. Some wore their Sunday best, but most were shabbily outfitted. One poor soul was even wearing cardboard shoes. I averted my eyes, feeling sick and also fortunate at the same time.

Gemma yanked me from where I had rooted and led me toward a series of numbered buildings. Dense bushes with tops flat enough to play mahjong on lined a brick pathway. People in business attire cast us curious looks. I was glad I had insisted on ironing our cotton tea dresses before we went out for our pretend meeting with a customer, an excuse Ma had accepted with a tired nod. Not paying attention to details like a crisp collar might have us mistaken for another kind of girl.

At a building marked 4, a heavy metal door led to a suite of offices, where we were met by a tall young man with a crop of longish brown hair. He appraised us with heavy-lidded eyes that drew in the world without giving much back, underscored by faint purple shadows that indicated someone who stayed up too late, either making merry or worrying excessively. His skin was so pale, it was almost translucent. "I'm Jack Lyman, Emil's assistant."

Emil Serège was the director. Hettie had sent us right to the top.

"I'll take you to see him," Jack continued. "He's in the archives." The man had a quiet way of talking, as if he preferred the listening end of the conversation. I didn't think Jack was the sort of man Lulu would've been attracted to. She'd always seemed more taken by the everyman's hero, like Douglas Fairbanks, than the mysterious stranger who met you on a moonlit bridge, like Rudolph Valentino.

We followed him down a hallway with gold light fixtures and wood-framed windows offering peeks into offices. A door swung open, letting out a swath of people, some in suits, some in costume. How did Gemma expect to find clues in this jungle?

"Any tips for nailing this audition?" she asked Jack.

He flipped back his hair, showing ink stains on the sleeve of his yellow shirt. "Whatever you do, don't tell him how much you love Carey Stone. He wants professionals, not lovestruck fans, working for him."

Gemma threw me a wide-eyed gaze. Carey Stone was also the everyman's hero type, and unlike Douglas Fairbanks, he was still single. But Lulu wouldn't date her costar, would she? As for Carey, a relationship with Lulu could kill his reputation as America's heartthrob. A liaison between the two would have to be kept secret.

"Sure," said Gemma. "But is he as dreamy in person as he is on the screen?"

Jack let out a snort. "Oh yeah, he's dreamy." We arrived at our destination, and he opened the door. "Ladies."

Shelves that reached the ceiling held all manner of curiosities—a mermaid tail made of plaster of paris, a crate filled with Los Angeles Angels baseball caps, a taxidermy turkey. Jack led us down a row of wigs that I swore looked like a parade of rodents. Gemma pointed to a bright-pink one and then to my hair, her eyebrows lifting as if to ask if I was in the market for such a thing. I rolled my eyes at her.

At the end of the aisle, a man in an argyle sweater-vest, corduroy knickers, and bright socks was watching a security guard shake out a fur coat. I put the director at thirty-something, with brown hair that stuck up in tufts, like he frequently pulled at it, a tan face, and a long chin. He took the coat from the guard. "Thanks, Finn. That'll be all."

Finn tipped his cap to us, his red face bright under the fluorescent lights. His lengthy legs crossed to the exit.

Jack tucked his hands under his arms and ticked his head at Gemma. "Emil, this is the gal Hettie told you about."

Gal, indeed. Everything about Hollywood was free and easy, even the introductions. Gemma punched out a hand. "I'm Gemma Chow, and that's my sister May."

Emil, who was examining the white fur, barely looked up. "Right. Sorry to disappoint, but Hettie spoke prematurely. I have all the line-readers I need." He had the hoarse voice of someone accustomed to yelling, and his body language suggested a man who was stingy with his attention unless you earned it.

Gemma made a noise of disappointment. "Won't you reconsider? I have much to offer. I am very good at standing and talking for hours at a time. And I have a good work ethic. I always give two hundred percent, so you'd be getting twice the value for your money. I can also sing, ride a horse, play the tambourine"—her eyes bobbed up to the long ceiling light, maybe searching for her other virtues there—"crack eggs with one hand, and juggle."

Emil's shrewd eyes began to wander. They were the color of money, and he seemed to be spending quite a bit of them on me. I felt myself straightening up, my neck becoming long, my face becoming an unreadable palette. I hadn't wanted to step into a spotlight, but now that one was on me, I wasn't going to let this puffed-up ringmaster dismiss us so easily.

"Plus, I come highly recommended by your own star," Gemma added. I forced my eyes not to roll at that exaggeration. Finishing her pitch, Gemma put her hands on her hips. Her smile swung like a parakeet on its perch. But Emil was still looking at me.

"At least let her read something for you," I ordered more than suggested, putting on the air of a schoolmistress dealing with a school bully.

Emil's argyle vest straightened against his trim figure. "What was your name?" The long chin swung toward me, bringing a smile that was all Hollywood, with straight white teeth that never seemed to end.

"May Chow."

"What do you think of this coat?"

"I'm no expert on fur, but it looks . . . warm," I said frostily. "The collar points could be turned out more, and topstitching fur just adds unnecessary holes to the leather, but that's a personal preference."

He grinned. "It's fake. Lulu refused to wear animal products. I wanted to keep it in *A Far East Affair* as an homage to her, even though Juanita hates it."

I had to admit, it was a thoughtful gesture—unless, of course, this Emil was a murderer. He swept his hand across the fur, almost lovingly.

"Lulu should be remembered," I said as evenly as possible.

His gaze flicked to mine and grew canny. "*You* have presence, as we like to say."

"*Presence*," Gemma echoed.

The director shifted around, looking at me from different angles as if I were a car he was thinking of purchasing. "Something you're born with. People look at you when you walk in the room. You have a good voice, clear as ice and smooth enough to skate across." He made a sliding motion with his hand. "Maybe I could even use you as an extra." He glanced at his assistant, who casually slouched against the end of the aisle. Jack hitched a shoulder.

Suppressing a smile, Gemma tapped her chin. "May reads the newspapers real good."

I gave her a hard look. She was not going to sell me out like this. Any fallout from this acting venture was not going to be on my shoulders. We had agreed that she was the one auditioning. She was better at digging around, getting mouths to open up, like those clammers on Malibu Beach. As Emil continued to appraise me, she made wild gestures behind his back. I ignored her.

"May *is* quite busy," said Gemma.

"Very busy," I agreed. It was about time she heeded me.

"But if you could make it worth her while—" Gemma added before I forced a loud cough, cutting her off.

"The pay is five dollars a day," Emil purred.

I stopped coughing. On good days, we only made four dollars doing the hot work of selling flowers.

"Done." Gemma clapped her hands as if rubbing off dust. I felt myself grow hot, like a radio that's been played too long.

Emil extended his hand to me. "Well, time is money. Be on set tomorrow at eight, no makeup. We'll need to take your picture and have you fill out some forms."

His hand suddenly looked like a bear trap. I shunned Gemma, who was blaspheming heaven with her praying gestures. Jack's cheeks had hitched up in amusement.

I focused on the high rows of mystery boxes. Harsh lighting painted all the odds and ends on the shelves with an unnatural glow. Could I really accomplish anything here? More importantly, how would the business stay afloat without me? Of all the ways we'd deceived Ma, going into show business was beyond the pale. She might be tempted to marry me off to the first bidder.

Yet here was one small thing I might do for Lulu and Gee Fa. One little wind I could blow against the gust that threatened to sweep us all away. Though I could already feel regret's cold shadow, I shook Emil's hand.

22
GEMMA

AFTER DROPPING MAY BACK AT HOME, I STEERED toward the coroner's office, plodding but determined. No Good thought we had cast bad luck on Chinatown. We would show him.

Both Ma and May seemed to have bought my excuse of taking the Mule to get her engine checked. May had been distracted, maybe worrying over her unexpected role as a Hollywood extra. Ma had barely looked up from her abacus and ledger, where she'd been spending a lot of time lately.

After driving half a mile, I arrived at the Hall of Justice, which housed the coroner's office. The Chinese cut a wide path around the towering monolith, as the former lumberyard was where the lynchings during the Massacre of '71 had taken place. Many ghosts lived here. If that wasn't a good enough reason to steer clear of the fortress, its white granite blocks were the color of death. All of that, together with an unlucky number of floors—fourteen—spelled disaster.

Yet minutes later, I was standing under the middle of three arches, about to enter, my shoulder bag clutched to me.

In China, arches were inscribed with great achievements or family honors. Ba knew a man who had built one to commemorate his wife's chastity—not something I'd want to be remembered for. But these arches, with their plain, unforgiving stone, did not sing praises, only warnings. *Go back. Flee. You can't bribe your way out of the Hall of Justice.*

I shuddered, trying to shake those thoughts free like rain from an umbrella. A feeling of being watched picked up my posture. I glanced behind me, catching sight of a sleek bronze car parked by the curb. When had that car arrived? Suddenly, it shot off, as quick as an arrow.

I breathed out my jitters. *Just act confident and don't overthink.* Didn't I do my best work on the fly? Sometimes too much thought was like overstirring egg drop soup, and instead of golden threads of egg suspended in broth, you ended up with a foamy mess.

Besides, I was on a winning streak today, getting May hired as an extra, and I wasn't going to fumble now. There was no reward without risk.

Inside, a grand lobby spread before me. Marble columns drew the eye up to an opulent coffered ceiling, sparkling with gold. A security guard stood at a counter talking on a telephone. I hurried by, not making eye contact. People marched in and out of polished elevators, presumably looking for justice. Well, I was one of them.

A directory informed me that both the district attorney and the sheriff sat in this building. My scalp started to sweat. More reason not to get caught here. They might think *I* had a hand in Lulu's death. The coroner's office sat in the basement, where it was probably easier to roll the bodies in and out.

Rather than stepping into one of those vertical coffins—I never liked elevators—I descended an echoey staircase to the bottom level. A smell occupied this area, a chemical odor that made my throat bunch. Unlike the grandeur of the lobby, this floor was clinical, with white walls and tile floors for easy mopping. Past the vertical coffins, a set of double doors popped open, letting out a few men in white coats who eyed me warily. The doors opened again, this time revealing a policeman. *Steady, girl. Remember the horned cucumbers.*

"Are you lost?" asked the officer, a man with tabbed sideburns and a gruff voice.

A vertical coffin opened, and the white coats disappeared into it, taking their staring eyes.

"I'd like some information about a deceased person."

"Hall's closing."

"Please, sir, she was my sister." I certainly hoped I wouldn't have to bribe him.

He fidgeted with the sleeves of his uniform. "Well, I'm just about to lock up, but if you make it quick."

Past the double doors, a hallway lined with offices spread out on either side. The closest room was marked CORONER'S OFFICE in black letters across its glass windows. Inside, a dark-haired woman in her thirties sat at a desk. I rolled back my shoulders and entered. With file cabinets filling the walls on either side of her windows, the place felt cramped, especially with the thought of all those criminals in the jail on the fourteenth floor.

"Good evening. I'm Lulu Wong's sister, and I would like to see her coroner's report."

"Oh?" The woman's sharp beak of a nose lifted. She reminded me of a hen with her jerky way of moving her head. "My condolences. Your family should've received the report already."

"Yes, but I was hoping there would be more information in her file."

"Who are you, exactly?"

"Bettina Wong." I bowed my head mournfully to hide any tells—I could lie, but May was the real actor—and prayed no one was keeping track of Lulu's sister's age.

"I'm sorry, but it should all be in the report." Her eyes darted toward the file cabinet on her right, where a tiny key had been left in the lock.

"I have it on good authority that there might be more to the report. If I could just get a look at the file—"

"Who told you that?" Her eyes grew smaller.

"Our, er, family physician." Her expression lost its bite, and I pressed on. "Yes. Dr. Frederick Winter," I heard myself say.

"Oh, Dr. *Winter*, of course." That name sure changed the weather. Now there were sunbeams lifting off her. "Let me check." She scooted neatly out from her chair and exited the room. Through the window, I watched her mince her way down the hall, barely causing her plaid skirt to move. She entered another windowed room, where a man with the gaunt look of an undertaker was talking to two others, a policeman and a hulking man in an ill-fitting suit the color of rust.

I caught my breath. It was Officer Kidd and Detective Mallady.

My heart became a hand trying to climb out of my chest. I grabbed the doorknob. But then the tiny key in the file cabinet caught my eye.

In my head, May screamed for me to flee, but I ignored her. Neither Mallady nor Kidd had seen me yet. Releasing the knob, I pulled the little key from the lock and dropped it in my pocket. That little act was probably enough to send me to the fourteenth floor. Tripping over my feet, I slipped back out the door. What exactly was my plan here?

Keeping my head down, I blew down the hall, feeling as out of control as a misfired cannonball. I hadn't been made yet, but the secretary would tell Mallady about Lulu's "sister" waiting in her office, and then the search would be on. Maybe they'd even send out dogs. Dobermans.

Reaching the double doors, I twisted the knob but felt no give. The guard had locked them! There must be another way out. I turned into another hallway, this one dim and cooler in temperature. At least it looked deserted. Instead of offices, a series of strange glass doors lined the wall, each slanted inward at the top. I nearly screamed at the sight of a pair of feet behind one of the windows. Each cabin held a gurney covered with a sheet.

Hurrying by, I took a deep breath. *Bodies, they are just bodies. Get ahold of yourself. You don't let the living scare you, so why should the dead get the privilege?* The glass doors ended at a regular door, this one of carved wood. My sweaty palm slipped against the brass knob. The door was unlocked. Hearing no protests, I pushed my way in.

The room featured a tufted velvet couch and a chandelier. It was likely a waiting room of some sort. A vase of stargazer lilies threw out a scent so sharp, I felt it behind my eyes. Heavy curtains on either side of the room might hide me while I sorted out what to do. I crossed to the farthest curtain and discovered a counter with a sink, cups, and a cookie jar. Good enough for me.

Before pulling the curtain closed, I glimpsed a clock on the wall—just before six o'clock. They were probably searching the building right now. I couldn't leave yet. I just had to stop breathing so hard and slip out when their guard was down. I resolved to wait until dark.

No reward without risk—what had I been thinking? There was also no fall without folly either, you numbskull.

Every noise caused me to stiffen, from the gasp of the vent to the groan of the ceiling tiles. I swore I heard the stabbing barks of Dobermans. I was sweating so profusely it was possible they'd find only a puddle of water when they got here. All my sweating built up a thirst. I used my hand to cup water from the faucet into my mouth. Then I grew hungry. I resisted the cookies.

I tried passing the time by thinking about twenty-one down from Sunday's crossword, with its stumper of a clue: *It takes time to sink in.* Only four of the nine letters were connected to the rest of the puzzle, and I had only gotten two of them.

The only word I could think of was GRAVEYARD, which made me sweat more.

Peeking out from the curtain at the clock, I nearly wept when I realized only twenty minutes had passed. The hallway lights had been switched off, making the room even darker. The lilies were cloying. I didn't care if I was caught. I couldn't stand being on this floor with all these dead people another second. I felt my way across the room, reaching the curtain closest to the door. A hard surface lay beyond it—another door?

Scooting aside the curtain, I discovered a window of some sort. Maybe this was a way out.

I felt along the window and found a light switch, which I flipped on. A light bulb cast a yellow glow in front of me. Through the glass, I made out the distinctive shape of a woman lying faceup.

I nearly bit my tongue, trying not to scream. Her face had a melted look about it, with the flesh of her cheeks hanging down by her ears. This was no waiting room. This was a crypt!

Switching off the light, I darted to the door I'd come in through. Had I been breathing dead people fumes all this time? I felt sick. Throwing caution to the wind, I charged out, ready for them to slap on the handcuffs.

But the hallway was empty.

I fled back the way I'd come, past the slanted windows with the dead bodies, then toward the coroner's office.

The hallways were dim, and the blinds had been drawn on the office windows. I should head for the nearest exit. Mallady was probably lying in wait behind the door.

But what if he wasn't?

I took a deep breath. I needed to get ahold of myself. There were no live bodies after me, no dead ones either, as far as I knew. And I would not get another shot at this.

With a glance over my shoulder, I slid into the coroner's office. I felt along the wall for the light switch. The light was like a jolt to my vision. Squinting, I looked around for a smaller desk lamp but came up empty. A new building like this wouldn't have something so antiquated as a desk lamp, of course.

The file drawer was unlocked—no surprise, since I had the key. Skimming the files, I went straight for the Ws. There were several Wongs. Lulu's file was raised slightly, as if recently put away.

I opened the file, and all the papers slid out—damn my shaky hands. Admittedly, this wasn't my best plan. I quickly gathered the papers, trying to figure out what I was looking at. A copy of the coroner's report was among the contents, lab results, then a paper with AUTOPSY REPORT printed in bold letters across the top, the original form still with its carbon paper attached, though the replicate sheets had been torn away. I scanned the paper.

Voices had started up down the hall again. I began to panic. They would catch me red-handed. I returned the papers to the manila file. A bit of blue from the carbon paper smeared my finger. What if I took the carbon paper, with its impressions of what had been written on top of it? Surely no one would miss the carbon, which was usually discarded anyway.

Crossing to the desk, I tore a piece of paper from a notepad, then used it to protect the inky side of the tissue-thin carbon paper. I rolled the two sheets together, then tucked them into my purse. Then I returned everything to the file cabinet.

Now, what to do with the key?

I dropped it into a dish of paper clips and other odds and ends. Perhaps the secretary would think she'd accidentally dropped it in there.

Switching off the light, I returned the way I came. On a desperate whim, I tried the double doors again and was surprised to find they were unlocked. I cautiously opened them. Seeing no one, I hurried past the vertical coffins to the echoey staircase, holding my breath. Invisible eyes seemed to track me. I took the stairs two at a time, swearing I heard footsteps following me.

In the lobby, the security guard no longer stood by his counter, but was pacing the front entrance. I ducked back into the stairwell, flattening myself against the wall. Was he looking for me?

The ring of a telephone echoed over the tiles. The security guard answered, and words were spoken. His footsteps drew closer. *Please, ancestors, let him not use the stairs.*

He continued past the elevators, and soon I couldn't hear him at all.

Wasting no time, I dashed through the entrance. Sweet night air filled my nostrils, and I shot from the building like Babe Ruth's last homer, not looking back.

23
MAY

MA COVERED THE DISHES CONTAINING OUR LEFTOVERS, glancing at the empty spot where Gemma usually sat. "Moses is taking a long time. Hope there's not too much wrong with the truck."

"I'm sure it's fine," I said, even though I wasn't sure at all. I couldn't help feeling that Gemma was, yet again, up to no good. She had deceived me once today already. I glanced at Peony, whose gaze slid back to her bowl even though she'd already eaten every last grain of rice. She had the look of someone who'd left the door to the chicken coop unlatched.

From a cupboard, Ma brought out a pink pastry box. "This came for you earlier."

"Open it," Peony urged.

I untied the red string, revealing eight winter-melon-filled cakes, each flat disc stamped in red with the character for "double happiness."

Peony's mouth fell open, even though she hadn't finished chewing. "Sweetheart cakes! Read the note." She pulled out a small envelope.

"*Dinner at Fragrant Bamboo?*" I read carefully, though my mouth had gone dry. Wallace was sure taking pretend-dating seriously. "*P.S. Please enjoy these cactus bugs.*"

"Cactus bugs?" Ma's tone was disapproving, but the grin feathering her face told a different story. "Do you enjoy his company?"

I hid my deceiving face in my bowl, not really tasting the food as it went in. "We've only been on one date, Ma."

Ma wound the red string from the pastry box around her finger. "Sometimes it only takes one date to know. Peony, why do you keep looking at the time?"

"No reason," she said, though her legs had begun to jitter. I slid Peony a questioning look, but she avoided my eyes. "Bettina came back to school today," she informed Ma. "We all hugged her, and Mrs. Shelley gave her a book of poems."

"Good. It can't be easy." Ma lifted herself by her belly and crossed to the window. "Do you think Bettina would like to spend a few nights here with us? Perhaps we can cheer her up, and it might give Wong Tai some needed time to herself."

Peony wiped the crumbs off her smile. "I think she would. I'll ask her."

The door unlatched and Gemma burst in.

"There you are, sister," I said through my teeth. "We were beginning to think you'd eloped with Moses."

She laughed a little hysterically. "With all those commandments to follow? No, thank you. Hello, Ma. Sorry to keep you waiting."

Ma clucked her tongue. "I like to eat dinner with *all* my girls, you know."

"Sorry, Ma," said Gemma, bowing her head. "But the Mule's working great now."

"Fine. Eat. I need to wash up." Rubbing her belly, Ma retreated to the hallway bathroom.

Peony had pulled apart a sweetheart cake, getting pastry

flakes all over the table. Gemma filled her bowl and helped herself to the note from Wallace. "Wallace *loves* you."

"Pretend-loves," I hissed. "I'll have to call it off. Ma's getting her hopes up too high."

As if she wasn't being obnoxious enough, Gemma reached over the table and picked a cube of tofu out of my bowl. "I'd say that's premature. Maybe the pretend-dating will lead to real-dating."

The memory of Wallace folding himself on top of me tapped nervous fingers in my belly. "How do you know I want that?"

"It doesn't take a detective."

Peony giggled, spilling her tea and then howling. With a sigh, I tossed her a tea towel.

Gemma shoveled rice in, talking with her mouth full. "Live a little, May. You have a charming young man sending you sweetheart cakes. Go fetch that juicy steak."

"We're not going to Clifford's."

"I didn't say you were." Gemma pumped her eyebrows.

I shunned her. The remaining tofu in my bowl suddenly looked watery and unappetizing.

Ma returned from the bathroom, then disappeared into her bedroom. Soon, her snoring rumbled through the walls.

Peony ran to our bedroom and returned with a small white leather box with a snap hinge. On the inside of the lid, the words JANIS JEWELERS were stamped in gold. "Bettina said Lulu always stored her earrings in this box. She doesn't know who gave them to her, but she thinks Lulu started wearing them sometime after her birthday in March."

"He must have been wealthy to afford such a gift," I said. A Hollywood type, perhaps.

Gemma rubbed a finger over the box's velvety interior. "We'll have to pay this Janis Jewelers a visit. Though a fancy jeweler like that will need some convincing before spilling customer secrets."

"Now that you've committed me to a full-time gig, when exactly would we do that?" I groused, smelling a scheme that I probably wouldn't like.

"Still working on it. Don't worry your pretty head."

Peony brought up her legs to sit cross-legged, her knees bouncing excitedly. "I interrogated Chin Chin this morning—that's the ladder maker's daughter." Gemma and I both leaned in. "Chin Chin thinks she saw a man in a dark overcoat in the Mercantile lot exiting Lulu's car. He smoked and used the broken toilet as an ashtray. And then, about ten minutes later, she saw a sporty-looking two-seater enter the alley. The man closed the toilet lid, got in the coupe, and left. She couldn't see the car well enough, or the driver."

"A getaway car," Gemma murmured. "Cole Stritch is a smoker."

I began clearing dishes from the table. "We have a clear motive for him. He had access. But why did he wait so long to strike? She got the role in March. And how did he do it?"

"This might give us clues." From her cloth shoulder bag, Gemma produced a rolled sheet of paper. She unrolled it to reveal a tissue-thin piece of carbon paper. "It's the carbon paper from the autopsy report."

A clamoring like the banging of a metal spatula against a wok had started up in my head. "*Where* did you get that?"

She ignored me. "It's got a bunch of medical jargon, and then there are these letters and numbers floating off to the side." She pointed to the right side of the page, where the imprint was barely legible: *FH 15 cm / GA 15 / PE & palp confirm.* "It's as if someone was writing on a different paper *on top* of the form."

Peony pulled at her chin. "Looks like a measurement."

I stood by Gemma's side, my fists on my hips. "You're avoiding my question." She gave me a sour look, then started talking. By the time she had finished recounting her misadventure in the coroner's office, I was ready to throttle her. "Unbelievable. Just unbelievable."

"Yes, it was like I'd been locked into the underworld. All those dead bodies lying there like fish on ice with their—"

"Not that. You didn't just visit the coroner's office. You *broke* into it." I dropped back into my chair and decided to let Gemma finish cleaning up the kitchen.

"That's the shocking part of this story? I also bribed a policeman. What's the difference?"

"You probably broke a hundred laws with your stunt, and you could've gotten us in real trouble," I sputtered. "What if someone *did* see you? And now we're harboring a stolen document."

Gemma's eyes narrowed over her rice bowl. "Maybe not a hundred laws. Besides, I wouldn't have had to break them if this city actually cared about justice. Whose side are you on?"

I glowered at her, resenting the smug tilt of her head, even the flippant way her collar tabs turned up, like shrugging hands. "I'm on the side of our family. You're always looking out the window, never thinking about what's inside the house. What would we do if you were thrown in prison? Springing you out would leave us in the poorhouse, not to mention break our parents' hearts. We'd be disgraced." My chair made a grating sound as I stood again, my head ringing with thoughts of catastrophe.

She leaned back, taking my measure like a tailor asked to dress a horse. "And you're so fixated on what's inside the house that you ignore the storm brewing outside. You think keeping us safe means walking inside the lines. But I have news for you. The lines aren't keeping us safe. They're keeping us locked up."

My chest heaved, and I had a strong urge to pinch her. Peony sat still, watching us battle without moving her head. I crossed my arms. "You," I told Gemma, "are a jobajoo." Her eyes flashed, but I didn't take it back. She *was* a freight train, not caring about anyone else as she sped along her track. I jabbed a finger at her. "Lie to me again, and I'm off the case." It wasn't an empty threat. I had lost a friend, but I would not lose my family.

24
GEMMA

GUITAR MAN MADE THE FRONT PAGE. AS MAY BORE US
toward Capsize Pictures for her first day of work, I held the latest
copy of *The Observer First* tight with two hands and read aloud:

Live Turtle and Lulu Wong Earrings
Found on Chinatown Suspect

*Los Angeles—Police agents have arrested a homeless
man, Gee Fa, known around town as "Guitar Man,"
for the murder of Lulu Wong and believe they have
solved the case. A witness claimed to have seen the
sixty-one-year-old vagrant lurking around the dilap-
idated horse stable at the heart of Chinatown where
the actress's body was discovered over a week ago.*

*Among other damning items, a search of Gee Fa's
guitar case produced Miss Wong's earrings and a
live turtle. Sources say Lulu Wong was afraid of
reptiles. The district attorney intends to prove the
suspect committed a felony murder in the course of
stealing Miss Wong's earrings by scaring her with
the turtle.*

"They planted those earrings on him," May said grimly. With an iron grip on the wheel and her neck jutted forward, she looked more like a farmer's wife hunting down a chicken than an ingenue on the brink of discovery. I continued reading:

> A coroner's report indicated that Lulu Wong died of a heart attack under suspicious circumstances. A heart attack arises when the flow of the blood to the heart is blocked due to an unhealthy lifestyle of too-rich food and alcohol, drug use, or, in some instances, an extreme response to fear.

I was tempted to throw the paper out the door. "Lulu wasn't scared of *reptiles*. And drug use? It's all baloney." My head pounded, as with the noise of an impending train.

Rabbit-ear dents appeared on May's forehead as she frowned at the road, ignoring a young man on a motorcycle ogling her through his driving goggles. "I wish we could find the young woman I saw Guitar Man with at the Plaza, the one in the cloche with the guinea feather."

"How do you know she was a young woman if you couldn't see her face?"

"Hemline. Midcalf."

That figured. "Maybe Mr. Moon knows? I'll stop by today and ask him."

The rabbit-ear dents hadn't disappeared by the time May pulled to the curb by the Capsize Pictures archway and I took her place in the driver's seat. "The receptionist we worked with at the French Hospital might be able to connect us with a doctor who can tell us what that coroner's report means. But be careful. And I meant what I said: no more lies."

"Yes, yes, I know." I already had the perfect doctor in mind, but she didn't have to know that. "See you at five. And good luck."

DOUBLING BACK THROUGH CHINATOWN, I DROVE PAST THE horse lot, dismayed to see a new sign nailed to a post.

```
City of Los Angeles
Notice of Demolition of Public Nuisance
Apablasa Stables
Scheduled for: October 15, 9:00 a.m.
```

Public nuisance, indeed. Sure, its days housing horses were over, and kids no longer played there. But it couldn't all end in a faceless train station, full of people on their way to someplace else. It just didn't seem a dignified end.

Once at the Barajases' farm, Angel helped me process the flowers, making leaves fly twice as fast as me and May put together. "Where's your sister today?"

"She had some errands to run," I lied, hoping it wouldn't get back to Ma or Ba.

"If you speak to your papa, tell him I got his note, and of course you may use my handcarts to help you move. Just let me know when you want to pick them up."

"Move?" All my insides ground to a halt.

"Sí, didn't he mention it?" His thick eyebrows drew up as he wrapped twine around a bundle, his arms a blur.

"Of course. It just slipped my mind." I worked my finger out of the twine I had tied around it.

"I have a cousin who lives in East Adams. He's wild about street racing, so be careful when you cross the street." He grinned, though it was hard to tell if he was kidding.

By noon, I had sold only a third of my flowers at City Market. It wasn't just the late start but an unfocused mind that had set me back. I shoved buckets into the truck bed, banging my thumb and cursing.

We were moving? Why wasn't *I* consulted? If Ba had told me, I would've remembered for sure. Had May known? No wonder Ma had been poring over the ledgers. Maybe No Good had finally convinced her that moving her bad-luck daughters out would be better for Chinatown. But Ma had been the one so set against leaving. What could have changed her mind?

Before heading to Westlake Park for the doctor's opinion, I stopped by Half Moon Bakery. Baskets of buns were half-empty, though the glass case with the fancier desserts still looked full. With the lunchtime rush, I had to wait several minutes before talking to the baker.

"One chicken bun, please," I said when I reached the front of the line.

He scooped one onto waxed paper. "They are a little flat. The news about Gee Fa had me overkneading."

That was my entry. "Mr. Moon, the last time May was here, she saw Gee Fa sitting with a woman wearing a cloche with a guinea feather. May said she's not from Chinatown, and she wasn't even sure the woman was Chinese, but she thinks she was a young woman. Do you remember seeing her?"

He tapped my nickel absently on the counter. "I'm sorry, no."

"Do you think she was from the flophouse?"

He coughed. Such matters weren't discussed in the company of ladies. "I haven't seen Gee Fa with a woman since Shao."

"Shao?"

"His wife. She was as lovely as a vase. But she died in child-birth many years ago. Before your time. It is why his brain went mixed-up." He tapped his head. "Still, mixed-up brain doesn't mean he's a killer. Let's hope Mr. Yam's new petition will get him released."

Another petition. Poor Mr. Yam had certainly been busy. "What happened to the child?"

"Don't know."

The line began to grumble behind me, and I stumbled out of the shop, my head filled with more questions than when I'd entered. They would just have to get in line behind the more pressing ones.

25
GEMMA

WESTLAKE PARK LOOKED POSTCARD PERFECT AS always. And if I was going to see the doctor, I might as well try to off-load some inventory beforehand.

I pulled the Mule underneath the shady palm, more jerkily than May would have done it. I hated deceiving her once again, especially knowing how things lay between us, but I didn't have time to behave, with a murder to solve. Lives were at stake. Ba had put May in command of the business, not only because she was the oldest, but because she was reliable with the everyday things that businesses needed in order to run. But we were dealing with matters outside the scope of the everyday.

If the family was a dragon, Ba was the head, providing direction; Ma, the body, connecting all parts; and May, the wings, helping us fly the course. I was the tail. Though the wings thought they were in control, it was really the tail that steered. The tail was also capable of striking on its own.

After setting up shop, I sold a dollar bouquet right off the bat to a family getting their picture taken by the lake. As they departed, a tall, pale man in a houndstooth driving hat appeared a few feet away from me, his hands in the pockets of a suit that looked too warm for the day. He skimmed my offerings.

"Does she favor any particular color?" I asked him.

His unblinking eyes appraised me coolly from a face that was all edges, down to its yellow triangle of a beard.

"We do have some lovely hydrangea."

He barely glanced at the showy flower head I lifted to him. "Tell me, where's yer father?" A Scottish accent stretched his English out of shape.

"Why do you want to know that?" My body tensed, my internal sirens beginning to ring.

He shrugged, and a thin smile broke over his face like a hairline fracture. "You are rather young to be runnin' a business by yerself."

"My business is none of your business." I stepped back, glancing around. Besides the boaters, several hundred yards away, I was alone. He could easily overpower me if he had a mind to. My feet began to dance under me in case I needed to make a run for it. I hoped he would leave.

Two figures approached from the boathouse, and I stopped jittering about. I wasn't sure if I was aggrieved or relieved by the sight of their navy uniforms. Coppers. I recognized the muscular policeman with the dark scruff who had reminded me of a Rottweiler. But his partner was not the smaller fellow with the mean look of a Chihuahua, though this new man did look familiar. He glanced about nervously, scratching his cheeks.

It was Officer Kidd. What was the rookie doing off his beat? Had he been following me? Perhaps he had seen me at the Hall of Justice after all, and now he'd come to shake me down.

At least the Scot had retreated to a bench ten paces closer to the lake and pulled out a newspaper.

I smoothed my moist palms down my apron, feeling the bump of money in my pocket. Five dollars in the purse, plus the one I had just made. *Smile. Don't bolt yet.*

"I remember you," said the Rottweiler, glancing around him, as if forgetting he was the one everyone else should be watching out for. His dark eyes slid to Officer Kidd. "Mickey and I caught her selling here last week."

Kidd tugged at his collar, still uneasy in his uniform. "I remember her too. Aren't you a bit far from Chinatown?"

"Hello, Officer Kidd," I chirped, desperately hoping he hadn't seen me at the Hall of Justice. "Three miles is hardly far, unless you are an ant."

"You brought your permit today?" asked the Rottweiler, his head swiveling. He struck me as the kind of man who had to be shown things a few times before getting it.

I squared my shoulders. "If you'll remember, my sister is in charge of the permit, and as you can see, she's not here today." Several women eyed us as they hurried by. The police were scaring off my business. "I do appreciate you stopping by." I handed them each a rose and a dollar.

The Rottweiler pocketed his money and shot Kidd a smile. "For a repeat infraction, it'll be three dollars each."

I coughed. "That's highway robbery."

"No, that's the cost of doing business without a permit," the Rottweiler returned with a sneer. "Pay the fee or get your permit." So he wasn't so slow. Maybe his partner's absence had emboldened him, and he was swinging around his weight for the rookie.

"The city won't give us a permit," I huffed, feeling the blood rush to my head.

The Scot lifted his eyes from his newspaper, watching me.

The Rottweiler's five-o'clock shadow stretched longer. "Well then, that narrows your choices. Quickly now, we have a park to patrol."

With a grimace, I emptied my purse. How would I explain a five-dollar shortfall to Ma? At least I could use the leftover pot-holder money to make up for some of it. She wouldn't check the purse until the weekend, so I'd worry about it then. Kidd gave me an almost-apologetic smile.

"After all that heavy lifting you did arresting the wrong killer on the Lulu Wong case, I hope you're catching a nice break from detective work," I couldn't help saying.

A thread of something canny slipped through Kidd's gaze. But then he glanced toward the lake, noisy with ducks. "I'm just a beat officer, ma'am." He tucked his money in his pocket.

"Mind you, the new patrol takes over in an hour, and I heard they charge twice what we do." The Rottweiler grinned a short-toothed smile, then lumbered away with Kidd in tow. Maybe fleecing a helpless girl made him feel more like a man. Good riddance to them both.

On his bench, the Scot was back to reading his newspaper, though I knew he was still watching me with those unsettling frosty eyes. I sniffed the roses. The scent was supposed to soothe the mind, but I didn't feel any better.

A pair of afternoon strollers milled around the truck but lost interest, and I wasn't in the mood to chase a sale. Six unlucky dollars in bribes. I might as well call it a day, especially with the Scot refusing to move along. Begrudgingly, I packed up the Mule.

Freddie Winter's office lay just outside the park and across the street. I had taken the liberty of looking up the address in the business directory last night.

I managed to park in front of the adobe Mission Revival build-ing without bumping the curb. After freshening my lipstick, I pulled the carbon paper from Lulu Wong's autopsy report from the glove compartment.

Beside the building's single arch entrance, a brass sign with the words OFFICE OF DR. FREDERICK WINTER, GENERAL PHYSICIAN released a cold shot of energy through me. The door opened, and a well-dressed woman in dark sunglasses looked me up and down before breezing by. Suddenly, my simple rose dress felt dated and prissy, and my black shoes looked scuffed. I began walking back to the Mule but stopped. Since when had Gemma Chow let anyone intimidate her?

Airing my skirts, I about-faced and strode to the door again. I was just here to ask a few questions, nothing more. It wasn't as if I was calling on a lover. I snorted loudly.

"Are you waiting for a written invitation?" A voice drifted down from the second story.

Freddie was leaning against the sill, staring down at me through the open window. How long had he been watching me? I hid the bloom on my cheeks under a layer of righteous indignation. "I wasn't sure I had the right address."

"And here I thought I wasn't going to see you again. Please, let me get the door for you."

With that, he disappeared. Chastened, I pushed open the door myself.

A leather sofa and two chairs conspired around a table with a crisp newspaper. Terra-cotta floor tiles formed a diagonal pattern. The only doctor's office I ever visited was Dai-Sang's bare-bones shop, where you simply stuck out your tongue and offered your wrist. This place seemed much too formal for sticking out tongues. Plus, there were no herby smells, just lemon furniture oil. On the wall hung a diploma from Harvard University with the name FREDERICK WINTER centered among a sea of calligraphy mumbo jumbo.

I wondered if I could've gone to a university if Ba hadn't

gotten sick and I had stayed in school. I'd enjoyed French and was always being picked to write the math equations. Of course, then I'd have to do battle with all the men whose big-thinking heads thought women's heads were too little. No, thank you.

A desk at the far end of the room was occupied by a gray-haired woman on the telephone. Her lively brown eyes ran over me. She covered the mouthpiece and said, "Do you have an appointment?"

Freddie breezed down a staircase, as fresh as a sail in a gabardine suit. "Mrs. Hightower, Miss Chow has a consult with me that I forgot to mention."

"Very good, Doctor."

"Shall we?" He gestured toward the stairs. "Oh, and Mrs. H, would you mind bringing Miss Chow and me refreshment? Lemonade?"

I recovered my speech. "Oh, I won't be staying long."

He crooked an eyebrow, then nodded at Mrs. H. "Bring us the whole pitcher."

Upstairs lay a suite of rooms. A woman in nurse's garb sat in an office, writing notes, while in another a young man stretched on a built-in wall ladder. Freddie gestured to the space that looked out onto the park. Inside, a padded table occupied one end, while a desk and two visitor chairs anchored the far side. Behind the desk, a skeleton hung from a stand.

I took the chair farthest from the skeleton. "Are you running a circus here?"

"Why? Have you come to join?" He left the door open.

"Not if I have to get hooked up to that." I eyed an alien contraption by the wall opposite the window, consisting of a chair and an assortment of tubes.

"If you keep hydrated, you'll never need to get 'hooked up'

to that. That's a colonics machine, for flushing out the bowels."

Flushing out the bowels? This place was certainly a house of fun.

Instead of sitting, he took up a post by the open window, which must be a favorite perch of his. I wondered how much this elevated view of Westlake Park had set him back. I bet those coppers never shook him down.

"I apologize if that makes you uncomfortable," he said.

"I am fine. It's just that you must see your share of, er, bottoms."

"Ah, there you go again, adding some color to my— What did you call it? Dull and dreary life. My spinal traction in the other room is also quite popular."

Mrs. H entered with the lemonade pitcher and two glasses, then exited in a bustle of skirts.

He handed me a glass. "Bottoms up."

Despite my initial reluctance, I thirstily gulped the lemonade. An assortment of framed photographs adorned the wall behind Freddie's desk, the most prominent of which showed a man who was a heavier version of Freddie with a toothbrush mustache. It must be his father. I pulled out the carbon paper from the autopsy report. "I wondered if you could help make sense of this."

His eyes dug into mine. "I'm afraid to ask, but what is that?"

"The autopsy report, like you suggested."

"I don't remember suggesting—"

"I didn't think anyone would miss the carbon sheet. If you could just take a peek and tell me what all those medical bits mean."

"Gemma, it is a crime to steal such things."

"I didn't say I stole it. Besides, as a doctor, aren't you supposed to keep my secrets?"

His frown pulled down his ears. "If you were my patient."

"I'm sorry. I didn't want to come, but you're the only doctor I know, and Lulu was our friend."

"I thought they arrested a suspect."

"The wrong suspect. The man they have would never do such a thing."

The bumps of his jaw twitched. With a mighty sigh, he lifted the paper by the corners and held it up to the window. "Cause of death is myocardial infarction, otherwise known as a heart attack. 'Pronounced lividity of back, buttocks, and back of the legs' simply means blood pooled in those regions." He glanced back at me. Afternoon sunshine formed a halo around him. "Miss Wong died on her back, about twelve hours before you found her."

We'd found her sometime after 6:00 a.m. on Monday, which put her death at 6:00 p.m. Sunday. We'd been painting the truck there at the time, making it more and more likely she'd been killed in her home. Hettie only lived ten minutes away, and Lulu wouldn't have left for her rehearsal at 7:00 p.m. with Hettie and Carey yet. Lulu's visitor had seen her at four, so the visitor would've been one of the last people to see Lulu alive. Maybe it was the visitor who had killed her.

"This series of checkmarks on the left side correspond to body systems, like respiratory, urogenital, digestive—they all seem to check out. Toxicology notes indicate no drugs, alcohol, or poison were present."

I nodded, feeling relief that Lulu had not died by painful strychnine poisoning, like Dixie Doors.

"I'd say that the report is remarkably unremarkable." He set the carbon paper back on his desk, then glanced out the window, his face a mask. With his hand resting on his hip, he looked like he could be posing for a Sears catalog ad.

"You're thinking thoughts that you're not sharing."

"Sometimes 'myocardial infarction' is kind of a catchall term for when you don't know the cause." He shrugged. "Autopsies aren't infallible. Sometimes you can't get a good sample of blood or tissue, or it degrades. Any number of things can affect the results."

"Her mouth was a little puffy. Why didn't the report mention that?"

"How do you mean, puffy?"

"Well, her lips looked like this." I made pouty lips toward him. His gaze fell to my kisser, where it stuck for at least a second. The floor seemed to slip around under me, and I ground a toe into it. I cleared my throat. "Like she was kissing someone."

"Were there any other marks on her face or perhaps her neck?"

"Not that I noticed."

He frowned. "It would've had to be a vigorous kiss in order to bruise lips."

Now I couldn't help staring at his lips. How did his teeth grow so perfectly straight? I shook myself free. "Is it possible to die from kissing?"

"That depends on if you ask a doctor or a poet."

"Are you a poet?"

His jaw twitched again, but this time a half-cocked smile appeared. "In my opinion as a doctor, I have never heard of anyone dying from a kiss. Certain chemicals, like poisons, could cause tissue swelling, but as I said, no poisons were noted."

"Could the report be wrong?"

His gaze rested longer on me, but then he looked up at the stucco ceiling. "It's always possible. The coroner's office has been a bit of a zoo lately with automobile accidents on the rise.

Anyway, I'd think they'd want to be extra careful with a famous person."

I snorted, lemonade fumes going the wrong direction.

"Are you okay?"

"Yes. I'm sorry, for a moment I thought you were serious."

"I am serious." He sat on his desk chair and crossed one leg over the other. "She was beloved. People are watching this case."

All my excess energy seemed to drain down my legs into the carpet. "I'm sorry, but you've been misinformed. Some in this city are hell-bent on railroading us out of our homes and will do anything to make sure it happens, including making it look like Chinatown ate its own. Sure, the city might care about a famous person, but not if she's Chinese."

A bit of frost had crept into my tone. Freddie casually triangled his fingers in front of him, a king in his tony Westlake domain who didn't need to care about people like us. I swallowed my anger. He was still doing me a favor.

I faced the report to him and pointed. "What about those numbers and letters slanting off on the side?"

Holding the paper up toward the light again, a line like an exclamation mark appeared between his eyebrows.

"Well?"

Setting the paper down, he pointed at the readings with a pen. "'FH,' or 'fundal height,' means the distance between the pelvic bone and uterus." He circled his pen around the pelvic region of the skeleton behind him. "'GA' means 'gestational age,' which the examiner put at fifteen weeks. 'PE and palp' means the examiner conducted a physical exam and palpitation to confirm." His expression was grim. "Lulu was pregnant."

26
MAY

BY NOON, THE ONLY THING I'D DISCOVERED ON SET WAS that I would need to mix a baking soda solution for my underarms, which, due to the stage lights, were experiencing a runoff to rival a spring melt. I'd been standing on the set of a teahouse, waiting to bring tea to an arguing couple: the dashing Carey Stone as a shipping heir, and Juanita, in Lulu's old role, as a tea waitress named Chang-Rae. I was surprised to learn Juanita had no Spanish heritage but had simply chosen the moniker as a stage name. I had yet to dispense the tea, or talk to Carey Stone, or notice anything that would help us solve Lulu Wong's murder. I hadn't even seen the other Chinese extras yet, who were not needed today.

On the fifth take, Emil popped up from his canvas director's chair. "Cut! The devil, Juanita, you're overacting. Deliver it more casual-cool, like Lulu, or you'll give away the ending." Emil sank back into the chair, which I feared would break under his frequent ups and downs. Someone with violent outbursts might certainly be the murderer, but why would he want to kill his star? I needed to do better than that.

"Lulu this, Lulu that. I'm not Lulu." Juanita threw out her long pale arms and stamped her feet. She possessed the kind of fine-boned face that cameras loved, but none of Lulu's nuanced

acting. Clad in the narrow Chinese dress, she looked as misera-
ble as an albatross caught in a fishing net. Her eyelids were taped
to look Oriental, which made her look more like a parody of a
Chinese girl than an actual one, and it pained me to see. Not all
of our eyes were slanted like that. They should've given one of
the Chinese extras a chance.

"No, you are certainly not," Emil said scornfully, then jumped
up again. "But you're an actress, aren't you? So act. Hold on, hold
on. Someone, her goddamn wig is slipping."

A woman rushed to adjust Juanita's wig. My knees had locked
into place, and I could feel my pancake makeup melting off me,
probably staining the mandarin collar of my own cotton sheath.
At least I had an enviable view of Carey Stone, with his blond
locks and a jawline sharp enough to cut paper. His looks could
kill, but what about the rest of him?

"Action!" cried Emil.

The Technicolor cameras with their hubcap-sized reels
started rolling. I gripped my teapot, waiting for my moment
once again. I'd need to do some digging. I cursed Gemma for the
dozenth time, for stranding me here. She was the one with "flexible teeth," as we called it, good at stepping into conversations
and working truths out of people.

Jack Lyman, standing by one of the raised lights that seemed
to be cooking the set, was the logical starting place. As Emil's
assistant, he knew everyone, and it seemed that whenever
anyone had a question, they'd ask him rather than face the loud-
mouthed Emil.

Carey Stone held Juanita's slim hand. "I'd never let her come
between us," he pleaded with the sincerity of a choir boy.

"A mother is the fiercest of animals," Juanita returned, this
time so casually I nearly laughed.

"Cut!" Emil growled, so fiercely I nearly dropped my tray. "Everyone, take five. Someone get me an aspirin and a seltzer."

Two women ushered Carey Stone to a mirrored vanity, where he was primped and watered, while others drifted toward the salami and cheese platters. Setting down my tray, I edged my way to Jack.

Emil's right-hand man seated himself on a tufted sofa. He crossed one of his long legs over the other, but sighting me, he uncrossed them again and sat forward. "May Chow, wasn't it? Have we scared you off the pictures yet, or bored you to death?" He patted the seat next to him.

I carefully arranged myself so that the slit up the side of my gown wouldn't reveal too much. "I admit it is more sitting around than I expected." Who knew the life of an actor was so up and down? Long stretches of tedium while you waited for other people to do what they were supposed to do, interspersed with the occasional firecracker just to make sure you were paying attention.

"So why are you really here, Miss Chow? Yesterday, you looked like you'd rather pull a woolly mammoth out of a tar pit."

Here was my chance. But could I trust Jack? Though I'd initially figured him as the dark and mysterious type, despite his light coloring, I changed my mind on that. He was surprisingly easygoing and likable, a yin to Emil's yang. But what if he'd had something to do with the murder? Maybe behind those jaded hazel eyes, one slightly larger than the other, lay a maniac. I shivered and edged closer to the sofa arm. "Yes, well, it was just unexpected."

"I'd say it was a lucky strike. You've got a good face, and I see the way you study people, like you want to understand them. The job pays well if it doesn't kill you." His gaze wandered to where Emil was smoking with the crew.

The door couldn't open much wider. I released a couch pillow I had been gripping. "I wondered if you knew if, er, Lulu Wong was having any problems here?"

His eyes rolled toward me, followed by the rest of him. The sofa shifted as he angled to face me. "Lulu? Is that why you're here?"

"She was a childhood friend. We're trying to understand what happened."

"Didn't the police catch the guy?"

"The wrong guy. We're not confident they even investigated."

His light eyebrows touched. "Sorry to hear that. Well, what's your question?"

"How well did you know her?"

His breath seeped out like the stale air released by opening a window. Something sad tiptoed across his face. "Probably better than most."

"Do you know anyone who could've wished her harm?"

He played with a vein on the back of his hand. "Lulu got along with everyone. Very professional, always came prepared, never forgot a line. She was in top form. Poised to take on the world."

"Someone had been stealing her scripts."

Jack nodded. "It happens. Jealous actresses are a dime a dozen. But I don't know of any specific threats against her."

I glanced toward Juanita, who was arguing with Emil as a woman in an apron powdered the starlet's pert nose.

Jack peered at the starlet but shook his head. "I doubt you'll sniff blood from that one. Juanita was shooting a Western when it happened."

"I understand Lulu's manager, Cole Stritch, also represents Juanita."

He nodded. "Stritch is well known."

"Was Lulu happy with him?"

"She never talked about him. I've never met the man myself."

"How was her relationship with Emil?" A big director like him was used to getting what he wanted. Maybe Lulu had done something to displease him and he hadn't been able to control his anger.

Jack's eyes grew pinched, and I worried I had overstepped. Emil was his boss, maybe even his best friend. If Jack told him I'd been snooping around and Emil was the killer, I had just given him a new target. I *really* wasn't cut out for detective work. This was all Gemma's fault.

"Emil? I doubt it. His profits started draining away the moment Lulu died. Paid a fortune to hire Juanita away from that Western. Capsize put all their chips on this movie," Jack continued. "If it fails, Emil's name is mud."

"What about Carey Stone?" I glanced toward the vanity across the room, where he was holding up his chin while someone powdered his neck.

Jack laughed. "I'm sorry, but I say Emil's more suspicious than Carey."

I frowned. What was that supposed to mean? Carey was definitely Lulu's type. I would need more convincing than that to drop him from our list of suspects.

As if sensing us talking about him, Emil glanced over. He signaled to Jack.

"There's my cue." Jack stood and rolled out his shoulder, his gaze far away. "In the last scene Lulu did, Chang-Rae chooses to forgive the lover who betrays her, even though her parents disapprove of her decision. Lulu's performance was falling flat. Emil asked her to think of a moment when she'd stuck up for her beliefs against her parents' wishes." He shrugged. "She hit the bull's-eye on the next take. Afterward, she told me, 'You know, Jack, Chang-Rae just taught me how to do the right thing.'"

I stared at his retreating figure. Who had betrayed Lulu? And had doing the right thing gotten her killed?

LATER THAT NIGHT, INSTEAD OF GOING TO BED IMMEDIATELY after dinner like usual, Ma gathered us into the living room. Gemma swept a crocheted blanket off the couch, but Ma didn't take the freed space. Instead, she paced the room, fanning herself. Peony slid onto the couch instead.

"Toy Tai offered us a room in her house in East Adams, and your ba would like us to accept."

Peony grabbed her knees. "I don't want to live there."

Gemma threw me a look, but I focused on Ma.

"Won't charge us much." Ma lifted her low hair bun and fanned the back of her neck. "Plus, you know she helped with all your deliveries. The baby will be in good hands."

"Why does the baby get a say?" grumbled Peony.

"Peony," I chastised, even though I understood her frustration. All my thoughts around the baby were directed toward the work it was causing, like all the diapers I had yet to sew. Ba had already left when Ma learned she was pregnant, and the baby, who should be a cause for celebration, had only been a cause of worry.

Gemma's fingers poked through the loose weave of the blanket, though I'd told her a million times not to do that. "But moving means letting them win. This is home. Remember what Ba always said? 'Uprooting a tree with strong roots can kill it.'"

Ma scoffed. "They will not kill us." She moved toward the window. "Your ba always loved this view, and I hoped he could come home to it." With a sigh, she turned around again.

Ba's voice rasped in my ear. *You must convince your ma to move . . . I must be able to count on you.*

If there was any time to speak up, it was now, but my mouth felt like an Indian seed pod, fluffy with cotton. I didn't want to move either, but sacrifices had to be made for the greater good. Ba was the head of the family, and he'd always done his best by us. That was good enough for me. I tugged the blanket from Gemma and folded it into a neat and even square, avoiding her gaze. "It's a good opportunity. It's closer to City Market."

Gemma gasped at my betrayal and reached out to pinch me, but I sidestepped her. She was so predictable, and anyway, I didn't deserve to be pinched for something out of my control. Her arms tightened and her chin jutted. "But farther from our suppliers, and anyway, that's not really the point."

I set the folded blanket on the couch arm. "It'll be easier to move before the baby comes."

"Who says we have to move at all?" Gemma cried.

"Girls, enough. I haven't decided yet." Ma's loose pant legs lifted as she lowered herself beside Peony, revealing her swollen ankles. "Toy Tai expects an answer by Friday. I will tell her my decision then."

27

GEMMA

WHILE WE WAITED FOR MA TO FALL ASLEEP, I FOLLOWED the traitorous May to our bedroom. I didn't even bother hiding my disgust from her and tried to make as much noise as possible folding laundry upon our bed. Even my scandalous news about Lulu's pregnancy, which I'd not had a chance to share yet, no longer felt like a burning coal on my tongue. May, on the other hand, managed to set up her ironing station against one wall with barely a squeak. We had disagreed on many things, but on the train station we had always been united. Just because Ba had a change of heart didn't mean we could abandon the fight. He was sick, but he'd be coming back soon.

I couldn't help remembering the time he'd come home with a bruised backside. He'd slipped off the roof he'd been repairing, which could've been fatal. Ma was so upset she burned the soup, but Ba assured us, his brown face cheerful, that he and gravity were old friends. Nothing much would keep him down.

Peony sat with her legs stretched out on her bed, gloomily staring at her feet as if they were half-drowned kittens.

"Go check on Ma," I told Peony.

Rather than squeezing by the ironing board and the foot of the big bed, she rolled over the mattress, messing up my piles, then blew out the door. I shot May another frosty glare. She licked her finger and tapped it to the iron, eliciting a sizzle. The sound annoyed me, a reminder of her mettle. I didn't have the nerve to touch a hot iron like she did.

While I waited for Peony to return, I picked up my half-filled-in crossword puzzle from Sunday's paper, mulling twenty-one down: *It takes time to sink in.*

It had to be GRAVEYARD. Still, it didn't feel right. Coffins sank, but did graveyards? I didn't fill it in.

May snapped out a damp shirt, eyeing me. "Before you burst into flames, I meant what I said. We have to be practical."

"Said the farmer to his chicken just before the axe fell. Also said Judas in the Garden of Gethsemane."

"You can be mad all you want. But family comes before principles."

I stabbed the newspaper with my pencil. "And this is where our family lives."

Peony darted back into the room and closed the door, nodding at us.

"Our brick is here," I continued, my voice louder. "We can't just leave our brick. How are we supposed to show the city this is our home if we're not living in it?"

Peony rolled over the big bed again and bounced onto her small mattress with a series of squeaks.

"Ba signed the Three Coins proposal." May bent over the board so I couldn't see her expression.

"Hold the horses. Ba said Three Coins would buy disaster."

"Yes, well, things have changed." Steam hissed as May ran the iron over the shirt.

I set down the crossword. "What do you mean?"

"Ba sent me a letter. His new treatment—pneumoperitoneum—carries risks. It would give him peace of mind to know we were settled . . . just in case the worst happens."

All my muscles unwound, and my energy seemed to suck out through my soles. Ba had been in the sanatorium for longer than the doctors had thought he would be. Was he so badly off that he required such a risky treatment?

"You mean if Ba dies?" Peony asked in a small voice.

"Yes." The word fell gently from May's mouth. She stood her iron and sat beside Peony. "Though we hope that won't be for a *very* long time. Who knows, maybe the treatment will work, Ba will come back tomorrow, and we can take him out for that malted milkshake."

I stared at a potholder without seeing it, the fight drained out of me. Ba couldn't leave us. I wouldn't let him, even if I had to personally escort his soul back from the Bridge of Seven Treasures, where the virtuous crossed into heaven. I still wasn't convinced we had to move. But being mad at May wouldn't help anything.

"Well, we're not moving tomorrow," I said, boxing up my worry for now. "And until then, we focus on solving this murder." I rolled out my news that Lulu had been pregnant and watched their somber moods vanish. "That would explain why Lulu had been feeling tired, as Hettie mentioned. Whoever the father is," I mused, "maybe he didn't want the child, so he killed them both."

Peony began to bounce. "If the boyfriend gave her the earrings, Janis Jewelers will know who he is."

"Hold on a minute." May hovered the iron over the board, her gaze running me down. "Who told you Lulu was pregnant?" Leave it to May to be distracted by non-important details.

"A doctor, of course."

"From the French Hospital?"

"Do I know any other doctors?" I asked, avoiding a direct lie.

"Which doctor?"

"Dr. Winter. Emil would've fired her, if he had known she was with child." I sped on before she could think of more questions concerning Dr. Winter. Would she really remove herself from the case if she found out I'd lied to her again? I didn't want to find out.

May had begun railroading a dish towel. "Jack didn't think Emil did it, but he didn't know about her pregnancy. He said she was in top form."

I nodded. That pregnancy changed everything, especially if Emil was the boyfriend.

May recounted her conversation with Jack. "Her character, Chang-Rae, had taught Lulu how to do the right thing. Maybe the 'right thing' had to do with her baby?" She set down the iron and wiped her forehead with the sleeve of her nightgown. "Jack doesn't think Carey Stone's a suspect either, but I didn't get a chance to talk to him personally yet. I will tomorrow, along with those Chinese extras. They weren't in today."

"I'll follow up on the satsuma mandarins," I said. Peony let out a loud sigh and flopped onto her back. Feeling left out of the investigation again. "Do you think Bettina could get us some of Lulu's clothes for a ruse? We might need to go jewelry shopping."

Peony rolled onto one shoulder. "I'll ask her. Bettina's spending two nights with us starting tomorrow, and she's in bad shape. Her ma refuses to come to the funeral. She still thinks Lulu isn't Lulu."

How would Wong Tai ever get closure without burying her own child? "When is that funeral?"

"Mr. Stritch arranged it for Monday at Rosedale."

Rosedale Cemetery, just a few miles southwest of Chinatown, was the final resting place for many of the Chinese, as it was open to all races and creeds. I groaned. "If she's buried, there goes Mr. Yam's petition for another autopsy. It's bad enough they think they already have her killer."

May's nose wrinkled as if detecting a bad odor. "And if Mr. Stritch did it, doubly bad that a killer be allowed to plan his victim's funeral."

I counted on my fingers. "Five more days to solve the case. Let's make them count."

MORNING LIGHT SEEMED RELUCTANT TO FILL THE MERCANTILE lot, where the broken toilet stood like a lost sheep among the junk, its lid stained and cracked. Why did the suspect close the lid after smoking? It seemed a strangely responsible thing to do. A crow landed by the busted shutter, which now looked like a skeleton with a broken rib cage. I flipped open the toilet lid before my imagination got the better of me.

Empty bottles and dirt filled the cavity. I pulled out the bottles one by one. At the bottom of the pile, I found two cigarette butts, one half-smoked. Using two sticks like chopsticks, I fished them out. Both were stamped in gold with the word LIBERTÉ, a brand I had not heard of. It sounded expensive. Imported. I wrapped the butts in a bit of newspaper. I didn't know what to do with them, but potential evidence like that shouldn't get lost.

A tiny movement caught my awareness, a change in the light, as though something had passed behind me, casting a brief shadow. I whipped around. Was someone watching me? The stillness rang loud in my ears. I shot back to the Mule, feeling exposed. In my haste to get going, the gears ground, and the engine died. *Easy, you ninny.* I restarted, chastising myself for letting my fear get to me. Whoever the killer was, he wouldn't kill a broad in broad daylight, surely?

I got rolling. Soon, City Market came into view, its hustle and bustle recalcifying my spine, even though I didn't make my turn tight enough and had to saw the Mule back and forth before getting the ship in the harbor. People edged away, shaking their heads. I hoped someone would invent a self-driving car one day, because I would be the first in line.

Before I set out my flowers, I brought Mr. Takashi a milk bottle of colorful roses for his table. He lifted his cowboy hat and smelled the blooms. "Maybe this will help me attract more customers, eh?"

"Slow for you too?"

He grunted. "Wanted my sons to go to college, but they'll have to help on the farm a while longer. Well, maybe that Roosevelt will get himself elected and shake things up."

"Ba likes Roosevelt too." Too bad most Chinese couldn't vote.

Mr. Takashi pulled a piece of paper from his apron on which was written an address. "Satsuma is uncommon around here; most are imported, but not for another month or two. Mr. Sunshine is the only grower I could find. But he's a bit of a drive."

AFTER ANOTHER DAY OF LACKLUSTER SALES, I PACKED UP AND
headed to Mr. Sunshine's in the city of Montebello, ten miles
southeast. Hot air blowing in through the open doors was nothing compared to the hot breath of the road hecklers crowding
me from behind, trying to get me to speed up. One gave a two-
note whistle as he passed, and I served it right back. Driving was
truly for the birds, especially driving when female. Most driv-
ers were male. I tried to keep my temper in check by focusing
on the gently sloping hills for which Montebello, or "beautiful
mountain," was named. Apple orchards boasted fruit, while the
apricot trees had gone quiet. Stretches of dried grass alternated
with vibrant fields of leafy stuff that would probably taste good
in the wok.

Following the rough map Mr. Takashi had drawn for me, I
reached a grove of orange trees, with their distinctive round
shapes, and then a barn with SUNSHINE GROWERS painted on the
side. I parked the Mule in a gravel lot, thankful there were no
lines to fit into.

Men in straw hats glanced up from their work in the orange
grove when I approached. A wave of nerves rushed through me;
I hated the feeling of being outnumbered. But I'd had my limit of
harassment for today. I rolled back my shoulders. If I could drive
down the road myself, why couldn't I walk down it on my own two
feet? Surely a man named Sunshine couldn't be too shady. Hardy-
har-har. Besides, if a woman had to wait for a man to accompany
her before going anywhere, we'd never get anything done.

"Good afternoon," I projected in my most confident tone. "Is,
er, Mr. Sunshine here?"

The man nearest the barn stuck his spade in the ground and
lazily approached. His leathery skin reminded me of wet clay
through which a comb had dragged deep lines. I put him at

forty-something. He whuffed out a seed and wiped his mouth on the back of his hand. "Who's asking?"

"Gemma Chow of Chow's Flowers."

"Didn't order flowers."

The other workers had stopped their activities and were watching us. "You're Mr. Sunshine?"

"You look disappointed."

"Of course not. I was, er, wondering if you sell satsuma mandarins."

"Satsuma, huh." His alfalfa-green eyes crimped, as if remembering something. "If you want satsuma, you'll have to wait till December like everyone else." He gestured to the row of trees closest to the barn, whose trunks were skinnier than the orange trees, with foliage hiding yellow-orange globules.

"Do you know of anyone selling them ripened now?"

"Can't be done." He smacked his lips in distaste.

A small man in overalls and a checked shirt emerged from the barn carrying a mug, his face shaded by a wide-brimmed hat.

"Actually," I said, "someone I know received satsumas as a gift a week ago."

"It *can* be done," said the newcomer, who turned out to be a Mexican woman. I relaxed a notch, knowing a female was about. "He's just cheap." Her dark eyes sparkled under thick eyebrows. "Won't spend on the chickens. His mother told him the secret."

"Don't need no pecking chickens in my life. I've got you," said Mr. Sunshine. He reached for the woman's mug, but she pulled it away. "I'm just fooling," he hastily added. "You're a good woman, Maria."

She released the mug and he drank thirstily.

I cleared my throat. "So your mother knows how to fruit satsumas early?"

Maria slipped her hands into her overall pockets. "She's the only one we know who can do it." A dimple marked her smooth brown cheeks. "But she's not the one who sold them to your friend."

"Why's that?"

Mr. Sunshine snorted. "Last I heard, she has dementia. She could be dead for all I know."

"Where does she live?"

"No idea. She disowned me when Maria and I got married twenty years ago. And as you can see, we've done quite well"— he raised his mug to the nearest tree—"without her money. Back to work, everyone! I'm not paying you to stare." He shoved the mug at Maria and stomped away. Maria regarded me curiously, then began to head back to the barn.

"He seems angry," I said, suspecting she knew more than she let on.

Facing me again, her round shoulders twitched. "She wasn't kind to us, but people can change." She cut her gaze to her husband, back to digging his hole with zeal. "Last we heard, his mother was living in Beverly Hills."

My jaw loosened. Thousands of people lived in Beverly Hills, but was there a connection between Lulu's visitor and Mr. Sunshine's mother? If so, I needed to find it before it no longer mattered.

28
MAY

AFTER A DAY ON SET, I HAD SEEN ENOUGH OF THE director, Emil, to know he came in two volumes—loud, and louder. Plus, he swore like a longshoreman. But on my second morning, the loudest thing about him was his lime-green socks. And somehow, that seemed worse. His eyes sparked like two lit fuses, and people moved about as if the place were rigged with explosives. Even Juanita didn't complain when Emil corrected her for the third time.

With his uneven temper, maybe he *was* the murderer. He might not have had a financial incentive, but if he was Lulu's boyfriend, maybe he'd snapped in a jealous rage. He'd certainly admired Lulu.

"Juanita." The man's thin upper lip curled with irritation. "Your boyfriend has just canceled your secret trip. You're worried, but you don't want him to think you are worried. Miss Vance—help her." He gestured at an older lady with the posture of a ballerina standing nearby, then stalked off. Juanita left her chair and followed Miss Vance.

I squeezed my teapot, and the lid rattled. Carey Stone, who had been watching me from the table with a curious expression, gestured at the now-empty seat. "These damn stools are like sitting on thimbles, but better than standing. This might take a while. Miss Chow, was it?"

Even after hours of standing by him, I still felt a thrill shoot through me at his mention of my name. *Stop gaping. This is the chance you've been waiting for.* I set the teapot down and slipped onto the stool.

"I hear you knew Lulu." Carey's voice was as smooth as water between fingers.

"Yes." Word traveled fast. I glanced at Jack, who was adjusting a spotlight. I hadn't pegged him for a blabbermouth, but then again, I hardly knew him.

"Relax. Jack only tells me his secrets, and I won't tell a soul. Got too many of my own." He winked, and I lost my train of thought.

"Ahem. Hettie said you and she were supposed to rehearse with Lulu at your place the night she was killed, but you switched plans because your place was a mob scene."

The dark-blond slashes of Carey's eyebrows lifted. "Yes. Fans can get overzealous. It makes me sick to think of her being hurt while we were reading our lines. She was a real doll."

I made a sympathetic noise, adding, "I had thought Hettie said it was the press bothering you."

"Did she?" A muscle in his cheek twitched, and he shifted on his stool. "Press, fans, they all look the same when they're screaming your name."

Was it my imagination, or had my question made him uncomfortable? His gaze skittered away from me to Jack again, who seemed to be appraising how his spotlight fell upon us. Being hounded by the press was different from being mobbed by overzealous fans. The former suggested a scandal. But what scandal had been breaking?

A secret relationship with Lulu, and a baby on the way? If he was the boyfriend, had he killed her to protect his reputation as America's heartthrob?

Yet, it would've been near impossible to kill her at six o'clock, transport her to the stables, where we were painting the truck, without us seeing him, drop her Cadillac in the Mercantile lot, and return to Hettie's place in time for their rehearsal at seven, unless he'd had an accomplice. Vital pieces were still missing from this story.

Carey recovered his composure, rubbing a thumb across his pillowy bottom lip. "Whoever did it has a lot to answer for. This whole production has boarded an express train to sinkhole city."

"What do you mean?"

"Delays cost money, and Juanita doesn't understand this role. We should have finished this scene by now. What happened this morning might be the final nail in the coffin."

"What happened this morning?"

He blinked. "Ah, I guess the extras don't get the call sheets. Hettie Bright jumped ship." He watched me absorb the shock, adding, "She joined *Big Apple Blues*."

"Is that another movie?" He probably thought me the dullest pin in the cushion.

"Not just a movie. It's rumored to have a million-dollar budget." That was a lot of zeros. "What's it about?"

"A wealthy Manhattan couple and the Shanghai madam who tries to push the wife off the Empire State Building. Hettie is playing the madam."

I groaned. "Sounds charming." Hettie would have to get her heavy-lidded round eyes taped, like Juanita.

He spread his hands over the table and leaned closer. "Summit Studios first offered Lulu the role, but she refused. She said

she was done playing villains. Next thing I hear, Capsize Pictures comes a-courtin' her with *A Far East Affair*. Both me and
Hettie signed on not long after, even though it was a smaller role
than she's used to. Lulu was a meteor, and we both wanted to
grab her tail, even at half salary."

"Three bright stars. Summit Studios must have been worried."

He chuckled. "They threatened lawsuits, but they had no leg
to stand on. But as we like to say where I'm from, sometimes a
prairie fire just changes direction. Lulu's death changed Summit's fortunes overnight."

Summit Studios certainly benefited with Lulu gone. But who
at Summit Studios? There could be hundreds of people. "But . . .
why would Hettie leave?"

"The usual reason, I suppose."

"Money?"

He nodded. "A hundred thousand is what I heard. They're
even covering the costs of her breaking her contract."

Something sick bubbled inside me as I wondered if I'd been
played by her. I stared into the cup, as if there were actually tea
leaves in the bottom for me to read. If money was the only reason for Hettie leaving, what did that say about her friendship
with Lulu? Maybe now she could buy herself that castle Mr.
News had joked about, Hettie's Castle.

I placed my hands around one of the teacups, even though it
was cold. "Has Summit Studios come to you?" I asked carefully,
knowing I was treading on delicate territory.

"No." He studied his fingernails. Was that anger darkening
his brow? Did he resent not being asked as well? "But even if they
had, I would've said no."

"Why is that?"

"Let's just say, I'm not their type and they're not mine."

How could the handsome and talented Carey Stone *not* be somebody's type? Everyone had secrets, but what were his?

The room had gone strangely quiet. Carey took the teacup from me and gently pulled my hand toward him. I felt myself getting trapped in the glittering depths of his blue eyes, watching me with a strange intensity. All my thoughts homed in on the feeling of his hand caressing mine, his fingers touching my palm as if he were trying to pass me a secret message. Closer he came, bringing the scent of herbs and musk. My pulse jittered. I thought I might swoon.

"Wh-what—" I attempted words.

"Cut!" yelled Emil. "My God, this day's finally getting better."

Back to reality, I snatched my hand from Carey's, still feeling the warm imprint on my fingers. The whole room was watching us.

"They started filming a few seconds ago," said Carey. "I was just giving them a little extra."

"Miss Chow, was it?" Emil cut in. "I said you had presence and I meant it. You and Carey were like two pieces of bacon up there. Sizzling. Everyone, take five. Miss Chow, how would you like to be in pictures?"

MY HEAD BUZZED AS I HIKED TO BUILDING 6, WHERE I HAD arranged for the Chinese extras to meet me in their dressing room to chat about Lulu. The walkway between the warehouses teemed with people on their way home.

Hollywood was knocking once more, and once again, I felt the hand of Lulu guiding me. The pay would be a whole eight dollars a day. With that, we could definitely do better than East Adams.

But I wasn't an actress. Was I?

I had enjoyed, no, *loved* playacting with Lulu. And though I would never admit it to Gemma, I'd felt a strange sense of satisfaction after our recent charades—at Westlake Park, the police station, the Pannychis—maybe even exhilaration.

So what was really holding me back?

A memory bubbled up, of Lulu and me riding the Angels Flight funicular up steep Bunker Hill. My stomach had fluttered like wildflowers in a breeze, and we had huddled close at the front of the car, where it seemed safer. As we rose higher, I was sure the cable would break, sending us crashing down the mountain. We finally reached the top. Treetops formed a richly textured green carpet all around us, but the roof blocked most of the view. We'd have to move to the railing, twenty feet away, to see anything.

But neither of us could make our feet move. "If we act brave, do you think we will be?" I asked doubtfully.

Lulu reached out a tentative toe. Together, we shuffled to the back.

The Los Angeles Basin spread wide before us like a hand-loomed skirt, a slick ribbon of river running through it. The mountains beyond looked spun from gold. Letting go of my hand, Lulu clamped the rails. "Hello, world, I'm Lulu. Pleased to meet you. Don't drop me."

"Salutations, sky," I added. "I'm May. You're looking a little blue."

We giggled, and at that moment, I felt as light as a balloon and ready to sail away.

But what would Ma and Ba say? A family was like a kite—pull one string even a little, and the kite changed directions. They expected grandchildren. Acting might suspend marriage, maybe even ruin my chances for it altogether.

A man grabbed me, and I yelped, nearly falling. An attacker?

"Easy, miss." The man set me back on my feet, his work boots gripping the pavement. The cart of props he'd been wheeling drifted to one side.

"Pardon me," I murmured, chastising myself for being so distracted.

What if taking the role made *me* the murderer's next target? I had to stay focused and aware of my surroundings.

Reaching the dressing room, I shook off grisly thoughts of being bashed over the head or knifed in the back. Emil had given me a day to think about it. He'd tucked his business card into my hand, telling me I should call him tomorrow and let him know my decision.

I knocked on a metal door. It swung open, releasing the scent of rose cold cream. A girl wearing a slip stuck her hairpin between her lips and gave me a no-nonsense handshake—one pump. I warmed to her instantly, the way I did to all no-nonsense people. She jammed the hairpin into her hair. "Come in. You must be May. I'm Patty Q." She had a quick way of speaking and moving, like she had a train to catch. "That's Fanny Ma"—she nodded toward a girl rubbing her face with cream—"and that's Yuki Hirami."

Yuki quirked an eyebrow at me in the mirror, where she was sitting on one of four stools. It didn't surprise me that one of the Chinese extras was actually Japanese. I didn't know any of these girls, though probably a connection was only a handshake away.

Patty Q finished pinning her hair. "So you don't think that Guitar Man character killed her?"

"No. We think he's a convenient scapegoat."

From a clothes rack, she slipped a cotton dress off a hanger. "That doesn't surprise me at all. It struck me as a cooked-up story. I mean, scaring her with a turtle? She loved animals.

Anyway, we're glad someone's looking into her death. We were all fans of hers, you know. Fanny and I came all the way from San Francisco for the chance to be in a movie with her."

Fanny rubbed her hands of the excess cream and approached, giving me a little bow. With her downy cheeks and soft eyes, and an attractive female roundness all over, she didn't look like she could kill a spider, much less a person, but I couldn't rule her out on looks alone. "We heard Emil wants you for Chang-Rae," she said in a soft voice.

News sure traveled fast. With Hettie gone, Emil had proposed that Juanita fill Hettie's role. Her elated shriek at the suggestion was still making my ears ring. I would step in for Lulu's old role. "Yes. I haven't decided yet."

Yuki slid off her stool and slunk over, her hair falling like a waterfall around her shoulders. With her haughty manner and eyes that were watchful even when not looking, she put me in mind of the ravens in the old Plaza fountain. "Lucky you. Congratulations." Her voice was husky with irony. Unlike Fanny, she could easily be cast as a villain. Still, that didn't make her one.

Patty Q stepped into her dress. "Don't be rude. May's way prettier than you, and anyway, you're too short."

"Lulu wasn't tall," Yuki sniffed, returning to her perch.

"Taller than you," Patty Q snapped back. "They chose us because we're shorter than her. Makes her look taller."

Lulu's visitor had been my height. Unless the neighbor had been wrong, none of the extras was Lulu's visitor—not to mention, a funeral dress didn't seem like the kind of garment any of these girls would've worn. But that didn't mean they hadn't stolen her script, or worse.

Or maybe Lulu's visitor wasn't Oriental, only someone whose eyelids were taped. I sucked in my breath as the field widened once again. If the visitor was the murderer, perhaps she had hoped to implicate a Chinese person with the disguise. It seemed a twisted thing to do, but so was murder.

Losing interest in me, Yuki took out a peacock-blue compact and began powdering her face in the mirror. Light from the bulbs around the mirror made her skin shimmer like it was dusted in gold.

"That's not the new Fox Stardust Powder, is it?" I asked, noticing that none of the beauty products on the counter had the distinctive peacock-blue packaging of Fox Cosmetics.

Yuki's puff paused for a fraction of a second. "So what if it is? Fox products make me feel like a million bucks."

Patty Q crossed to Yuki and put her face up to the other girl's. Swan-necked and fair, Patty Q had the practical, even features of one who kept her word, while Yuki's pouting expression expected *you* to keep yours. "Why are you giving Otis Fox your hard-earned money?" Patty Q demanded. "He doesn't like Chinese, and I bet he doesn't like Japanese either."

Yuki snorted. "Who cares, as long as the products keep you looking youthful? It's all those natural ingredients they use. They started the company from Mrs. Fox's herd of twelve goats, and have you seen her skin? She looks thirty but she's probably fifty. Her son, Philippe, is pretty dishy too. I saw him on a political ad."

"Don't tell me he wears Stardust Powder too. Give me that." Patty Q grabbed the compact. Peering at her reflection, she tapped the powder to her face.

The door burst open, and the fourth Chinese extra slid in. She was as tiny as Peony, her slender neck holding up a perfect moon of a head. With her rosy cheeks and snug-fitting dress, she looked like she could've walked off the Prosperity cigar box. "I asked them about offering tea once in a while instead of coffee, but they said no. Oh, you must be May. I'm Suzy Daisy from Fresno." She was as bubbly as champagne, without a hint of guile.

"Nice to meet you," I said, taking her small hand.

With a bored grunt, Yuki began brushing her hair.

"So what do you want to know about Lulu?" asked fast-talking Patty Q.

I perched on a love seat. "How well did you know her?"

"Not well," said Suzy Daisy. She turned her back to the demure Fanny, who helped undo her necklace. "But she went out of her way to be nice to us. We begged her to show us how to cry on demand, and she told us to think of something so sad, it hurts to think about."

A memory tugged at me. Hettie Bright had mentioned seeing the Chinese "backgrounders" crying after talking with Lulu. So they hadn't been arguing, only acting.

Patty Q plopped down onto a stool and began braiding her hair with even tugs of her fingers. "I thought of when my grand-mother died last year."

Fanny filed a fingernail, and her gaze grew wistful. "I thought of my parents having to close their restaurant for good."

"I thought of what would happen if I could never afford a mink coat," said Yuki with a smirk.

"Did she ever mention a boyfriend?" I asked. "Did you ever see her with anyone?"

The women shook their heads.

Patty Q fit a felt beret over her head. "She was always work-ing. Like me. I've got another job to get to. Toodles." Shouldering a large bag, she grabbed her jacket.

As the door closed behind her, I couldn't help wondering if

she was in a hurry because of the job, or because my questions were making her uncomfortable.

"Do you know if anyone here had it out for her?" I tried again with the three remaining extras. "I'd heard someone was stealing her scripts."

I watched the women's expressions carefully. In the mirror, Fanny's hazel eyes floated up to the right corner. Suzy Daisy, unbuttoning her dress, shook her head. "She seemed a real nice person. I wish all the stars were that way."

Yuki admired her reflection, turning from side to side to see herself from all angles. There was something crafty about her. But maybe I only thought that because she clearly didn't like me.

"Had you heard anything, Yuki?" I asked, annoyed at her indifference.

"Oh, please. Hundreds of girls would kill to be her. You should be asking who *didn't* have it out for her." She stood and grabbed a jacket from a wall hook. "Well, it's been fun, but I have a bus to catch."

"One last thing—why did you all quit after Lulu died?" I asked.

"We thought if there was a killer out there, maybe they'd be after us too," said Suzy Daisy. "But Fanny said we owed it to Lulu to stay strong."

Fanny pivoted on her stool, and her face was mournful. "She called us 'movie stars in training,'" she said in her quiet voice. "She hoped one day she wouldn't be the only Oriental face on the screen. If I ever need to cry in the future, I will think of her."

If Fanny was acting, she was good at it. The problem with talking with actors was that you never knew for certain when the camera started rolling. In a city full of them, finding the truth would be as easy as grabbing the wind.

29
GEMMA

"SLOW DOWN," I TOLD MAY, WHO WAS DRIVING AS FAST as a firecracker from the studio. After my haul to Montebello, I was already feeling queasy.

"We're late, and Ma's no fool," May snapped back, though she slowed a notch.

I forced my mind back to her description of the Chinese extras. "We have bubbly Suzy Daisy, practical Patty Q, demure Fanny, and spicy Yuki. So who stole Lulu's scripts?"

"I'm not convinced any of them did."

"I'd put my money on Yuki. She sounds like a character."

"Well, she wasn't happy when I—"

"When you . . ."

"I mean—" May's driving gloves tightened around the wheel. "Never mind."

I crossed my arms tight. "What's holding up your hat? Air? Or are you keeping secrets?"

She lifted her nose, as if to keep her thoughts from spilling out. "Let's get back to your day."

"A dead end. Those mandarins were our only link to Lulu's visitor."

"Just because someone has dementia doesn't mean they can't answer a question. Mr. Sunshine's mother might still have some faculties. We can look through the phone directory for a Sunshine in Beverly Hills. It's a long shot, but it doesn't cost much to take."

We parked, then unloaded our floral supplies. In front of the herbalist's shop, Mr. Yam and No Good were listening to Dai-Sang read a letter and didn't even notice us approach.

". . . *unable to accept your proposal for the Three Coins development project, as there is insufficient evidence that it is in the city's interest at this time.*" Dai-Sang folded the letter, his scholarly face grave.

So the city council had spoken. There would be no alternative neighborhood for the Chinese.

"*Insufficient evidence,*" Mr. Yam echoed in disgust. "We sent them a fifty-page document, signed by a hundred of our business leaders, and they reject it after less than a week?"

No Good crossed his arms over his potbelly. "There will never be a time when we are in the city's interest. We should fight back. Deface their businesses. See how they like having eggs thrown at them."

"When you go to dig a grave for your enemy, dig two," intoned Dai-Sang.

Noticing us drawing closer, No Good's scowl dug in like a spade in baked earth.

"Evening, Mr. Ng, Mr. Yam, Dai-Sang," May greeted politely.

The friendly lines in Mr. Yam's cheeks returned, and he gave us a small bow. "You are coming home late."

No Good grunted. "Girls should be helping their ma with the meal."

"Girls *are* helping with the meal, just not in the kitchen," I growled back, clutching my tote of floral supplies closer.

"These girls are very responsible," said Mr. Yam. "When we

were their age, we were catching bass in the river, or throwing dice."

"Women should know their place." No Good's long black mustache flapped like a crow trying to take flight. "You've gone soft, and look what their bad luck has brought you."

"What does that mean?" My tote slipped off my shoulder.

Mr. Yam clucked his tongue. "It is time for Mrs. Yam and me to find another place." He glanced down the street toward One Dragon. "More of the ceiling has crumbled, and the landlord will not fix it."

"But where will you go?" May clutched her hat to her head, as if a fickle wind might knock it away.

"There are many options. Do not worry." Mr. Yam gave us a smile that did not assure me. I hugged myself tightly, already feeling the loss.

Dai-Sang's expression darkened, and he busied himself moving his turtles back into his store.

"Your problem is you should have worried more." No Good crooked a yellow fingernail at Mr. Yam, the only nail he kept long. Then, whiskers twitching, he strode away, his flat-footed gait smacking the uneven pavement.

Mr. Yam watched him. "Don't mind him. He has become a grumpy old trout, stuck in his narrow stream. He loved a woman once. But she chose someone else. So he is bitter."

Who could blame her for not wanting a sourpuss like him?

Dai-Sang returned, holding a small feed sack, and began sorting through his trays of citrus peel, which had been drying in the sun.

"Of course," Mr. Yam mused, "everyone loved Shao."

I sucked in a breath, and May threw me a questioning glance.

"Mr. Moon told me Gee Fa's wife was named Shao," I said. *She was as lovely as a vase.*

"Yes." Mr. Yam's face twitched, as if busy with too many thoughts.

Dai-Sang's fingers moved deliberately, picking strips of dried peel and placing them in the feed sack. "She was taken too soon. Baby was too big."

My mind began to take a detour down a twisted alley. Shao had chosen Gee Fa over No Good. "Exactly how bitter is Mr. Ng?"

Dai-Sang sniffed one of the peels and tossed it back. "If you're wondering if Mr. Ng was the person who tipped off the police, let us not speculate."

I swallowed the sour taste in my mouth. Betraying a country-man was like yanking a rose off a bush despite the thorns. If he had done such a thing, may the guilt shred him inside.

"What happened to this baby?" May asked Dai-Sang.

"Gee Fa was in no state to care for a child. I believe the orphanage took her."

"Her?" I asked, my mind flying to the young woman May saw Gee Fa talking to at the Plaza fountain. Where had she been all these years? May chewed her lip, maybe thinking the same thing.

Mr. Yam's short chin levered up and down. "Yes. I think it was a girl."

"Have you seen Gee Fa?" May's eyes drifted to a loose button on Mr. Yam's shirt.

He shook his head. "He is being kept in the Hall of Justice, and is not allowed visitors. Not even a smoke." I scowled. Gee Fa hated going into buildings, and I wasn't sure how he would stand being cooped up, much less on the fourteenth floor. "But his petition received one thousand, one hundred, and nine signatures, a good number. I delivered it to the Hall of Justice last night."

I blew out a breath. "Great magnolia, that is an impressive number."

Mr. Yam hooked his thumbs into the waistband of his worn trousers. "Yes. Took much paper."

"Let us hope the petition will be loud enough." Dai-Sang handed May the feed sack. "Give these to your ma. Good for nausea."

She dipped her head. "Thank you, Dai-Sang. Good night, uncles."

Before going into our building, we touched our family brick. Then we quietly ducked into May's sewing room so she could change from her simple dotted dress back into her work clothes.

Ma was out on the balcony when we at last arrived, unpinning sheets from our clothesline. Bettina and Peony stood at the stove, aprons tied, dropping dumplings into boiling water. They hurried over as we stripped off our shoes and hats. Steam from the pot had fogged Bettina's lenses. I embraced her, which was like hugging a damp coat.

"Bettina brought Lulu's clothes like you asked," whispered Peony. "But they might need alterations."

Ma returned from the balcony and waddled over. "You're very late, daughters." Her hair was held back by a handkerchief, and beads of sweat dotted her nose.

"We are sorry, Ma." May handed her the sack of dried peel. "Dai-Sang said the city council has rejected the Three Coins proposal."

Ma tsked her tongue. She opened the feed sack and took a short sniff.

"And Mr. Yam said he and Mrs. Yam are moving," I added.

"That one, I knew about. Mrs. Yam told me." She picked my tote of garden tools up off the floor and brought them to the sink for rinsing. "No need for sadness. Maybe they will find a place in East Adams too, and we can see them often."

"*If* we move to East Adams," I said.

"Yes, if," Ma added.

I wanted to ask her about Gee Fa's daughter, but talking about a daughter born under such tragic circumstances might be unlucky for Ma. She turned back around, one hand still on the sink. "A doctor named Frederick Winter called you today, Gemma. Why are you seeing a doctor?"

I nearly stumbled pulling off a stocking. May threw me a look full of daggers. We rarely got business calls. People just knew to stop by City Market if they wanted anything. I busied myself lining up my oxfords, then turned around, my face as composed as a tea tray. "Oh, he was just thinking to order flowers for his office. I'll return his call tomorrow."

"But he said to come by his office at your earliest convenience. He said you knew the address. I never heard of a doctor's office ordering flowers." Ma leaned against the sink, watching me.

"Well, yes, it's becoming quite fashionable. In fact . . ." I drew out my words, sensing an opportunity. Next to me, May's face had turned to stone. "May and I have been prospecting new ways to sell the flowers. So . . . we might have a few late days like today. I hope that's okay?" I held my breath. This white lie would either be brilliant or a bust.

Bettina began wringing at her apron, maybe sensing my lie. Peony, laying out bowls on the table, gave her a reassuring glance.

Ma shook her head, pulling loose strands from the handkerchief. "You girls are working too hard, doing the work of many sons."

My smile faltered. The trouble with white lies was the oily coating they left behind. May took a step away from me, as if expecting lightning to hit me on the spot. "Don't worry, Ma. May's face does half the work for us." I pinched May's cheek, and she batted me away.

That was close. Suddenly feeling too warm, I escaped to the balcony to finish taking in the sheets, but also to puzzle out why Freddie had called. He must have had some revelation about the case. He certainly hadn't called to order up new flowers.

AFTER A DINNER IN WHICH I BARELY TASTED MA'S STEAMED FISH and bok choy stir-fried with pickled turnip, Peony caught my eye and announced, as we had planned, "Bettina wants to help me wash the dishes."

"But you are our guest," Ma protested.

"I like w-washing dishes," said Bettina.

Ma patted Bettina's hand. "A wife who enjoys her housework is a treasure in the house."

"Thank you, Bettina and Peony," May replied smoothly. "That will give me time to finish some stitching in the sewing room."

"I'll help you," I added. In the privacy of May's sewing room, we—well, *May*—would start tailoring Lulu's clothes to fit me for my ruse at Janis Jewelers tomorrow. I wished she could come with me. May's presence gave credibility to barefaced lies, and we needed this ploy to yield results.

Ma grinned her missing-tooth smile. "I'm glad you're finally taking an interest in sewing. Maybe I'll join you. I haven't listened to music in a while."

I propped up my smile. Of all nights to sit with us, why did it have to be tonight? "That would be nice, Ma."

Setting off for the room down the hall, we dragged another

chair, an extra lamp, and a sheepskin rug for Ma's feet. While I settled Ma into the chair, May discreetly hid the dotted dress she had stashed there earlier behind one of the calico curtains.

The open window let in a swinging tune that, far from getting Ma sleepy, caused her shoulders to swing from side to side. "Your ba likes this 'ragtime.' He says it makes him feel young." Her swaying slowed. "So tell me, how many sales at City Market today?"

While May draped her dress form with a length of cloth, I began babbling about our made-up day at City Market. Then the conversation turned to May's date with Wallace tomorrow night at Fragrant Bamboo.

"Wear green," said Ma. "Green means harmony, and we all hope for a harmonious union."

"Yes, Ma," May replied, suddenly looking a little green herself.

After what seemed like an endless loop of stabbing my fingers and tying knots, a sleepy song called "Wabash Moon" drifted in from the building across the way. Ma yawned. "Time for bed."

I helped her back to our apartment. While Peony and Bettina waited for Ma to fall asleep, I snuck Bettina's valise back to the sewing room and set it on May's sewing table.

Leather buckles slid silkily apart in a cloud of jasmine perfume, revealing colorful dresses that begged to be petted. "Butter and eggs," I murmured.

I expected May to fall upon the clothes. Instead, she drew back. Sadness shrouded her face. "It doesn't seem right to wear her things."

"These might help us find the person who gave Lulu those crane earrings." I drew out a wine-colored dress with geometric diamond patterns and held it to me. "Anyway, you're not going, so you don't have to wear them."

May lifted out one of chocolate silk. "Actually, I got the day off tomorrow. They don't need us every day."

"You just started, and you're already getting a vacation? Not that I'm complaining." A two-woman act was much more convincing than a solo. "So who do you think they'll get to replace Hettie?"

"Why do you think I'd know?" she said a little too defensively. I peered closer, but her face was as inscrutable as her dress form. She batted me away. The wooden spools in her basket tutted as she rummaged through them. "After the jeweler, we can visit that doctor of yours as well. I wonder why he was so desperate to see you."

I lifted the wine-colored dress over my head, my pulse quickening uncomfortably. It seemed the doctor's path was crossing mine yet again, which both pleased and irritated me. The crepe de chine poured over me like cool lemonade.

"Who is he, anyway? Is he going to charge us for his services?"

"Just a doctor, and I don't know." Freddie might not charge us, but this would definitely cost me in sisterly trust if May recognized him from Westlake Park.

The door opened, and a double-peaked mountain of Bettina and Peony under a single cream-colored blanket stood in the doorframe.

"Good heavens," said May.

The pair made their way in, and I feigned horror. "It's alive. It's moving. It's alive, it's alive, it's alive!"

Peony grinned at my Dr. Frankenstein impersonation. That movie was one of the last we had seen before Ba had taken ill. Bettina hardly seemed to hear me.

They alit on the sheepskin rug, watching May button me into

Lulu's dress. Bettina glanced away. "M-my ma keeps making Lulu's f-favorite tofu dish." The girl was still stuttering.

"She won't be like that forever." Peony nudged closer to Bettina. "Just like my ba. He's sick right now, but he'll get better."

May hiked up the shoulders of my wine-colored dress, pinning them higher. Lulu had been longer in the waist. "That's right. Our job is to buoy them up so they can float on their own again."

"And then we can all go out for malted milkshakes," added Peony.

"I want to try the new rocky road," I said of the new chocolate ice cream with snips of marshmallows and nuts. "I heard it was invented to cheer people up during these gloomy times."

Bettina studied the bumps of her knees under her nightgown. "Lulu used to take me for ice cream after work every F-Friday."

May's face folded sympathetically, and she clucked her tongue. Poor Bettina. Perhaps she needed to be useful. Being useful was the best way I'd found to drive away the gnats of anxiety, which hovered over too-still waters.

"Say, Peony, could you grab the phone directory?" I asked. "I want you girls to help me look up a Mrs. Sunshine in Beverly Hills."

Peony ran out and returned a few seconds later with the book. Flipping to the right page, she began moving her finger down the names. "Abraham Sunshine, Court Sunshine, Sunshine Growers, Sunshine Laundry . . . nothing in Beverly Hills, though."

Bettina flipped the blanket hood off her head. "Sunshine is a funny name. We have a neighbor named Mrs. Sonenshein."

I glanced back at May, whose hands had fallen away from me. "Describe her."

"She's older and lives by herself across the st-street, a few doors down. I haven't seen her for a few m-m-months."

"Does she grow mandarins?" I asked.

"I d-don't know."

Was it possible this Mrs. Sonenshein was Mr. Sunshine's mother? A son who was disowned might change his name. He might even choose a similar but catchier name, like "Sunshine," for his citrus business. We were closing in on the answer, as sure as May was cinching the fabric around me. Hopefully, tomorrow would bring a ray of enlightenment.

30
MAY

EVEN BEFORE WE SET OFF FOR JANIS JEWELERS IN THE Mid-Wilshire district, Lulu's chocolate silk dress was sticking to me. This might be Gemma's most ridiculous scheme so far. "I hate deceiving Ma," I informed her. After City Market, we had snuck back into our building to change in my sewing room, being extra quiet just in case Ma decided to venture out.

In the passenger seat, Gemma patted on her lipstick with her finger. "I don't like it either, but think of it this way: Everyone is a little good and a little bad, and what matters is the final tally, which I hope won't be for a while."

"I'm sure a lot of crooks would agree with you."

Traffic forced us to a crawl in the downtown corridor, where stone buildings in the Beaux-Arts style leaned in on either side like disapproving elders. A fight seemed to have broken out in the lunch line of a soup kitchen, and the wails of a crying baby set my nerves on edge. That could be us, scrapping for bread heels, our cramping bellies reducing us to blows.

My breathing came easier as we turned into one of the dim tunnels out of downtown, where the scenes of desperation were replaced with cooling cement. At last, the palm-tree-studded Westlake neighborhood drew up around us. A signal halted us by a handsome bronze Pierce-Arrow. While Gemma stridently defended our pending misdeeds, the driver, a tall man with a pointy blond beard and sharp cheekbones, stared openly at me, something menacing in his gaze. I went as still as a jackrabbit, longing for the light to change. Perhaps it was the combination of our fine clothes and smart berets contrasted with this old jalopy that had caught his attention. Still, it was never good manners to stare.

". . . four more days until they bury her, and I'm not giving up without a fight. Why, the day you give up the fight is the day you find yourself in a basement with your toes sticking out like shriveled grapes and your face looking like a tin of shoe polish." Gemma frowned at a bug on the windshield. "We should be thankful for the fight, because the alternative is worse."

Janis Jewelers occupied the same block as the luxury department store Bullocks Wilshire, with its streamlined façade and copper-sheathed tower that could be seen for miles. With the building of that shopping palace, more luxury shops had begun moving out of downtown to this quieter neighborhood, where there were no soup lines or people with cardboard shoes. I longed to live in a quiet neighborhood one day, but in Los Angeles, quiet came with a hefty price tag.

I parked around the corner in front of a new apartment building and out of sight of Janis Jewelers. After adjusting the belts of our dresses, which I'd hemmed to midcalf to drape at the perfect angles, we made our way down a sidewalk that sparkled like it'd been dusted by Fox Stardust Powder.

"Remember your story?" asked Gemma, marching alongside me.

"Yes, I remember." We were gambling that the shopkeeper didn't know the identity of the person for whom the crane

earrings had been purchased. I would play the troubled recipi-
ent, and Gemma would play my sister.

She elbowed me. "I would do the tragic one, but you're more
tragic than me."

"Thanks," I muttered. I hadn't told Gemma about Emil's offer
because I wasn't ready to fight that battle yet.

Windows with cranberry awnings were the only spots of
color on the stony walls of Janis Jewelers. A doorman pulled
open the door for us, his face as expressionless as a cantaloupe.

The smell of heavy perfume daubed the air. A customer like a
stout version of Greta Garbo, with her dark waved bob and pancake hat, admired a stunner of a necklace in a mirror.

On the other side of the counter, a shopgirl clasped her hands,
making the ruffles of her apron quiver. "Truly, it speaks for itself."

The jewelry displayed in the cases looked no different from
the painted-glass pieces women wore to imitate the movie stars,
but with heft and depth. Those were real gems, as real as the
pain of Gemma pinching my arm. She nodded toward a man
who had been inspecting a gem through a loupe.

Sighting us, he quickly wrapped both objects in velvet and
slipped the bundle into a drawer. "Good afternoon." The last
word fishtailed up, as if the question of whether it would be
a good afternoon was now in doubt. He straightened his her-
ringbone vest and smoothed back his black hair, which was
divided neatly into two shares atop his head. "May I help you?"

Gemma showed him our white jewelry box. "Earlier this
year, my sister received a pair of gold crane earrings from Janis
Jewelers—"

"It is Jan-*nee*, after our family name," said the man, his French
accent high in his nose.

"Par-*dohn*, Monsieur Jan-*nee*," Gemma said respectfully, sliding her eyes to me. "Anyway, the earrings were given to her by a mysterious gentleman, and we were hoping to learn his name."

Monsieur Janis clutched at his bony fingers. "I am sorry. We never disclose our client list."

"Yes, but I hoped you would make un exception pour l'amour." Gemma pressed a hand to her heart. The bit of French she had picked up at school was painful even to my ears. "Tell her, sister."

I lowered my gaze to the jewelry case, displaying cocktail rings of all shapes. "You see, I was married to a man I despised." I shuddered. "He treated his bulldog better than me, slapping my hand if I tried to feed the ducks, yanking me along if I wasn't walking fast enough."

Gemma made a disgusted sound, and her beret wagged back and forth. I took a deep breath through my nose, as if trying to calm myself.

"I do not see what zis has to do with us." Three lines had appeared in Monsieur Janis's forehead. He moved closer to his telephone, perhaps in case law enforcement was needed.

I quickly continued, trying not to let my alarm affect my performance. "Well, one day, my husband was scolding me over the roast beef I had made for our picnic, and a young man who I'd often seen in the park stood up from his bench. He'd overheard." I chuckled in embarrassment. "Half the park overheard. I watched in amazement as he stuck something into the knot of a tree, then tipped his hat to me."

The shopgirl held up another necklace, but Greta Garbo had begun watching us through her mirror. Monsieur Janis was staring. I couldn't help noticing a bit of carrot stuck between his teeth.

"It was a letter addressed 'To the lady who married a bull-dog.'" My gaze fell to the combed carpet with its fleur-de-lis design. "Over the next few months, this young man would leave me notes—nothing scandalous, of course, but encouragements, sometimes poems to lift my spirits. And then, one day, I found the crane earrings."

Greta Garbo twisted around, making no pretense of watching us.

"That was the last I heard from him." I imagined something sad—Ba lying in his sickbed, weak and afraid, his wasted lungs barely rising, no one there to comfort him—and my eyes filled with tears and my nose prickled with warmth.

"It's okay, sister." Gemma patted my arm. "Take my hankie."

Swallowing down the lump in my throat, I took it. Monsieur Janis was stretching out his neck in quick jerks, at a loss for how to react to my sordid tale. At least he was no longer looking at the telephone. "Where are ze earrings?"

"Alas, my husband found them, and, well, I can only assume he gave them to his mistress. They ran off a few months ago."

Greta Garbo gasped and pulled out a fan. The shopgirl had drifted closer.

"The maggot," added Gemma.

"Good riddance to bad rubbish," said Greta Garbo.

I sent the woman a grateful nod. "I just want to thank the man who helped me through such a difficult time."

Monsieur Janis tugged at his tie. "Our policies have remained ze same for twenty-five years. We do not divulge client names."

I closed my eyes as if the news had physically hurt me. I even managed to hiccup.

"However," he continued, "you may leave a note, and if zis client visits again, I will pass it along."

That certainly seemed reasonable. But if Lulu's boyfriend was the killer, we didn't want to leave a trail back to us. We should've thought of that. Now what?

"It would be quite improper for us to leave a note with a stranger," Gemma said with the indignation of a schoolmarm catching a cheater.

Monsieur Janis's eyes bobbed to the side, and I could see him trying to work out who the stranger was—him or the gentleman in the park? His eyes narrowed like ventholes cut into burlap. Was he onto us?

Gemma caught my eye and jerked her head toward the door. Dabbing my eyes with the handkerchief, I trailed her to the exit.

The late-afternoon sun shone a warm spotlight on me, and the rattling leaves of the ginkgo trees sounded like applause. Despite our dead end of a visit, my breath sailed freely in and out of my lungs, and my limbs swung with ease. It had been liberating to be able to control the hot and cold of my emotions like the taps on a sink.

Gemma blew out one of her ridiculous whistles through her teeth. "*He* was a load of unhelpful, even if he did have a fancy accent. But that performance deserves a medal. You were born for the screen, sister."

"It was a touch overdone," I said modestly, knowing this was my opening for coming clean. But was I ready? Gemma would push me to do it, but I had to make this decision on my own.

She picked a leaf off the seat, then hopped into the passenger seat, her face lifted like the figurehead on the prow of a ship. She was a woman in charge of her destiny. She'd been born in the Year of the Tiger, after all, which made her brave and confident. Knowing what you wanted was half the battle in life, because the sooner you figured out that, the sooner you could go about getting it.

As much as I was still sore at Gemma for her deceit and recklessness at the coroner's office, some of her arrows as of late had hit their mark. I did make decisions based on how they affected others, to the point that sometimes I barely knew what I wanted for myself.

Ma and Ba would be scandalized if I accepted the job Emil was offering. But despite Ma's disapproval when she had come upon Lulu and me playacting, she'd smiled when she'd seen Lulu's face on the billboards. We'd all been proud of her, the first daughter of Chinatown.

"Why are you just sitting there?" Gemma pushed her hands at the steering wheel. "Get this hunk of junk on the road. We need to see the good doctor before his office closes."

"I have something to confess."

31

GEMMA

MAY SAT PRIMLY IN THE DRIVER'S SEAT, AS IF SHE WASN'T the world's biggest hypocrite. Scolding me for my visit to the coroner's office when she'd been pocketing a whale of a secret.

"A starring role in *A Far East Affair*?" I sputtered. The delicate angles of her face shifted, half-pleased, half-embarrassed. I stifled my annoyance with her. Save that pony for a better trick later. "Don't tell me you accepted."

"You don't think I should accept?"

"An hourly rate for a starring role? Lulu Wong got forty thousand dollars. Okay, you're no Lulu, but you're no garden-variety snail. You're an escargot, which is French for 'slugs in butter.' At least let me negotiate something a little better for you. Remember?" I tapped an incisor. "Flexible teeth."

"It's a lot of change."

I scoffed. "The world changes around us every day. Just keep a foot planted, and you'll end up standing where you want to be instead of where the wind blows you. Ma will be furious, but she'll get over it once she realizes you're doing something you love." That might take a lifetime, but why dwell on the negative? "You've been handed a gift, and this time you can't turn it down. Remember the slippers?"

May groaned.

One year during the Chinese New Year celebration, two baskets had been set in front of a brass statue of the smiling god of wealth, for the children to pick out a gift. One basket contained thimbles, while the other contained bamboo slippers in bright colors. Everyone wanted the slippers. By the time it was May's turn, only one pair of slippers remained. And though she really wanted them, she took a thimble so that the fishmonger's sniveling daughter could have them.

"This has nothing to do with those slippers, Gemma—"

"We didn't even like that brat," I rolled on. "Always such a martyr. You never take for yourself, even when it's your turn. Anyway, this might be a good time for you to admit how much you admire my ideas. My vision. My uncanny ability to sniff out opportunity like a piggy to a truffle. If I hadn't pushed you—"

"Gemma!" she whispered loudly.

A young woman who looked like a utensil with her spooner hat and gray dress appeared at the corner, waving a white cloth. "Excuse me?" she called.

It was the shopgirl, holding her apron. She hurried toward us, taking in the Mule with quick darts of her hazel eyes. Would she figure us for fakers?

May folded her gloved hands in her lap with the cheerless mien of a woman rubbing at a stain that won't come out and said, "Yes, hello?"

The shopgirl glanced behind her. "I couldn't help overhearing your story and, well, I wanted to help out. You see, I remember this man."

"Oh?" May asked, managing to sound breathless, hopeful, and guarded with a single vowel.

The shopgirl nodded. "He had the earrings made special. Said you would appreciate cranes. Maybe he knew how much you liked the ducks in the pond, as we don't get cranes here in Los Angeles."

"What was his name?" I cut in.

"Actually, I don't know. Only Monsieur Janis spoke with him."

Was the man trying to keep his identity secret? "Well, what did he look like?"

Her hands stopped wringing at her apron, and she looked pointedly at May. "Don't *you* know what he looks like?"

May cleared her throat delicately, and I quickly replied, "Just trying to make sure your guy is our guy."

The shopgirl's eyes shot up, searching the brim of her hat. "Well, he had brown hair and a medium build, not big and not small." She had the voice of a girl sitting on a porch swing who had all the time in the world.

I snorted. "Not big and not small, that narrows it down."

May gave me a look that said, *I will pull off your shoe and stuff it in your mouth if you don't behave.* I ignored her. There was a murderer on the loose. Our neighborhood was on the verge of being railroaded. I didn't have time to dance around people's feelings. "Was he in his twenties? Thirties? *Nineties?*"

"He could be in his twenties. But I only saw him from the back, so he could be in his thirties or forties too. Monsieur Janis took him into his office, and he must have left out the back door."

"Could you give us a little more?" I growled. "Any distinguishing features? A hunch? A lisp? How did he smell?"

May kicked me.

"Goodness me, I don't remember his smell." The shopgirl scratched her hat. "Oh! But he had a real smooth way of talking, like he'd be good at romancing and sweeping you off your feet."

A dimple large enough to hold a penny appeared in her cheek, and she began to sway as if music were playing. "Maybe he's a movie star."

May sighed dreamily, managing to keep in character. "That sounds like my admirer. Very romantic."

"He certainly showed his Schnauzer a lot of love."

I fought the urge to lift off the girl's spooner and throw it like one of those discuses we'd seen pictures of from this summer's Olympics. "Why didn't you tell us he had a dog?"

The shopgirl's mouth fell open like a sagging pocket. "Again, I assumed you knew that, since you saw him at the park."

May glared at me. "Yes, of course. I knew he had a Schnauzer, with a beautiful gray coat."

The shopgirl's eyes narrowed. "Actually, it was a white Schnauzer. Very rare."

May fiddled with her skirt. "Ah, well, perhaps it only looked gray in the, er, shadows."

The shopgirl crossed her arms. "Say, how is this helpful to you?"

May leaned back in her seat, no longer bothering to hide her annoyance with me.

I pasted on a smile. "It tells us we're on the right track. And as our father always says, you can reach the right destination on the wrong track, but rarely the wrong destination on the right track."

As the shopgirl searched her hat brim again, May started the engine. "You've been most helpful. Thank you ever so much." We drove off. Once out of earshot, May sputtered, "You nearly tipped our hand—maybe you even did."

"She was getting on my nerves. Not big, not small? Good at romancing?"

"She was just trying to help. You know what your problem is?"

"No, May, why don't you tell me? I'm dying to hear."

"You're intolerant of anyone who doesn't do things your way." She gunned the motor past a line of cars.

"So?"

"Now she has a bad opinion of us. We could've persuaded her to get the stranger's name out of Monsieur Janis."

"You mean, like, bribe her?"

May snorted. "As a last resort. Some people do things because they're nice people."

My head was getting hot. I pulled off my wool beret and fluffed my hair. "I doubt someone like her would have the subtlety to pull that off. Turn here."

"But I thought we're going to the French Hospital. To see your doctor?"

"Actually, the doctor's office is just across from Westlake Park."

May's face became a frown, but she swung toward Westlake Park, still none the wiser but somewhat more suspicious.

"Maybe I should go alone," I said once we'd parked. May was definitely going to recognize Freddie from Westlake Park, and then *I'd* be the hypocrite.

"Why? You planning to rough him up too?" Ignoring me, May slid out of the car and marched down the sidewalk.

"Suit yourself." I resisted the urge to check my appearance in the mirror and bustled after her.

Inside the office, I was surprised to find a woman stretched out over the couch, her flared pantsuit making her legs look as long as telephone poles. The woman glanced up at us. It was Max Factor, Freddie's ex-girl.

My heart dipped a little. What was she doing here? I thought they were history, but perhaps they were back on. I was suddenly glad for my smart outfit, even if it was a lie. Of course, unlike her, who looked so comfortable in her threads I bet she could wear them to sleep, my clothes suddenly felt like they were wearing me.

Max Factor's Cupid's-bow lips parted, and her long, dark lashes whipped back against her pale skin, sparkly with powder. "Heavens. You two China dolls look familiar."

"You must have seen us on a shelf somewhere," I muttered, focusing my gaze on her fleshy money nose.

May would've chastised me for being rude if she weren't so busy staring at Max Factor, probably wondering where she had seen her before. "Evening, miss."

"Please have a seat," Mrs. H called from her desk. "I'm sorry, but he's running behind."

Wonderful. Now we had to sit like chumps across from Max Factor.

The leather chair gave a stuffy sigh when I sank into it. May tucked her dress neatly beneath her before gently lowering herself, avoiding the chair belch. She glanced up at the adobe ceiling, painted with pastels and swirly designs.

On the table, the newspaper looked untouched. The headline caught my eye.

Park Named After Edith Newman, Late Wife of Maurie Newman

I pulled the paper closer. May read alongside me.

Elysian Park just got rosier. In a ribbon-cutting ceremony featuring strawberry punch and a five-layer angel cake, newspaper magnate Maurie Newman dedicated a newly developed corner of the park, "The Garden of Angels," to his late wife, Edith, a project sponsored by the Rose Growers of Los Angeles and the Newman Trust. "She made life beautiful, and now she will continue to bring beauty even in death."

Edith Hamish Newman, a lifelong gardening enthusiast, was killed in a train accident involving the Union Pacific Railroad four years ago. She was 42.

"He mentioned his wife in his speech," said May, turning the paper over for more of the article, but there was nothing else.

I blew out a breath. "He may be corrupt as sin, but that's a tragic way to cash in."

Max Factor adjusted a pillow behind her head. "If you're talking about Edith Newman, it *was* tragic. Her heel caught on the railroad track, and the case is still in litigation. She should've just left the shoe."

I bristled at being eavesdropped on. "Panic deadens the brain. Have you never seen roadkill?"

Max Factor snapped her fingers. "I've got it." One of her pink fingernails crooked my direction. "You're the two who were selling flowers in the park." May stiffened beside me, recognition sharpening her features. Max Factor leaned in. "Do you have any on you now?"

I leaned in as well and lowered my voice to covert levels. "No, but we do have some black weed. The good stuff." I gave her a wink as if I could actually slip her some opium across the table.

The sound of shoes thumped down the stairs, along with the sound of Freddie's voice. "I'm converting the backgammon parlor into an exam room, so next time you visit, you won't have to scale these stairs." Freddie appeared, helping an elderly woman climb down.

May and I both stood.

The woman stepped off the last stair and stretched out her hunched back. "I wish your parents could see how your braces got me back on my feet again. God rest their souls." Her crinkly eyes grazed the three of us. "Why, your dance card appears full, Freddie."

He humored her with a polite laugh, though his face was drawn, as if he had slayed his share of dragons for the day. His tie had been loosened and the top button of his shirt undone.

"Ladies," he addressed us with a curt nod of his head. As he passed, I smelled soap. It reminded me of when he had danced me across the patio of the Beverly Hills Hotel. He opened the door for his patient. "Mrs. H will wait with you for your taxi."

After the two women exited, Freddie opened his hands at us. "May Chow, I presume?"

"Yes." May's eyes slid to mine, where they stayed for two counts of a knockdown. She'd figured out this was no coincidence. That I had lied to her. But she wouldn't back out now, would she? We were too deep in the investigation. Plus, she had hid something material from me as well. Maybe thinking similar thoughts, she breathed out a heavy sigh. "How do you do, Dr. Winter?"

"Very well."

Max Factor still lay sprawled on the couch. "Hello, Freddie." She tilted her head like a teeter-totter, causing her blond curls to bounce around her face.

"Ophelia. I'll be with you shortly. Feel free to help yourself to whatever you need. You know where the kitchen is."

"What I need isn't in the kitchen, darling."

Freddie ignored that. He seemed to be dodging my eyes. "Shall we?" He gestured to the stairs.

May's eyes burned my backside all the way up that creaky hill of shame. Once inside Freddie's office, May discreetly swept from the colonics machine to the skeleton. Freddie gestured for us to sit, then folded himself into his own desk chair. He tented his elegant fingers together, a thin, unamused smile appearing on his lips. "So, Miss Chow," he said, meaning me, "the coroner's secretary called me. I used to work there, if you'll recall. Apparently, I told Lulu Wong's sister that she would be allowed to see Lulu's case file." His eyes flicked with sparks of anger. In my head, I heard a violin play the kind of angsty rhythm used in a movie just before a knife falls.

"Oh." A burning sense of mortification warred with anger over my stupidity, and I wondered if it was possible to melt into a chair. No wonder my mentioning his name had put a glow on the coroner's secretary's cheeks. "Well, I had to get that carbon copy somehow. A man's life is at stake." Poor Gee Fa. I couldn't help wondering what had become of Little Leaf.

May was sitting as straight as a pin. "What she's saying is she's *sorry* she caused you such great inconvenience. We are very thankful for your help understanding Lulu's autopsy report."

The newspaper on his desk was folded back to the Sunday crossword puzzle. It gratified me to see that his twenty-one down hadn't been filled in yet. I still hadn't figured it out either. *It takes time to sink in.*

"You're welcome. Also, I confirmed that Lulu was pregnant."

My breath fell out of me. "How?"

"I examined her," he said through his teeth.

"They let you in, just like that?" Mr. Yam had spent a great deal of effort circulating the petition for another autopsy, but had all we needed was one well-connected doctor?

He ignored me. "I also confirmed the blow to the head, though I don't think it was hard enough to kill her. I already sent my report to the district attorney."

I reached for the desk, feeling a shift in this case. Surely a report from a doctor like Freddie would show that material facts were missing. Assuming the district attorney wasn't dirty, the scheme would begin to unravel. Freddie's eyes were stern, rippling with thoughts.

May cleared her throat. "Doctor, that was good of you to go out of your way."

"Yes. Some powerful people might not like you for that," I added. Maybe a wealthy doctor didn't have to worry about making enemies the way we did, but if anything happened to him, I would feel responsible.

"Freddie?" said a voice from the doorway. Ophelia. "I'm getting tired."

"I'll be right with you, if you don't mind waiting downstairs for me."

Instead of retreating, she strolled in. She could walk where she wanted and never hear a protest. "But why have you kept me waiting so long?"

"I hardly expected to see you," he said coolly. "Please."

"Please, *dearest*. You used to call me 'dearest.' "

He grimaced. I barely knew Freddie, but he was definitely not the type to air his dirty laundry; he probably didn't even do his own laundry.

May stood, even though I hadn't finished asking my questions. "Well, we best be on our way, given your prior engagement." There she went again, obeying social niceties when there were more important issues at stake.

"One last question, Freddie," I said, rising as well.

May gasped at my use of his familiar name, and I could feel her eyes boring into the side of my head.

I shunned her. "In your numerous strolls around Westlake Park, do you remember seeing a white Schnauzer? It's a rare variety."

"Schnauzer?" Freddie rubbed his head, looking momentarily confused as all the bodies in the room shifted around, May herding me toward the door like a sheepdog and Ophelia moving to the window, where she swiveled the glass closed. At least he could count on his skeleton to stay where it was. "Sorry, I—"

Ophelia returned to Freddie, rubbing his back the way people do when someone's choking, though I never understood how that helped anything. She was like a piece of lint you can't shake off your fingers. "I've seen a white Schnauzer, the sweet thing with its cute beard. I remember thinking that you and I should get one when we're married."

Freddie unhooked his arm from Ophelia's.

"Did you get a look at the owner?" I asked. May had stopped pulling at my sleeve.

Ophelia's laugh was like the tinkling of ice in a silver goblet. "Goodness me, these don't sound like medical questions. But I don't remember much about the owner. He was a medium sort . . ."

I rolled my eyes at May. "Do you remember around what time they were walking?"

"In the evenings after five, I'd say. I suppose he is one of those *working* fellows." Ophelia reached up and tickled Freddie's chin, then grinned wickedly at us.

He dodged her finger. "Heaven forbid."

"Now, let these ladies be on their way. Your *next* appointment would like you to take her out to dinner." Ophelia sank into a chair and crossed her legs, making herself right at home.

"Again, we appreciate the trouble you've gone through for us," said May, yanking me from my spot.

My annoyance at Ophelia's obvious marking of her territory was making it hard to think. We were here on important business, and she was making goo-goo eyes. I was sure I had more questions to ask the doctor, but right now, I couldn't think of a single one.

32
MAY

IT WAS LATE BY THE TIME WE LEFT DR. WINTER'S OFFICE, too late to drive across town and expect Mrs. Sonenshein to answer the door without first calling the police. We would have to save her for tomorrow. Plus, Wallace would be arriving soon for our dinner at Fragrant Bamboo. Ma might go into labor early if I failed to show up.

Gemma insisted on driving home, even though I knew it would take twice as long. To my surprise, she found all the gears and knobs without trouble.

"Are we just going to ignore the giant Freddie in the room?" I asked when she maneuvered us safely onto the road.

"Yes."

"How did you know he was a doctor?"

"He must have mentioned it."

"You mean when you were conning him into buying that orchid at Westlake Park? Or were there other conversations you've had together? You seem to know him pretty well."

"Not that I recall. He's just an acquaintance," she added casually, though she'd gone stiff, her arms now tightly welded to the steering wheel.

"I hope it stays that way," I grumbled. "You lied to me again." I tried to muster more indignation, but I could see she was upset.

Plus, we both knew I wouldn't abandon the investigation like I had threatened when we were so close.

"I'm sorry. I know I put you through a lot, but I try to be good, most of the time."

"You shouldn't go trusting strange men like that."

"Oh, come on, he's a doctor. And he doesn't have a white Schnauzer."

"But he does have brown hair and a medium build, not big and not small. He's a smooth talker, and I bet he's good at romancing."

She snorted out a laugh that said I was being ridiculous. Maybe I was, but I had seen the way she looked at Freddie's girl, Ophelia. As Gemma motored past closing shops, their cheer buckets sorely in need of replenishing, a memory floated into my mind of a silk phoenix kite for which Gemma had been saving her pennies as a girl. One day, as we passed the import store, we saw another little girl lifting the kite out of the window display. Gemma stood at the doorway, her face set in the same stony grimace as now, watching the little girl's father buy it for her.

Gemma had always been the hungry type. I thought about the slippers I'd let the fishmonger's daughter take. I was the hungry type too, but I also cared about what others thought. Sure, I didn't always get what I wanted. But maybe what I actually wanted was for other people to be happy.

I didn't push the issue. What was the point? Leaving aside whether such a well-heeled professional would marry a flower seller, it was still against the law for whites to marry Chinese. They could only employ them. Was that the reason Lulu had kept her boyfriend a secret?

A truck swerved close, and Gemma laid on the horn, but I

barely heard it. *"Maybe he's a movie star,"* I said, remembering the shopgirl's words. "Carey Stone's a movie star."

Gemma snorted. "That's a thin thread by which to hang a body. Plus, Carey Stone's blond."

"Dirty blond. His hair could look brown in the shadow of a hat, and he has *a medium build, not big and not small.* A girlfriend could hurt his image, especially a pregnant Chinese one. Those kinds of secrets might be worth killing over."

"Great magnolia, you're right." Gemma laid on the horn again for no reason at all. "But does he own a Schnauzer?"

"That horn is not a percussion set," I snapped, though my head swirled with thoughts. Costars fell in love all the time. Look at Mary Pickford and Douglas Fairbanks.

Gemma slowed as we drew closer to Fragrant Bamboo. Someone had strung up new paper lanterns outside the famed eatery to replace the ones the wind had blown away. "I can think of someone who knows a lot of secrets. Tonight, you and Wallace can turn up the heat on Cash Louie." A grin alighted on her face. "You're only on a pretend-date, after all."

AN HOUR LATER, WALLACE WAS PULLING OPEN FRAGRANT Bamboo's wide door, freshly painted red. All traces of vandalism had been cleaned up, restoring its image as a chic hideaway. Even as I looked furtively about for Cash Louie, I couldn't help noticing that Wallace's forest-green sweater matched my dress. Had his mother chosen it for its harmonious color too? His trousers were neatly ironed, breaking at his worn black-and-white saddle shoes.

He misread my look as I crossed the threshold. "Don't tell me you don't like the shoes."

"They're nice."

"I thought we weren't playing that game. They're pathetic."

"Alright, they're pathetic. Why do you keep them?"

"These were the shoes my ba wore when he opened his factory. I guess I'm sentimental. Ma keeps trying to throw them out, but I hide them at night. I like things with soles."

I couldn't help smiling, thinking of Gemma's terrible puns. He handed me into one of the tall U-shaped booths that made you feel you were in your own private train car. "Do insects have souls?" I asked.

"Definitely the praying mantis."

I let out an unladylike laugh that made him laugh back. I couldn't help thinking this Shangri-la for people with secrets seemed an appropriate venue for our pretend-relationship. Mid-room, a fountain above the bar functioned to both block the view of the other side of the room and provide a watery shushing that hid conversations. The place was only half-occupied, with waiters outnumbering the patrons, but it was early, not yet six o'clock. I hadn't yet seen Cash making his rounds, and I hoped he wasn't absent today.

After consulting with the waiter, Wallace folded his hands and lifted his face to me. "So what's your act of rebellion?"

I snorted. "I don't have one."

"Of course you do. You're not exactly the sheep type."

"Sometimes I . . . pretend to have mending to do so I can escape to my sewing room." I withheld mentioning Stuffy the dress form.

His smooth face grew mirthful angles. "I hate to tell you this, but I think your family already knows that."

"Fine, maybe I am a sheep type."

"No way. A sheep type wouldn't pursue this investigation with such determination."

I groaned softly, all my worries suddenly rounding my shoulders. "I constantly question if I'm doing the right thing. Who's going to listen to us if we do find the killer? Plus, if my parents found out about our investigation, it would crush them." I gripped the leather seat. If Ba knew we had deceived him, would the stress make his tuberculosis worse? Would Ma's health suffer too? And the baby's? Despite all our setbacks, our family had persisted because our parents knew they could entrust us with so much. "They might never trust us again."

I sucked in my breath, somehow feeling I had revealed too much. Wallace might think me overemotional. It was rude to burden others with one's troubles.

To my surprise, he slipped a warm hand over mine, setting my pulse aflutter. "One of the hardest things I ever had to do was tell my father I wasn't going to follow him into the business." His teeth snagged his lip, then he let out a mild chuckle. "That I was going to research honeybees. Ba spent my whole life teaching me how to run his company. I figured he'd disown me. I expected it."

"Your parents are proud of what you do."

"It took time. But our parents are tougher than we think."

I hoped that was true, but I didn't want to test it.

Waiters set before us a treasure trove of roasted duck, fried rice with slivers of sweet pineapple, and char siu pork. Wallace and I shared a grin, suddenly coconspirators about to rob a bank. I couldn't remember the last time I'd eaten in a restaurant. Wallace dished me some glossy bulbs of bok choy.

"Did you know bok choy needs bees for pollination?" he said with the eagerness of a child showing a pet lizard.

"I didn't." A smile tugged at my lips.

"I'm sorry, I get a little too excited about the bees."

"Well, *I* get excited about restaurant food." I tilted my head like a lady dropping secrets. "Did you know char siu pork turns that color because of its red bean curd marinade?"

He picked up a slice with his chopsticks. "If you're trying to ensnare me with your culinary knowledge, it's definitely working." His hand paused before the morsel went into his mouth, and he peered at the meat's trademark red coating. "This marinade has been enhanced with dye."

"Cactus bugs?"

He nodded.

"I guess you'd better not bring your boss here."

"Unless I want to be the boss." He pumped his eyebrows. "If the cactus bugs don't get him, the garlic shrimp will. All arthropods have chitin."

While we feasted, I updated Wallace on our investigation.

"I'm glad the doctor spoke up," he said. "If people know that Lulu was pregnant, maybe someone will come forward. I'm just sorry that Wong Tai will have to find out this way."

"She's still not in her right mind. Bettina says her ma wants that 'poor woman' buried as soon as possible." Peony and I had each held Bettina's hands while Gemma gave her the news of her sister's pregnancy, expecting the worst, but the girl had taken the news on the cheek. Hadn't shed a single tear.

Wallace's forehead knit, his eyes drifting to a black lacquer post painted with bamboo reeds. "When Wong Tai's husband left, she had a similar break. Do you remember?"

"No."

"In sixth grade, she showed up at school with a parasol, even though we hadn't finished class. Said Lulu's father was going to take them all to the beach, though we knew he'd already left. Perhaps Wong Tai had the same reaction when Lulu died. With loss so great, perhaps it is a mercy to retreat somewhere else while . . ." He searched for the words.

"The heart heals," I finished, and he nodded. "But Monday is the burial—"

"May Chow and Wallace Moy?" said a hearty voice. Cash Louie strolled toward us, his "wealthy" face with its tall forehead and big nose—two features that bring money—expressing delight, his meaty hands outstretched. "A good pairing, like sweet and sour."

"Hello, Ah-Suk," said Wallace, using the Cantonese word for "Uncle." He half stood and shook the man's hand over the table. "It's been a while."

"You grew up. And I grew out." The man clapped his hands over his round belly and laughed. A red vest had been cut extra wide for him.

"A mark of success," said Wallace congenially.

"And how's your father, May?" Cash's joviality evaporated.

"They are trying a new treatment on him. We are hopeful he will come home soon."

"Good, good. A family shouldn't be without their king."

"Ah-Suk, we were sorry to hear about the vandalism."

He scowled. "Fortune does not come twice, and misfortune does not come alone. Lulu was a good soul. This case should've been solved by now. Her car was found in the Mercantile lot, and everyone's looking at me. Business had been slow, but it's fallen even more."

"Do you have any idea why she came to Chinatown?"

Cash frowned. "May I join you?"

"Of course." I scooted closer to Wallace to make room, while Wallace moved closer to me. We bumped in the middle. "Oh!"

"Sorry," said Wallace.

We managed to coordinate our efforts, and Cash slid in next to me. His eyes were "loose," always scanning the room, as if on the lookout for important people to greet. "All I know is Lulu didn't come here that night. Sure, she still dined here now and then, but she hadn't come for a few months. I went down to the station and told Detective Mallady that myself."

"Did Lulu ever come here with a boyfriend?"

"No. If she had a boyfriend, I didn't know about him. You're asking better questions than Mallady."

"He didn't seem interested in solving this case at all," I lamented. "They just wanted to find someone from Chinatown to pin it on."

"Yes. And even if they can't pin this crime on Gee Fa, the smear is not good for Chinatown or our businesses." He straightened the gold tablecloth and pushed the soy sauce, chili sauce, and sesame oil into a tight grouping. Ba said Cash got his start as a busboy, and old habits must die hard. "I'm afraid the battle over Chinatown will be lost sooner or later. But there are ways to win the war."

There was that word again. *War*. Cole Stritch had accused Lulu of asking for a war that would take both of them down. "What do you mean?" I asked.

"I mean that people think the Chinese are to blame for everything. Why?"

"That's how the newspapers portray us."

"Yes, and other booster propaganda. You want to create a monster? Put it in print. But if you want to give the monster a heart, you go to the movies." He slid back his head, giving him an extra "good luck" chin.

Wallace set down his teacup. "Change public perception through the media."

"Precisely." Cash folded his arms.

Dixie Doors had been elevated from local beauty queen to kitchen cosmetics genius by the time the newspaper had finished reporting on her death. "So how do we do that?" I asked.

"You make a generous donation to the right people. Allies. Wallace knows."

Wallace slowly nodded. "My parents donate to the Chinese American Citizens Alliance, a group trying to change perceptions of Chinese Americans. They publish the *Chinese Times*."

I nodded at the name of our newspaper. For a family who had left Chinatown behind, the Moys still cared about its welfare. Perhaps one never really left Chinatown, the same way you could never rinse a flower of its fragrance.

Cash matched his fingertips together. "Others of us take a more unconventional route."

"Unconventional how?"

Cash's head tilted to one side, then the other, as if weighing the thoughts inside. "My business is built on privacy. If it gets out that Cash Louie spills secrets, I would be a Cash-less Louie. Let's just say, Hollywood for most people means movies and glamour. Behind the scenes, however, is where the real theater lies."

The shush of the fountain seemed to move my thoughts along. So Cash fought the "war" with strategic donations to important movie people. "Lulu said she was done playing villains."

"Yes. *A Far East Affair* was a big role not just for her, but for all of us. A Chinese girl playing a *heroine*. It's never been done."

This had to have been the war Mr. Stritch thought Lulu was "asking for." Lulu had been an agitator, dismantling perceptions about the Chinese in the best way she knew how. Mr. Stritch didn't want to be a casualty of this war. He was a smoker, so he fit the description of the person Chin Chin saw in the Mercantile lot. Still, if he was the killer, why he had waited so long to strike?

"Would it be correct to say that Capsize Pictures was one of Chinatown's 'allies'?" I asked.

"That would be a correct assumption."

"And therefore, its rival, Summit Studios, must be an enemy."

Cash's attention returned from its detour around the room, and he nodded. "Another correct assumption."

So we had been on the right trail. "And who's the general in charge of Summit Studios?"

Cash's eyes became hard. "There are many generals. But if you are looking for the treasury that funds the generals, his name is Otis Fox."

AFTER DINNER, WALLACE TOOK ME TO GRAUMAN'S CHINESE Theatre for an after-dinner stroll. Before the elaborate pagoda, palm trees grew from the forecourt where movie stars' footprints were enshrined in concrete. People crowded the cement tile where Lulu had stood, trying to fit their feet into her size-five impressions. A little girl with chestnut curls placed violets by a nearby lotus-shaped fountain, where more bouquets had been left. Tributes to the fallen star.

Wallace took my hand, tugging me toward Lulu's spot. Her shoes had left two teardrop shapes punctuated by heel marks. "It's ironic, isn't it? The mark she left on the world is way bigger than those little prints."

I hung back. I could never stand in her shoes, much less fill them.

I got tired of other people holding the reins. So I took them back. Act like you have power, and you just might get it.

A stone dragon challenged me with its gaze from where it

hung thirty feet high above the entrance. A decision awaited me, and this time, I could not let other people guide my hand. I'd have to make my parents understand that this was not only good for our family, but for our community. If I didn't take Lulu's role, it would be given to a white woman with taped eyes. And I wanted to do it. Maybe Gemma was right about the bamboo slippers. Just because I liked giving people what they wanted didn't mean I couldn't also take something for myself once in a while.

Lulu had been on top of the world. But she'd used her vantage point to shoot the wind, bending it in a new direction. I hadn't stayed a part of her life. But I could ensure her legacy.

33
GEMMA

WHILE MAY WENT ON HER PRETEND-DATE, WHICH I hoped for her sake would end with a pretend-kiss—she needed to loosen her stays—I used the hallway phone to call Hettie Bright. I was half-glad when the starlet didn't answer. I hadn't found a good way to bring up her change in employment other than *Hey, dollface, why'd you jump wagons?*—an approach that could easily end with a "None of your beeswax" and the slamming of a phone in my ear. Then again, we weren't here to make friends, but to find enemies.

When the operator returned, I asked her to connect me with another number, one I had snuck from the business card in May's purse. My heart tapped nervously along with my feet.

"This is Emil," the man on the other end boomed. I glanced down the hall at our door, hoping Peony and Bettina were keeping Ma occupied in our bedroom, the farthest from the telephone.

"Good evening, Emil. This is Gemma Chow, May's sister."

"I remember you." His voice sounded guarded, like a man who had noticed a bee flying around him.

"I'm calling to discuss the fee for my sister's services."

"Do you always negotiate for her?"

Only when the baloney train comes to town. "I want to make sure she's treated fairly."

His voice grew louder. "Eight dollars a day is very generous. May I remind you the extras are paid five dollars a day."

"The extras don't have to memorize lines. Not to mention, your other stars don't get daily wages." My throat suddenly felt as dry as the Mojave Desert. This could easily go south. My meddling might cost May her job entirely, and I knew she wanted to take it.

A sigh gusted through the receiver. "What are you proposing?"

"Sixteen hundred dollars per month for three months, paid up front, and if more time is required, a premium to be negotiated." That worked out to eighty dollars a day. I held my breath, hoping I hadn't overshot. I had made the calculations based on no more than the relative cost of baby's breath compared to long-stemmed roses. You could do without the filler, but the roses were the main event. They worked the room, and they cost about ten times as much.

A long pause followed, during which the bee somehow flew through the telephone cable to my end.

"Eight hundred a month for three months."

I squeezed my fist in victory, knowing better than to push my luck further. Plus, eight was a lucky number. I kept my tone unimpressed. "I will let my sister give the final approval. But there is a last condition. You might've heard that the police arrested someone for Lulu Wong's murder, but we think they have the wrong guy. My sister is understandably concerned about her safety. We would like a security guard assigned to protect her." Carey Stone was a strong suspect. He had been "rehearsing" with Hettie Bright the night Lulu was killed. Would she have covered for him? Or worse, perhaps the two had conspired to rub out Lulu, she for personal gain, he because a baby would cramp his style.

"We do have security guards. I'll see that she gets special attention."

After we hung up, I kicked up my heels. We could buy a lot with three months' salary at that rate. Maybe one day, our own house. Perhaps the winds were finally changing in our favor.

AN HOUR AFTER MA WENT TO BED, MAY RETURNED HOME, smelling like Goobers and with a flower in her hair.

"You look like you rode a cloud." I set up her iron for her, knowing she always thought better with a hot block of metal in her hand. Bettina helped her out of her clothes, and Peony brought her a warm towel.

"Did he kiss you?" Peony's face wrinkled in disgust.

"Of course not." May scrubbed her face and neck, then announced, "I have decided to take the job."

I unleashed a grin. "That's good, because Emil's going to make you rich." I fed her the figures and caught her when she swayed.

She batted me away. "You should've asked me before you called him. What if I didn't want to do it?"

"But you do, so no harm, no foul." She couldn't yank the grin off me if she held it on both ends and swung on it, but I stepped out of her reach anyway. "Relax, tiger." I held up my hands. "I told him you had the final say. He expects a call tonight."

She sucked in her breath. "Well. Forty dollars a day is quite a sum." Folding the towel, she pressed it to her face, as if to press out her disbelief.

"Yes, you're a cash cow. Now, what else did you find out?"

She took her place by the ironing board at the foot of our bed. I dumped a basket of clean clothes onto our mattress. We were once again running low on things with wrinkles. Peony sat on the floor, ankles on her basketball. Behind her, Bettina sat on her bed, brushing Peony's hair with a determined look. I was glad to see that the color had returned to Bettina's cheeks, and there was focus to her movements. *Shush, shush.* Her hairbrush moved in even strokes.

May flicked water onto a shirt and railroaded it. Then she recounted her evening, leaving out any juicy tidbits about Wallace. "The person at Summit Studios who benefits the most from Lulu's death is none other than Otis Fox," she concluded, a cloud of steam forming around her.

"It's not looking good for that weasel." If he didn't already have a personal reason to want Lulu dead, now he had a business one. It wasn't surprising that Otis Fox bankrolled one of Hollywood's main studios. Maybe it was even how Fox Cosmetics had gotten such a toehold in the industry.

While May bent over the ironing board, I squeezed more wrinkles into a pair of trousers. "So the odious Fox lures Hettie Bright to Summit Studios. Capsize Pictures, an ally of Chinatown, had put all its chips on *A Far East Affair*. The loss of Lulu was bad, but Fox needed Hettie to sink Capsize, once and for all." I tossed the wrinkled trousers to May like a steak to a hungry dog.

She attacked it with ferocity. "Of course, theories won't help get Gee Fa out of prison. But Wallace's parents have funded a lawyer for him."

"That's good of them," I said brightly. I was liking Wallace and his parents more and more.

Peony tilted back her head, putting slack in the braid Bettina was plaiting. "Fox's life would be easier if he didn't hate Chinese people so much."

"So would ours." I poked my finger into the frayed hole of a sock.

Peony chewed her lip. "Well, I hate him back."

"That's the spirit." I chucked the holey sock into the mending basket.

May rolled her eyes, always superior.

"I hate him too," Bettina said in a quiet voice.

All my insolence drained away. Though I'd been joking with Peony, Bettina's hate was no laughing matter. It was only natural to hate the person you thought had robbed you of your sister and her baby, and it wasn't going to go away on its own. Bettina needed us to bring the killer to justice as much as Gee Fa did. "Ladies, we're putting this day to bed soon, which means there are only three days left until the burial. We need all hands on the pump. Otis Fox is at the top of the laundry pile and harder to reach." I placed a pair of rolled socks atop the laundry I had folded. "If we eliminate a few pieces at the bottom, maybe the one at the top will be easier to take down." I tugged out a dish towel from the bottom of the stack, and the socks rolled off. "Tomorrow, I'll troll the park for the Schnauzer and pay Mrs. Sonenshein a visit. May, you dig around on set and see about that jobajoo Cole Stritch. He's a big agent, and someone might have some dirt on him, or know what kind of cigarettes he smoked. Liberté isn't a common brand. But don't talk to Carey Stone. He already knows you're investigating. Better he thinks you've given up on the case."

She nodded, her jaw a grim line as she resumed sawing away. Emil had promised a security guard, but I couldn't help worrying about the visibility May's new role might bring her. She was no longer just an extra. If the script stealer was the killer, would she set her sights on my sister?

Bettina had finished Peony's braid, and both girls were staring at me with the intensity of soldiers awaiting a command. "What about us?" asked Peony.

"Let's see the tiger note again."

Peony handed me the folded paper she'd been using as a bookmark.

Tiger roars; mountain tumbles. I will remember your words and deeds.

"The tiger rules the jungle," I mused, studying the loosely written, uneven characters. "But did Lulu help this person, or hurt him? Maybe Mr. Yam can identify who wrote this." I returned the note to Peony. "You two can ask Mr. Yam about it on your way to school tomorrow."

Peony tugged at the parts of her hair that Bettina had pulled too tight. "We want to go with you to talk to Mrs. Sonenshein."

"Mrs. Sonenshein knows me," added Bettina. "She'd want to help."

May made a disapproving noise. "I'm sorry, but no fieldwork for you two. It's too"—she licked her lips, perhaps considering her words—"risky."

I nodded, for once agreeing with May. It was bad enough that May and I were hunting down criminals and lowlifes without adding two whelps to the mix.

Peony stuck out her lip. "But you said I was helpful, and Bettina is Lulu's sister."

"We don't want Bettina's ma to find out she's investigating," I pointed out.

Bettina set fists upon her knees. "Better that than not finding who killed her."

I couldn't help noticing she was stuttering less today. If I were in Bettina's shoes, I'd want to be at the front of the investigation too. Still . . . "If the killer is associated with Mrs. Sonenshein, it could be dangerous. I'll drive you home tomorrow after school, and you can watch me from your window and keep your eye on your ma. How's that?"

"What about me?" Peony complained.

"You'll keep an eye on our ma," said May. "A pair of watchgirls."

"I'm always the watchgirl," Peony muttered, exchanging a look with Bettina.

I sank onto the bed. "The bigger problem is, even if we find anything, who would believe us?"

May snorted. "I believe I made that point before we started this investigation."

"Yes, well, I'd been hoping we'd find a smoking gun and the person holding it, but it hasn't worked out that way just yet," I said irritably. "If only we knew someone with power, someone upstanding who won't hide in the shade."

"You mean like a sunflower?" asked Peony.

"Right. We need a sunflower."

34

GEMMA

AFTER A DISTRACTED MORNING SELLING FLOWERS AT City Market, I returned home to look in on Ma. She was kneading dough at our kitchen table.

"You need more happy baby herbs?" I asked. "I can pick up some later."

"Sit down and fold. Better an ugly wife than a bad cook."

I groaned. Why'd she always pick the most inconvenient times to improve my wifely attributes? It was already three o'clock. Bettina and Peony hadn't come home from school yet, but they'd arrive any minute now. I couldn't waste daylight with my arms stuck in flour when I had a killer to catch.

Ma gestured at the dough. "Fold, then push. Don't forget the fold. Without the fold, you don't get the flaky layers, and there's nothing worse than a lead pancake." She touched her chin. "Except a pancake with syrup on it."

I wasn't driving down that dead-end street. Ma thought Americans ate too many sweet things, and to her, pancakes should be savory. We divided the dough, rolled it flat, then sprinkled in sliced scallions and sesame seeds, followed by more rolling. I looked at our wall clock, wishing to be on my way.

"I have accepted Toy Tai's offer," Ma said quietly. "We can move in little by little."

I clenched my teeth, hating the changes blowing in but help-less to stop them. The scallions were making me cry. I was rolling them too hard. Ma was tearing up too.

"Sorry, Ma. I have a lead arm." I expected her to agree, but she just waved me off. It occurred to me it wasn't the scallions making her cry. "Ma, are you okay? Is it the move?"

She shook her head.

"Ba?"

She gave me a tight smile. "I'm sure he'll be okay." It sounded more like she was trying to convince herself.

"Of course he will. The doctor said pneumoperitoneum was a promising treatment." We were expecting a phone call any day with an update on Ba's condition.

She wiped her eyes on her apron. "Better get those happy baby herbs," she joked.

I wished I could lift away her worries. Instead, I was add-ing to them, though she didn't know it yet. I wasn't sure how we were going to explain May's new job. In fact, I still couldn't believe May had actually agreed to it, and half expected her to change her mind. But standing up for Lulu Wong was for all of us, including our new little recruit coming down the gangway. Ma would understand. It was as if Lulu's death had widened the outlook, like stepping up on a ladder and seeing a little farther beyond one's own street.

I glanced at the clock: 3:45. "What's taking the girls so long?" The school was only a short walk away.

"Did Peony not tell you? She said Wong Tai was taking them home. She wanted to make them dinner, and then she'll drive Peony home tonight."

"Oh?" She hadn't told me that. *I'm always the watchgirl,* Peony had muttered. She'd been mad at being left behind, even after her lightning strikes of brilliance, and now she was up to no good. I scrubbed my hands with our cake of soap, trying to scrub away my annoyance. "Ma, I think I'll check on May, see if she needs help with . . ." What excuse had we made for May today?

Ma's rolling slowed. "You said she was taking a class on how to use a sewing machine."

"Right. Maybe I'll try to learn the machine too."

She cornered me with her gaze. "This seems almost too good to be true."

I grabbed a light sweater and attempted an easy smile. "Better an ugly wife than a bad seamstress."

I motored past several commuters in my haste toward Beverly Hills, cursing Peony for putting this wrinkle in our neatly ironed plans. At least my driving was improving. With all this gadding about, I'd be ready to drive the new highway connecting Los Angeles and Pasadena, once they got around to building it.

All was quiet on Andromeda Lane. The trees flickered their late-afternoon shadows over the houses. Pigeons roosted on telephone lines, eyeing me with suspicion. Mrs. Sonenshein's blond brick abode with shuttered windows lay across the street and a few houses down from the Wongs' red stucco house. But the sight of a red Cadillac in the Wongs' driveway had me pumping the brakes. Was Cole Stritch back? I parked, then slipped out of the Mule.

Wong Tai answered the door. A dress of thick yellow cloth hung in folds around her, like melting beeswax. She blinked in confusion.

"Good afternoon, Wong Tai."

"Hello. I hope you aren't here to take Peony home. I haven't even started cooking yet."

Smoke drifted to my nose, a scent that was more rotten fruit than tobacco. Cole Stritch was definitely here.

"I had some errands to run out this way and figured I'd say hello."

"How nice. I'm sorry, though, I'm a little busy. The girls went for a walk around the neighborhood."

Wonderful. They had already started the gumshoeing.

"Would you mind if I got a glass of water? I'm a little parched."

"Of course. Come in."

Cole Stritch sat at the kitchen table, his arms spread over the top as if staking a claim to it. Light from the bowl chandelier reflected off his pomaded head, and papers littered the table.

"Cole, you remember Gemma Chow?"

He grunted, which could as easily mean yes as no, or could just be the clearing of voluminous phlegm. Jobajoos never cared about the noises they made. "A few more signatures, and I'll be on my way."

Wong Tai filled a glass and handed it to me, then sat at the table and shuffled through the papers. I shuffled my mind for how to play this. I was good on the fly, but I wished I'd had time to think this through. I couldn't just go about issuing accusations—not to mention, if Cole was the killer, I didn't want him to set his sights on my family.

"So you didn't sell the Cadillac." I shifted my gaze between Mr. Stritch and Wong Tai, equally interested in their reactions. Wong Tai scribbled her signature, barely seeming to hear me.

Mr. Stritch's eyes narrowed, probably remembering our dustup. "I never said I was selling it."

"You did. You said ownership had been 'transferred.'"

Wong Tai glanced up from her papers. "Yes, I transferred it to him." She glanced at my open mouth, and I quickly shut it. "Cole is going on a road trip," she added, as if that should explain things.

"Where are you going?" I asked. Was he on the run? It wasn't going to be easy to catch a killer who'd already taken flight.

"Florida." Annoyance seemed to ooze out of every pore of Mr. Stritch's large face. His black mustache twitched like a rodent digesting poison.

"Cole is retiring, at long last," Wong Tai said, to supplement his stingy response.

"So you won't stay to see Lulu's killer brought to justice?"

"Just what are you suggesting, young lady?" His heavy brow bunched.

Wong Tai looked up sharply. "Lulu is not dead. Besides, they already caught the killer of that poor young woman. You know, that beggar showed up last month out of the blue asking if Lulu wanted to play baseball. He is touched." Wong Tai tapped her pen to her temple. "It was only a matter of time before he snapped. I'm just glad it wasn't her."

A sick feeling plucked at my insides. It wasn't the first time Guitar Man had ventured out of Chinatown. He'd gone to West-lake Park and was ordered to leave for scaring people. But he wouldn't hurt anyone. Wong Tai was the one who had lost touch with reality.

Yet had our own bias caused us to overlook something crucial? Though I hated to even consider it, Gee Fa could be fear-some when he was upset. Had he visited Lulu? The memory of him swinging his guitar case at the bricklayers who had laughed at him flooded my thoughts. Had he swung his guitar case at Lulu with his pitching arm? If he had killed her, he was certainly strong enough to carry her to the horse lot.

Still, they had planted her earrings on him. The city's hands weren't clean, but what about Gee Fa's?

I licked my lips. "So Lulu turned him away?"

"No. She drove him back to Chinatown."

My head clattered with too many thoughts. Cole Stritch had begun gathering papers and stuffing them into his briefcase. I barely noticed the pack of cigarettes that had been lying under one of the papers until he stuffed it into the pocket of his black jacket. The words STRAMONIUM CIGS were printed in block letters on the label. I'd never heard of that brand before, but it certainly wasn't Liberté. *Stramonium* sounded almost medical.

Frowning at me, Mr. Stritch got up noisily from his chair. I stood too, not just because Peony and Bettina were at large, but because I needed time to think. "I should run those errands."

Once outside, I looked around for the girls. Seeing no one but a man watering his plants, I slipped over to Mrs. Sonenshein's house and tried not to worry. Camellia bushes trimmed her walkway, and a single poplar cast a screen over her lawn. A cedar fence closed off the backyard, hiding all but the tops of a couple cedar trees.

I pulled a lever, which yielded a quiet gong.

The door opened, and I braced myself, belatedly wondering if I should've brought a weapon.

Peony and Bettina stared back at me in their now-wrinkled school uniforms. Each of them was clutching an orange fruit that I would bet was a satsuma mandarin. Between them, Bettina held the arm of an old woman with a hunched back that put her at the girls' level. A fine quilted housecoat embroidered with gold thread draped her form. "Who's there?" Her cloudy blue eyes squinted beyond me. She was blind.

"It's my sister Gemma, just come to, er, pick me up." Peony threw a toothy, apologetic smile my direction, but I was not amused.

"Don't tell me you want a mandarin too, girl. I don't have many ripe ones left."

"No, ma'am, though they are beauties." I eyed the one Peony was holding with its shiny loose skin and a navel that puckered like a kiss.

"Mrs. Sonenshein never sells them," Peony offered smugly, as if her unearthing that fact could justify her naughtiness.

"This is what keeps my skin looking good," cackled the woman.

"Do people ever try to steal them?" I asked.

"Hmph. I got a line of cactus for anyone who thinks to hop *my* fence."

From what I could see still standing outside the front door, the wood-paneled hallway featured wall hooks hung with jackets, and a painting of still life. Beyond, a clutter-free living room consisted of a plush couch and a coffee table with padded corners, probably so she didn't injure herself. It didn't look like a home that housed a murderer. "My compliments to your housekeeper. Your home is immaculate."

Mrs. Sonenshein didn't answer. She'd dropped Bettina's hand. "What are you doing in my house?"

"Mrs. Sonenshein, it's me, Bettina Wong, your neighbor. You gave us satsumas."

The woman's head swung back and forth like a turtle, and her mouth began to gape. "I never did. Have you come to rob me? I shall call the police." Her eyes had peeled open all the way, and she took a step back.

"Of course not, ma'am. We were just leaving." Gritting my teeth, I jerked my head back toward the sidewalk. The girls set their mandarins on a side table and hastily exited.

The shutter of one of the windows flickered. A young Chinese woman in a black maid's uniform peered out at us. She looked to be a few years older than me, with a mouth like a daub of pink paint and rectangle eyes that conveyed a watchful demeanor. Then, as quick as the flash of a camera bulb, she was gone, though her image still left an imprint in my mind. Who was she? I'd never seen her before.

"Esther! Call the police." The door shut with more strength than I expected. But not before my eye caught on a hat hanging on a hook: a felt cloche with a guinea feather.

35
MAY

MY NEW ROLE NETTED ME MY OWN DRESSING ROOM
with a lighted wall-to-wall mirror that made me feel trapped
with myself. Every time I tried to read the script, my gaze would
crawl to my reflection, and I would have to do battle with all the
doubts brewing there.

How was I supposed to investigate Lulu's murder while carrying a film? Had I made a mistake? The burial was in three days.
Now was the time to throw all the coal in the fire.

Feeling like a tiger was sitting on my chest, I set down my
script, then went in search of Carey Stone, who'd been on set all
day. I'd promised Gemma not to talk to him about the murder,
but surely I could find out if he owned a white Schnauzer without mentioning our investigation.

Outside my door, Finn, the tall Irish security guard assigned
to watch me, straightened to his full height. "Miss?"

"Hello, Finn. Have you seen Carey Stone pass this way?"

Finn glanced down the hall toward a ficus plant. Carey's
dressing room lay just around the corner. "No, but it's lunchtime. He may be back in his room."

"Of course. Why don't you take your break?"

"I shouldn't be longer than thirty minutes. Sure wish these
rooms came with locks."

"I'll be fine." The only place I'd been alone all day was my dressing room, where Finn had been a constant sentry. "Thank you."

Finn headed toward the exit, while I made my way toward Carey's quarters, closer to the main studio. Rounding the corner, I was surprised to see Jack standing at Carey's door. Dressed in slouchy pants and a wrinkled oxford, he glanced around him, his longish hair swinging about his face. I shrank back behind the ficus plant before he saw me. Through the screen of leaves, I watched him reach for the doorknob. Then, with a last look around, he slipped inside.

A tingle of energy traveled up through the back of my neck. What was he up to? Carey and Jack were friends, but why was he acting so secretive?

Ordinary May would mind her own business. But Ordinary May had been replaced by someone with a gold sign on her door, engraved with her name. I padded down the wine-colored carpets to Carey's room, one of only two in this hallway.

They were arguing. Jack's usually mellow voice was talking faster than normal.

I inched closer, trying to hear.

"They know. It's only a matter of time." Carey's normally silky voice had become strained and high.

"Calm down," Jack said sharply. "No one knows anything. Act like everything's normal and it will be."

What secret were they harboring? Panicked voices behind closed doors meant big secrets. Maybe deadly ones. Carey had been rehearsing with Hettie the night Lulu was killed, but an accomplice could've done the job. I had trusted Jack too quickly.

Carey groaned. "It's all coming down."

The double doors at the end of the hall opened with a

sucking sound, and a petite figure in a yellow tea dress glided through them.

"Oh, hello, May," Suzy Daisy called out, the round face that belonged on the Prosperity cigar box brightening. "What are you standing there for?"

My cheeks flamed as if the word *eavesdropper* had just appeared in neon lights over my head. The conversation between Jack and Carey fell off. "I was just on my way to my room." I made tracks in that direction before either man came out, demanding to know what I was doing.

The Chinese extra trotted to keep up with me. "Oh, good, because I was coming to see you."

"Oh?" We reached the sanctity of my chambers, and I held open the door. "Come in."

Inside, I took a swiveling stool by the mirror while Suzy Daisy cautiously perched on a tufted chaise longue, glancing about with wide eyes. Her gaze alighted on a shelf piled with beauty products.

"I didn't know Hettie dyed her hair." She nodded at a peacock-blue bottle whose contents had smeared its label like blood. "This used to be her dressing room, you know."

"No, I didn't know." Looking around, I noticed more of the distinctive peacock-blue Fox products around the room. Perhaps they had also belonged to Hettie, as Capsize Studios wouldn't order the products of its enemy.

Suzy Daisy jumped out of the chaise longue and began examining all the Fox Cosmetics. "Here's Mrs. Fox's cold cream, *made with goat milk for a dewy, fresh complexion*," she read from the label. She picked up a compact. "Oh, look! Stardust Powder." Opening it, she dusted her cheeks with the accompanying puff. "Wish I'd invented this. We've got mica mines up in Fresno."

"My ma has cousins in Fresno. The Los of Lo Orchard."

Her now-glittering cheeks lifted in pleasure. "Oh yes, I went to school with Theresa. Double happiness for her recent marriage." She set down the compact and returned to her perch.

Just as I'd thought, we were only one handshake away from a connection.

"Thank you, we're all happy for her." I folded my hands, waiting for Suzy Daisy to speak.

Her knees began bouncing under her yellow tea dress like two rabbits under a tablecloth. "I remembered something I thought you might want to know. About Lulu. In case it helps find her killer."

"Yes? Anything will help."

"The last time I saw Lulu was the Friday before her"—her legs stopped bouncing—"passing. A man I never saw before picked her up from the studio after hours."

I gripped the stool, feeling something shift. "What did he look like?"

She tapped her chin with a polished nail. Her thin eyebrows reminded me of tiny knitting needles, weaving an array of expressions. "It was dark, so I couldn't see too well. But I remember he was muscular and blond like Tarzan, and he drove an Alfa Romeo coupe, apple green. I don't know if he was her boyfriend, but he had his arm around her like he owned her." Her eyes grew big, and she rubbed at her arms. "He helped her into the car, and they drove away, fast, like they didn't want anyone to see."

This Tarzan didn't sound like the medium-sized brunet who had bought Lulu's earrings. "Did the man, by chance, have a dog?"

"I didn't see a dog."

Was it possible that Lulu had two secret boyfriends? Perhaps one had killed her when he found out she was with child with the other. Maybe this new fellow had a wife too. I began to sweat, thinking about the endless jungle of possibilities.

Oh, Lulu, if it was true, why did you need two men in your life?

Someone knocked, and before I could answer, the door opened again.

The acting coach, Miss Vance, angled her narrow face at me, not a single wrinkle on her alabaster skin. Suzy Daisy got to her feet. "I should get back to rehearsal."

"Of course. Thank you, Suzy Daisy."

"You're welcome. Friends help each other out," she said brightly, then slipped out of the room.

After watching her go, Miss Vance peered at me with an expectant gaze, as if waiting for a formal invitation to enter. "Miss Vance," I greeted her.

"Are you alright? You look like you forgot to turn off your stove." Her lips pursed into a red dot.

Pushing aside the turmoil in my head, I summoned a smile. "I'm fine, thank you."

The woman folded her hands in front of her. "Emil wants me to run through the scene work with you." She enunciated carefully, as if each syllable must be polished up, like silverware, before it was laid out. "Any questions on the script?"

"Actually, well, I noticed a lot of kissing scenes." Lulu's prior roles had never been particularly amorous. We had heard it was illegal. Even white actors dressed up as Chinese weren't allowed to kiss white actors.

She hooked up an eyebrow. "I hope you don't have a problem with kissing."

My face warmed like a heating brick. "It's just, I was surprised that it would be allowed."

Miss Vance stared through a spotted fur stole hanging on a rack along with an assortment of clothes. Tracing a finger through her tightly pulled hair, her severe manner softened. "It's stuffy in here. Come." She marched back out the door.

Just as with her speech, her walking was also measured. I felt like a hay truck on a country road as I followed her swanlike figure out to a courtyard, where several tables and sun umbrellas bloomed. On either side of the courtyard rose loaf-shaped warehouses, which I'd learned were called "soundstages."

Miss Vance hailed the attendant of a rolling cart. "Two lemonades, please, Bertie."

The man popped the lids off two bottles and handed me one. I followed Miss Vance to a table. People smoking cigarettes cast me long glances, taking in my homemade plaid skirt and my sweater knitted from sales-bin yarn. I'd styled my hair in a French knot, hoping it would make me look more sophisticated, but I just felt like a schoolgirl trying to pass for older. The name *Lulu* had made its way to my ears numerous times since I'd arrived this morning, and I knew the comparisons had begun. Just sitting down at the table seemed fraught with peril.

"So have you taken acting lessons before?" A strand of Miss Vance's silver hair had pulled loose from her tight bun, and she smoothed it back with a finger.

"No."

This displeased her the same as a bad odor, but she waved the unpleasantness away. "You have an expressive face, so you're ahead of the game. The hardest part is memorization. Chang-Rae is a woman of few words, but each word is important. You can thank Lulu for that." She nodded to passersby calling greetings and sliding me knowing looks. It occurred to me that caring what people thought of you wasn't an asset in this industry, and I would need to develop a tougher shell, like a cactus bug.

"It seems Emil had much confidence in her."

"Yes. I'm not entirely sure how, but she was able to get approval rights over her character's storyline, and she wanted a role that would break some rules. She wanted Chang-Rae to be a complicated woman who, at the end, would make audiences weep." She squeezed her fist.

My soles flattened against the tile. Sadness began to creep in like rainwater. There was so much I wanted to ask Lulu, but I would never have a chance.

"The studio balked at the kissing, but she fought hard for it."

My gaze lost focus. It must have been so mortifying for Lulu to bring up such matters, much less fight for them. Had she been considered a troublemaker? Perhaps she'd hoped a kiss might soften her roles or add an element of humanity.

"In fact, Emil had just approved it before she died. Such a shame she'll never be able to do them."

My head jerked up so quickly I nearly pulled a neck muscle. Had the kiss been the tipping point for Mr. Stritch? The reason he'd waited so long to strike?

I cleared my throat. "Lulu must have had a good agent. Cole Stritch, wasn't it?" I tried to act as casual as possible. They could be best friends for all I knew.

"Yes, old King Cole." Miss Vance held up her lemonade. "Here's to the new Lulu, then."

I clinked my bottle with hers and tried not to grimace. Now I'd have to bring him up again. The lemonade painted a cold stripe down my throat. "Actually, I was thinking about asking Cole Stritch to represent me, but I can't abide the smell of certain cigarettes. Do you what brand he smokes?"

Her eyes narrowed, and she took another sip from her bottle. "I have no idea what he smokes."

Wonderful. Now she thought I was a prima donna.

"I wouldn't get your hopes up, though. I heard he was moving to Florida. Might've already left."

My bottle nearly slipped from my loosed grip. Leaving town, or skipping town?

"Now, show me how you'd drink that lemonade if you suspected someone was trying to poison you."

It didn't take much acting to look nauseous.

WHEN I RETURNED TO MY DRESSING ROOM, I WAS SURPRISED TO find the door open. I cautiously approached, hearing Finn's familiar lilt. He laughed. He must be familiar with whoever was inside.

A woman with ginger curls was packing the spotted fur stole into a valise, into which she had packed all the peacock-blue products in the room.

"Hettie?"

She twisted around and struck a pose, good enough for a magazine cover. A vogue striped pantsuit made her legs look endless. "Hello, May. Pardon the intrusion. I left some things."

"I'll just wait outside," said Finn, edging past me.

Hettie gave me a smile that was one-half smirk. "I heard congratulations are in order." Gone was the haunted look I'd seen at the Pannychis. Instead, the actress radiated good health, with shiny curls and a blush to her skin.

"I have you to thank for it, and congratulations on your new role, as well." Opportunity rang a silver bell. I wished Gemma were here. She'd know how to play this hand without spilling cards all over the table. Then again, maybe it was better to drop the artifice and just be honest. That's what I was best at anyway. "I have to admit, I was a little surprised."

"Oh?" Her green eyes squeezed a fraction, getting my meaning. "I think Lulu would be happy for me. It's not easy being a woman in this industry. The clock is ticking on our looks. We have to grab what we can." She briskly shook out a pair of knickers and added it to her valise. Her face softened, and she rubbed the glossy fabric of a silk shirt between her fingers. "Plus, with her gone, working here is just depressing."

"Yes, that must be difficult." I paused, wondering if I should continue pushing the issue. She seemed genuinely distressed. Then again, she was an actress. "You do know that *Big Apple Blues* was backed by Otis Fox?"

"Yes, I'm aware. But I try to stay out of politics. Such dirty business." She twiddled one of her poison-red curls with the unconcerned air of someone who never needed to bother herself with politics. It threw dust in my face and left a sour taste on my tongue.

"Indeed. Especially when murder's involved."

Her cheeks pinkened, and the silk blouse slipped off the hanger. "What do you mean? Are you implying Otis had something to do with her death? I thought they already found their man."

I shrugged. "Their man. Not the *right* man. Lulu's death worked out for Fox. It's no secret how much he hates Chinatown. Not only did *A Far East Affair* threaten Summit Studios' number one release, it showed the Chinese in a good light. He could easily have had her erased."

I watched her carefully for any reaction, but her face seemed to drop all emotion, like a handkerchief off a balcony.

She returned to her valise. Was she hiding something or just

annoyed at my questions? "If you ask me, I think you're bark-
ing up the wrong tree. The Foxes hosted the premiere party of
Lulu's and my first movie together, *Fast Fortune*, a year ago. I'd
never seen Otis Fox so charming, offering her his happy dust—of
course, she didn't do drugs—and showing her his art collection."
Hefting the valise, she checked her appearance in the mirror,
rubbing at a bit of lipstick stuck on her tooth. "Maybe the truth
is more complicated than you think."

She breezed out, leaving behind a trail of question marks.
Lulu would act professional, but she would never be friendly
with people who sought the destruction of Chinatown. I wanted
to go home and talk over these new developments with my sisters. But I was expected on set any minute now, and I still needed
to memorize my lines.

The script lay on the counter where I'd left it, facedown. My
pulse began to nudge up. Had I left it that way?

The paper felt cool under my grasp, the typewriter ink giving
off a thin, metallic scent. I flipped it over with a hand that suddenly felt unsteady.

The words *YOU'RE NEXT* were written in red pen across the
front page.

36
GEMMA

AFTER MRS. SONENSHEIN SLAMMED HER DOOR ON US, we hurried back to the privacy, or at least the false privacy, of the Mule.

Peony pulled Bettina into the passenger seat next to her. "I know you're mad, but we're not helpless."

"No, but you are thoughtless. There may very well be a killer in that house, and now she knows who you are. Thoughtless, reckless, and selfish."

Peony tied her arms into a knot. "Sort of like you, when you went to the coroner's office."

My breath huffed out of me. I resisted the urge to yank her braids. "That was different." Was it? *You are a jobajoo,* May had said. My high horse went saggy in the saddle. "Fine. But don't do it again."

"Alright, I won't," Peony said gamely. She was a better egg than me.

"We have to make ourselves scarce just in case she did call the coppers. You two go back to Bettina's house. You can keep an eye on Mrs. Sonenshein from your window, but don't go back there. Promise?"

After assuring me they would behave, the two scampered out of the Mule, but quickly shot back to my door. "We almost forgot," said Peony. "Mr. Yam said the tiger note looked like Gee Fa's writing."

I swore the Mule sank lower at the news.

"Is that bad?" Bettina twisted at her skirt.

I propped up a smile. "Not necessarily. I will have to think about it."

I lit out for Westlake Park, my brain racing in several directions at once, like dogs on leashes held by a single hand. The woman named Esther who Gee Fa had spoken to at the Plaza was living in Lulu's neighbor's house. She must have brought the satsumas. Was she his daughter? A person her size didn't match the description of the person Peony's classmate had seen in the Mercantile lot, but if she had killed Lulu, Gee Fa could've helped her dispose of the body. The idea loitered, like a dog you didn't know would heel or bite your shins. If they had killed Lulu, that would be a double tragedy that even I couldn't stomach unearthing.

But what of the letter? *Tiger roars; mountain tumbles. I will remember your words and deeds.* A threat, or a thank-you?

Boxy motorcars and shaggy trees reeled by, marked at regular intervals by telephone poles. I forced my jittering limbs to be still. Without a motive, I refused to believe either Gee Fa or Esther were involved. There were too many missing clues in this crossword for the others to fall in place just yet.

I parked in my usual spot at Westlake Park, managing to avoid bumping the curb this time. The paths were mostly deserted, and the uneasy feeling of being watched whipped my head in both directions. Don't be silly. This is a public park. I pulled out my basket of flowers. As Ba was fond of saying, many a flower has charmed a tiger, and peddling flowers would give me an excuse to stroll the lake path. I looked toward Freddie's office. The Chinese believe people who meet again and again are tied together by the red string of fate—one that is permanent, not like the fickle winds of change. The red string of fate was the reason Ma thumbed her nose at dating. If you were meant to be together, you would eventually meet.

Move. You are not connected by the red string of fate to that pretentious, condescending, yet admittedly helpful doctor, who seems to have gotten quite snaggled in a ball of yarn himself with Ophelia. Inhaling some calm, I set off, offering smiles that didn't always net one in return. Dogs sniffed me and sometimes barked, but none were white Schnauzers.

Now empty of people, the boathouse's red candlesnuffer roofs had turned dusky, and boats peeked out from their garages like crocodiles. A flash of white caught my eye. It was a knee-high dog, briskly padding beside a man in a dark duster down a pathway that led to the edge of the park. Was it a white Schnauzer? I couldn't be sure.

I followed, hoping Schnauzers were friendlier than Dobermans. Thick palm trees stood in silent judgment on either side of me. With his black fedora, the man—probably half a foot taller than me—walked with a purposeful stride that caused his duster to billow. The dog walked slightly ahead of the man, so that it was hard to get a good look at either man or beast.

Exiting the park, the pair crossed into a residential area. Waiting for several motorcars and trucks to pass, I hurried after them. But by the time I had reached the sidewalk, they were gone.

I continued walking until I reached an alley where they might have disappeared. The alley appeared to be abandoned, bordered on either side by warehouses with fenced-in lots. The only thing that moved was a tin can, batted around by the wind. I had lost them.

I crept along a wood fence, on alert for any sign of beast or man. Nothing. I decided I should return. Girls shouldn't be out on their own in strange neighborhoods after dusk, not that I ever let that stop—

A hand clamped around my arm. I gasped and dropped my basket. Light-blue eyes bore down on me. It was the man who had approached me at Westlake Park three days ago. The Scot. But he wasn't wearing a duster, but a coarse suit with his familiar houndstooth driving cap.

"How dare you," I gasped, terror shooting through me. "Let me go or I will scream."

"Go ahead. There's no one to hear you." He jerked his chin toward the warehouses, his yellow triangle beard like a caution flag. "The workers have gone home now, haven't they?" He twisted my arm, squeezing it so tight that my fingers went hot. I whimpered, but the man only tightened his grip.

"You're hurting me!"

"What's yer interest in Lulu Wong?"

"What's *your* interest in her?" I struggled to shake him off, but the man's grip had welded onto me. Was this the man who had killed Lulu in cold blood? He certainly talked like a killer, his voice cold and detached, the voice of a man reading bingo numbers. I tried to use my weight to break free, but I was no match for him. My arm tingled, losing circulation. "We only want justice for Lulu," I gasped, forcing myself to remain calm. *Don't you dare let fear draw a target on your chest.*

"Why do you think you'll find it here?"

"She was dating a man who owned a white Schnauzer."

His face remained expressionless. "You think he did it?"

"With the way you're manhandling me, I'm beginning to think *you* did it."

"Lulu was killed by someone she trusted. Someone who wanted to replace her."

"How do you know that?" I stopped struggling. My heart was beating at breakneck speed, and I forced it to still.

He ignored me. "Am I right that yer sister has been offered Lulu's role in *A Far East Affair*?"

I gaped, finally shaking my arm free. "Have you been spying on us?"

"So it's true, then. You'd better watch yer back. As you've seen, girls are easily replaced. Girls like yer sister."

A bronze car motored down the alleyway at a too-fast clip. I shrank away so quickly I stumbled painfully onto the concrete, hearing fabric rip. The car braked hard. A door opened, and the Scot jumped in, slamming the door with a metallic clank.

Then the car sped away in a shower of dirt and exhaust that burned my nostrils. My basket lay in a broken heap of wicker and torn petals. I got to my feet and hugged myself. *Stop shaking, you ninny.* Who was the Scot to Lulu? Not the boyfriend. This man was dangerous, and not the sort I imagined Lulu caring for. Perhaps someone working for the boyfriend or another interested party.

It was hard to think. I stumbled back to the park, feeling feral and out of place. I'd gotten too close to the truth, and it had nearly run me over.

Reaching the sanctity of the Mule, I wished for the millionth time we had transportation that included doors. *You meat cleaver, what if something had happened to you? How would Ma, in her condition, have managed? How would Ba, in his condition . . .* I buried my head in my arms and let out a sob. *Steady. Steady. You're no good to anyone falling apart.*

"Miss Chow." A dark figure spread himself over the passenger doorway, blocking the purple sky behind him, his face cast in shadow.

I grabbed at the gears, not remembering how to operate them. Was it the Scot again, come back to finish the job? Or the killer?

37
GEMMA

"YOU'RE LIKE THE CYCLONE ROLLER COASTER," THE stranger continued, his voice thick with disapproval. He shifted, and Freddie's familiar haughty gaze landed on me. "I can't help standing in line, even though I know I'm in for a crick in the neck." His voice softened. "Gemma. What's wrong?"

I nearly laughed in relief. "Why would you think anything's wrong?" I said brusquely. "I'm not a damsel in distress, you know. I'm a perfectly capable person. And I must be getting home now."

Freddie had already rounded to my side of the Mule. "You don't look fine. Slide over. I'm taking you to the office." He slid in, forcing me to scoot over.

"But I am fine," I said in a voice too tightly strung. "What are you doing here?"

"Taking a walk, like I often do. What are *you* doing here?"

I breathed through my nose. *Get ahold of yourself. He probably thinks you've gone into hysterics.* "What time is it?"

Freddie smoothly started the Mule and coaxed her from the curb. "Half past seven."

"I must go. I'm expected at home." May might intercede, but she'd be in a snit, expecting the worst of me.

"First we make sure you're okay. You can use the phone in my office."

Two minutes later, we had pulled up to his office building, and he was unlocking the door. He switched on the lights, then led me to Mrs. H's desk, where he handed me the phone receiver.

While I waited for the operator, he disappeared into the kitchen at the back of the office. Moments later, I was being connected to the phone in our building hallway. It rang and rang.

Freddie emerged from the kitchen with a headache bag and a glass of water, his eyes bright with worry. I turned my back to him.

"Gemma, you're injured. There's another phone in my office if you want to try later. At least let me examine your arm and leg."

"My leg?"

I looked down, only now noticing the tear in my trousers. He took me by the wrists and turned over my palms, which were scraped and bleeding. "This has to do with Lulu Wong, doesn't it?" His tone was flat, the words more a statement than a question.

He placed the blissfully cool headache bag in my hands, then led me up the stairs. At the top, he touched my arm as if to help me, but I gasped in pain.

"Hurts there?"

I gritted my teeth, feeling tears rush in. "Nope, barely felt it."

Inside his office, the shades had been drawn and his desk chair neatly pushed in. I eyed the examination table. I was definitely not getting up there to be inspected like the underside of a car.

Thankfully, he didn't mention the table, only pulled out one of the conversation chairs, which I gratefully dropped into. He slipped off his dark pin-striped coat and hung it over his own chair, then crossed to the sink and washed his hands.

The crossword puzzle still occupied the corner of his desk. More of the puzzle had been filled in, including an additional letter for the clue that still eluded me, twenty-one down. *It takes time to sink in:*

That meant the answer wasn't GRAVEYARD, unless the "I" was wrong.

One clue had been circled, four across. *Our best supporters:*

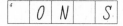

Freddie had written the word *patrons* on the side with a question mark. But that didn't fit. There were too many letters, and they were in the wrong places.

"Now, let's see this arm. Do you mind?"

I shook my head. He unbuttoned my sleeve, rolling it up with care. An angry red mark banded my biceps. "Somebody did this to you."

"Really. I thought it was a troop of howler monkeys. They get mad if you don't yield the light."

His fingers were light and cool, lifting my wrist and brushing his fingertips along the length of my arm while he inspected. Goose bumps broke out on my skin. "Tell me. Not about the monkeys."

I tried to think of a good lie, then wondered why I bothered. He already knew I broke into the morgue. There wasn't much else you needed to form an opinion about a person other than that they broke into the morgue. So in as few words as possible, I explained about tailing the dog, which literally was a walk in the park.

He took the chair next to me and held the headache bag to my arm. The scent of soap and something musky percolated to my nose. There was something angry in his expression. Judgmental as always. He would never have to take on a murder investigation himself because the police were meant to serve people like him.

"The good news is, give it a week, and you'll be right as rain. The bad news is, you're as infuriating as—"

"As a crossword puzzle you can't solve?" I was angry too. I didn't ask to be grabbed and shaken. "The answer to four across is bones. Our best supporters are bones. If you had asked for his point of view"—I flicked my nose toward the skeleton—"you could've gotten it. But no one listens to people who have to stand in the background. I just hope he wasn't one of your patients."

He glanced from the crossword to the skeleton, then sighed. "With your permission, I can disinfect those cuts on your knees while you try again." He pushed the telephone toward me.

"Fine." I requested the connection. While the hallway phone rang, Freddie knelt and inspected my leg in the infuriatingly thorough way he liked to analyze things. I couldn't think straight.

Someone answered. "Hello?" said May's voice.

"Finally." I put on a tone of false aggravation. "It's Gemma. I'm at Dr. Winter's office. Dog watching took longer than I expected."

"Is Peony with you?"

"No, Wong Tai is taking her home after dinner. There's a long story there."

"Ma got as mad as a hornet when we didn't come home

together. How was I supposed to know you were 'joining me' at the 'sewing machine class'?"

"What excuse did you give her?"

"I'm out of excuses, so you'd better think of something. She went to the herbalist for the happy baby herbs."

I wilted, remembering I was supposed to get those herbs for her. At this hour, Ma would have to knock on the door of Dai-Sang's apartment behind his shop. "I'll see you soon."

Despite my twitching about, Freddie dressed the road burn on my knee as efficiently as May trimmed and wrapped a bouquet of gladiolas. He made short work of the shallow wounds on my palms as well, cleaning, dabbing an ointment, and bandaging. Medicinal smells filled my nose.

"What's stramonium?" I asked, remembering Cole Stritch's brand of cigarettes.

"Is this related to the murder investigation? Because I'd rather not encourage more risky behavior."

"If you don't tell me, I shall find the answer somehow."

The air cannoned out of his mouth, and his movements became brisker. "Stramonium is a toxic weed used since ancient times to treat a variety of ailments. People smoke it to treat their asthma or emphysema."

"Would someone smoking these also smoke tobacco?" Liberté cigarettes, for example.

He frowned. "If they are motivated to smoke stramonium, I would guess they have advanced lung disease, and it would be quite irritating to do so."

Would someone with advanced lung disease have had the lung capacity to kill Lulu?

"Anyway, stramonium is falling out of favor. I say, moving to a humid area is best for those with severe emphysema. Of course, not everyone can afford to move to Florida."

Cole Stritch was retiring in Florida.

Freddie pressed an adhesive bandage into place. "All done."

"Thank you." It occurred to me how nicely he was dressed. Rose-colored collared shirt, with a matching tie. Freshly shaved too, it appeared. "I shouldn't take more of your time. Wouldn't want to keep Ophelia waiting." I got to my feet, and he rose as well.

"Not Ophelia." He scoffed. "I was on my way to the bar I know the district attorney frequents every Friday." He dug a finger under the silk knot of his tie and loosened it. "I hadn't heard from him, you see."

That stalled my tongue. He had gone out of his way twice now. "Well, thank you," I managed to say.

Peering down at me, his clinician's gaze looked suddenly lost.

Ma always said my feet moved faster than my head, but as with fledging birds, sometimes nature just told you when to jump. His hands were open, inviting. In that moment, a feeling that was neither push nor pull, go nor stay, clutched at me. My mission had always been to catch the world and bring it back to my family's doorstep. But in this moment, I'd thrown out a net for something I couldn't possibly want.

May had warned me not to trust strange men, but Freddie wasn't really a stranger anymore. I pushed out thoughts of my sister, who was the last person I wanted to think about right now.

His serious eyes watched me draw closer, something tender in his expression. "How did you blow into my life?"

"Trouble rarely announces itself." I drew closer still, crooking my face up to his. His surprised exhale caressed my skin.

Before I closed that crucial distance, my eye caught on one of the framed photographs on the wall, hung under the portrait of

Freddie's father. It showed Freddie standing on the threshold of his office, shaking the hand of man with a gummy smile.

Was that . . . Maurie Newman of the *Observer First?*

"Why is Mr. News shaking your hand?"

Freddie's gaze drifted behind him to the photo. He rubbed at his brow, like a man gathering his thoughts. "Er, Maurie was one of my sponsors. He put me in touch with the right people to get my practice started."

"Really? You never mentioned it."

"Hadn't I?" He lifted one of those cultured eyebrows.

"No. Not at the Pannychis when you told me who he was."

He cleared his throat, a sound that put me in mind of a deck of cards being straightened. "I don't make a habit of spilling my life story to perfect strangers, even ones as charming as you."

My blood cooled. Was I swatting at imaginary flies? His nearness made it hard to think. "I should go." The soft carpeting plucked at my feet.

"At least let me drive you home."

"I'm quite capable."

"Gemma. Gemma, wait!"

I hobbled back to the Mule, the sweet anticipation of kissing Freddie flattening into something melancholy. A little sugar in the teapot was how business got done here in Los Angeles. Had he accepted a little sweetener in his tea?

Even if he hadn't done anything illegal, the reminder that he ran in different circles than me, circles I would never have access to even if I wanted, shook something loose inside me. A relationship here was doomed to fail. Maybe if I was Lulu Wong, I could approach him on equal footing. Maybe if I'd been born with sky-high legs and a fleshy nose, things would be different. But I was just me, a grumpy, slightly banged-up, cheeky chit from Chinatown.

38
MAY

I PACED OUR KITCHEN. GEMMA HAD BEEN CAGEY ON the phone, and I wished she would hurry up and get home so I could get mad at her in person for what I suspected had been reckless behavior on her part.

I would wait until after scolding her to tell her about my vandalized script.

The culprit had not been found. Emil had considered the script defacing a practical joke, though he did agree to get locks installed on the dressing room doors. Was Suzy Daisy the mischief maker? She'd had an opportunity while I was sipping lemonade with Miss Vance. Hettie Bright? She could've done it before Finn returned. I doubted it was Carey or Jack, who seemed to have more worrisome matters on their mind than tampering with my script. When not on set, I'd kept my distance from both of them. Their conversation had certainly sounded damning. But how would we ever prove if they had blood on their hands?

Peony burst through the door, casting me meaningful looks. Behind her, Wong Tai looked as brittle as an apothecary bottle, standing with Bettina in our hallway.

"Thank you for bringing Peony home," I told the woman.

"Won't you stay a moment?" I couldn't not invite her in, even though Ma hadn't returned from the herbalist yet.

"I would like that." Wong Tai's tired eyes momentarily lost their grippy look.

Peony pulled Bettina into our apartment by the hand. "You can see Venus from my window. I'll show you."

Wong Tai watched the girls disappear into our bedroom, then glanced at our stove, stacked with clean pots, four faded aprons neatly hung along a cracked wall that even emperor-yellow paint could not hide. She looked out of place here with her elegant shawl, and though I'd always taken pride in our tidy housekeeping, a trickle of embarrassment made its way up my collar.

"I just brewed some chrysanthemum tea." I gestured toward our table.

"That sounds lovely."

After hanging her shawl, I poured. The last time I'd seen her was over a cup of tea.

She inhaled the steam. "Daughters are a family's greatest treasure. You have made this house a home."

"Ba says home is not a place."

"When Song left us, it was Lulu who kept me from drowning." Her dove-wing hands clenched tight. "She told me she would buy a big, beautiful house where we could forget our troubles. She was the one who pulled us out of the sea. I never told her what a good girl she was."

I couldn't help noticing her use of the past tense. Had she finally accepted Lulu's death? She was wearing white—a thick knit with a wrap-around design. "I'm sure Lulu knew how much you appreciated her."

Her face crumpled a little, like a sweet pea feeling the wind.

"We argued. That is why I went to my cousin's in Anaheim. She had gone behind my back. Helped that beggar, even after I told her not to. And then he killed her."

Beggar? "Gee Fa?"

She flinched. "She always looked up to him."

She'd sometimes play ball with our gang, Wallace had said. *Guitar Man taught her a killer swing.*

I gripped my knees, feeling something shift. "How did Lulu help Gee Fa?"

Her eyes became razor blades. "Got his daughter a job with our neighbor," she said hotly.

The young woman I'd seen at the Plaza.

All noise fell away. The always-present rumble of the train. The girlish chatter in the next room. Emil had asked Lulu to think of a moment when she'd stuck up for her beliefs even when those she loved disagreed. *You know, Jack, Chang-Rae just taught me how to do the right thing.*

Wong Tai covered her hands with her face. "It's my fault. I should've given her a better father."

"Of course not," I muttered. After all these years, the man continued to inflict his injury on this family.

"Ma, come and look at Venus," Bettina called from our bedroom.

Composing her features, Wong Tai finished her tea, then made her way to the bedroom.

As I refreshed the teapot, the front door opened. Ma shuffled in, looking a little off-balance in one of Ba's stretched-out cardigans. Her hands held a paper bag of herbs and a newspaper, which she thrust at me. "What is the meaning of this?"

It was the *Observer First*, the Friday evening edition. The headline shouted in bold:

RAILROADS' FINAL PLEA DENIED
City Orders Construction of
Union Station to Begin Immediately

So it had happened at last. They were forcing us out. "Chinatown—"

"Not that. This." Ma stabbed a finger lower down on the page at a glamorous photograph of Hettie Bright. My eyes caught on a postage-stamp-sized image set in the corner of Hettie's picture. It was me, not smiling but with a slightly startled look. It must have been the employment photograph they had taken my first day as an extra. The accompanying article read:

Upheaval at Capsize Pictures with Hettie Bright's Move to Summit Studios

In shocking news from Hollywoodland, Summit Studios announced that America's sweetheart Hettie Bright would be joining the cast of its upcoming film Big Apple Blues, *despite a prior commitment with Capsize Pictures'* A Far East Affair, *currently filming. The death of Lulu Wong, her costar, halted production of the highly anticipated Capsize release, but only briefly. "With Lulu gone, it was just too difficult to go on," said Miss Bright.*

Sources say an unknown talent, May Chow, will be assuming the role previously played by Lulu Wong, while the actress Juanita will take the role previously played by Hettie Bright.

I wanted to hide the article. I wanted to tell Ma it was all a misunderstanding, but her lips had gone white with fury, beads of sweat framing her face.

"You're a movie star now?" She spat the words out like bitter seeds.

"No, not a movie star. It's a job, Ma. A good job. It'll pay many bills, and we won't have to worry so much about the baby."

"Who's worried about the baby?" She angrily tossed her happy baby herbs on the table, spilling them. "You? What good will herbs do in a house full of lies?" I was vaguely aware that Peony, Bettina, and Wong Tai had emerged from our bedroom. Noticing them, Ma squeezed her temples. "I'm sorry, Wong Tai. I didn't know you were here."

"What's the matter?" Wong Tai reached for the newspaper, and I was tempted to throw it out the window. Instead, I let her have it.

"May has much to answer for," Ma said simply.

"I'm sorry, Ma," I pleaded. "We wanted to tell you. We were just trying to—"

"We?" Ma cut in.

Bettina, standing by the stove, began tugging at her wispy braids, her eyes wide behind her glasses. "It was my idea. I—"

"Told us there were opportunities as extras," I hastily cut in, not wanting Ma to know about our amateur investigation, which would worry her more than me being an actress. "We thought it might be a way to make some extra money."

The paper made a dull thud as Wong Tai dropped it on the table. Ma paced to the window and back, her anger radiating off her like the heat from a potbelly stove. On my other side, Wong Tai was taking deep inhales through her small nose, her lips pinched into a knot. Fire and ice.

"The role just . . . happened," I said. "We didn't mean—I never meant—"

Ma threw out her hands, then caught the small of her back. "You are the oldest! You are supposed to know better. What will Wallace think?"

Wallace already knew of my work as an extra, and I doubted he would mind, but this wasn't the right time to mention that.

"Think of your reputation once word gets out that you're an *actress*," she fumed, speaking the word as if it left a bad taste. "Strangers will ogle you on the screen. They will think you are loose."

"I'm sorry, Ma."

Her gaze slid off me, as if she couldn't stand the sight of me. She hissed a loud rebuke, gripping her stomach as if it were a miniature world I had knocked off its axis.

"I knew you had a low opinion of my daughter," came Wong Tai's voice, the warm base notes taking on razor-sharp edges. She cast Ma a hard look as the itch of old injuries flared. "But it seems the stone has hit the sender."

Ma turned her astonishment on Wong Tai. "I admired Lulu and would never speak harshly against ghosts."

"She is *not* a ghost."

The women eyed each other, two tigers meeting in the jungle. Bettina looked like she wanted to cry, and Peony was patting her shoulder.

The door opened.

Gemma limped in, looking like she'd stepped off a battlefield. Her trousers were ripped, with one pant leg rolled up, revealing a white bandage around her knee. Her hands were also bandaged. Worst of all, her eyes were swollen like maybe she'd been crying. I hadn't seen her cry since we were children. She pushed the hair off her face with a knuckle. "What did I miss?"

39
GEMMA

WONG TAI BLAZED AWAY, TOWING A TEARFUL BETTINA behind her. Ma's face bore a streaky flush, and she sank into her rocking chair, waving me toward the couch with her newspaper. Peony and May fetched supplies and got to work sponging grit from my "tumble."

"I just decided to go for a drive. My straw hat blew out the side and the light was red, so I jumped out to fetch it," I babbled. "I didn't see the bike coming by."

The newspaper landed with a thud on the table in front of me. I gasped. "Railroads lost?"

"Worse," Ma said darkly.

What could be worse than that?

My body went numb as my eyes roamed the rest of the page. A quick look at the next headline and the picture of May, who photographed well, despite her surprised expression, told me everything I needed to know.

Ma sat eerily still, her hands wrapped around her stomach, looking like a dragon-lion hoarding a ball of gold. She clucked her tongue. "Who bandaged you? Never mind, I don't believe anything you say anymore." The rocking chair started up. "How did you manage to sell flowers when she"—Ma nodded at May sitting beside me—"was off being a movie star?"

Peony hugged her knees. I began to protest, but May shushed me. I ignored her. "The business is still sound. We've had to make a few adjustments, but it won't be forever. Plus, May's new job—"

Ma waved her hand at me as if wiping dirt from a window. "You talk as if this can continue. What will your father say when he reads the newspaper?"

May hung her head. "You have every right to be disappointed. We were wrong to deceive you."

I scowled, knowing May wouldn't fight, even though it meant throwing away the opportunity of a lifetime. Especially now, when we needed the income more than ever.

The faint ring of the phone sounded from the hallway. Ba must be calling.

We all rose, but Ma slashed a finger at us. "No, no. You will all stay here. I'll answer it."

Peony pulled Ma out of the chair, and Ma briskly crossed to the door. It swung shut behind her, as sharp as a rebuke.

"What's the real story?" said May, fitting my flannel nightgown over my head. "You didn't even bring your straw hat. It's hanging there on the rack."

I kept the tale simple and emotionless, knowing May would overworry.

Peony held lukewarm tea to my lips. "So the Scot and whoever he's working with must not trust the police either. Otherwise, why have they been tailing you?"

"Good question." I glanced at the door, wondering how Ma was breaking the double-bad news—the railroads, and May—to Ba. "It couldn't be a coincidence that the Schnauzer and the Scot were at the park at the same time."

May buttoned my sleeves. "So you think they're connected."

I shrugged, though the movement was painful. I must have

pulled a muscle in my shoulder. "My guess is that the Scot's working for the man who owns the Schnauzer—Lulu's boyfriend. I just wish I'd gotten a better look at him."

"Which means Lulu's boyfriend is a vigilante," Peony breathed.

"Or he's a murderer looking to cover up his tracks," I pointed out.

May finished my sleeves and sat back, causing the couch to sigh. "That seems excessive. The police already think they have their killer. If the boyfriend did kill her, all he needs to do is lie low. Maybe he really is trying to find out who did it." The delicate planes of May's face had shifted into a troubled expression. "One of the Chinese extras, Suzy Daisy, said she saw a muscular man who looked like Tarzan escort Lulu away in an apple-green Alfa Romeo coupe the Friday before she was killed. Suzy Daisy said the man was acting possessive and whisked her away fast and secret like. She didn't see a dog."

"Two boyfriends?" Peony chewed on her lip. "But . . . Bettina said Lulu took her for ice cream after work that Friday, like they always did."

"That's right," I said. "Could Bettina have gotten it wrong?"

"We need to stop investigating," May stated, staring at the ceiling. "Ma doesn't trust us anymore, and you were attacked. We can't even report that without paying a bribe."

"That noodle was just trying to scare me," I said, though my words lacked punch. "We're so close."

"We should be proud of ourselves for getting this far," May said in a too-breezy tone, the kind that hurried you along before you noticed anything wrong. Was she hiding something from me? She never directly lied, but lies of omission were a different matter. "We ruled out Cole Stritch as our suspect, and you said Dr. Winter was going to talk to the D.A. tonight. That's good of him."

My heart bent a little. This investigation had led down many paths that I could never unwalk.

"I would bet the woman who brought the satsumas was Gee Fa's daughter," May continued, pulling socks onto my feet. "Wong Tai told me Lulu helped her get a job with their neighbor, against Wong Tai's wishes."

Peony nodded vigorously. "We *saw* her at Mrs. Sonenshein's. Her name's Esther. If Gee Fa wrote the note, he must have been saying thank you. Lulu was the tiger whose roar could make even mountains tumble."

Work was hard to come by for low Chinese girls. A position in a beautiful house with room and board was coveted. A weight lifted from my chest like a too-heavy blanket. Gee Fa was no killer, and neither was Esther.

"Gee Fa always did speak in poetry," mused May.

The door clicked, and we all jumped to our feet. Ma poked her head in, one hand still on the knob.

"Is he still on?" I asked. "Could we talk to him?"

She nodded. "He wants to talk to you, Gemma, but don't keep him on long. He's very tired."

I hurried out to the telephone, with Ma, May, and Peony trooping along behind me. Ma refused the stool, instead pacing the hall, her woven grass slippers making shuffling noises on the linoleum. I took the stool, and May spread a blanket over my lap. Peony held the receiver to my ear. "Ba? How are you? Is the treatment working?"

"It has only been a week," he chided in a whispery voice. My heart squeezed to hear him sounding so small. "More time is needed. Did you figure out twenty-one down yet?"

"No."

"Ha! Well, don't expect me to tell you." He somehow

mustered indignation, even while whispering. "I guess I am still smarter than you."

"But not for long," I lobbed back, though I didn't really feel it.

I heard him swallow water, and he cleared his throat with effort. The knowledge that even joking was painful for him put an ache in my side.

"Your ma says you have been hiding things from her. That May is now an *actress*." He pronounced that last word as if it were in another language.

"I'm sorry," I said. "We just didn't want Ma to worry."

Ma stopped her pacing and made a sucking sound with her teeth. May winced.

"But you knew that she—*we*—would disapprove," he said.

"Yes. But it's a good opportunity, Ba. Times are changing. Movies can show us in a new light, a better light. Plus, May's talented, and they're going to pay her eight times what we make in a month." I was speaking fast, but I needed to get it all in while I had the chance. "And don't worry about Chow's Flowers. Sure, I've had to donate a few bunches here and there"—Ma, now standing with her back against the wall, frowned up at a yellow ceiling bulb—"but our business is kicking along."

"How are you running it by yourself?"

"You know I was doing most of the work anyway. May's just there for looks." May pinched me, despite my delicate state. Ba began to cough, a rattling noise that went on for at least a count of ten. "Ba, are you okay?"

"Time without my family has made me reflect." He sighed. "May is number one cloud fighting day-to-day battles. Number two cloud must take the long view. That's you, planning from behind." He paused, maybe feeling the tickle of another cough, or perhaps choosing his words. "Does May want to be an actress?"

"Yes, she wants to be an actress." May's eyes met mine, and she stopped chewing her lip.

"Hold the phone so everyone can hear," Ba instructed.

After repeating the instructions to Peony, she held the phone out, and we all leaned close to the receiver.

"I am a lucky man to have three beautiful clouds in my sky." Ba's raspy sigh rattled again. "What I want is for all of you to follow your hearts, even if it means finding new skies to explore. Life is too short to spend living someone else's dreams."

I glanced at May, who cast her surprised gaze at Ma. Ma frowned at a crack along the wall, a grumpy note of acceptance sounding in her throat.

"Ba, do we have to move to East Adams?" Peony spoke into the receiver.

"Well, third cloud, the city council rejected the Three Coins proposal. But sometimes moonlight makes friends with a darkened path. There is a rumor that help may be coming from an unexpected source."

"What source?" I asked.

"I do not know yet, but Gemma, one last word with you?"

I put the phone back to my ear. "Yes, Ba?"

"I know you are too smart to jump out of a truck for a hat. Whatever you are *not* saying, please be careful."

I didn't know whether to be alarmed or cheered by the fact that he could still see through me, even from miles away. "Yes, Ba."

Number two cloud must take the long view. I had always been good at looking at the big picture. But somehow along the way, the big picture had flickered out of focus, and I'd been unwilling to adjust my lens. May was right. We were walking too close to the fire. I could never forgive myself if something happened to my family.

40

MAY

SATURDAY MORNING FELT UNTIDY, WITH PATCHES OF fog spread over the sky like wet newspaper on cement. Ma had served us breakfast in silence. She had swallowed my "movie star job," as she called it, without further complaint, but I suppose she had more than one coyote howling at her at the moment— not just Ba's health and the baby, but also our impending move. The landlord had given us a week to clear out.

I hadn't told my sisters about my vandalized script after all. Gemma would insist that we continue the investigation if she knew I was being harassed. At the Esteemed Friend planter, I touched our family brick after her, hoping the positive family energy we'd rubbed into it over the years would comfort me. But all I felt was cool, rough stone. Even the gardenias seemed to be withholding their perfume.

We went about our purchasing from one of the smaller growers in silence. I kept seeing Lulu in everything. A cloud the shape of a kiss. The coo of mourning doves. A woman driving a convertible that was neither a Cadillac nor red. I had failed Lulu. I had been the one closest to her. That Ba had convinced Ma to let me stay on for Lulu's role was more bitter than sweet, knowing I couldn't quite atone for abandoning her, as long as her killer walked free.

"Has the sun risen in the west? You just made a lane change without signaling," Gemma chided.

"I can't let it go. Who was stealing her scripts? Who drove her car to the Mercantile lot and smoked cigarettes? Who killed Lulu Wong?" The world rushed at me, and though I was in the driver's seat, I couldn't help feeling that I'd lost control. I slowed, drawing closer to the horse lot.

"We're doing the right thing." Gemma's words sounded like how sponge cake tasted, oversweet and full of air. "Hold the horses, aren't you supposed to be the one saying that? Wait, did we switch brains?"

I barely heard her. A green bulldozer painted with the words HAZE BROTHERS and men in overalls and work gloves had collected in front of the horse lot. It was demolition day. The day Chinatown would start to fall.

Gemma braced herself against the bench. "Pull over. I want to imprint the horse lot in my mind before they take it away."

I applied the brakes, easing the Mule to the curb. Behind the bulldozer, a man in a dark suit was leaning against a navy sedan. He waved his fedora at us, looked both ways, and clopped across the street in his cowboy boots.

His overly scrubbed face looked familiar, peering into the truck at us.

"Officer Kidd," Gemma said dryly.

The man screwed his fedora back onto his head. He must not be on duty today. "Hello, ladies." He jerked his thumb toward the men. "Big day."

Gemma jutted out her chin. "And you're here for the show? It's a strange way to spend your day off."

He held up his hands. "I have nothing to do with this. I was actually waiting here to see you two." There was a seriousness on his face that I didn't remember from our past encounters. He pulled his wallet from his pocket, then passed three dollars across me to Gemma. "This belongs to you."

She pinched the money between two fingers. "You really are a rookie. You're supposed to *keep* the hush money."

"Not all of us in the department are crooked. I know you've uncovered information on Lulu Wong's murder."

Gemma frowned. "How do you know that? Have you been spying on us?"

"Keeping my eyes sharp, more like. How else do you think you got clean away that night at the Hall of Justice? I saw you go in and made sure you could get out."

Gemma's breath huffed. "I did see you. But why?"

"Like I said, not all of us are crooked. In fact, some of us are hoping to clean up the department, but on the hush. See, a grand jury was convened with the power to hand down indictments on any city official—the police chief, the mayor, even the district attorney."

I matched Gemma's cynical gaze, not sure I was hearing right. "They tried that before, but all the jurors were paid off."

"This time's different." He took a business card from his jacket, pinching it between his thumb and forefinger. "See, the foreman's Clifford Joust."

My posture loosened. "Of Clifford's Steakhouse?"

"The same. He's rich enough not to be bribed, and he's serious about cleaning up the city. And he wants to talk to you two." Officer Kidd's fedora jerked at us.

Gemma placed a fist under her rigid chin. "Why should we believe you?"

He watched a falling leaf spin in the air between us. "You don't have to. But if you choose to, Cliff will be at the restaurant tonight, and he's expecting you." He handed me the business card from Clifford's Steakhouse, then returned to his car.

I started up the Mule again, the gears in my own mind whirring and clicking. "If Clifford is the foreman, maybe that's why you saw him with Philippe Fox that day in his restaurant. He was looking into the foxhole."

Gemma's eyes tightened. She tucked the dollars into our money bag. "Or he's in bed with the Foxes."

That was a grim thought, but one that couldn't be ignored. But perhaps, at last, the right players had joined the stage. We might not have found Lulu's killer, but we might root out the evil that had let her murderer walk free. An evil that had offered up an innocent man for the crime. An evil that wouldn't even wait for people to get out of the way before bulldozing their neighborhood.

From the seat of his sedan, Officer Kidd touched his hat at us, then steered his car away.

"We have to follow this lead," I said. "Clifford Joust might be our sunflower. Someone who won't hide in the shade."

"You don't have to convince me. But what's our plan for Ma?" Gemma added, more to herself than to me. She slapped her knee, grinning. "The plan's name is Wallace. You haven't seen him in, what, two days? An eternity for lovers. And you can get a steak dinner out of it. *If you want her to say yes, take her to Clifford's.*"

I didn't bother to honor that with a response, focusing instead on navigating through the universe of City Market without hitting any customers or stalls. Heads turned as we rolled to our space, and some people waved. That was odd. People were usually too busy this time of the morning to socialize.

After parking the Mule, I hauled out the folding table we kept in the stall, walking backward as I dragged it.

"People are waving at you," said Gemma. "Golly, I think they missed you. Or . . ." Gemma covered her mouth with a bandaged palm.

Make-Me-a-Deal looked up from his table, where he was chalking prices. "Hm, the movie star has arrived. Shall we roll out a red carpet?"

So that was the reason for the funny looks. Mr. Takashi in his white cowboy hat began to clap, and other vendors joined in.

A smile broke over Gemma's face. "The red carpet's not necessary, but May does give autographs, and those might be worth a fortune one day."

LATER THAT AFTERNOON, I RANG WALLACE ON THE HALLWAY telephone. His mother answered. "Hello, Mrs. Moy. It's May Chow."

"Hello," she greeted me coolly. "I'm afraid Wallace is not available."

"Oh? Would you mind telling him—"

"I'm sorry, May. I have decided it would be better for you and Wallace not to see each other."

"But—"

"A girl like you is too independent to make a suitable match for my Wallace."

I coughed, not quite sure I'd heard right. Me? The dutiful oldest daughter, too independent? Was it because I was calling Wallace, instead of the other way around?

"Anyway, I trust you will have many other suitors in your career."

Career. This was about the news article. "I see, but if you don't mind—"

She hung up, a last rebuke, and the disappointment howled

like a wind in my ears. I stared in shock at the phone receiver. Had Wallace seen the article too? He'd known I was working as an extra, but I hadn't told him about my new role yet.

My thoughts would not hold together, like unruly stems. Why should I be upset over a relationship that was fiction, just another lie, like so many of the ones I'd already told? I could hardly expect Wallace to fake a relationship with someone who would generate so much controversy. Still, I had hoped . . .

Someone behind me cleared her throat. Ma stood a few paces away, her hands deep in the pockets of her apron, her face grave.

I replaced the receiver with finality, like closing the door to a room you will not be entering again. How long had she been standing there? "Ma, that was—"

"I heard."

Shame clouded my vision. I doubted her opinion of me could fall much further. "I—I'm sorry, Ma. I guess he wasn't, or I wasn't—"

She gathered my hands together, seeing the hurt in my face, and whatever stitches were holding her tight suddenly loosened. "There is no need for apologies." She stood a whole hand shorter than me, but at that moment, she looked powerful enough to command a fleet. "It is *they* who should be sorry. Your ba was right. He said, 'We do not raise the flowers for their blooms, but for their tough roots.' You have that. All my girls have that."

A feeling that was both giddy and grounded lifted my soul. I'd been walking a narrow path for so long that I'd forgotten how much I needed her support. Her strong arms wrapped around me, arms that could hold a miniature world without dropping it.

41
GEMMA

DINNER WAS WELL UNDERWAY BY THE TIME WE ARRIVED at Clifford's Steakhouse, a neon sign of its name lighting the brick façade. May pulled a hastily cobbled together basket of flowers—mostly mums and pine cones—from the flatbed. Clifford's needed an autumn arrangement, and we'd come highly recommended. That's what I'd told Ma, anyway.

"You mean someone's paying you for that rubbish bin?" She'd stopped her packing and rubbed her stomach as if it were a crystal ball and she was trying to divine the truth of my words.

"Yes, this is considered *à la mode*," I lied.

Ma took a deep breath. "I expect you back by six for dinner."

It was already well past five. I had to admit, even with my busted moral compass, I was feeling the pinch of lying after all we had put Ma through last night. But here was our chance to collar villains, including those who had robbed Lulu of justice. Maybe even free a man wrongly accused. It was just one conversation.

A footman opened the door, ushering us into a lively Saturday-night scene.

"They're playing Gershwin," May whispered, looking toward the piano at the foot of the stairs.

"Smell that," I moaned. "Steak with a perfect char on the fat, with roast potatoes and gobs of butter."

The same maître d' with the military bearing that I had seen on my prior visit rested his sharp eyes on our floral arrangement, which looked shabby compared to the garlands wrapping the posts and the miniature potted pine trees twinkling with lights. "It's nice to see you again. You may set that right there." The host nodded at a side table, then glanced up to the second floor, where Mr. Joust leaned over a carved railing, surveying the dining room. "That's him. Please go right up."

Spotting us peering up at him, Mr. Joust waved, his trim white beard a brushstroke on a rather rectangular head. The pianist nodded at us as we ascended, the velvet runner silencing our steps.

Mr. Joust met us at the top of the staircase, his blue eyes curious. He wore a tuxedo with a rose in his lapel, and in his hands he held a leather book. "Thank you for coming." He gave a short bow and gestured to a table by the railing. His gracious manners reminded me of Cash Louie and must be a job requirement for a restaurateur.

A waiter pulled out heavy leather chairs for May and me. Mr. Joust seated himself and set his book on the table—a Bible. Seeing my confusion, he smiled. "I gave up the ministry because I liked money too much. Are you hungry? How about some steak tartare? It's a house specialty."

"That sounds lovely—" I began to say, when May kicked me, despite my injuries.

"I'm sorry, Mr. Joust, but we don't have much time," she said primly. "Our mother expects us home."

"It's Cliff, please." He signaled a waiter. "I'll get right to the point. As head of the grand jury, I'm the chief gardener digging

out the bad seeds and stubborn weeds in this city. We finally have
an opportunity to pull out one of the most pernicious vines with
one big yank. Once he yields, his whole network will dry up."

"Who is this vine?" I asked.

"Otis Fox."

I glanced at May, who had gone still, before asking, "Is that
why you met with Philippe Fox?"

His stroked his beard. "Ah, yes, the day you visited. I'm afraid
the answer I give will lead to more questions, questions I'm not
at liberty to answer. Do you still want to know?"

"Yes," May and I said at the same time.

"Simply put, I agreed to fund his political campaign. As for
why, you will simply have to trust me."

He tapped his Bible, and a verse floated into memory, some-
thing about how a home divided against itself cannot stand.
Perhaps that was Cliff's strategy. It wouldn't surprise me if one
Fox was willing to sell out another.

The waiter returned with glasses of Coca-Cola, tinkling with
ice. I put mine to my lips. No sense letting it go to waste. I supposed if we didn't trust Cliff, we wouldn't be here enjoying his
libations, which easily could've been poisoned had he meant us
harm. And anyway, at least for now, the enemy of my enemy—
Otis Fox—was my friend. "I thought it was the prosecutor's job
to investigate, not the foreman's."

"The grand jury can conduct its own investigation on whether
sufficient evidence exists to charge someone with a crime. Some
of us take an expansive view on that." He drummed his fingers
on the table, his nails tidy and trim without a hint of dirt.

"Do you believe Fox had anything to do with Lulu Wong's
murder?" May asked, not touching her drink.

"I don't know. But I have no doubt that Lulu's is one of many cases that will simply be pinned on the most convenient of suspects, as long as the weeds continue to throttle the truth."

May gripped her hands in her lap. "What do you need from us?"

Cliff leaned his forearms on the table and spoke directly to May. "I need *you* to attend a party."

"A party?" May's eyes slid to mine.

"Yes. Tomorrow. At Mr. Fox's residence."

May's back hit the chair with a thump.

Cliff opened the Bible and read, "*The wicked accept a bribe in secret to pervert the ways of justice.* That's Proverbs." He closed the book and patted it. "That's Otis's entire racket. He bribes city officials to give lucrative contracts to private businesses. He gets a cut of those contracts, which he uses to continue his bribery scheme. City officials receive private sector fat, and subpar businesses get a leg up. It's a scheme as old as Adam and very hard to catch when only cash is used. But . . ." He took a sip of his Coca-Cola, then dabbed a starched napkin to his lips. "Recently, one of the businesses, Haze Brothers Demolition, failed to cough up the funds."

My mind flew to the bulldozer we had seen this morning. I could feel my eyebrows pinch, not surprised in the least that Otis Fox had a financial stake in the razing of Chinatown.

"So instead," Cliff continued, "Otis took a prized work of art from Mr. Haze—*Jardin Oriental* by François Lefevre." Opening the Bible, he slid out a photograph of the painting. In it, Chinese women in silk robes sat on the edge of a pond. The most striking element in the picture was not the women, but the koi fish in the foreground. "You see, Otis has quite an affinity for Oriental art."

I snorted and some of the carbon gas fizzled up my nose. "Fox doesn't know whether to love us or hate us."

Cliff nodded. "I'm told that several years ago, the Foxes showed up unannounced at a popular Chinese restaurant and were turned away by the proprietor because he didn't want to rush his other patrons. Perhaps that's where Otis's feud with Chinatown started."

"Cash Louie?" I exclaimed.

Cliff folded his napkin into a neat triangle again. "Cash is a good friend. He should've expanded his empire by now, but Otis's reach is wide, and no one outside of Chinatown will rent to him."

I glanced at May, looking tragic in the soft yellow light of the antler chandeliers as she fingered the photograph of *Jardin Oriental*. I never expected a successful man like Cash to have troubles, but turns out, there was a lot I didn't know. It was as if Lulu's death had rolled the outside world up to our front door, a giant tangled ball of yarn. "So where does May come in?"

Cliff took another considered sip of his drink, taking his time swallowing. "Otis is hosting a soirée to get his investors excited about Summit Studios' new movie, *Big Apple Blues*. Lots of back patting and hand shaking. Hettie Bright will be there. We want May to be there, too." Both May and I began to protest, but he held up his hands defensively. "Before you say no, the task is simple. You'd simply keep your eyes open for that painting. If you see it, that's enough probable cause to get a search warrant. The painting is proof he's on the take. The threads will begin to unravel."

"They'd never let me in the door." May's expression had begun to crimp, and her knotted hairstyle had loosened.

He chuckled. "You're a VIP now. Otis would be beside himself if his rival's big star showed up at his gala. That's a feather in his hat. Once you're invited in, you have every right to be there."

He riffled through his Bible and tapped his finger on a page. "As Matthew instructs us, *If those living in a house welcome you, let your peace come upon it.*"

"Why can't *you* do it?" I asked, the warm feelings I'd had for Cliff beginning to evaporate. Sure, he made it seem like he had the angels on his side, but what was another Chinese girl to him? A necessary expenditure in the war of weeds?

"On the chance we don't find the painting, I will need to continue my efforts in other ways, and I can't afford to arouse suspicions." He lifted his face and held the pose, like one of those stone angels in the cemetery.

But Lucifer was an angel too, before his great fall. "Let's go back to the part where Otis hates Chinese people," I said. "How do we know she'll be safe?"

"Loves and hates. You said it yourself. May showing up at his house raises his profile. Plus, how would it look for Otis if something were to happen on his own property to an unaccompanied woman?"

"Unaccompanied?" May and I exclaimed at the same time.

"Sending May by herself will disarm Otis. He won't suspect her true purpose. Of course we'll have agents nearby. She'll be quite safe."

I eyed the Bible. "Would you swear it on that book?"

A smile played at his lips, and he flipped open his Bible again. "James tells us not to swear, neither by heaven or earth or by oath. But if it were my own daughter, I would have no trouble sending her."

I glared at his Bible, my hand squeezing my cold, empty glass. It still sounded like a terrible idea, sending an innocent like May into the heart of the enemy. She was a good actress but hardly a spy. I wasn't even sure *I'd* have the stomach for that.

On the other hand, two of our main suspects would be on this stage—Otis Fox and Hettie Bright. Might this be our shot to get at the truth? Lulu would be buried two days from now. There was still time for justice to be served.

But at what cost?

"You'd be doing Los Angeles quite a service," the man continued glibly. "In Matthew, Jesus says that when giving to the needy, do not let the left hand know what the right hand is doing—"

I set my damp fist upon the tissue-thin pages of his book, having had enough of his sermon. "The thing is, Cliff, you're not sending *your* daughter into the lion's den, but *my* sister. I have another sister, but this one's pretty useful to me."

"How old is your daughter?" May asked, ignoring me.

"Twelve, and I hope to leave her a city that's in better shape than it is now." He frowned at the ring my fist left on his page, his self-righteous fervor dimming.

Peony was twelve.

May scooted to the edge of her chair again. "I'll do it."

I blinked at May, but she and Cliff were matching stares. I'd become invisible.

I stood. How dare she try to leave me out of this? "Now who's looking out the window instead of at what's inside the house?" I fed May's words back to her. Diners had begun glancing in our direction.

"Sit down," she growled. "I am looking at what's inside the house. And there's a lot more than just us in there." Folding her thumbs, her gaze became placid, but I knew a hundred thoughts bubbled behind her eggshell complexion. The bribes we paid, the permits we were denied, the homes we could not buy.

Though my annoyance still made my head ring, I sank back

into the too-large chair. "On one condition, then." Both turned to me. "That I come with her."

Cliff rubbed the sides of his beard. "I'm sorry. May on her own will cause enough of a stir. I'm afraid the two of you together will be an unnecessary distraction."

May nodded. "What if Gemma came as an attendant? No one ever notices the help."

Cliff's gaze rolled to one side, and he nodded. "I might be able to arrange that. Let me make a few calls." He held out his hand for May to shake, then offered it to me. I crossed my arms. I certainly hoped he was the saint he held himself out to be, but if not, I wasn't going to shake hands with the devil.

42
MAY

THE LIVING ROOM COUCH BOUNCED AND SHIFTED, PULL-
ing loose the stitches of the baby blanket I was knitting. I couldn't
tell who was more agitated, me or Ma sitting beside me. Cliff
was certainly resourceful. He'd arranged every last detail of
tonight's operation, including having Cash Louie's wife spend
the day with Ma and put her up for the night.

The rumble of the approaching noon train rattled the windows. It whistled an obnoxious hurrah. Gemma, watching for
Ma's ride, whistled back. For once, her unladylike screeching
didn't annoy me.

Ma gestured at Peony, who finished buckling Ma's valise,
then hauled her up from the couch. "It was nice of Lan-Ying to
arrange an outing for me, but it is bad luck to celebrate early.
Last minute too. With all this packing!"

"It's not for the baby," said Gemma. "It's for you to have a little
fun before the baby comes."

Ma made a sucking sound. "A little fun. I don't need fun."

I frowned, losing count of my stitches. Was that motherhood,
all duty and no play? I couldn't remember the last time Ma had
gone to the Chinese opera that she loved so much, or even visited with friends. Everything she did was for us.

"I *am* having fun," she proclaimed, switching strategies.

"Lan-Ying is too American. Remember the last time I visited her? She wanted us to play 'tennis.'" She made a harsh sound at the back of her throat. "And I don't understand why I must stay the night either."

I set down my knitting. "She wants to take you to the new breakfast place in Santa Monica. They make pancakes."

Ma tried buttoning her silk jacket, but her stomach was in the way. She sniffed. "Waste of money. They probably pour syrup on them."

AN HOUR AFTER MA LEFT, A WHITE VAN WITH THE WORD CATERING on it stopped in front of our building. Gemma would be arriving at the Foxes' mansion separate from me, as part of the catering staff. We would have to play things by ear and wait for opportunities to present themselves. I was grateful Gemma would be there as extra eyes, and to confer with on the sly.

"We don't take unnecessary risks," I reminded her, straightening the collar of her catering uniform—a white jacket with brass buttons, black pants, and her hair tied back by a black silk scarf.

Gemma shrugged me off and pulled the curtain of our window closed. "Of course not. You'll be on display. People will be watching you. Your part is to be your dazzling self, while I snoop around the sidelines."

"*Safely* snoop."

"Sure, *safely snoop.*" She winked at Peony, who was sitting on her basketball, arranging chrysanthemums for the garland she was making.

I expected Peony to grumble about wanting to go with us, but to my surprise, she seemed engrossed in her project. "This is for Lulu."

I knelt and put an arm around her thin shoulders. "The king

of flowers is a good choice for the queen of Chinatown." Perhaps Peony was realizing that even off the battlefield, she was making a difference. Maybe the littlest cloud would one day outpace us all.

After the catering van carried Gemma away, I dialed the long-distance operator from our hallway telephone. While the operator found the route to Fresno, I fidgeted on the stool.

Something had been nagging at me, like a collar that kept flipping up. Bettina had mentioned that Lulu took her for ice cream every Friday. But Suzy Daisy said she had seen Tarzan pick Lulu up from the studio on Friday night. They couldn't both be right. And my money was on Bettina.

The phone rang, and I jumped up to answer it. "Hello?"

"May, it's Wallace."

My heart performed a little skip dance. Had he called to apologize for his mother's behavior? Or to tell me goodbye himself?

"I wanted to call you yesterday, but would you believe? My boss had another bout with cactus bugs. He licked a postage stamp of an American flag. That's twice I've saved his life. But I didn't call to talk about cactus bugs." He sounded nervous, all the words coming out in a rush. "We're honest with each other, right?"

"Sure."

"My honest feeling is that we shouldn't pretend-date anymore."

My heart pinched. "I know, and I appreciate you telling me yourself."

"Why wouldn't I? So, when can I take you out again?"

"I thought we were done with pretend-dating."

"I meant for a *real* date."

"Oh." Complicated feelings whirled inside my stomach like laundry in a spinner.

A voice broke through. "Your call to Fresno is ready," said the operator.

"Wallace, I'm sorry, I'm expecting this call."

"Ah, forgive my intrusion," he said, sounding disappointed. Then he was gone.

I could barely concentrate when Theresa Lo's familiar matter-of-fact voice burst through the wires, sounding tinny. "Hello?"

"Hello, Theresa? It's your cousin May Chow. How are you?"

"I'm well. What's the emergency? I hope it's not your ba—"

"No, he is well, thank you." I spoke quickly to make the three-minute rate window for a long-distance call. "I wanted to ask you about one of the Chinese extras in the film Lulu Wong was filming when she died. Her name is Suzy Daisy."

"Tragedy about Lulu. I'm not surprised Suzy Daisy went into acting."

"What do you mean?"

"You know I don't like to gossip."

"Of course, but this is important. You have to trust me. I will tell you more in a letter."

Crackles of static filled my ear, and Theresa sighed. "Okay. Well, Suzy Daisy has a flair for embellishment. In third grade she told everyone she had won a new Webster dictionary, which she actually stole from the library."

"Lots of kids do crazy things."

"Then there was the autograph she said she got from Rudolph Valentino."

"Oh?" That did sound rather odd.

"And the latest, a new wealthy beau out in Hollywood."

"What wealthy beau?"

"She said he looked like Tarzan. But we know that's a lie. Her roommate said there is no beau."

I sucked in my breath, feeling foolish for trusting Suzy Daisy so quickly. Whether Tarzan was a real person or a figment of her imagination, Suzy Daisy was not reliable. I would not be surprised if she was behind the script pranks. But was she a killer?

"Thanks, Theresa."

"Stay out of trouble, May."

It was much too late for that.

43

GEMMA

THE FOXES' GRAY STONE BEVERLY HILLS MANSION WAS
even more absurdly symmetrical in person than in the diagram
of the property Cliff had given us. In addition to the two wings
flanking a rotunda, there were ten camellia bushes per wing,
all carved into rectangles like blocks of butter, two chimneys,
and even two mailboxes. The symmetry felt almost sinister, as if
chosen purposely to hide something crooked.

A young man named Ulysses, one of four male servers, mis-
took my gawping. "Shucks, they all look the same after a while,"
he said in a Southern drawl. "Sure you're going to be okay there,
miss?" Light-brown eyes, an even tone with his skin, dipped to
my bandages.

I smiled at his concerned face. "It looks worse than it is. I'm
perfectly fine." I gamely took a pile of linens and marched to a
side door after the others.

Besides the servers, there were two cooks in gray dresses
and aprons, all led by our captain, Mrs. Souza. With her steady,
plowing manner, the woman reminded me of a steamboat, her
tremendous apron bow like the waterfall off the back paddle.
She had accepted my addition to her staff with a patient nod of
her head. Had Cliff greased her palm? What had Proverbs said
again about bribes? Something about perverting the ways of

justice. Maybe one needed to fight fire with fire and all that.

The side door led directly into the kitchen, where a woman with a high pile of graying blond curls surveyed us as we entered with our loads. She reminded me of a high-strung pony the way she strutted about. "Afternoon to you all. I am Mrs. Fez-Percy, the house manager. Mind your shoes aren't muddy."

The kitchen was bigger than our entire apartment and boasted double stoves and four iceboxes—enough for a flock of chickens. The acrid stench of bleach soaked the air. It was exactly the wrong smell for a kitchen.

Mrs. Fez-Percy led us into a "lodge" with showy furniture that crammed too many styles between four walls, silk wallpaper of garish yellow, and shiny art deco floor tiles. As they say, old money inherits houses, new money buys them. From there, we passed into a rotunda. I ignored the piano, my eyes picking apart the oil paintings lining the walls. Maybe I'd find *Jardin Oriental* before May, who wouldn't be arriving for several more hours. The top knave, Otis Fox, would fall, and so would his house of cards.

"The only thing you may touch in this room is the floor when you circulate through it." As Mrs. Fez-Percy rattled off her rules, I caught sight of an oil painting of the Foxes on the far wall. The artist had done a dapper job capturing Otis Fox's piercing black eyes and the sharp lines of his face, along with his wife's statuesque elegance. Between the two stood their son, Philippe. The future politician was just a kid of twelve or thirteen here, looking slightly restless, probably having better things to do than pose for a portrait. Would he be here tonight? We still didn't know how he figured into Cliff's plans.

"Do you think he's actually killed anyone?" Ulysses whispered beside me.

My head jerked up, nearly dislocating my neck. Did he know about my covert mission?

Then I realized he was frowning at a suit of armor by one wall, and I relaxed. "His mouth is wired up, so I guess he'll never tell."

"You will confine yourself to the kitchen, the lodge, and this rotunda," Mrs. Fez-Percy was saying. "The west wing is private."

That was the wing that housed the bedrooms, though Cliff doubted *Jardin Oriental* would be there. More likely it was hanging somewhere it could be admired, like the movie room or the library. In any event, Cliff had assured us May would not need to check the private wing, which he considered risky.

Even Mrs. Souza's gaze was beginning to glaze over as Mrs. Fez-Percy droned on. "You must keep the appearance of busyness, and if you are not busy, then—" She suddenly stopped her prancing and stood as straight as the suit of armor. "Mrs. Fox, this is the catering staff, ma'am."

Mrs. Fox strode in from the west wing, already dressed for her party in a midnight-blue beaded gown with a matching jacket that, instead of shrinking her dimensions, made her even more imposing. White-blond hair that didn't match her dark eyebrows swirled daringly around her head, making her festive makeup pop against her goat-milk-nourished skin. "Thank you, Mrs. Fez-Percy." Her long shoes clapped about the wood floor as she appraised each of us, her face animated. She caught one of the cooks, a wholesome milkmaid type, staring at her, and her eyebrows flared.

The girl lowered her eyes, closed her mouth, and curtsied.

Mrs. Fox nodded approvingly. "Now, tonight is a special celebration." Her voice was commanding, the kind of voice that could call the cows home. "It's my son's twenty-fifth birthday.

We shall have a cake brought in, and my good friend Florence Foster Jenkins will be stopping by to sing 'Happy Birthday.'"

Murmurs of astonishment rippled out among our small group. Florence Foster Jenkins was a soprano whose terrible singing had not deterred her popularity, but I wasn't thinking about her right now. Philippe would be here. Theories began to form in my head. He was twenty-five years old. Brown hair, medium build. I couldn't imagine why Lulu would keep company with a Chinese hater, but I would definitely be watching him.

"Please have champagne ready and attend to your duties without stopping to watch or gape, as some of you are doing now. Am I clear?"

"Yes, ma'am," we all murmured.

Mrs. Fox's green eyes, shaded with a bold cobalt blue, probed me. "Why are your hands bandaged?"

I kept my focus on a beaded choker around the woman's throat. She smelled of vanilla musk and smoke. "I had a little scrape, but I'm fine."

She snatched my wrists so quickly I gasped. The beads on her sleeves clattered as she turned over my palms. Abruptly, she released me. "You don't seem fine. The bandages are unsightly. Do you want our guests to lose their appetite for the food you will be serving them?"

I gaped. "Of course not. I—"

"You're dismissed." She slapped her hands together.

The pronouncement hit me in the chest. The other servers looked at their shoes while, beside me, Ulysses sucked in his breath.

Mrs. Souza took a deep breath. "I'm sorry, ma'am. We can't get an extra server on such short notice," she said in her soft voice that still somehow carried. "Could she maybe help in the kitchen, out of sight? Plenty of work to be done there, even if it's just stirring the sauces."

Mrs. Fox's painted mouth thinned. "I hardly know how she will do that."

"My fingers work fine," I piped up, trying to keep the pleading out of my voice. "It's mostly my palms."

Mrs. Souza smoothed her hands over her apron. "We can use all the help we can get to make your party a success."

Mrs. Fox cracked her neck from side to side. "Very well. *Out of sight*. Carry on." She gestured dismissively, and Mrs. Fez-Percy ushered us back to the kitchen.

I should have been thankful I could stay, but now how would I look out for May? I would just have to keep my wits about me. Safe snooping had gotten riskier.

44

MAY

THE HEAVY DOOR OF THE FOXES' MANSION CHALLENGED me to knock. It stood like the final mahjong tile, the one that could trigger the players' walls to fall, causing fates to come crashing down.

I could never have guessed that the twisted path of Lulu's murder investigation would lead me to the front door of Chinatown's enemy number one, wearing a gown of cream satin under a velvet cloak from Bullocks Wilshire department store. But such were the strings of fate that Ma so believed stitched lives together. Lulu and I were knotted together with a shiny red ribbon. Perhaps tonight, at last, I could help set her free.

The night played with my hair, which I had worn loose, and I clutched my new beaded purse tighter. I glanced behind me. Somewhere on the extensive driveway that ran down the hill, Cliff and Officer Kidd were watching me from a black Pontiac sedan. Go in, find the painting, then leave. It sounded easy, but things that sounded easy were never so. Especially since we had a second mission in mind—a last-ditch effort to track down Lulu's killer. One of our main suspects, Carey Stone, wouldn't be here, but I could at least ask around and find out if he owned a white Schnauzer.

My mind flitted to Wallace, whose call I hadn't yet returned. If things went south here, he would never know how I felt about him. It didn't sit well with me, but there was nothing I could do about it now.

The door suddenly opened. A gray-haired butler blinked at me, his white cravat like an Easter lily at his throat. He must have been standing there watching me all along through some hidden peephole. "Good evening, miss."

The rotunda in which he was standing suddenly grew quiet as guests swung their attention to me. Even the Bing Crosby look-alike at the piano seemed to croon a little softer.

My throat dried up. I moistened my lips, to which Gemma had insisted I apply Lulu's Noir Red. A gesture for the sister we would not leave behind. "Good evening. I'm May Chow."

A man came into view. Otis Fox's thin loop of a mustache shifted, marking his surprise. "Yes, you certainly are." He spread his hands dramatically, giving me a glimpse of the purple satin lining his tuxedo.

I pinned on a false smile, remembering my prepared words. "I hope you don't mind. Emil said I should stop by and introduce myself. He wanted you to know there are no hard feelings."

"That son of a gun." He looked behind me, probably expecting an escort. Seeing none, a smile grew on his lips. "You are most welcome. Please come in."

I hesitated, my survival instinct putting up a final protest. This man, with his goblin-like grin, had made great efforts to erase us from Los Angeles, had maybe even killed Lulu Wong. We were in his lair. If I said the wrong thing, faltered in my role, things could sour very quickly. But Gemma was already inside. She was here to back me up, the second cloud.

Behind the scenes is where the real theater lies, Cash Louie had said. Well, this would be the biggest performance of my life. The stage never felt so large.

My gold pumps bore me forward. There was power in being tall, but these three-inch heels made me feel like a tent pole. The butler's sleepy eyes widened when I resisted giving him my cloak. But keeping it would only make me stand out more, so I let him have it.

My breath caught as I took in the walls of the rotunda, covered in art. I didn't see *Jardin Oriental* anywhere. The pianist was filling the room with music as sparkling and golden as the champagne that arrived on the tray of a waiter with dark curly hair. The ceiling was painted with a heavenly panorama, like an Italian chapel. In the middle of the room, ladies in bright silks lounged on a round sofa. Both truth and beauty lay here, hidden in the details.

I didn't see Gemma, or Hettie.

"You're the talk of the town," said Otis Fox, his voice slightly hoarse, probably from all his speech giving. "The new Lulu Wong is what I've heard."

Hearing him speak her name drove pins in me, but I tamped down my feelings. "I'm afraid the town is mistaken. I haven't even made a movie."

He tsked. "Hollywood people never turn down a compliment. It's bad for business. How will people believe in you if you don't believe in yourself?"

"I can only believe in myself if I am not telling falsehoods," I said lightly.

His lips thinned to a slash, and he held up his glass to me. "To not telling falsehoods, then."

"Indeed." We drank. I'd never had champagne before, and not just because it was illegal. I didn't care for the way bubbly drinks bit at my mouth.

"Let me introduce you." He guided me to a group of guests

admiring the art on the walls. I lost the names as soon as they were given to me, except for one, a man with blond hair shot with silver and a hale manner. "Please meet Mr. Maurie Newman. He's a dirt-scooper, but we tolerate him." Here he was again, Mr. News, the owner of the *Observer First*.

"Whaddya mean, you old Fox?" he wheezed, his face shiny with the auburn glow of bourbon. "I've been saving your fundament since college." Saving his backside how? He gripped my hand with his damp one, and I had to stop myself from pulling away. He'd never been an outspoken opponent of Chinatown, but he had poisoned the water against us with his selective storytelling. Not to mention, he had bribed Mallady not to investigate Lulu's murder. "Miss Chow, the name on everyone's lips. You have some pretty big shoes to fill. Lulu was a light that went out too soon."

The conversation trailed off, and for a moment, it felt like I was surrounded by exotic fish, staring at me with their unblinking eyes. My breath sat high in my chest, and I forced it to move. "Yes, and may she always live in our memories."

"Indeed." He pressed his lips into a smile.

Otis Fox, watching us carefully, lifted Mr. News's glass from his hand and replaced it with another from a passing waiter. "May there be a silver lining to this tragedy." His grave tone did not fool me for an instant. He lifted his own glass at Mr. News. "Union Station."

My cheeks pinkened, wondering if I was missing something. Otis Fox was obsessed with tearing down Chinatown. For him, the measure wasn't about the trains. My head swam with too many thoughts.

Mr. News's wife, Edith, had been hit by a Union Pacific train, a case that was still in litigation. The railroads would have to cough up lots of money for the new station, including Union

Pacific. A clear motive cut like a fin through my reckonings. Mr. News certainly had an interest in sticking it to the railroads he blamed for his wife's death. He was in Chicago the night of Lulu's murder, but he had enough money to pay someone to do the job for him. All trace of joviality had left the newsman's face as he ground his gaze into mine. Was it the booze? Or something more menacing?

Otis Fox signaled for more champagne, a smug expression frothing his lips.

I couldn't help myself. "It won't be much of a silver lining for Chinatown." I relaxed my grip on my glass before I broke it.

"My dear, you are now above the riffraff. You no longer need to care."

People snickered, watching me for my reaction. Anger slithered through my gut, but I held my temper, reminding myself I wasn't Gemma. I had a purpose here. People were counting on me, and I would not get another swing at the ball.

"But tell us what you know of the latest scandal." Otis Fox swept his arm dramatically.

"What scandal?"

"Carey Stone. People have been seeing him around town with Emil's assistant. Carey and his Jack-a-dandy."

The partygoers blurred in front of me. Carey wasn't Lulu's boyfriend. He was Jack's. *They know. It's only a matter of time,* he'd said. The news that America's heartthrob preferred men would end his career. I was relieved Carey hadn't killed Lulu, but the sight of people making fun of him made my jaw clench. "I don't keep up on gossip."

A woman with long gloves drew a puff from her ivory cigarette holder. "He's finished. How's anyone going to stomach him as the romantic lead?"

"Actually, I stomach him just fine." Time to do what I came here to do. "Movies are like fine art." I gestured toward the paintings. "You see what you want to see."

"Well said, my dear," said Otis. "Are you an art lover?"

"Indeed," I said smoothly, even though I'd never been to a gallery. "Do you have any Oriental art?"

"Many pieces. I have an eye for it, you know. I can show you a few, if you'd like?"

"I would love that."

We all followed him to an adjoining room. Here, the party was in full swing, with guests draped around the furniture, laughing and eating. By a marble table, Mrs. Fox with her eye-catching makeup and beaded dress handed out cosmetics tied with ribbon from a basket. Perhaps Gemma was in the kitchen. At least she was doing a good job keeping out of sight.

Noticing me, Mrs. Fox made her way over. "How charming," she purred, squeezing my hand with a firm grip. If she was surprised to see me, she hid it well. "The new Lulu. But, darling, you've chewed off your lipstick. This new formulation is very moisturizing." From her basket, she handed me a peacock-blue tube of lipstick, unlidded it, and rolled up a newly shaved waxy cylinder, shaded a barely-there pink.

Closing it, she handed me the glossy tube. It felt like an expensive jewel in my hand. No wonder Yuki had been so smitten with the Fox products.

"Why, thank you," I said, marveling again at the power of fame to improve one's standing.

Otis Fox opened his hand toward a blue-and-white vase tucked into an alcove. It measured about a foot high and was painted with the "hundred flying cranes" design, showing the birds in flight. "Don't let him go on too long," she told the half dozen of us gathered around the vase, feeding her husband an indulgent smile. "We're having cake soon." As he shared the story of how he acquired the rare Ming piece, she continued doling out her gifts around the room.

By a set of dark floor-to-ceiling windows, a familiar figure had tied her arms around a young man, playfully trying to get him to kiss her. It was Hettie Bright, her ginger curls messy around her pale skin. The man gently pushed her away, and when he turned, I recognized the Foxes' son, Philippe. The budding politician had the good looks of an Italian gondolier, with a smattering of dark whiskers around his chin and circles under eyes that hinted at late-night secrets.

A server approached, the same young man with curly black hair who had served me champagne. "More?" he asked, even though my glass was still full.

"Actually, this doesn't agree with me. Would you please take it?"

"Yes, miss." He set my glass on his tray, then dropped in my ear, "Gemma says she will meet you by the garden shed in ten minutes."

I blinked in surprise but nodded. Had she found the painting? I hoped she hadn't done anything foolish.

But now Philippe and Hettie were making their way toward our group. My toes began to clench. I had told Hettie about my suspicions over Otis Fox, and certainly hoped she hadn't mentioned it. And why was Philippe glaring at me, his face twisted as if he couldn't stand the sight of me? Hettie pulled a cigarette from a packet—not Liberté—and batted him with her fingers, as if asking for a light.

"Who is this, Father?" he asked, not taking his eyes off me.

Pulling a matchbook from his pocket, he struck Hettie a tiny flame.

A forgotten detail flickered before me. Lulu had filed her nail on a green matchbook from Clifford's Steakhouse. Had *Philippe* given it to her? Was he the boyfriend? He fit the shop-girl's description with his medium build and brown hair. A sour taste coated my tongue, and I knew it was from more than the champagne. If he was Lulu's lover, Philippe could have a strong motive if he didn't want the child, especially if he had another girlfriend, like Hettie.

"This is May Chow—don't you read the papers, son? She is Emil's replacement for Lulu Wong."

"That's quite nervy of her to show up here."

Hettie blew out smoke, then pulled a bit of white fluff off Philippe's tuxedo sleeve. "Oh, stop, Philippe. May is perfectly sweet. We're all friends here, aren't we? Now shake hands."

Philippe's eyes had become resentful. Defiant. All my muscles tensed, and I forced myself not to retreat. Why was meeting me so offensive to him?

Come on, May, act. This is what you're here for. "It's nice to meet you." I extended my hand, conscious of all the eyes on me.

He didn't take it. My posture crumpled, like a pansy feeling a hot wind. They would see me as weak. Maybe even an impostor. I wasn't one of them, only a pretend one of them.

But then Lulu's voice once again whispered in my ear. *Act like you have power, and you just might get it.* I tucked my hand away and met his challenging gaze.

45
GEMMA

I STOOD BETWEEN THE GARDENING SHED AND A SHRUB, watching the guests mingling through the windows. The cold air felt good on my face, after hours of hooking peeled shrimp over bowls of ice and arranging lobster on tiny squares of toast, some of which was now digesting in my stomach. As a Buddhist, Lulu Wong must have always left these events hungry.

Come on, May. Ulysses had assured me he'd passed on my message. Break time would be over in fifteen minutes. I needed to tell her my suspicions about Philippe, and that she could use the diversion of the birthday cake and Florence Foster Jenkins to snoop if she hadn't found the painting by then.

A near-full moon threw its reflection over a long swimming pool, which rippled under a breeze. The faint sounds of "I Wanna Be Loved by You" floated from the house, and with them came thoughts of Freddie. Curse my traitorous heart. He'd been an unexpected knight, but I hoped he'd ride on soon. Sometimes the red string of fate got snagged. You had to just keep on moving and time would work it out.

As if called by my thoughts, a figure, as lean as a knife in his tuxedo, approached the window. Freddie? My jaw sagged and my heart banged, somehow relocating to somewhere between my ears. What was he doing here?

Personal physicians to Hollywood stars are always invited. When the champagne starts flying, someone's bound to fall off a roof.

He stopped, and his gaze seemed to affix itself to me in my servant's garb, a shrub poking my behind. But of course, he couldn't see into the dark. I fought the urge to make myself known to him, say something cuttingly witty. *Why, Doctor, you can hear the blood whooshing in my veins if you listen varicosely.*

The sight of Mrs. Fox appearing at the window beside him chilled my thoughts. Freddie's presence at the Pannychis was one thing, with several hundred in attendance. But this was a private party. The Foxes would've had to invite him personally.

Before I could work it out, the sound of footsteps drifted from the other side of the pool. All my senses perked. A dark figure made his way down the length of the pool, continuing deeper into the property. Glancing behind him, he let out a two-note whistle. A bark answered, and then a dog came running up. A white dog.

A Schnauzer?

The shrub was trying to eject me, but I pushed back, wanting to wait for May. But maybe she couldn't get away. And if I had just seen a rare white Schnauzer, then the boyfriend who had given Lulu the crane earrings had to be Philippe.

I shook my head, still resisting the idea that Lulu would have anything to do with Chinese haters. Still, I had to find out. Ignoring my gut, which urged me to stay in the bushes, I emerged from my hiding place and crept along the pavement, heel-to-toe so my oxfords wouldn't make a sound.

With the moon lighting the way, I passed a copse of trees until another gray stone structure rose before me, several times smaller than the main house. I remembered from Cliff's diagram that a guesthouse lay at the back of the property, though he had discounted it as unlikely to contain the painting.

The door was wide open. I hovered by the entrance, not breathing as I listened for sounds coming from inside. But there didn't seem to be anyone at home, with only dim sconces lighting a foyer.

"I thought ye just went," came a male voice with a Scottish accent from somewhere behind me. It was the voice of my attacker. My bones threatened to come loose. A dog whined. "It's that cream puff ye ate, ye dumb crane. I told ye not to, but ye didn't listen."

Crane? Perhaps the dog's name was Crane.

I looked wildly around me for an escape, but there was none. My feet quickly hustled me into the house, even though I knew I would regret it.

The place looked more like a business than a guesthouse. On the left lay a meeting room with a table and chairs, and on the right, a laboratory of some sort with colorful bottles lining built-in shelves and a central walnut desk backed by gold velvet curtains. Ahead lay a dark room that I wasn't keen on exploring. I ducked into the laboratory-office, where I could at least hide under the desk or behind the drapes. The drapes might better mask my smell. Maybe I could even open the window behind them and escape. I just hoped a sick dog had more important things on its mind than sniffing me out.

Spreading open the curtains, my heart sank when I realized there was no window behind them, only a wall hung with a single painting inside a gold frame. *Jardin Oriental.* I nearly let out a hysterical laugh. We had found what we came for, but at what price?

I straightened the fabric to cover me just as the Scot's footsteps broke over the threshold. The scrabbling of claws followed. "Let's fetch ye some real food." The front door closed with a whump.

Footsteps moved deeper into the house, but not paws. My heart pumped as fast as someone bailing water from a sinking boat. My breath fogged my face as I inhaled fumes of stale cigarettes and vanilla musk, and my silk hair scarf felt sticky with sweat. It was curtains for me, like they said in the gangster movies. Except that these curtains were really going to kill me. With little airflow and me gusting like a bellows, I would suffocate. I'd escaped one pair of curtains already this week, and I doubted my luck would hold. Desperate for air, I pulled one panel back a fraction.

Crane was still in the foyer.

Watching me.

46
MAY

PHILIPPE FOX'S EYES SANK INTO MINE AS HEAVY AS anchors. Hettie released the fluff she had picked off Philippe's jacket, and it floated away. Lint? Or fur?

I nodded toward the Ming vase. "Do you like cranes?" I asked Philippe. "In our culture, the birds represent long-lasting love and fidelity."

"Isn't that funny?" Hettie grabbed a shrimp off a server's tray and popped it in her mouth. "Philippe has a dog named Crane."

All my blood rushed to my head. So Philippe *was* the boyfriend. Lulu had been dating the son of the man who was Chinatown's enemy number one. No wonder she had kept it quiet.

His gaze narrowed, glinting like iron. "Miss Chow, I wonder if I might give you a private tour of the library."

My heels wobbled. Surely he wouldn't pull the trigger, so to speak, here in the presence of all these people, all of whom would be witnesses to this tense confrontation. I tried to keep the tremor from my voice. "I would love that."

Gemma would have to wait. As Philippe led the way toward the west wing, I tried not to think about how I was taking one of those unnecessary risks I had warned Gemma against. But here was my chance to finally understand how things had gone so wrong for Lulu. To help her in death, when I had been neglectful in life. I couldn't, *wouldn't* miss my chance.

Watching us go, Hettie's smile fell off her face and she sucked at her cigarette. We passed Mr. News, sniffing a cigar that another guest was holding under his nose. Was he a smoker? Probably, given the blissful look on his face. But what brand of cigarettes did he favor?

Instead of the library, Philippe showed me into a study taken up by a leather sofa and a pedestal desk. An ornately carved ceiling put me in mind of a coffin. He locked the door behind him, the snick sounding like the cocking of a gun. He wheeled on me. "You certainly have nerve, showing up here."

My heart jumped, and I forced myself to breathe. "Lulu was a friend. We just want to find out who's responsible for her death. And with the way you're behaving, I wouldn't be surprised if it was you."

He snorted. A lock of his brown-black hair fell into his face, and he blew it back with an abrupt whuff. "She told me about you. How you were an even better actress than her. How you should've been the one who made it."

The sofa bumped me from behind. Lulu had thought I was better than her? Yet she'd tried to pull me up after her. *Girls from Chinatown have to help each other out.* I pushed aside the sadness gathering in me. This was not the time for regret, especially with Philippe's eyes burning like two coals on my face.

"I think you killed her," he spat. "You even 'found' her body."

I straightened my back. "You're paddling a canoe to the top of the mountain when you could just walk. Why would we risk our lives looking for a killer the police have no interest in finding? Maybe *you* were so ashamed of your feelings for her, you killed her. You were behind the attack on my sister. She was following you right before the Scotsman grabbed her. You sicced him on her. I could have you arrested."

Even I could hear the empty tin-can rattle of my words. How exactly would I do that? Ask to use his telephone? But he looked abashed. It was the look of someone who'd had his heart seams ripped beyond repair. "You knew about Lulu and me. How?"

"I didn't have to beat the information out of anyone, if that's what you're asking."

"I'm sorry that your sister was injured." His eyes lost their glare. "Lulu is the one who wanted to keep us secret. She didn't want it to affect my political career. I would've given it all up for her." He pulled at the back of his neck with both hands, the part that our herbalist said hurt most when sleep was lost.

"Lulu would never support a politician who wanted to tear down our community," I said archly.

He crossed to the desk, upon which rested a model train paperweight. He hefted it, and I shrank back, as if he might attempt to throw it at me. "Three Coins," he said, staring at the weight. Three Coins? Was he talking about the proposal for a new Chinese neighborhood? To my relief, he set down the train. "Lulu knew the forces were stacked against Chinatown."

"Thanks to people like your father."

To my surprise, he nodded. "The only way Three Coins will succeed is if I'm elected to city council."

"You would stand against your father?"

"*Fox for Progress.* I hoped for a better future for us. Lulu and me."

I went still. Ba had mentioned a rumor that help for China-town might be coming from an unexpected source. Was that source Philippe Fox? *Sometimes moonlight makes friends with a darkened path.*

"So if neither of us did it, who did?" Philippe asked.

"Hettie Bright's teacup certainly received a heaping spoonful of sugar."

"She could've gone to Summit Studios anytime she wanted."

I steadied myself against the sofa, my sweaty palms slipping on the leather. "And lose her reputation as America's sweetheart? Now people consider her move the act of a grieving friend who lost a sister."

He stiffened like wet starch under a hot iron. "I've never known her to be greedy."

"Maybe it's not greed. She certainly isn't shy about her affections over you." He grimaced, and I knew I'd hit a nerve. "How did you meet Lulu?" I pressed.

"I met her here, during the *Fast Fortune* party. She was hiding in the garden, but Crane sniffed her out. Lulu didn't care for parties."

I'd never seen Otis Fox so charming, showing her his art collection, Hettie Bright had said.

"Of course, then she went to the hospital, and I thought I'd lost her before I'd even gotten to know her."

"Why did she go to the hospital?"

His lips pursed, as if this was a secret he shouldn't tell. He glanced toward the door. "Things got a little out of hand. Hettie had a little too much of the powder, you see."

"Cocaine?"

He nodded. "Hettie got the idea that Lulu might look good as a redhead, so she dabbed a bit of the hair dye samples my mother was giving out on Lulu's hair when she wasn't looking, as a joke. Lulu started breaking out in a rash. She would've died if we hadn't gotten her to the hospital in time."

I ran a dry tongue over my equally dry lips. Wong Tai's voice slipped into my head. *Too red, like Hettie's hair. Even the doctor warned her about it.* It wasn't the Cadillac the doctor had warned Lulu about. It was the red in Hettie's hair dye. Red dye from the cactus bug was harmless, unless you were allergic.

Anyone at that party would've known Lulu was allergic to red dye. But we didn't see a rash on her body when we found her. My shoulders had started curling forward, as if I'd been handed a sack of laundry too heavy to carry. How would I sort it all out in time? "Who else knew about the baby?"

"Baby?" His focus sharpened.

"You didn't know."

His face clouded, and he seemed to draw inward, his dark lashes knitting together, mouth tight. Then his expression collapsed, and his head became a grave pendulum, swinging with disbelief. "No. No, I've been away in Sacramento . . . She was dead when I got back." His voice cracked. Slumping against the desk, he hid his face in his hands and drew in a shaky breath.

I couldn't help feeling sorry for him. Ba said secrets were like little fires you carry in your pocket, and this newest blaze had caught him right in the breast.

Someone knocked on the door. "Mr. Fox, are you in there?" said a man.

"Yes, what is it?"

"They're expecting you in the rotunda, sir."

"I'll be there shortly." Philippe rolled out his shoulders. Before opening the door, he said, "Give me a few minutes' lead, if you want to avoid an entrance."

I nodded and he left. I caught sight of my reflection in a wall mirror. My hair hung in limp strands, and I had chewed my lips dry. The powder I had applied earlier looked streaky. Digging around in my beaded purse, I did my best to reform my appearance, then returned to the party.

Back in the rotunda, people had gathered around a three-tiered cake dusted with gold, presided over by the Foxes. Hettie, seated on the round sofa with peacock-blue cosmetic samples strewn around her, watched Philippe embracing his parents, his politician's face firmly in place.

The piano played an introduction, and then a lady in a burned velvet dress began to sing "Happy Birthday." Guests joined in, though not Hettie, whose eyes looked extra large as she dabbed on lipstick in a mirror held by her neighbor. The color was a shade too dark for her skin, looking like a slash of blood. With a scowl, she wiped her mouth on a napkin.

A cheer went up, but I hardly heard it as my mind wheeled back to the abandoned stables. There'd been a bloodstain on the crisp sleeve of Lulu's pantsuit. But maybe it hadn't been blood at all. Maybe she had tried to wipe something off, like her lipstick. But why ruin a perfectly good outfit? Why not use a napkin, or the back of her hand, at least?

The room became a colorful blur in front of me. Lulu's Noir Red had been specially made vegetarian for her. But what if she hadn't been wearing Noir Red? When we found her, Lulu's lips had been pursed, one could even say puffy.

My gaze traveled to an oil painting of the Fox family, showing Mr. and Mrs. Fox on either side of their then-teenaged son. Otis Fox's dark eyes seemed to mock me. Despite being shorter than his wife by several inches, the painter had depicted the man as equal in height to Mrs. Fox, with her almost-shocking white-blond hair and tiger-green eyes. No one was smiling in the painting, though there was a fondness to the way Mrs. Fox held her arm around her son's shoulders.

The memory of a recent conversation echoed in my head.

Uncle, what did the driver look like? Gemma had asked Gee Fa.

A white demon.

I glanced to where, moments ago, I had seen Mrs. Fox, the first lady of a cosmetics empire, warmly embrace her son.

She was missing.

I needed to speak to Gemma, who must be wondering why I hadn't met her at the gardening shed twenty minutes ago.

Past the guests crowding the rotunda, I returned to the lodge, my movements jerky, my thoughts spinning. The waiter who had passed me Gemma's message was clearing a table. "Would you mind passing Gemma a message?"

"Sorry, she's not back yet. Mrs. Fez-Percy is spitting nails."

She must have still been waiting for me. A sliver of fear dug into my chest. I hurried through the kitchen, hardly noticed by the busy staff, who were probably feeling the pinch of being one caterer short.

Just off the pavers that led to the swimming pool stood a stone shed whose wooden doors only reached halfway up. "Gemma?" I hissed just in case she was hiding.

Only the leaves answered, a rattling symphony moved by an invisible conductor.

But then a dog barked.

47
GEMMA

CRANE FIXED HIS SIGHTS ON ME, HIS EYEBROWS RAISED and his bristly beard quivering with curiosity. I put my finger to my lips, as if he could understand me. His ears screwed tightly forward. Was I friend or foe? I didn't move a muscle, save for my eyes, as I cast about for an escape.

Before me on the ornately carved walnut desk stood a framed photograph of a boy with dark curls. It must be Philippe Fox, and this must be his father's office, with its heavy desk and clinical feel. Silver trays lined counters on either side of the room and held all manner of instruments—pipettes, jars of cotton gauze, tweezers. I'd never thought of Otis Fox as a scientist, but creating cosmetics would of course require lab work.

My eyes caught on a blue pack of cigarettes on the desk. I'd never seen a pack that color before. In the dim lighting, I made out the word *Liberté*.

Crane's head pivoted toward the entrance. The front door opened. Quickly, I closed the curtain, my heart in my throat. All my risky behavior was finally catching up with me. The Scot was dangerous, and now I'd given him the chance to finish me off once and for all. *Foolish girl!*

The Scot's heavy steps approached from the kitchen. "Ma'am. I was just getting Crane some real food."

Ma'am?

"Sean, we no longer require your services," said a woman's voice. It was the kind of voice that could call the cows home. A voice from the Midwest. "You're dismissed."

"Wot?"

In the stunned moments that followed, my own mind grasped for understanding. What was *Mrs. Fox* doing here?

"H-have I done something?" the Scot, or Sean, continued. "I've been with yer family for years. Don't that deserve an explanation?"

"Let's just say, your loyalty is to me, not my *son*. I know you've been keeping his secrets. Now go before I call the police."

After a long pause, Sean's long strides clopped back over the threshold, the door closing behind him.

Mrs. Fox crossed to the desk. A drawer slid open, and something solid was dragged out, sending a thrill up my spine. My knees quaked. I stifled the urge to scream.

"You can show yourself," said Mrs. Fox. "I can see the curtains moving."

Why had I come out here by myself?

"I didn't want it to come to this, but you left me no choice. You and your sister, meddling."

I couldn't outrun a gun, which I knew she was holding, even before I heard the click of the hammer. But I wouldn't go down without a fight. May would know I was missing. She'd find me. I just had to draw this out to give her time. Slowly, I pulled back the curtain.

Mrs. Fox mockingly appraised me from the other side of the desk. The sight of the demented grin on her recently touched-up face made me nearly lose my water. She held the gun loosely, almost cradled it. The woman had grown up homesteading, where firearms were a part of life.

Steady, girl. Don't let the panic deaden your brain. "How did you do it?" I asked, trying to keep my voice from quavering. Didn't criminals always want to confess their crimes?

"I thought you were the brighter sister." Her shoulders lifted and then dropped. "I would explain, but I have a birthday party to get back to." The gun lifted its nose at me.

"Actually, I figured it out." My words tumbled over each other. I hadn't figured out anything, except that I was going to die if I didn't speak. "Your son was dating Lulu. You knew he had gotten her pregnant."

She didn't react, her face as cool as a block of ice.

"A relationship with a Chinese girl, to say nothing about a baby, would destroy your husband's reputation. Everything he stood for would drain away, and his vast empire would crumble. So you went to her house, killed her, then used her own car to drive her to the stables."

She snorted out a laugh, a jolting noise like the slam of a broken shutter. "*His* vast empire? I made the formulations. Stardust Powder, cold cream, eye shadows. It was all *me*." Her mouth, painted a deep purple-red, pushed out the last word as if expelling a seed. It was human nature to want to correct each other. "Lipstick was my specialty, my top seller. Even Lulu couldn't resist it."

My mind stalled. What was she talking about? "She only wore Noir Red."

"Except when she died. Lulu was wearing a red I call Beta." A measure of pride crept into her voice.

I knew from school that beta was the second letter of the Greek alphabet. It seemed a strange name for a lipstick. "She would never wear your lipstick," I tossed out, baiting her.

"I paid her a visit when I knew my son was out of town, when I knew she'd be alone. I told her I approved of the relationship, and I even told her I supported the building of a new Chinatown—Three Coins, was it called? To show my goodwill, I gave her a tube of my new 'vegetarian' lipstick, Beta." She began to tug at her short hair, pulling the ends into jagged tips, giving her the look of a mad scientist. "I suggested she try it on. Naturally, she wanted to please me, her new ally, so she eagerly complied."

"You poisoned Beta."

"That's the beauty of it. I didn't *need* to poison it. I just gave her my regular formulation. Lulu was deathly allergic to the cochineal insects used in red dye."

I swallowed hard. Lulu wore only Noir Red because the formulation had been made vegetarian for her. In trusting Mrs. Fox, she had unwittingly died by her own hand. *Push it aside, keep talking.* "How did you know she was pregnant?"

"After the good doctor told me about her nausea, I knew. You don't grow up on a farm without knowing when a gilt's going to farrow. Anyway, relationships run their course, and Philippe would have tired of Lulu soon enough, but a *baby*." She grimaced. "No yellow baby would stake a claim in my fortune. Can you blame me?" Her words were coming faster, and her free arm lashed about. She was getting worked up. "When she started going into shock, she hit her head. Oops."

On the drawer. With the red dye poisoning her, Lulu had fallen, succumbing to cardiac arrest. Mrs. Fox had waited until dark, then dropped her off at the abandoned horse stables. Peony's classmate thought she'd seen a man in the Mercantile lot. But she had actually seen Mrs. Fox, a tall woman with a grudge against Cash Louie, leave the car where it could do some damage.

My breath sat high in my chest, and I could no longer feel my feet. "People will find out. You won't get away with this."

"I have before. I called that lipstick Alpha. That one used strychnine."

Strychnine. "You killed Dixie Doors."

She shrugged and her beads clattered. "Mixing mica into cosmetics was a clever idea. Her Shimmer Cream had promise. But I knew someone like her would demand more than her share."

"You're a monster," I gasped.

My horror caused the woman's lips to stretch thinner, and her face became gleeful, her nostrils flaring as if smelling blood. "Non, une chimiste."

It seemed fitting she'd use the French word for "chemist" to describe herself, a woman whose life's work was to powder and shadow the truth, especially when the truth was too horrible for words.

Don't dwell. Just get out of here.

I could fake right, then go left, like Peony did in basketball. But even if the first shot missed, the second one wouldn't. And we were far enough from the main house that no one would hear the gun. "So . . . Lulu had a doctor."

"Yes, a handsome one." Mrs. Fox's eyes turned mirthful. "But of course, you already knew that."

"No." Something cold pooled in my gut. My face stung as a photograph of Freddie shaking Mr. News's hand appeared in my mind. *He put me in touch with the right people to get my practice started.* My lungs began to accordion shut, all the air squeezing out. A pretty face, a clever tongue. Was that all it had taken to undo Gemma Chow? I was such a fool.

"Who do you think footed the bill for his gorgeous office? All that experimental therapy he tries?"

Perhaps the "sugar" Mr. News had offered was more like quicksand, hard to escape.

Twenty-one down. It takes time to sink in. QUICKSAND.

"I knew having a doctor in my pocket would come in handy one day," she crowed. "Doctors aren't paid near what they should be for all the ugliness they see. Still don't believe me?"

Numb, I shook my head. He'd taken an oath to do no harm.

She mock sighed. "Love makes fools of us all."

"Did Freddie know you killed Lulu?"

"He knew he'd breached patient confidentiality by telling me patient secrets. But you were his downfall. You rubbed his nose in the mess. He showed up tonight asking all sorts of questions."

Don't believe her, my gut ordered. For all I knew, this woman was baiting me. The gun flicked, like an adder.

"I wish I had a parting gift for you, but I gave my last tube of Alpha to your sister. Her lips were criminally dry, and sure, Alpha's poisonous, but it's also filled with emollients. The best part is, besides a touch of sheen, it's invisible."

"No," I croaked, my insides catching fire. Is that why May hadn't met me? Was she dying this instant? My legs nearly gave way.

"It will take a good fifteen to thirty minutes for the seizures to start, but once it touches the lips, there's no way to stop it. I have really invented the perfect crime."

Despite my trembling, the euphoric trill of the madwoman's speech filled me with rage. I took a tentative step toward the side of the desk, but her gun nosed my direction. She aimed her sturdy arms. Arms sturdy enough to carry Lulu into an abandoned horse stall.

"It wasn't that perfect," I said. "You forgot about the earrings."

The earrings had told us that Lulu's death wasn't a simple robbery gone wrong. Earrings in the shape of cranes . . . Like the dog's name. *Crane.*

Two-note, parrot, train, come-hither, whistling was my specialty. I tightened my lips and blew, just like I'd heard the Scot do. But I must not be the master of whistling I'd thought, because instead of coming hither, the dog only lowered himself onto the floor. Mrs. Fox glanced back at the Schnauzer, now burying his head under his paws, and laughed at my weak attempt at distraction.

Feeling myself wobble, I clutched at the curtain behind me. Something clattered. *Jardin Oriental.*

"Now, move away from the painting." She waved her gun. "No sense ruining good art."

My insides were melting into a puddle of fear, but one defiant thought remained. If this was the end, I wouldn't hold still for her to shoot me, like some frightened animal. Acting mostly on instinct, I whipped opened the curtain, exposing the painting. With no time to waste, I grabbed it off the wall and held it before me like a shield.

"This is one of a kind," I tossed out, peeking around the picture, which was big enough to cover my vital parts. My nails dug into the wood frame. The painting felt too flimsy and light in my hands to actually do any good as armor, but I clung to the ridiculous hope that if I wasn't framed for a break-in, this frame could help me make a break for it.

"Don't be silly. Put the painting down."

I inched around the desk, gambling.

"Actually, I don't give a fig for that ugly picture." She leveled the gun.

I threw *Jardin Oriental* at her. She dodged, and *pop!* went the gun. The sound of breaking glass crashed behind me, and the framed canvas bounced harmlessly off her. Another *pop!* exploded in my ear as I barreled into her, spilling her backward.

Something metallic scratched across the tiles. The gun? I felt myself falling.

I sank onto the tiles, the sound of the gunshot ringing in my ears. Had I been hit? A hot ache in my side pulled all my awareness to it, an intense searing pain that made me cry out.

I didn't want to die alone. I didn't want to die at all, but we didn't get to choose things like that. Forcing my mind away from the pain, my eyes took in the broken glass around me; my nose caught the whiff of chemical smells that made me wince. All was chaos and pain.

I closed my eyes and asked for my family.

An image of Ba answered, his ready smile the best part of his brown face. There beside him were Ma, Peony, and May. I sent up a brief prayer for her deliverance tonight. *If you make it through tonight, dear sister, you'll have to make them understand. It was for us. Our family, Lulu, Chinatown, the baby. All of us.*

I was vaguely aware of three men stumbling into the scene. Philippe Fox seemed to be yelling at his mother, who was cowering on the floor. His man, Sean, had leashed Crane and was dragging him away. And another man was bent over me.

"Gemma," Freddie pleaded, his tears splashing on my face. "I'm sorry. I'm sorry." His cool but trembling fingers probed my side, and the pain erased the picture in my head.

I moaned, not wanting him to touch my injury, though I could feel the warmth of my blood spreading down my side.

I could barely look at him, his sensitive scholar's mouth twisted in anguish, his bow tie pulled loose. He'd had a hand in Lulu's death, whether he knew it or not. The irony that he was now trying to save me made a laugh bubble up, though it came out as a gurgle. Removing my apron, he bundled it into a square and pressed it to my side. "Hold this here," he instructed, placing my hand over the cloth. He removed his tuxedo jacket and pillowed my head.

"Never mind me." At least my voice still worked. "You need to find May," I urged, watching his face grow more alarmed. But nothing was more important than this. "Make sure she doesn't put on the lipstick."

48
MAY

AFTER HEARING GUNSHOTS, I'D KICKED OFF MY HEELS, dropped my purse, and run to the guesthouse, heedless of the stones cutting my soles. Halfway there, I was met by a surprising figure. It was Dr. Winter, bare of jacket and with his white shirt soaked in blood. I shrieked, clutching at my heart. Was he the murderer?

"The lipstick," he panted, grasping at his head. "Did you put it on? She poisoned it."

"Lipstick?" Were these the unhinged ramblings of a madman? The peacock-blue tube Mrs. Fox had given me inserted itself in my head. *This new formulation is very moisturizing.* I touched my lips, on which I'd recently applied . . . Peony's plain old beeswax. "No." Relief and a little bit of hysteria made me fidget, sweat dribbling down my face despite the chill air. "Where's Gemma?"

"In the guesthouse. I need to call for an ambulance." He hurried away, leaving me to imagine the worst. Was that Gemma's blood? Was the killer, who surely must be Mrs. Fox, at large? It didn't matter. I had to find my sister.

"Gemma?" I stumbled into the guesthouse, my stomach rising in my throat. A dog barked from somewhere, sounding strangely far away in my head.

In a room to the right of a foyer, Mrs. Fox was on her knees, pleading with Philippe, whose face was twisted in fury. The woman's lipstick had smeared, making her look almost clownish, and she was missing a shoe. "Philippe, she was an intruder. She was trying to steal from us."

"No, she wasn't," he croaked.

Beyond her, Gemma lay crumpled by a walnut desk. Blood had spattered the ground by her side. A gun lay like a dead pigeon on the tiles halfway between Mrs. Fox and me. I let out a strangled cry, putting the scene together, my pulse hammering in my ears. Gemma had been shot.

Both Philippe and Mrs. Fox turned toward me. Mrs. Fox's eyes were resentful, as if I'd interrupted a private meeting. Her eyes strayed to the gun. I'd never held a gun, let alone fired one, but even if I had to join Gee Fa in prison, she would pay for this.

Mrs. Fox lunged for the gun. She was closer, but I was standing. I kicked it from her grasp. It skidded along the floor, hissing like an asp, but Philippe reached a foot out and stopped it. He collected it, a half-mad expression contorting his features. My heart seized. When all was said and done, did he have the backbone to condemn his own mother, or would he turn the gun on me?

He opened the chamber. One by one, the bullets clattered onto the tile like metal tears.

I ran to my sister. "Gemma," I called, trying to keep the horror from my voice. The front of her catering jacket was soaked with blood, and she was holding a bundled apron to her side.

"Lipstick?" she gasped, her horrified eyes fixed on my mouth.

"No. I didn't put it on," I assured her. My eyes had begun leaking.

Her face, which had been screwed up tight, relaxed. A relieved breath rushed out of her mouth. "That's good, sister. Oh, that is good." She braved a little smile.

"Philippe," Mrs. Fox pleaded. "Philippe, you have to listen to me."

"No more lies, Mother. You've done enough."

Gemma's eyelids were fluttering closed. I was too late. "Gemma, stay with me," I begged, drowning in dread. I lifted her hand from the apron, replacing it with my own. Two more men entered the scene: Clifford Joust and Officer Kidd.

Mrs. Fox glanced around at all of us staring at her, then at Gemma, limp before me. The woman sat back heavily. With Philippe now wielding the gun, she grabbed her missing pump from where it had slid near a credenza, holding it as if it were a handle with which she kept her grip on the world. Her defiant face gleamed with sweat. "I had no choice. That girl was going to ruin your life."

She meant Lulu, but Gemma was all I could think about now. Had I just sacrificed a sister to get justice for another? If so, the cost had been too great.

"Don't leave us, Gemma," I moaned. "Many great things still await. Don't you want to meet the new baby?" My tears splashed over her pale face.

"This is it, sister," she labored. "But we did it, didn't we?"

"Yes, we did." My jaw shook with the effort it took to not bawl.

"This would be . . . a good time . . . to tell me . . ."

"Yes, sister, anything." I leaned closer, not wanting to miss a single syllable.

"How much you admire me."

"Admire you?" I held her close, as if trying to push all my life force into her dying body. She was my better half; life without her would be half a life. "You are my hero. You're the bravest, smartest, cleverest—" I choked, unable to go on.

One of Gemma's mischievous eyes popped open. "Keep going."

I drew back, and her shoulders began quaking. She was laughing. "You're faking!"

A smile split her face. "Freddie said the bullet only grazed me. But don't squeeze me so tight. It hurts."

I wanted to shake her, but instead, number one cloud kissed number two cloud's very hard but big-thinking head.

49
MAY

THE DAY LULU WONG WAS LAID TO REST SHOWED UP LIKE
any other, without pretense and full of promise. Just like Lulu.
She never considered herself a star, but somehow, like the sun
warming the earth, she'd created a kind of magic in the world
because it was what she was meant to do.

I watched the interment at Rosedale Cemetery from a distance.
The ceremony was private, and I was glad to see Wong Tai in
attendance, clutching Bettina to her side. But after the cars left,
when the shadows were growing longer, I made my way across the
trim expanse of green, the lawn quieting my footfalls. Headstones,
mausoleums, and even a few pyramids studded the grounds.

The fresh scent of the chrysanthemum garland that Peony
had made, tied gayly with ribbons, reminded me of the hope
always being born into the world. Ma had been plenty angry at
our foolish "monkey brains" behavior. But later, to calm all our
nerves, Peony had served some of Dai-Sang's soothing tea without spilling a drop. Watching Gemma sleep, Ma had clucked
her tongue at the triumphant grin curving number two cloud's
mouth, even at rest. Gemma really *was* the bravest—and, yes,
cleverest—of sisters. Maybe Ma knew we were growing up.
That mistakes might be made, but progress was something you
viewed from the sky, not the ground.

Besides a few mourning doves pecking the ground, Lulu's grave site was empty of visitors.

LULU WONG
March 14, 1911—October 2, 1932
Not a star, but a meteor.

Kneeling down, I arranged the garland around Lulu's headstone like a stole around the shoulders of a fine lady. A lump in my throat formed as I thought about her nearness. *I am here with you, my friend, and I will carry a piece of you in my heart forever.*

I bowed my head and closed my eyes, returning to that day on Roosevelt Highway. I remembered how the ocean had danced before us, her profile as resolute as carved jade.

See, sometimes you can't just open the front door to air the house. Sometimes you have to come from the side, through a window. Sure, it's work to lift it, even a crack. But once you get your fingers under it, the lifting gets easier. And when the sweet breeze fills the spaces, change will follow.

Thank you, dear sister, for cracking that window.

WHEN I RETURNED TO THE MULE, A SLIM FIGURE IN A GRAY SUIT was leaning against the doorframe, his hands in his pockets. Wallace. Hearing me approach, he got to his feet and slid back his fedora.

"Gee Fa's lawyer told us what happened," he said hoarsely, reaching for me. "They released Gee Fa this morning. Are you okay?"

"Yes, I'm okay," I answered weakly, but only because the sight of him waiting for me made my insides begin to spin.

He pulled me into his arms, his breath releasing as he drew

me closer. "May, my true feeling is, I felt sick when I heard what you did last night. I should've been there. I should've helped you—"

"You didn't know what we were going to do." Wallace's shoulders felt solid, like a sturdy ladder.

He frowned, his dark eyelashes hooking together. "No, but I should've been honest with how I felt about you sooner, and maybe you would've been honest with me."

Palm trees shivered in the breeze. The roar of the ocean sounded near. I inhaled deeply, catching the scent of cut grass and something musky. "Well, I'm being honest with you now. And my true feeling is . . ."

He went still, his gaze foundering upon mine.

"I like hearing about honeybees," I finished.

His face broke into a smile, but he made his voice serious. "Did you know a male honeybee dies after mating with his queen? His abdomen gets ripped out . . . Well, what I'm saying is, I would let you rip out my abdomen, if you wanted to."

I could not resist fitting my lips against his goofy grin.

His kiss was tender, promising something more, his nose nuzzling mine. Releasing me, he cradled an arm around my shoulders. A mourning dove cooed. Together, we gazed out toward Lulu's grave site, a place filled with rest and light.

Epilogue
GEMMA

TWO WEEKS LATER

ONE BY ONE, MAY, PEONY, AND I REMOVED OUR CHEER buckets from each threshold that had been a part of our world—the herbalist, the cobbler, the tofu seller, and so many more. It was said that the Garnier Building on the Old Mexico side of Alameda would be spared.

"They can kick us out, but they can't have our cheer buckets," I announced, ignoring the dull ache in my side where Mrs. Fox's bullet had grazed me.

"One more." May steered us toward One Dragon. Peony led the way, her arms strapped around a stack of our red pails. I held our family brick, which the bricklayers had cut from the Esteemed Friend planter for us.

The Yams had already cleared out, taking their statue. We'd see them again. The election was next week, and though the Fox name had taken a beating, Philippe Fox was still in the running. The Three Coins proposal might yet be viable. And even if Chinatown was no longer a place, it would always be a community.

At the end of Apablasa Street, the stables had been demolished, and a pile of rubble waited to be hauled away. A figure with the shape of a jug made his way from the lot, his guitar case swinging and a cupped hand extended in front of him.

"Gee Fa!" cried Peony. "What do you have there?"

"A ladybug." He showed us the tiny beetle on his palm. He'd acquired two black eyes during his week in prison, which had faded to yellow splotches. "The best things have wings, and no cage will hold them." He grinned, showing us a mouthful of crooked teeth.

The insect took off, and Gee Fa ambled after it. Not everything that flew had wings.

May set down her buckets, and we waited for her to unhook the last red pail, which Ba had nailed into the wall beside One Dragon's entrance.

The real sinners were in their cages now. Mrs. Fox had been charged with the murders of Dixie Doors and Lulu Wong. With the mountain of evidence against her, not to mention the testimony of one very disgruntled Scotsman who had served the family for years, she couldn't bribe her way out this time. The prosecutor didn't even need the cigarettes I'd collected from the Mercantile lot.

Mrs. Fox was the keystone whose collapse caused the other bricks to fall, including Otis Fox, the driver of the getaway car, who was more a figurehead than a mastermind, with a weakness for Oriental art. Mr. News couldn't save his old chum's fundament this time, not with Mallady charging *him* with bribing a public official. Mallady's hands weren't exactly clean, but at least the crane earrings he had planted on Gee Fa had been returned to the Wong family.

Of course, we weren't naïve enough to think that new foxes wouldn't replace the ones being evicted, but this was the City of Angels. Maybe one was watching over us.

Another face popped into my head, uninvited, as always. Freddie had been disgraced, and his office closed, but at least he'd tried to do the right thing in the end. I touched the wound on my side, remembering his competent fingers. I didn't wish him ill. Everyone was a little good and a little bad. Who could say how the final scales would hang in the end?

For now, I had great plans.

"Why do you look like that?" May asked, cutting her eyes to me.

"Like what? As delightful as dandelion? As clever as clover?"

May coughed. "As crafty as crocus, more like." She worked at the bent nail that trapped the bucket in place.

"I know where I'm going to plant this brick." I held it out, letting the sun warm it.

"Where?" Peony demanded. "Toy Tai won't let you plant it in her garden."

"No, not there. I'm thinking Pa-sa-de-na." I mimicked Ma's overpronunciation of the word. May's face tightened like a corset. Stepping up to her, I placed a sloppy kiss on her cheeky-chit cheek. May was good for me in the way baking soda was good for gas bubbles, and wherever she went, there I would be. "The trouble with you is that you lack vision," I continued. "Your petit ami lives there." Bug Boy had certainly been useful lately, helping us move to Toy Tai's and distracting May to keep her from suffocating me with her mothering. "The houses have big yards. We could set up a canopy and two rocking chairs, one for Ba to take in the dry, warm heat, and one for Ma and Bin Wun."

Another cloud had joined the crew earlier this week, to whom we had given the American name Bliss. Judging by her cry, she would be the fiercest one of all.

May's face became thoughtful. "Ba would like that." The pneumoperitoneum seemed to be working. Ba had started to gain weight, and his coughing had improved. "But could we afford it?" she added doubtfully.

"Sure. You're bankable." After the news of her role in *A Far East Affair* broke, the movie offers hadn't stopped pouring in. I poked May in the ribs, and she broke character, a feather of a smile floating up on her face.

"I like Pasadena," Peony grunted, taking a turn with the Yams' bucket. It was one of the older ones, rusty on the inside, with a few stubborn flowers still clinging to the bottom.

"Wait," I told her. "That one's not just a cheer bucket. It's a here bucket. It's saying, *I'm here, and I'm not going to leave.* I say we let it be."

May rolled her eyes and Peony giggled. But both picked up their cheer buckets, and together, we walked shoulder to shoulder down a street that knew our footsteps. The winds of change had carved a new path for us, and that new path was up. I gazed into a sky full of fire. Separately, each cloud can block the wind. Together, we might determine its flow.

AUTHOR'S NOTE

THE CHARACTER LULU WONG IS LOOSELY INSPIRED BY ANNA MAY Wong (1905–1961), considered the first Chinese American Hollywood movie star, whose career, spanning forty years in silent film, talkies, radio, stage, and television, had been largely unrecognized until recently. Frustrated by the stereotypical and frequently villainous roles she was offered in the United States, she was quoted as saying, "When I die, my epitaph should be: 'She died a thousand deaths.'" Orientalism was popular during the Golden Age of Hollywood, ensuring that stereotypical depictions of Asian Americans would have far-reaching effects, even to this day.

I chose the razing of Los Angeles's Old Chinatown in the 1930s because it was a perfect example of the power of publicity to erase a community. Voteless and unable to own land, the Chinese were at the whim of booster literature from newspapers like the *Los Angeles Times* and tourism brochures, which depicted them favorably or unfavorably, depending on the city's developmental agenda. When calls for a union station went out, focused on the transportation nexus that was Chinatown, there began a complicated and litigious battle between railroad heads and city officials as to how this would be accomplished, with no say given to the Chinese whose homes were the ones up for demolition.

Do I think three lowly Chinese girls could have influenced the destiny of an entire community? Yes, I do.

ACKNOWLEDGMENTS

JUST WHEN I THOUGHT I HAD GOTTEN THE HANG OF WRITING A book, this book killed me twice. Happily, I've reached the acknowledgments, which means I'm still standing after all, and I couldn't have done it without the support of some pretty amazing people. Jennifer Klonsky, Stephanie Pitts, Matt Phipps, Theresa Evangelista, Maya Tatsukawa, Cindy Howle, Christine Ma, Misha Kydd, Jacqueline Hornberger, Tessa Meischeid, and the entire team at Penguin Books for Young Readers, Kristin Nelson, Angie Hodapp, and the Nelson Literary Agency, you are all the butter and eggs. Jeremy Enecio, your cover art is extraordinary.

I'm very grateful to those who've blown their guiding winds into the cloudy beginnings of this manuscript, helping me shape it into a book. Shauna Rossano, I'm ecstatic to have your fingerprint once again on my work. Savannah Ly, Gemma and May thank you for your thoughtful analysis of them. Abigail Hing Wen, I appreciate your constant and cheerful willingness to lend me your eyes. Kelly Loy Gilbert and Joanna Phoenix, this story is so much better thanks to your scrutiny. Parker Peevyhouse, Kristi Wright, Evelyn Skye, Isabel Ibañez, and to all my local Bay Area writers, thank you for your support. To Sharon Levin for your wonderful book advocacy, Angel Barajas Magana for the use of your name, and Ava Razon for your speech expertise. And of course, Stephanie Garber, thank you for helping me wrestle the clouds.

Eugene Moy and the Chinese Historical Society of America, Gay-Quai Ming Yuen and the Chinese American Museum of Los Angeles, thank you for your dedication to keeping Chinese American history alive. Dolores, Wai, and Jonathan Lee, you've touched this story in so many ways, and I'm grateful for it. To my sisters in spirit who create with me—Angela Hum, Chenyi Lum, and Karen Ng—we still have a lot of fabric to go. Tony Cheng, Maureen Medeiros, Yuki Romero, Bijal Vakil, May Leong, Ariele Wildwind, Lia Theologides, ilana Lam, and the ladies of the Rivermark Book Club, special thanks to you for all the love. To the original fierce clouds, Laura Ly (Wise Cloud) and Alyssa Cheng (Beautiful Cloud), I (Charming Cloud) thank you for being a part of my sky. Evelyn and Carl Leong, I'm grateful for your constant love and support. (And for not guessing the killer, Mom!) Bennett, my kiddo, read this and know it is for your education. And last, Avalon, thank you for the brilliant title. May the clouds always bend to your will.

of course, Stephanie Garber, thank you for helping me wrestle the clouds.

Eugene Moy and the Chinese Historical Society of America, Gay-Quai Ming Yuen and the Chinese American Museum of Los Angeles, thank you for your dedication to keeping Chinese American history alive. Dolores, Wai, and Jonathan Lee, you've touched this story in so many ways, and I'm grateful for it. To my sisters in spirit who create with me—Angela Hum, Chenyi Lum, and Karen Ng—we still have a lot of fabric to go. Tony Cheng, Maureen Medeiros, Yuki Romero, Bijal Vakil, May Leong, Ariele Wildwind, Lia Theologides, ilana Lam, and the ladies of the Rivermark Book Club, special thanks to you for all the love. To the original fierce clouds, Laura Ly (Wise Cloud) and Alyssa Cheng (Beautiful Cloud), I (Charming Cloud) thank you for being a part of my sky. Evelyn and Carl Leong, I'm grateful for your constant love and support. (And for not guessing the killer, Mom!) Bennett, my kiddo, read this and know it is for your education. And last, Avalon, thank you for the brilliant title. May the clouds always bend to your will.